For Azusa

ISBN-13: 978-0998247441

Illustrations by Alex James

Whydidthechickencrosstheuniverse.blogspot.com

Rabbooks Publishing:
www.rabbitstudios.blogspot.com

Author's page: amazon.com/author/alexanderg.j

Facebook: facebook.com/rabbitstudiosbigpush

Why Did the Chicken Cross the Universe?

Alexander G. J.

ACKNOWLEDGMENTS

Special thanks to all the people who helped in one way or another, either by inspiration or perspiration, to place this book in your hands.

A special thanks to Melissa Ehman and Luke Neher for their tireless editing and support.

Novels by Alexander G. J.

Flaming Jackass: Sex, Drugs, and Pizza
Flaming Jackass: In Love
Mary & I: The True Story of Miss Mary Mack

CONTENTS

"Just an observation: I've never, ever, ever, ever, ever heard a female voice as the narrator of a movie trailer."

— Neil deGrasse Tyson (@neiltyson)
September 10, 2011

Chapter 1
Look Up!

My voice is that of a stern, elderly woman. Why did I say woman, you ask? Because if I were to say the word "narrator," the first thing to come into your head would be the voice of an elderly, stern, male actor—Morgan Freeman, perhaps? So, to eliminate that chance, you will hear my voice tell you all the thoughts and the comings and goings of all the characters.

Imagine that you are in a very, very dark place. This dark place goes on forever and ever. It's not nothingness. It's a substance called dark matter. Now imagine, before you there seems to be an endless amount of bubbles, as though you had been blowing soap bubbles in a dark room. Some of them are exactly the same and others are so different you would never think that they are related in some way. You see, these bubbles, some swirly and colorful, some bland and drab, are universes—surprise! The universe is a sphere! That's right, if you were to travel across the surface of the universe, you would end up right where you started–but wait! you say, what about those other bubbles? Well, those are the countless other universes. Some are completely identical to ours, with their own Earth and their own you. Others may be identical except for one thing, say, Hitler was never born or you managed to marry that high school crush you regret never having the courage to ask out. Not to worry, they ended up getting a divorce and becoming a homeless meth addict, with a hankering for wearing underwear on their head. See, aren't you lucky? But I digress. This is not a story about you, not in the least. If you start to zoom in on the 1,335th universe, the one that's a little blue…Not that one, the other one. That's right. Keep zooming…faster…faster still. Okay, at the speed you're are going, by the time you reach the Earth, our story will be over 989x999 trillion years ago, so let's go super fast. That's it. Now you're at the speed of light. Sorry to say but you're still too slow. Tell you what: see that thing that looks like a large golden ring? Go through that. I'll explain more about that later. Now, you've just traveled to our solar system. You know this from the obligatory shot of Saturn whizzing past and that red thing on Jupiter. There's Mars with its many useless land roving robot vehicles and finally, you come to that big, polluted, formerly blue marble that we all call Dirt or rather, Earth.

We're almost there. We get closer and we see North America. Oh-oh, looks like a hurricane in Cuba and another wildfire in California. That has nothing to do with the story but it's kind of interesting seeing it from space. Zoom in to California, not the smoky part in LA, but around the middle. There are so many urban and suburban grids of houses, roads, factories, and farmlands soon to be factories, houses and roads. Here we are finally coming to the place where our story begins, and about time, too. This is not LA or some big city like San Francisco but a small hamlet known as Pepper Mill. It's a quaint little town, which about 30 years ago didn't even exist. Sure they had a college, and of course the old pepper mill, but things didn't really pick up until the farmers sold off their property and the refugees from the horrors of the big cities came and built large houses and coffee houses, big box stores and small trinket stores. Then came gourmet food and bad chain food. In other words, it turned into just another American town. This ordinary town is due for some extraordinary events. Even as we zoom in to that independent coffee house right across the street from that chain coffee house that moved in and sucked 70% of their business away, events are unfolding that will determine the fate of the entire planet!

Do you see the young man at that table, not the African American with the red, thick-rimmed glasses, but the Caucasian at the table behind him? His name is Casper Cornbregger. This young man of average looks is waiting for someone. He appears nervous, looking around as if at any moment a cafeteria tray is going to whack him on the back of the head. This doesn't happen but if it did, his anxiety would be justified. He looked out of the window at all the young, double-income Newbie couples sauntering past. Strangely enough, they are on their way to telecommuting jobs at home. They're out walking their dogs and shoving electronic devices into their babies' faces to limit interaction with their kids, until they can be handed over to the nannies. Casper scowled in disappointment at the jumbo iPad in a baby stroller. He took a sip of coffee from Jack's Magic Beans Café. The café's roasts are much better than the chain place but he doesn't come here for the coffee. He comes here because he can study in peace without being interrupted by the cackling of Newbies as they talk about their trips to Tuscany and Tahoe, or how they are still breast-feeding their unvaccinated 12-year-olds to prevent autism. These thoughts put him in a temporary bad mood. He hates these spurts of bad moods. They seem to pop up when a significant event happens in the news. He can't watch TV or listen to the radio without hearing the words: Middle East, death, shooting, or disaster. Even when he goes on a temporary news blackout, the news always filters through from one of his friends.

Trying to take his mind off of his anger, Casper thought about his date with Lori. Getting a date with her was one of those unexpected bones that life throws the alley dog; Christmas in February.

An Asian female approached the table. She was not as tall as Casper, which was not the only difference: He is secular Jewish, she is an agnostic Buddhist; he likes the music played on college radio, she likes Joshua Bell and the Koto, his hair is black, short and usually looks like he just woke up in a bed made of static electricity, her hair, although also black and short, has a dyed pink strip in the front that usually has to be pushed out of her face. There is one thing they have in common: She sat across from him and they shared a table.

"Hi, Casper," she said.

"Uh, hi…Lori."

She had a scrawling look of disappointment on her face. Remember that look, for it will be repeated again.

"No standing up when the lady arrives, huh?" she muttered.

"Huh?" he asked.

"No holding the lady's seat or standing up?"

"Oh, sorry." He stood up. "I didn't realize we were living in the 1930s."

The girl muttered an insult under her breath. Casper only heard the Japanese word "baka." "What?" he asked.

"Oh, nothing. So, is this your favorite café?"

"No," he said shyly. "I just come here to study and my friend gives me free coffee."

"Oh, you're a student?…A cheap student."

"Y-yeah, at the university."

"What are you studying?"

"Well, I'm taking Astronomy, Physics, and Art for now."

"Art?"

"Yeah, I've always wanted to be an artist, but it's a hard field to make a living in."

"So you gave up?"

"Er—no, I still do art. I just do it more as a hob–" There was a tiny bell chime from Casper's cell phone. He looked at it and read the text message.

"Booty call?" the girl asked.

"Huh? What?" Casper was shocked and a little angry. "No! It's my mom."

He put his phone away and took a sip of his latté. Before he could put his cup down the phone pinged again.

"Persistent booty call," the girl complained.

"It's not a booty—It really is my mom!"

"What does she want?"

"She can't find the remote."

The girl turned her head sideways, the way a dog's would after watching a squirrel sitting on a telephone wire explode. "Do you live at home?"

"No, she lives 2000 miles away. She just texts a lot because my dad's not around. I guess I'm her substitute husband."

"Gross."

"That sounds kind of incestuous—forget I said that. No, I live with two roommates: One's a know-it-all, Japanese exchange student who can't make up her mind between premed and philosophy and thinks she knows more about American culture than we do, and the other is a science geek who thinks he's God's gift to the microprocessor." As Casper talked, the Asian girl moved her fingers like a hand puppet, its mouth opening and closing to simulate talking. "Problem?" he asked.

"Oh, you haven't asked me anything about me. Girls like it when guys show interest in them."

"Oh, uh—sorry," he said embarrassed. "How was work?"

"Terrible," she answered.

Casper didn't expect that. No one ever answers "terrible" when asked "How are you doing?" "Why terrible?" he asked.

"My pimp tells me that if I don't start bringing in more money, he's gonna put me in a steamer trunk and throw me into the river."

At this sentence, the African American behind Casper, who was obviously listening to their conversation, chuckled to himself.

"Huh," Casper said. "I thought you worked in the <u>record store</u>, Lori?!"

"Oh yeah, sure, sure, record store," she said with a very badly executed wink of her eye.

Casper lowered his eyes at her. "Anyway, Lori! What do you like to do?"

"Come on, Casper? What do you like to do? If you don't know by now, why are you on a date with me? These are things you should have covered when you first asked me out!"

"Okay, annnd…cut!" said the African American behind them. He turned around in his seat to look at them. "Worst-Date-Evuh!"

"Forget both of you!" Casper complained. "As if Lori is going to say she's a prostitute, or say baka—don't think I don't know what that means, Ami!" He pointed at the Asian girl, we'll call her Ami (pronounced Amy) from now on. "…And you, Don…" Casper looked at the African American. "Even you have to admit Ami was being a little hostile for a date."

"Casper, you have to be ready for anything she throws at you," Ami said. "Suppose she admits she has a wooden leg or her ex-boyfriend is a Hell's Angels/Nazi? Think of what I was doing as mental kung fu."

"What do you know about kung fu? You're Japanese," Don informed.

"Oh, I'm sorry, Japanese people are only supposed to know about karate, anime and sushi. Give me a freaking break, Don. Just because you're Black doesn't mean you only know about rap and basketball!" Ami countered.

"Rap?" Don returned the volley. "What is this, 1989?"

"Anyway!" Casper interrupted. "…Back to me! This was my practice date, after all!"

Ami looked serious. "Casper, it's stupid to have a practice date. It's not like a job interview. People are a heck of a lot more random than that; a butterfly flaps its wings."

"What?" Casper and Don both seemed confused. Across the street, a dog watched as a squirrel ran across a power line's transformer and exploded. The group looked in the direction of the explosion and then returned to their conversation.

"A butterfly flaps its wings? Chaos theory? Everything is connected?" Ami put her fingertips together. "Predicting what your dream date with Lori is going to be like and practicing for it is useless."

"Why?"

"Because, at this moment, let's say she's in a good mood—holy cow, she just got fired! Now she's mad! Holy guacamole! Her Hell's Angel ex-boyfriend found out about your date and wants to invert your pyloric sphincter with his fist!"

"Pyloric what?"

"Sorry…I'm thinking about this test I have on the gastrointestinal system on Friday—anyway, stuff's happening!" She waved her arms around, almost hitting Don in the eye. "You can't practice for life, you have to live it! Be yourself! Otherwise, she'll see right through that practice date of ours and chalk you up to being a fake."

Casper laid his head down on the table. "But I can't be myself, I'm boring."

"That's the spirit," Don said, rolling his eyes. "I'd sleep with you."

Ami patted his head. "Poor Casper…no self confidence." With a look of disgust, she pulled a piece of lint out of his hair and tossed it aside. Casper lifted his head to figure out why she had pulled on his hair.

"You know what you need?" Don asked.

"Face-lift?" Casper mumbled.

"No…Well, yes, but that's another conversation. You need a preemptive chance meeting."

"A what?" Casper asked, still a little angry from the face-lift insult.

"Ambush her at her job," Don suggested. "You say she works at that used record store, right? Happen to be browsing at some stuff, get some more info on her. Then you won't be all anxiety when the real date comes along; like a preemptive attack."

"That's a terrible idea," Ami countered.

"Why not?" Don asked. "If he's all crazy now, imagine what he's going to be like in four days? And we have to live with him! When he's heart broken, he doesn't sleep and when he doesn't sleep, he stays up 'til four in the morning blaring that freak'n TV—headphones, Casper, think headphones!…Anyway, he should get seeing her out of the way A.S.A.P."

Casper stood up and put on his backpack. "I hear what you're saying, but I'm going to completely ignore every word of it. Now if you'll excuse me, I'm going to a job I hate."

Ami looked at her cell phone. "Oops, I gotta go, too, before the library closes. Don? Can you get me one of those muffin things to go?"

"Only if you pay for it. My boss is getting sick of me giving free stuff to you guys." Don looked towards the counter. There was no one there but another barista like him, wasting time, exploring the inside of his nose with a straw.

"What's for dinner?" Casper asked Ami.

"Why are you looking at me? Just 'cause I'm a woman?"

"No, because it's your night to cook, Suzy Suffragette."

"Oh, right. Actually tonight we're supposed to go to The Pepper Grind and watch the big game."

"Oh, right." Casper rolled his eyes and made air quotes with his fingers. "The BIG game." I don't see why everyone is so excited about that. Every year they get to the playoffs and every year they drag their loser butts back home."

"Harsh," Don said. "Show some team spirit, Cap."

"Bah, humbug. The only thing I have faith in is, the more faith you have in humanity, the more it lets you down." Casper headed out the door. "See you guys at the bar."

Ami and Don looked at each other. They had very concerned looks on their faces.

Casper rode his bike down Main Street, towards his job at Big Red Groceries. When it came to the higher income Newbies moving into town, the only thing he was happy about was the upgrading of the roads with new bike lanes. When he was a kid, if he ventured out of his neighborhood and came within one mile of the downtown, he would be run off the road by a contractor's pickup truck, or insulted with: "Get outta the road! Hippie!" He never understood that insult. His hair was never long and he'd rather be set on fire than wear tie-dye. Perhaps it was the appearance of anyone <u>not</u> in a pickup truck. So much has changed: Pickup trucks are now SUVS, hybrids, and plugins, the ice cream shop was now called Yoghurt Yurt, the gun store was now a yoga center. Even the restaurant he went to for his bar mitzvah and got food poisoning that nearly put him in the hospital was now getting restaurant buzz for their fancy haute cuisine.

Big Red Groceries was another chain store. Its low wages and high expectations created more chain in the direction of slavery than retail. Casper has always felt that working in retail was akin to being a bit player in The Lord of the Rings saga. Big Red was, in essence, Mordor. The employees could be broken down into simple groups: The Hobbits (cashiers, sales floor people) who just want to make it through the work day and be left alone. The Elves (office people) who aren't evil or anything but want to make things easy for everyone and are therefore a little uncommitted. The Dwarves (disgruntled Hobbits): They hate their job so much that they don't care anymore. They're usually fired fast, so as not to spread their influence. Monsters (customers): Not all monsters are bad—some are quite cordial—but anyone who enters your personal space should make you put your hand on your sword and prepare for the worst. Trolls: people who do the grunt work (janitors, loading dock workers): usually underpaid workers. Wizards (head management): Are they good or bad? Doesn't really matter. Their goal is to kill the giant spider or dragon (Walmart, Target, Costco) and get hold of the other rings no matter what they have to do. It's best you stay out of their way or get hit with a lightning bolt. Humans (realistic supervisors and managers): whenever Casper hears any supervisors complain about any policies, or rule changes, he thinks: "Okay, they still have a realistic view of what it's like to work at a crappy retail job; therefore, holding on to their humanity." Golums (overzealous brainwashed workers): These are the worst of the worst to deal with on a daily basis. These are the employees who have sold their souls to the Super Devil and without a bit of irony, will use words like "team member" or "brand loyalty" and honestly believe any drivel that comes out of the Big Red manifesto. Gollums are very unpredictable because at any moment they'll grab the ring and throw you into the volcano. Casper's manager, Sue, is so much into Big Red that it was like she had absolutely no other life outside of the store. Casper wondered: "Isn't Big Red just a job? The only people who have any chance of any type of career are the Elves and Wizards."

Casper was called into the office for managerial chats more than once. He rarely smiled at the customers because most of them either never spoke or were in bad moods, especially the ones who only wanted to get out of the store and go home with their box of tampons, condoms or rectal itch cream. Putting a bitter-flavored icing on the cake was the fact on this long death march, customers, desperate for help and not finding it with the many non-English speakers, would latch onto him and harangue him with millions of questions about the products in sections of the store he had no idea about. Thinking about how illogical his job was made his mood sink from sad to depressed. To lift his spirits, he decided at this moment to break one of the rule of cashiers not speaking to each other.

Darla, the resident Goth girl, was stationed next to him on register #7. She was a year younger than he was and yet seemed to have her priorities more in order. She was taking classes in biology at the local collage and at night was the bass player in a band called: Jesus Christ Sushi Bar. Casper never had the nerve to see them in concert because they were always playing in clubs with names like The Acid Pit, Broken Arm, or The Outhouse.

Caspar watched as a female customer asked Darla for help. "Excuse me, are you open?" she asked. Darla took a second to think and looked the woman over.

"I'm sorry..." Darla finally responded. "...I like boys."

Casper and the woman were silent at first, until the woman, thinking that Darla was serious, corrected her. "No! I mean is your register free?"

"Oh, okay." Darla said, rolling her eyes.

As Darla rung up the woman's purchases, Casper felt a cold chill on his back. It was the type of feeling a chipmunk would get as a boa constrictor, slithering one inch away, was opening its mouth. He turned and spotted Sue, the manager, or "Team Leader," as they liked to call themselves.

"Casper?" Sue said. "Can I see you in the office, please?" Whenever anyone higher than a cashier said those words, Casper knew it rarely meant they were inviting you into the office to tell you what a good job you were doing, give you a big fat raise or ask for your opinion about their marriage woes. When Sue closed the door behind him, he wondered if this was it. Was this going to be the day that she tells him he's fired? This was a constant feeling while working in retail. Retail was like being fired, very slowly.

"How are you doing, Casper?" she asked.

The urge to say "Terrible!" came to his mind. "I'm okay."

Sue clasped her hands together. "You seem a little distracted lately. Is everything all right?"

The only thing that was distracting Casper at work was his attempt to ignore the fact that he was working in Mordor. Of course he couldn't say that, so he just said, "Yes."

Unwilling to relinquish her pursuit of an answer she liked, Sue continued to dig. "So no problems at home? Anything you want to talk to me about?"

"I'm sure there's nothing I want to talk to YOU about." This slipped out of Casper's mouth. It was the truth and everyone knows when your boss drags you into a mysterious meeting that could threaten your job, you can lie like Anne Frank at an Angry Guys with Tiny Mustaches convention.

Appearing a little perturbed, Sue pressed on. "I noticed that you've been coming in a little late for the past three weeks, and we also observed that you don't say 'hello' and 'thank you' to the guests."

Casper mentally rolled his eyes at the word "guest," was used instead of "customers." After all, you don't charge a guest $200 to sit on your couch and try to talk them into getting a credit card. Sue pulled out a sheet of paper. On it were written the many infractions of the store's policies, along with some things that just annoyed her. Casper was familiar with the ones she had just mentioned, but the others he never imagined she could have witnessed: talking to Darla too long, not putting peoples' bags in their carts, not asking people to sign up for credit cards, and many others. These could only be witnessed by the supervisors under her. They've obviously been keeping track of his every move. Casper felt like throwing up. It was one thing to avoid your boss observing you goofing off, but knowing that she had the Orcs spying on you was almost diabolical.

"This is an official warning. You're on probation for six months, at which time these things will disappear. I need you to sign the bottom of the paper to prove that I've discussed this with you and that you understand the consequences of not complying." She slid a pen to him.

Casper felt like he was signing his own execution papers. Even if he was to buckle down and become the employee of the month, what was his motivation? If he did a bad job, he was fired; but if he did a super job, they wouldn't drag him into the office and give him a vodka shot and reward—most likely they'd just think this was the way he was supposed to behave in the first place. He was trapped between the Devil, a rock, a hard place, and the deep blue sea.

When he left the office and headed back to the cash register, it took every ounce of strength he had not to keep on walking until he was outside.

His phone had a text message; it was his mom:
HOWZ WRK?

"When will she stop using 90s style texting?" He responded with:

WRK SUX.

What does SUX mean? she responded.

Realizing he might have overestimated her texting savviness, he switched to alphanumeric normality: It means sucks, he typed.

I am quite familiar with the word "sucks," son. I mean why does your day suck?

Oh, in that case. He typed:

TMI T2 YO L8R.

He tapped his phone off and returned to the front lanes.

"What was that about?" Darla asked.

"Warning to ship up or ship out," he answered while signing in to his register.

"Did they make you sign that piece of paper thing?"

"Yeah, have you had to do that?"

"At least three times. Don't think too much of it. Their memories of anything you do that's bad are almost as bad as their memories of anything you do that's good. Just act like super employee for two weeks and they stop watching you. Whenever they start to watch you again, that means that the big boss spotted you doing something and chewed them out for not doing their job. See, look…" Darla pointed to a couple of head managers talking to each other. One of them looked at Casper. Casper pretend to straighten a display of Halitosis Harry Garlic chewing gum. "Everyone is someone's slave. They spank the supervisors and the supervisors spank us."

"But why does anyone have to get spanked in the first place?"

"Human nature, Mr. C… human nature."

Casper looked at the managers. An older gentleman walked over to them. He heard one of the managers explain that he would try to have a report of some kind on his desk by noon.

"Spanked!" Casper thought.

Professor Pascal was around 40 years old. Casper didn't know for sure because his youthful disposition placed his age at around 28. He was also fit from running five miles every day to work. Whenever he explained something about the cosmos that really interested him, it would ignite a spark of enthusiasm that would radiate around the astronomy class like volatile knowledge fuel. Today's tinder involved the subject that had been dominating the news lately. Casper was sick of hearing about it, which was strange for someone in an astronomy class,

Pascal looked at the eyes of every student in the class as if he wanted to make sure they were hanging on to his every word. He hunched onto his desk like he truly wanted to fall forwards and land in the laps of those in the front row of the lecture hall.

"Well?" he asked, darting his eyes from face to face. "Did you see it?"

Most students nodded their heads, Casper did not.

Unwilling to accept head nods, the professor asked again. "How many of you saw it?"

About the same number of students raised their hands. Again, Casper did not participate in the survey. The professor finally took note of this.

"Mr Cornbregger. Why have you not raised your hand? Did you not go outside at night any time this week? Are you some type of reverse vampire?" Some students chuckled at the prospect of this.

"Well…" Casper said nervously. It wasn't that he was afraid of Professor Pascal, it was a feeling he had disappointed him by not doing the simple class assignment. "I've actually been at work during the peak viewing times."

"Well then…" Pascal walked from behind his desk. "Perhaps you can catch the next appearance of Pascal's Comet… Say, the next time it comes around, in two thousand years?" Again multiple chuckles were heard around the room.

"I'm sorry, Professor, but I just haven't had time to see it. I mean, it's a great discovery on your part and all, but to see it, you have to be waaay out in the middle of nowhere without all of these city lights around, and I don't have a decent car of any kind…"

Pascal sat on the edge of his own desk and crossed his arms. "Mr. Cornbregger, what do you think the most valuable element in the universe is?"

Casper thought for a second. "Er-ah, love?" The class let out a soulful "Ahhhh." A cute girl, who was extremely out of Casper's league, added: "That's so sweet."

"I see," said Pascal. "Love would be a good answer if you were a 1980's musician writing a power ballad, but this is real life. I mean what is the element that shoulders our every move? Something we are constantly swimming in? Something that affects the richest 1% of our population down to the rat that the downtrodden ate for dinner last night?" Pascal got really close to Casper's face. "If you could master this element in any way, you could drag your species out of the Paleolithic Era, faster than the abacus became a iPhone."

For what seemed like forever, Casper and the professor looked at each other. The expression "quiet enough to hear a pin drop'" could be used, except for the fact that the cute girl dropped a pin; she used it with a ball point pen to give herself mini prison tattoos —it was a hobby—to each her own. Anyway, no one noticed when it hit the ground.

"Matter?"

"Good answer…" The professor stood up and walked back to his desk. "…But not the answer that I'm looking for." He drew a picture of a clock face on the board. "Time, my overly romantic friend. Time is the god that slaps our infant behinds back into reality—every day! You can't escape it, we need it, and no matter whether you are in the 99% or the 1%, it ends you."

"I'm sorry, but what does this have to do with me?" Casper asked.

Pascal wrote on the white board what Casper had said earlier, and went over it, word by word: "'I'm sorry, –Professor, –but –I – just –haven't –had TIME– to see it.' —Time! Mr Cornbregger! Do you think that our existence here on Earth is so important, so meaningful, that all astrological events rotate around us? Of course not! Unless you are traveling at the speed of light, time for you is going to remain unaffected. Instead of seeing the comet with your naked eyes and experiencing something so old that it's like seeing part of the universe's placenta…"

There was a collective "Eww!" from the class.

"Sorry, bad example–but time is too valuable to waste, playing video games while staining your fingers with greasy, artery-clogging, carb-filled cheese snacks, or spending hundreds of dollars tipping strippers at the Pink Pony Lounge…" The look of shock on some of his student's faces forced him to stop talking about his tenure-threatening, after-work activities. "But, I digress. My point is, make—time! He circled the picture of the clock face on the board. "Time, my friends is what it's all about!" "It's why we get old, why we'll never travel to nearby solar systems and why our existence as humans has about as much impact on the universe as one grain of sand on the entire Earth…" Make better priorities! This is it! When you die, Pascal's Comet will be flying through the cosmos with or without you observing it. You're not in this class to NOT observe things., you are here because you look up at the night sky and you ask: What's a comet made of? What are black holes and why do science fiction movies have sounds in space?" Pascal stopped talking to answer a question posed by a student in the back row, a fellow with long, blond hair and glasses. Unlike most long-haired blond fellows with glasses, if he took them off, no one would say, "Mr Jones, you're beautiful!" They would just say, "Put your glasses back on. Your squinting makes you look like a creepy mole."

"Yes, Mr. Adams?" Pascal asked.

"Did I hear you right in saying we'll never get to visit nearby solar systems?"

"Yes, that's right."

"But…as a scientist, don't you think that's kinda, well, pessimistic? I mean, why not?"

"Time!"

"You mentioned that…like a Brazilian times. I don't get it. Are you referring to how long it'll take for us to develop the technology to achieve such a goal or the time to get there?"

"Actually, I was referring to both. I have complete faith in man's ability to create neat little toys and gadgets that achieve the nearly impossible and the skills to create horrific weapons that can kill a foreigner in a thousand different ways. But, remember, we are all slaves to time. Star Wars, Star Trek—what do they have in common besides armies of nerds following their every episode?"

"Lasers?" answered the cute blonde girl.

"No, we can already make lasers that that can turn a human brain into popcorn from a mile away."

"Aliens?" Casper answered.

"True, but no. Don't get me started on the way all aliens speak the Queen's English."

"Solving your problems through negotiations instead of military insurgency?" asked a voice from the back row. His identity is not important because this student will never be heard from again. Don't worry, nothing bad happens to them, it's just that he's extremely unimportant to the rest of the story.

"What? Who said that? No, that's not the answer," Pascal answered, a little confused that no one had seen that he was trying to link the subject back to time. "The answer is they both leapfrog over Einstein's theory of relativity in order to jump from galaxy to galaxy as if they were taking a bus across the street. Unless you had that wacky warp drive cog from Star Trek–bending space around like an origami crane–give me a break! We can't trust man to do the right thing with nuclear technology; why would you let Virgin Airlines control the fabric of space? Without some type of technological leap thousands of years into a future where we stopped fighting and put our money into the education system instead of turning peoples brains into popcorn, then there's no way you can get from A to B."

"What's wrong with traveling at the speed of light? I think we could one day have rockets that do that," Casper said.

"Assuming that your eyeballs don't fly to the back of your skull on ignition and you can overcome the fact that as you approach the speed of light you would either have to be zero mass to continue or have access to infinite energy; where do you plan to go with this inferior technology? The solar system would be fine; zipping to Pluto in four to seven hours. But what about a nearby star system like Alpha Centauri for example, 4.2 to 4.3 light years away? Hop in your light speed hot rod all you want, when you get back, allowing for exploration time and heaven forbid, not running into a pebble-sized asteroid shooting through your craft like a bullet, you're talking about eight years and whatever months! Almost nine years just to get across the street! Not many people would volunteer for that kind of mission: returning to Earth when your wife, who is now eight years older than you, has replaced you with your best friend—the one you asked to "look after" things. And your cute kindergarten daughter now has a tramp stamp tattoo, a boyfriend, a major attitude, and no idea who you are. I mean, sure, you could get a friendless, single, non-parent astronaut whose entire family is dead, but what a morbid resumé for a traveling companion. Face it dreamers, unless someone from your favorite sci-fi show hands you that warp drive whatever thing in a box and says, "Plug it in, but whatever you do, don't open it—you'll never figure it out," then we're gonna be stuck here on this cloudy, blue rock." There was a moment of silence as if every dream in the room was shattered all at once. "So, speaking of time, ours is up. I'll see you all next week. The class shuffled and rustled out. Casper lingered for a second.

"Sorry to dash any dreams, Mr. Cornbregger." Pascal seemed sincere in his apology.

"That's all right," Casper said. "You're right, we're stuck on this planet until we all die of some war or poison ourselves."

"Probably, but that doesn't mean you can't enjoy yourself while you're here. Like the Bible says: Jesus died for your sins, you might as well enjoy them."

"I may be Jewish, but even I don't think that's what Jesus had in mind."

"Casper, go see the comet. I'm not pushing it because I discovered it, got to be on the national news, may have a book deal or get to make a paid lecture about it in Paris next week…life is sweet! But I really believe it's important to look up in the sky on occasion. Like checking in with the Universe, like saying I know we may be an insignificant speck of lint, but we're still part of the fabric of space. What do you think of that? Lint, fabric, get it? I should use that in Paris."

Casper nodded yes and smiled. "Still don't have a decent, running car to get out of the city."

Pascal took a bus pass out of his wallet. "Here, borrow this. Take the number 37 bus to Baker's Field. It's a great view."

"No, I…"

"I said borrow this, not keep it. Go ahead, maybe it'll inspire you to create that warp star-drive thingy that'll drag mankind kicking and screaming into the future."

"What future? We both know how the book of humanity ends."

"Truth be known, Mr. Cornbregger, we really don't."

"Come on Professor, you can't cut on the TV without hearing some awful…"

Pascal put his hand on Casper's shoulder. "'The children now love luxury; they have bad manners, contempt for authority; they show disrespect for elders and love chatter in place of exercise. Children are now tyrants, not the servants of their households. They no longer rise when elders enter the room. They contradict their parents, chatter before company, gobble up dainties at the table, cross their legs, and tyrannize their teachers.' Do you know who said that?"

"You?"

"Socrates back in 469 BC…or some guy I met in the sixtiess. I'm not sure if he meant youth have always acted like animals or if it was grumpy old men have always complained about things. Either way, illegitimus non carborundum, Mr. Cornbregger—don't let the bastards grind you down."

With that, Professor Pascal left the room.

Casper rode his bike down what could best be described as the main street. On both sides of him, recession-proof businesses drew in the Newbies: buying expensive groceries at the place that sells truffle oil, browsing books at the chain book store and buying pricey baby clothes that will only be used for a month. The record store Lori worked in was one of the hold outs, not only from the changing face of the old boulevard but also one of the last holdouts from CDs and downloads. As Casper rode past it, he slowed the bike down. "Should I stop?" he wondered. "Would she see this as stalking?" An excuse had to be created. Perhaps he really was there to buy a record….a record which he couldn't play on any machine in his entire house. Going against his better judgment, he parked his bike and locked it up.

If he wore a hockey mask and had a knife in his hand when he walked pass the entrance of the record store, this would be the only way he could feel even more like a stalker than he did at that moment. A quick turn of the head to peek inside was about as subtle as a hammer against the front window.

Lori was 5' 2" tall, with long blonde hair that reached between her shoulder blades. Her face was pretty, not the kind of pretty for television but suitable for a catalogue for ladies hand bags. Her manner of dress can best be described as eighties' pop rock: leopard pattern leotard, black bra on the outside, tutu skirt and a pair of black Converses. She spotted him and smiled. Truth be known, she actually wasn't looking at him, but the guy walking behind him. Coincidentally, this was the same gentleman from Casper's class whose activities are completely insignificant to the story. If you don't believe me, perhaps we should follow his story instead:

His name is Greg Mathis, not to be confused with the African American judge on TV. This duplication of names has made his life a living hell. Enemies constantly nickname him "Judge" or "White Judge Mathis." Greg is on his way to the grocery store to buy some bread. With this bread he's going to make a peanut butter sandwich. A sandwich he will eat, ironically, while watching a re-run of the Judge Mathis show. In that time his girlfriend Samantha will call and ask if he wants to have dinner with her and her father at Shenanigans. Shenanigans is one of those restaurants where the underpaid waitress and waiters pretend to be happy in spite of having to wear lots of crazy buttons. These buttons match the walls, covered in crazy items like kayaks and stop signs. The walls match the crazy food, buttered, battered and deep-fried everything. During dinner, Samantha's dad will ask: "So, Greg, what have you been up to?" To which Greg will answer, "Nothing much."Focus on that answer if you will: 'Nothing much.' Greg has just given us the perfect example for why we should not follow his tale but focus more heavily on Casper's fate.

Casper's actions at this moment, although seemingly routine at this point, are going to lead to events which can change the lives of everyone in this town. It didn't seem like he was changing the fate of anyone but himself as he entered the record store. He knew it was a bad decision but, to him, it was a bad idea on the same level as eating clam pizza for breakfast, or washing whites and colors together. Not the kind of mistake that can completely ruin your chances with the girl of your dreams. Lori didn't acknowledge his presence in any way. He wondered if it was because she was at work and her boss might be watching her. There were no other bodies in the store except a bearded gentleman wearing a black T-shirt with a picture of a milk carton on it and the words "Have you seen me?"—again, an insignificant character. Casper pretended to browse some albums. He inadvertently started browsing the collection labeled Gay Disco. "Oh crap! She's going to think I like disco!" He quickly moved to the "Alternative" section which, strangely enough, had quotation marks around the word "alternative." For a long time, his glances over to her were ignored, as was his proximity. "Did I do something to offend her?" he wondered. "Does she not want to go on our date?" Eventually, he got close enough to speak to her.

"May I help you?" she asked.

This slightly insulting greeting fazed him. "Uhh, hi, Lori?"

"Hi," she said. They stood looking at each other for a long moment. It wasn't the kind of moment that leads to kissing, but closer to one that leads to a restraining order.

"Perhaps it was a joke," he thought. "Maybe I should play along?" he wondered. "How's it going?"

"I'm sorry," she said. After this, followed one of the few phrases that someone can say to you to spark a reaction that leads to suicide or homicide. It can only be taken as a form of insult, especially if one person in the party has invested far more time, money or love into the relationship, while the other person has been caught unaware of how important the relationship is. "Do I know you?" she asked.

Again, thinking that she was joking, Casper played along. "Casper? Casper Cornbregger?"

"You seem familiar, do I know you?"

The joke had gone a little too far and was entering devastation. "Y-yeah, we had a date tomorrow?" Casper smiled in a most painful way.

"Really?" She had a scowl on her face; not a good sign of joking.

Casper was without speech. Taking another shot that this could be a joke, he filled her in on the events leading up to the date.

It was last Saturday. Casper was at a party of one of his classmates, Gomorrah Sanchez. He had not been invited to the party because she liked him, but because she felt a party was a failure unless you have trouble walking through your apartment because there are so many people blocking your way. At one point, Casper had been trapped between the crowd coming out of the kitchen and the one coming out of the bedroom. Lori had also been a victim of the perfect storm of people, forcing her and Casper to talk to each other. For about an hour, they had discussed politics, the origin of the universe, and the sexual preference of Bugs Bunny. Feeling that the end of their time was approaching, Casper initiated a continuation of their conversation in another setting: next Saturday at Jack's Magic Beans Café. She agreed and wrote his name and phone number on a piece of paper. She placed this note into the pocket of her brown hoodie jacket with multicolored dancing teddy bears on it. This jacket is not only distinctive for its bad fashion, but it happened to be the same jacket Lori was wearing as Casper told her the entire story of their meeting.

Lori reached into her right pocket and pulled out the note. She unfolded it and read it. "Whoa! Look at that. You were right."

Feeling vindicated and still confused, Casper was prepared to restate the plans for their date, but Lori cut him off before he could finish one syllable.

"I'm sorry…" She looked at the paper to remember his name. "…Casper…Corn Bread?"

"Cornbregger," Casper corrected.

"Corn…Whatever, I'm sorry, but I don't remember any of our conversation."

"You don't remember?"

"Yeah, I'm sorry but I was totally blazed that night."

"Blazed?"

Lori put her index and thumb together and bought them up to her mouth.

"You were drinking from a straw?"

Lori looked a little angry and confused. "You know, ripped?"

"Ripped?"

Now Lori was just angry: "Hooted?…Blasted?… Zooted?… Blazed?… Blitzed?" With each of these words, Casper grew more and more confused, like she were speaking French into the ear of a German Shepard. "…Puff! Burnt? Hubbly-Bubbly? Muggled!? Taking on a number? Tighten my wig? Wacky terbacky!" Lori yelled as if she were on a mission to translate her night's activity into every language.

The fat bearded guy, who was eavesdropping on the conversation, interrupted Lori's tirade: "She was high on marijuana!"

Truth be told, after she used the word "blasted" Casper had already figured out that she had been high on drugs the night she spent so much time speaking to him. This would also explain her giggling fits when he mentioned the constellation "'Betelgeuse" and the way she ate an entire bowl of greasy, artery-clogging, carb-filled cheese snacks. Lori looked a little embarrassed. She gave the fat bearded guy a dirty look, then she excused herself, turned around and went back to work. Casper stood there in shock and confusion. In one conversation, Lori had gone from a dream date to one of the rudest rejections of his limited dating career.

To add confusion to insult, the bearded guy walked up to Casper and put his arm around him. "Don't worry, dude," he said. "She did the same thing to me." He proceeded to give Casper a hug. Then, taking things into a the fifth gear of weirdness, the guy began to weep. "Women can be so cruel!" he blubbered.

Fifteen minutes later, or however long it took for Casper to cheer the guy up in order to pry him off of his shoulder, Casper stepped outside. He knew he was feeling depressed and he knew when you are depressed, it can affect your memory as well as your emotional state. Therefore, it was of no surprise when he stepped outside and forgot where his bike was locked up. This was a reasonable explanation at first until he looked in all directions and didn't see his bike anywhere. "Oh, no!" you might be thinking, and you are right to utter such a cautionary prediction. He remembered putting a lock on it. The lock that cost more than the bike. The lock which could take a point-blank range shotgun blast without breaking. He remembers putting it around the bike. The bike into which he had put more money in upgrades and repairs than if he'd bought one that Lance Armstrong could afford. The bike was connected to the lock and the lock was securely fastened around a tree; the tree which was not there.

Casper walked over to the four-inch thick tree stump. He stared in disbelief at the amount of work someone would put into stealing his cheap bike and the speed at which they worked. The fact that there had been no sound of a chainsaw meant they must have used a hand saw and worked at amazing speed. "Wow," was the only word he could muster. At the exact moment he dropped his bicycle helmet onto the sidewalk (after all, he didn't need it anymore), a bus appeared at the stop, a few feet away from him. It was the #37, the one he should take to Baker's Field, the place with the best view of Pascal's Comet. As if they were moving on their own, Casper's legs walked onto the bus. He didn't know why he did it, but he did know where he did not want to be and that was on that sidewalk, looking at a tree stump after being rejected by an amnesiac pothead.

After a physiologically long bus ride, stopping at every object that looked remotely like a bus stop, Casper arrived at Baker's Field. It was dark—real dark. The kind of dark where stepping off the well-lit bus was like walking into a wall of black ink. It took a few seconds for Casper's eyes to adjust. Shoulders bumped into his as the day laborers pushed pass to get onboard. This was the sole purpose of the #37 bus, to transport the loads of mostly undocumented workers who serve as farm hands or nannies for the Newbies whose houses were too big to be placed inside the town limits.

The bus pulled off and headed back to town. It would be back for one last time in about an hour. This was long enough. There was no need to walk anywhere for a better view of the Milky Way.

Stretched before Casper's eyes was the quiet sea of blue and black, As if someone had spread a large black velvet blanket out and then dusted it with white talcum powder. Casper paused. This was something he rarely did. His life was always go here, do that! go there, do this! But here, there was nothing to do. There was no stressful retail job. There was no crazy amnesiac love crush, there was no deceased parent.

He thought briefly about his dad. There was something he like to say: People were books and bottles. If you look at either one, they can have great covers or labels, but those rarely tell you anything about what's really going on in the inside. A book may be popular because it's good, or its author just has a good agent; or a bottle of wine can have a great label and come from a famous winery, but if the bottle wasn't stored properly it'll taste like liquid death. These were not Hershel Cornbregger's exact words but they were his version of: "Don't judge a book by its cover."

This saying was not always true, Casper thought. If you see a book cover with a naked woman doing things that are illegal in Kentucky, you are not expecting Shakespeare. So surely, if a pretty girl has a one-hour conversation with you, wants to meet up with you and writes your name and number down, that is along the lines of paying a lot of money to see Citizen Kane and instead you are treated to an empty-headed action movie, where the hero does a kung fu move on the villain and the villain catches on fire, crashes through a window, lands on a gasoline truck that explodes and the hero says: "Rest in pieces!" You are angry that you wasted your money on this celluloid nightmare.

In spite of trying to find respite in his father's advice, Casper was still mad. The night was doing its very best to snap him out of his funk. He could see everything he was studying. He could see Gemini, Taurus, the Plough, Ursa Minor, Cassiopeia and Draco. It occurred to him at that moment that he should have brought his telescope. This realization reminded him of how confused and frustrated he was. He did not need a telescope to find Pascal's Comet. It was very prominent in the sky, like a big blue fuzzy street light. All of the other stars were merely co-stars (no pun intended). This was the second time in his life he could see a comet with his bare eyes. The first was when Comet Bibimbap (discovered by a Korean astronomer) made its way past Earth when he was five. He didn't understand what the big deal was. To him, being a small child at the time, of course comets passed by the Earth, all of the time. Just like unicorns ran through the woods, and he was pretty sure Superman would save him if the comet headed towards Earth. The fuzzy blue light was brighter than Comet Bibimbap. Actually, it was a lot brighter than he thought it would be and, perhaps, brighter than it should be. Casper was unsure of the reason Pascal had wanted him to see the comet. Did he think that staring at this cosmic marvel was going to change his view on life? Was he supposed to be inspired by the sight of a bunch of sand that had been traveling through the cosmos since the beginning of the universe? Was this supposed to push him to go out and change the world or himself; invent the Internet, write the Torah, lead a nation out of darkness? If anything, the comet made him feel small and stupid. His problems seemed insignificant and therefore made everything he was working for meaningless. "Nice try, Professor," he said, turning on his heel and walking back to the bus stop.

The bus ride home was spent thinking about the comet, more than when he was actually observing it. The brightness and its position bothered him. It was also too round. For a comet that was going to be passing quite far away, and never crossing the path of earth's orbit, it should look…well, more comet-like. He would ask Professor Pascal about this next week.

There was a test message from his mom:

@ ANT FAY HOUs 2 LOOK @ COMET. TOY.

It took him a second to figure out this message: It read: "At your Aunt Fay's house to look at the comet, thinking of you." It was weird that his mom knew more text lingo than a 90s teenager. It was like she had gone from 46 back to 16 even tough she had gotten a smart phone which could send videos, pictures and other attachments she never used. His mom was dealing with his dad's death a lot better than Casper: She was being more social and outgoing, joining clubs, exercising and embracing technology— albeit backwards. It wasn't so much she was trying to distract herself from the sad event, but it was like his dad's death was a warning shot across the bow. Casper wished he could start living like that right now, before gray hairs covered his head.

The bus entered the busy town square; something was going on. Small groups of people huddled in different areas: outside the bars, library–any place where people would usually congregate. 'What were they talking about?" he thought. He remembered there was a big sports game of some sort. Perhaps their team had won the "big game" or a world leader had been caught in such a salacious scandal that people had run in disgust from their televisions, to look for someone to talk to. Casper got off the bus in front of The Pepper Grind. This is where Ami and Don were supposed to be watching the game. Like the other places, there were groups of individuals gathered outside of it. He circumvented the obstacle and slowly made his way inside, squeezing in the even larger group.

There were two odd things about the crowd: they were mostly silent—not the audience one would expect to see for the "big game". Even if a player on your team's head came off right when they were about to score, you would at least be hearing some disappointed moaning and groaning.

He spotted Baboosh. Baboosh was the owner of the Pepper Grind. He was a dark-skinned fellow, originally from Yakistan, a country neither India or Pakistan had any interest in fighting over. In a normal situation, if he knew who you were, you couldn't enter his bar without him making a loud announcement about you and how glad he was to see you. Today, he was staring silently at the TV screen and drying a glass, which if it became any drier, would turn back into sand.

"Uh, hey, Baboosh?" Casper asked. "You seen Ami and Don?" Baboosh slowly pointed to a table near the middle. Casper looked at the TV screen. There was no "big game", just a shot of the sports stadium with lots of people in the stands. Two sportscasters were talking, but not about the game. "Did someone just drop dead on the field?" Casper asked. Baboosh ignored him and kept cleaning the glass, his expression, the same as if yes indeed, someone had just dropped dead on the field. Casper navigated through more people, their eyes fixed on the screen and expressions as if something bad had happened at the game. Casper never really cared about sports, but this scene had him very concerned. If losing this game was going to make people this depressed then perhaps next time he should be more supportive. Ami and Don were part of the zombie staring convention. The thing that completely freaked Casper out was Ami was grabbing Don's hand. As long as he had known these two, when they were not insulting each other, they were indirectly insulting each other. To see them holding hands was a signal the world was ending and Satan had just appeared on the TV to tell everyone to grab their ankles and put on their 3D glasses, because things were about to get real. "Uh, guys?…Ami?…Don?" There was no response. He had to tap Don on the shoulder to get his attention. "Don? What's wrong? Did an airplane crash into the middle of the field and kill our entire team?" Don looked at him. The expression was one of "How did you guess that correctly?" Before Casper could relish in his new found psychic powers, Don informed him of the truth.

"Th-they just found out that that comet? It ain't gonna pass by…It's heading here, Cap…It's gonna hit us…It's the end of the world."

Casper slumped down in an empty seat next to Don. He took a swig of beer. It was uncertain whether the beer belonged to Ami, Don or the large Hells Angel Natzi in a leather jacket standing next to the table, sobbing like a baby.

"So…" Casper asked. "Did we at least win the "big game?""

Chapter 2

What Do We Do Now?

A man goes to see his doctor, the doctor says: "I have some bad news and some very bad news."

"Well, give me the bad news first," the man says.

"You have 24 hours to live," The doctor says.

"That's terrible," says the man. "What news could be worse than that?"

"I've been trying to call you since yesterday," Says the doctor.

This story is perhaps the best way to describe the mood of every living person on the planet Earth as news spreads that their existence would soon be wiped away, the same as Tyrannosaurus Rex, the dinosaur and Tyrannosaurus Sex, a low budget horror movie with a very limited run. The experts predicted the whole planet would go through Elisabeth Kübler-Ross' five stages of death: Death, anger, bargaining, depression and acceptance. The problem with Kübler-Ross' list is that she forgot to factor in that humans, although fairly predictable creatures are fairly unpredictable in real world scenarios, especially when it comes to their potential demise. To give you an example: if I were to point a rusty dagger at your head right now and say, "That's the final time you take the last piece of cheesecake without asking—I'm going to end you!" After realizing: "Oh great, I'm going to die over a mediocre piece of cheesecake, couldn't it at least been a better dessert?" You aren't going to say, in perfect order: "No! I hate you! Come on!" Cry and then say: "Oh, well." There is going to be a mix of emotions twirling around your head like a 1930s Busby Berkeley dance number. More like: "No! No!" Cry; "Oh well, Come on! No! I hate you! Noooooo!"

Within 24 hours, a miracle happened. All major wars on Earth stopped. Soldiers almost immediately started to withdraw and tried their best to return home to be with their families. The wars in the Middle East ended in less than 12 hours. Japanese whaling ships turned around and headed back home. Crime in the U.S. dropped to its lowest level since the 1700s. Thieves realized it wasn't worth stealing something that was going to be smashed to pieces with everything else. Churches become very popular with agnostics and ex-convicts. The atheists held their ground by lots of drinking.

Getting the daily news updates about the comet proved difficult. Newscasters started calling in sick or standing up, while on the air, and walking away. After all, why sit behind a desk reading the news when you could be consuming large amounts of alcohol–sorry, I mean spending more time with your family? The radio broadcasts were mostly uninterrupted because radio broadcasters only needed to record their voices and could work out of their homes.

The world leaders sat in meeting after meeting deciding what to do; all plans were considered:

Plan 1: Evacuate all of the smartest people to an underground bunker, to emerge years from now when the smoke clears and repopulate the Earth. The problem with this plan, besides the fact that all secret underground bunkers in Antarctica were already reserved for world leaders, the 1% and their family, was that no matter what type of society you created, you would still need people to clean your toilets, fix your cars and shoot any zombies that tried to get into your bunker. With so many staff members doing the grunt work, surely one of them, most likely the guy with the gun, would realize: "Why in the world am I taking orders from this guy? Why am I not the new president of the Earth?"

Plan 2: Put the smartest people on Earth onto the International Space Station to ride it out until the smoke cleared. Once again, the tickets on the mostly Russian rockets to get there were already booked by Russian billionaires, their wives and mistresses. The only empty seat which could have been taken by a person of actual use for rebuilding a zombie-ridden, post-apocalyptic society was taken up by a wooden box containing a large amount of vodka.

Plan 3: "Let God sort it out." This was proposed by the top religious leaders on Earth. The strange thing about the term "religious leaders" is that the only religions represented were: Evangelical, Catholic, Baptist, Protestant and Jewish. There were no Mormons, Muslims, Buddhists, Amish or Flying Spaghetti Monster acolytes. You had to give them credit, though: no matter what, they stuck to the script of leaving everything to God and intended to stay in character until the end. Unfortunately, unknown to the general public, they had already secured bungalows in the secret bunker in Antarctica.

Plan 4: "Blow it up!" was the most popular course of action, more popular than the logical "let's blow up a nuclear weapon in space and let the force knock the comet into a different direction." The reason why had to do with the long-time addiction of the United States to action movies.

"Why would we nudge the comet in a different direction?" asked the U.S. president, and I quote: "This comet is a threat to all existence on Earth. We aren't going to say 'excuse me' to it! We need to show this comet and all other celestial bodies that we mean business!" That quiet pattering you heard is not polite applause, but the French and Australian ambassadors slapping their foreheads in frustration.

"Why in the world did people elect that guy?" Casper asked, turning off the TV. There were no added complaints from Ami and Don. Ami was on the phone trying to book a flight to Osaka, Japan to be with her mom; this was a futile effort. Besides the fact that everyone over two hundred miles from their birthplace were trying to book a flight; pilots had families too, and no interest in flying you home during their last days on Earth.

"Kutabare!" Ami yelled, pressing the end call button on her phone as hard as she could. Back in the old days, people could slam their phones down to end calls which would have been a lot more dramatic—but you get the gist.

Casper, Ami and Don were silent for a minute, each lost in the one thought that surrounded the globe.

"Cap?" Don asked. "What do we do now?"

"How would I know?" Casper answered, putting his finger tips together.

"Well, you're taking astronomy. Is it true? Is this it?"

"Depends."

"On?"

"Well...usually the size of the object is going to predict how much destruction it's gonna cause. Anything smaller than 150 feet won't do too much damage unless it lands on your town. When you get into stuff larger than that, say, one mile, we're talking nuclear winter, block out the sun, kill the crops, only the strong will survive, Mad Max type of stuff. And anything above that..."

"Above that?" Ami asked.

"Ten miles long? Equals mass extinction. Dinosaur killer."

"How big is that comet?" Don asked.

"Early reports say around five miles."

"Combo destruction?" Don asked

"Combo destruction," Casper answered, clasping his hands.

"What are they going to do?" Ami asked in a panicked voice. "Can't they just blow it up?"

"If they're smart, they'll detonate near it and nudge it in a different direction. But our stupid president has been watching too many end-of-the-world action movies and wants to blow it up."

"So what's wrong with that?" Don asked.

"Lots of tiny, fast moving pieces, the size of washing machines, heading our way?"

"Better than one big one," Don offered.

"I guess, depending on if it hits you or not," Casper said, sending yet another text message to Professor Pascal. There was, so far, no response. Pascal was a very busy man. Radio, TV, and what was left of the newspaper industry kept asking him the same, universal question: "What do we do now?"

"How long do we have?" Don asked. He stood up and looked out of the apartment window. They were lucky enough to live right on Main Street, near the coffee houses and the book store.

"Less than a week," Casper answered.

"Less than a week? Less than a week! That's not long enough!" Ami yelled. "I still haven't seen Machu Picchu, Angkor Vat and Graceland! I can't believe I'm going to die in this country, with you two!"

"Hey!" Don complained. "If you have to die, America's a great place to do it!"

"It's amazing that you never worked for the tourist board," Casper said.

"What about you? Casper? Don't you want to get home to your mother?" Ami asked him.

"Of course, but I'm in the same boat as you. No airlines are flying, which means driving in traffic with the entire freaked-out population of the United States all the way to the East coast. I'll never make it. The comet will have hit when I'm in Texas. Texas! Do you think I want to die in Texas?"

"What about you, Don? Don't you want to see your parents in Seattle? You could make it there."

Don was silent for a few seconds. "I already talked to them. They're going to spend the final day inside the church, praying."

"What's wrong with that?" Ami asked.

"Nothing, but…when the end of the world comes, I don't want to be inside. I want to be outside, enjoying the last breaths of fresh air."

"You seem to have put some thought into it," Casper said. "I'm surprised you didn't say, 'while holding a bottle of Jack Daniels.'"

"Of course, that's a given," Don added.

"You know…" said Ami, "…we can't go home but we don't have to stay here."

"What do you mean?" Casper asked.

"We can just walk."

"Walk where?" Don asked, turning around to face them.

"It doesn't matter. To the nearest state park? We'll take a tent; camp out, get some fresh air. If the world is ending, I don't want to spend it inside some tiny apartment either."

I have the need to point out that Ami has slipped from Anger into the Acceptance phase, while Casper and Don are still in Denial and Anger.

In Washington D.C., President Jimmy Jarrod, or "J.J." as his campaign posters read, was packing his suitcase to go to the secret bunker in Antarctica. He had given the order to fire missiles at Pascal's Comet. The mission was now dubbed "Operation Comet Freedom." His phone rang just as he's putting his favorite pair of boxer shorts, the ones with an American bald eagle, tightly grasping two cannon balls, into the case.

"Mr. President," the secretary said on the speaker phone. "It's Professor Pascal."

"Who?"

"The expert on the comet."

"Oh, right. Put him through."

There was a short beep and then Pascal's voice could be heard. "Mr. President?"

"Dr. Prosciutto, what can I do for you?"

"Pascal."

"Pass what?"

"Pa…never mind. Mr. President, I've just heard that you ordered the comet to be blown up with missiles."

"That's right, Doc."

"Mr. President, That may be a grave error. If you break it into pieces, we may see large, fast moving chunks pelting the surface of the Earth."

"Better than one big piece, don't you agree, Doc?"

"Of course. But Mr. President, I think it's possible to fire near, the comet and use the shock wave to throw the comet off course, just enough to pass the planet completely."

"Here we go again. What is up with this lovely-dovey liberal approach to comets?"

"Sir?"

"If we let this comet survive, it's going to come right back round again and destroy us!"

"Not for at least a thousand years."

"Exactly! And do we want our space children to say, 'Oh no, our ancestors let us down! How could they give that comet a hall pass and let it come around and destroy us like this?' I can't live with that, could you?"

"Mr. President, we're talking about a thousand years. The human race will be long gone by then."

"Oh please, have some faith, Doc. Humans are strong, like bionic cockroaches; you can't keep us down. In a thousand years our android butlers and sex bots will be doing all the work and we'll have flying jet packs to the moon."

There was a moment of silence from Pascal.

"Doc? Are you still there?" the President asked.

"Yes, sir. I urge you to reconsider. Your plan has dangerous repercussions. It'll be like hitting an iceberg with a stick of dynamite."

"Exactly! Ka-boom! Goodbye iceberg! End of story!"

"Not exactly, sir…"

"Listen Doc…" The President interrupted. "I gotta go, I'm… about to go open a school or execute a convict or something like that. Don't worry your pretty little head about anything. Let the big boys handle this. You just get to work on those sex bots."

"But, Mr. President, I don't…"

"So long, Doc." The President pressed the end call button hard. He turned to his assistant. "I thought I told you, no more phone calls from people who don't agree with me!"

Casper hated camping. To him, camping was like voluntary homelessness. It baffled him that people would choose to live in discomfort in order to take a break from their uncomfortable lives. Sure, the views were pretty, being in the woods of the California mountains, its majestic hills stretching out like an Ansel Adams photograph, but there was only one shower, at least a seven minute walk away, it was cold at night, and noisy, thanks to a family of raccoons having a gang fight with a family of opossums.

Ami, Don and Casper were not as alone as they wished to be. On the two-day hike to get to this spot from their home, passing by numerous people in numerous cars and numerous traffic jams, it never occurred to them that at one point someone else would give up on the idea of doing a mecca thing for their last day on Earth and leave the eighteen-hour traffic jam. It wasn't as crowded as a campsite would usually be at this time of year but the sheer presence of anyone else in your spot at the end of the world was kind of a spiritual killjoy. As you try to gather your thoughts and meditate about your life, you don't want to hear the sound of a jet ski on the lake, a man's voice yelling at his wife who just confessed to an affair she's been having for ten years, or the constant sobbing of a Wall Street banker realizing all of his money won't get him a seat on the Russian rockets to the space station. The worst thing about all of these noises was they were all coming from the same man—the only one to leave the traffic jam and in spite of the hundreds of other vacant campsites, the only one to park near Casper and his friends within ear shot. This fact was not lost on Casper, who brought it up yet again.

"Just ignore him!" Ami suggested, again. She put a log onto the fire. The orange glow of the heat warmed their bodies and illuminated the surrounding trees under the blanket of the night.

"I can't," Casper said. "Maybe we should kill him."

"WHAT?" Ami and Don exclaimed simultaneously.

"Yeah," Casper said, with a devilish look on his face. "Think about it. The police are ignoring the people. We won't go to jail because the world is ending. This is the perfect time to off people when they get on your nerves."

Ami got off of her log and moved further away from Casper.

"Cap? Besides the fact that if you kill someone, you die and go to Texas, murder is just plain wrong," Don said.

"Well, besides the fact that Jews don't believe in going to Texas if you die–wrong or right, what does it matter any more? Do you think that Newbie guy would hesitate to kill all three of us for our marshmallows?" Casper complained.

"You're scaring me, Casper," Ami said. "If you're serious, then I think you should move over to the Resident Evil campsite."

"Of course I'm not serious. I just find it interesting that we haven't heard any news about huge armies of people going around looting, killing or even getting rid of that enemy in the Middle East they've been fighting for forty years. I mean, did those end-of-the-world movies lie to us? Where's the rioting, the elderly Black president who does car commercial voice-overs, or Bruce Willis in a space shuttle, riding the comet like a cowboy on a bucking bronco?"

"You're complaining that there's no murdering?" Ami asked.

"I don't know, I guess I'm just confused by people's actions. I mean, when we had all the time in the world, we had wars, crime and all that, but, when we're all gonna die, we stop and think about how we shouldn't have murdered all of those Third World people or stolen all of that money? It's so lame! Why didn't Mr. Newbie next door clean up his act when he was in Vegas doing cannonballs in a swimming pool full of cocaine?"

"It wasn't in Vegas, it was Tahoe!" came a voice from the other campsite.

Casper was a little embarrassed that perhaps the Newbie had heard him plotting to murder him. "Anyway…" Casper lowered his voice. "…Why stop now? If you believe in dying and going to Texas, then by now you should have one of those tickets with a number on it, ready to be called."

"I hear what you're saying, Cap," Don said. "I like to think that God forgives everyone for all of their sins, even Mr. Newbie over there."

"Thank you!" came the voice from next door.

"IF they confess their sins and beg for forgiveness!" Don yelled back.

"Duh-oh!" the guy said.

"Well, personally I have trouble with the whole concept of the 'Western God' to begin with," Ami said, using air quotes. "I believe that if a unified spirit is everywhere and in everything then that's also us. And we shouldn't have been fighting wars or snorting cocaine mountains in the first place. We don't need a person or a building to tell us to be good; we should have been good for goodness' sake. God or no God!"

"I disagree," Don said. "I believe the Old Man has been watching over us all this time."

"That's the problem I have with religion. You said HE! God is a man? Is he an English-speaking White one, too? Does he look like Charleston Heston or Bernie Sanders? Why does God have to have a shape? We're talking about a force in the universe that's capable of creating planets! To the ants, we are God, do we look anything like them?"

"It's just a metaphor. People need an image in their heads–to think about when they pray or go to church," Don answered.

"And you think of a White man with a beard? Lord knows what you think about during sex."

"Whoa! How did we get from religion to sex?" Don asked.

"Aannnd scene," Casper interrupted. "I think in less than five minutes, we are going to find out if there is a White God or not."

"Is it time?"Ami asked, worried.

"Yep," Casper took out his transistor radio and cut it on. "The missiles should be hitting the comet right about now."

The voice of the college radio DJ, Skip Recordson (real name Daryl Rabinowitz), tuned in with a little static. "...NASA engineers all waiting for this moment. In fifty seconds, the three missiles will make contact with Pascal's Comet and shatter it into smaller, harmless pieces, the size of elephants, going a hundred miles an hour. Excitement is building here, as it is around the world, as everyone puts their hope in the United States' defense shield–thank you, Ronald Reagan! At this moment, churches have all gone silent in prayer, those stuck in traffic jams have come out of their cars in order to look up at the sky for something to see—perhaps expecting a bright light to indicate success, or perhaps no one wants to die inside of a Prius. I'm going to talk to Professor Pascal, the expert on the comet, who is at Mount Hamilton observatory in California..."

"So that's where he is," Casper said before being shushed by Don and Ami.

"...Professor Pascal. You're raising skepticism about the President's plan to shatter the comet. Why are you being such a buzz kill?" Skip asked.

"Well, Skip. I believe..."

"Sorry to interrupt, Professor, but I was told the missile is about to make contact. This is it, America! In twenty seconds we're going to find out if the Flying Spaghetti Monster is watching over us! I'd just like to say, it's been a privilege serving you all for all of these years, and to my ex-girlfriend, Sandy, I'd like to say: I told you, I'd never come crawling back to you, even if the world ends!"

Ami walked over and grabbed Casper's and Don's hands. Don closed his eyes. Ami looked up at the night sky. Casper did not. He knew that if there were any significant flashes, visible from Earth it would only be seen in Australia at this moment. He didn't want to ruin it for Ami and looked up also. The radio broadcaster went silent. In the background, you could still hear chatter from NASA, co un ti n g d own : 10... 9... 8... 7... 6... 5... 4.. 1..
And then silence. It was a silence like before the beginning of time. Everyone in the whole world held their breath. It reminded Casper of 9-11. When the first tower fell it created the reality that the second tower could also fall. Before that happened, it was like everyone in America was using whatever psychic, Charleston Heston powers they could muster to try to hold up that last tower. Casper's phone beeped a text message from his mom. He didn't have to read it. He knew what it said.

The silence continued until Skip said: "What? It did what? You're kidding!" Followed by a nervous laugh. "Uhh, ladies and gentlemen, I don't know how to tell you this, but the missiles... missed."

There is no record on hand for the most amount of people saying the same word all over the world at the same time, but at that moment, in their own languages, everyone in the world at the same time said:

"WHAT—THE—@#$*?!"

"L-lets go to Professor Pascal now for an explanation." Skip stuttered. "Professor, what happened? Is this what you were about to warn us about? Was this an ill-fated plan to begin with?"

"Of course it was an ill-fated plan, but what just happened actually doesn't make any sense...unless."

"Unless what, Professor?"

"Casper?" Ami asked. "How could they have missed?"

"Inferior technology?" Casper answered.

"Ladies and gentleman, I have Gil Bakers on the line from NASA to explain what happened. Gil?" Skip asked.

"Yes, Skip?"

"Gil, what happened?"

"No freak'n idea, whatsoever."

"Not a good answer." Casper complained before being shushed.

"I know what happened," Pascal volunteered.

"Professor?" Skip asked

"The data was all wrong."

"Professor?"

"I don't know how this happened or why, but unless this comet is able to move out of the way on its own, all of our previous data, including my own, have all been wrong."

"How wrong, Professor?"

"From what I can see by my new data, the speed is off, and the impact point has changed."

"How different are we talking about?"

"At its previous speed, on impact it would have taken us <u>all</u> out. Now it has the velocity to only take out an area the size of… Kenya. Matter of fact, that's probably where it's going to hit."

"Wait, Professor, you mean we don't have to worry any more? That it's not going to devastate the entire planet?"

"Well, yes, except for the poor people of Kenya of course…"

"Of course, but for the rest of us, we're saved, right?"

"There may be an ash cloud from it that'll cause extra freezing temperatures and an extended winter, maybe crop loss, famine in Third World countries, war, that kind of thing."

"But, except for a few extra months of skiing, we'll be alive?"

"Minus the end of Kenya, we should be okay…"

"YES!" Skip yelled.

Casper and Don high-fived.

"Why are you celebrating? What about Kenya?" Ami asked

"That's sad but hey, they're used to that kind of thing," Casper said smiling for the first time in days.

"Used to a comet destroying their <u>entire</u> country?" Ami asked.

"Yahooo!" Yelled the Newbie guy, crashing through the woods. He was holding a bottle of very expensive champagne and a bunch of plastic cups. "We're gonna live!" he yelled.

"What about Kenya?!" Ami yelled.

"Kenya, Schmenya. Who cares. They're used to that kind of thing!" The Newbie began to pour them plastic cups of the alcohol.

Don was silent. He had his back turned to them all and his head was lowered. Casper assumed he was either praying or didn't want them to see him crying for joy. Either way, Casper let him have his peace.

The two day walk back home took a little longer than they had expected. All of the traffic and people that were trying to get to birth homes on their way out, were now trying to get back to their regular homes.

Instead of being polite for fear that the almighty would judge them completely on their last week of behavior, people had no problem honking their horns, cutting each other off in traffic, using four-letter words, and one-finger expressions. The wars that had stopped, started up like someone had grabbed a record and let it come to a voice warping end and then released it to sound like a singing chipmunk with a machine gun Crime increased, too, as criminals took advantage of all the people that had abandoned their homes.

Casper and his friends trudged up the last flight of steps to their apartment. They were listening to the radio story of the Russian billionaires who took the rocket to the International Space Station. Apparently they overshot and were now heading into deep space and not expected to be heard from ever again. Meanwhile two helicopters carrying two American billionaires and two Congressmen who had voted against an anti-global warming bill, had their engines freeze up as they were flying in Antarctica, and then crashed into an iceberg; only the pilot survived.

"Wow!" Don said. "There is a god."

"God nothing. They were probably offed by the competition," Casper said. "War, murder, greed and theft. Nice to have the earth back to normal, huh?"

Ami unlocked the apartment door. It swung open to reveal their landlord holding Casper's TV. He was a bald, short, chubby man with a mustache. He always seemed to only wear wife beater shirts accessorized with red suspenders holding up his pants.

There was a brief staring contest.

"Mr. Campbell?" Casper asked.

"Oh…guys, how ya doing?" Campbell said, setting the TV down. "I was just checking to make sure no one stole anything out of your apartment while you were gone."

Casper, Don and Ami all had angry and shocked looks on their faces.

"I'll just let myself out…Nice to see you kids made it back, safe and sound." Campbell backed out and closed the door.

"Check everything!" Ami said.

"That's a given," Don agreed.

Casper checked to make sure his laptop computer was where he had left it. It was, but it had a $100 price sticker on it. "Nice to see that things have returned to worse than ever," he said.

In spite of being labeled with price tags, nothing was missing from the apartment. They decided they would start looking for a new place to live tomorrow. For now, it was tranquil to lay in their own beds, unhunch their shoulders and unclench their teeth. Casper slept soundly that night, like a boulder on the bottom of a warm lake. He wasn't awakened by the constant sounds outside of people returning to their homes. He was, however, awakened the next morning by a phone call at 10:00.

"H-hello?" he said groggily.

"Caper Cornbregger, please."

"Speaking."

"Casper, this is Sue, where are you?"

"I'm at home, you should know that, you called my home number."

"No, I mean why aren't you at work?"

"Work? You want me to come to work?"

"You were scheduled to be here at 9:00 It's now 10:00. You didn't call in."

"But…the world was going to end."

"It didn't, so now that everything is back to normal, you're late for work and this is going to count as another point against you."

"I'm being punished because the world was going to end?"

"You're being punished because you're on probation and you're gonna be late for work again."

"Late, because of the Apocalypse."

"Casper, I don't like your tone. This is exactly what I talked to you about in our meeting. I think it's best that you don't come into work today."

"Cool. Three-day weekend."

"That's not what I meant Cas—I'm saying we're gonna have to let you go."

"Go where?"

"Go nowhere. We have to <u>fire</u> you, Casper."

"Fired because of the Apocalypse?"

"We'll mail you your check." Sue hung up on him.

Feeling apathetic, Casper cut on his TV. The channels were all business as usual. Most channels were of course talking about the day the world almost ended, while ignoring the fact that an obliterated Kenya and a long winter could still have devastating effects on the entire planet. When they showed the current footage from Kenya, hordes of evacuees were trying to get out of town ASAP. There was chaos everywhere as grocery store shelves were stripped bare and looting set in. Even in the small village of Kiambaa, the news footage showed a hut door being broken down, two men entered and then ran out with someone's goat. There was also chaos in the bordering countries, some of which refused to accept the Kenyan refugees, sometimes using violent military force to repel them.

Casper was very confused about the news about the velocity of the comet. A typical mile-long object hitting the Earth would flatten everything from New York to Boston and then throw up a dust cloud big enough to block out the sun, which would wipe out the rest of life on Earth. Comets and asteroids do not slow down unless they are affected by outside influence. Even if the comet were moving at a slower speed, contained destruction in Kenya would only occur if it were moving in the lower hundreds; far less than 30,000 miles per hour. Casper hypothesized perhaps the comet had been blasted backwards by something in the past or the missiles exploded too early and the government was lying.

He went into the kitchen. Ami was there, eating toast with jam and reading a travel guide for Machu Picchu.

"Going somewhere?" Casper asked.

"Hecks yeah," Ami said before taking a sip of coffee.

"Don still asleep?"

"No, he went for a jog. I think it's going to be his new thing."

"And is traveling going to be your 'new thing?'" Casper turned the book around to see which part of it she was reading.

"You got it. I wasted too many years of my life between Japan and California, I want to see what the rest of the world is like."

"I have news for you. One summer I visited four different countries with my parents. Everywhere we went had a McDonald's."

"There's a McDonald's in Osaka, doesn't mean it's not an interesting town."

"I guess. I'd just like to go somewhere that's not so…here. You know? Somewhere so different that you can't even look at the garbage on the street and know immediately what kind of candy wrapper it is. That's my idea of getting away from it all. Like taking your mind and dipping it into a vast unknown, like finally letting go of all of your expectations."

Ami was silent for a second. "You really are an astronomer, slash artist."

"I guess…it's my new thing." Casper walked over to the cabinet to look for a coffee mug. "So, my job called—I'm fired."

"What? Fired for what?" Ami put her book down.

"Apparently, I was supposed to go to work today," Casper said, looking up.

"Today? Two days after near Armageddon?"

"Yep."

Ami raised one of her eyebrows. "Wow…Sorry? I think."

"Yeah. I'm over it. Before the comet, I would have been really freaked out to be fired from there. Nothing like a near-death experience to get your priorities straight. I guess now I'll have to find another crappy job."

"I hear the slaughter house is hiring."

"Bring it on!" He took a coffee mug off the shelf.

Ami looked worried. "Casper?"

"What's up, Ami-chan?" He frowned at the coffee stain in his favorite mug.

"They're not reporting the real story about the comet, are they?"

"What makes you say that?"

"Well, I'm no scientist but you can't slam a five-mile-long object on a country road without causing some major damage in the city, right?"

"You are correct." Casper crossed his arms. "The odd thing is, at the speed it's going they're saying that it won't destroy us—which is crap. Something that size should cause a nuclear winter—and why no worries about some major earthquakes on the nearby countries? Evacuate to Ethiopia all you want, it won't matter. They should just consider all of Africa as ground zero."

"But, how does a comet slow down suddenly?"

"I'd like to ask my teacher that if he ever picks up his phone."

"Maybe it's not a comet."

"Not a comet?"

"Maybe it's an alien space ship?"

"I wish, but no."

"Why not? It's dodging missiles and slowing down."

"It's not dodging missiles and it didn't slow down. They miscalculated its location and speed."

"But why not an alien ship? I thought you wanted to be a scientist. Aren't you supposed to be open to that kind of stuff?"

"I…I would like to, but I can't."

"Don't you believe in life in outer space?"

Casper poured himself a cup of coffee and sat across from Ami. "When I was a kid, I used to go into the backyard and climb up on the tool shed. I would lay on my back and stare up at the stars for hours, and when I did, I would have the same thought: I wished that aliens would travel to Earth and take me away. Every time I went up there that's all I could think of. Years later, I learned about light years, I discovered that the light from those stars I was looking at was thousands of years old. Like if they looked at our sun, they would be looking at the light shining on the Earth when Abraham was running around. That meant that no matter what, we would always be not only in different galaxies, but different times. We'll always be looking at each other's past. And the worst thing would be if those aliens were to travel to us and then go back home. Most likely, both civilizations on both ends would be gone thousands of years ago. Their friends, family, culture, everything would be gone. They would be cavemen on their own destroyed planet, bringing a human descendent, even less advanced than a caveman—a cockroach, perhaps?—to visit. Doesn't sound like much fun for anybody."

Ami started reading her book again. "You must be a LOT of fun at sci-fi movies."

"Nowadays, Don always goes alone."

Casper took a walk around town to see how things had or had not changed since the "Near End," as the press had dubbed it. The only change he could see was an absence of half the population, probably still stuck in the various traffic jams. Further into the town circle he saw a car crashed into the window of the Yoghurt Yurt, and some graffiti on the city hall. "Odd" he thought. Odder still, he saw Lori walking towards him, holding a white plastic bag. He was really not in the mood to deal with her or whatever explanation for the plastic bag she had. He cut into a blind alleyway. Before he could find a way out, he heard Lori's voice coming closer and closer. She was talking on her cell phone. Casper looked for somewhere else to go. The fire escape ladder overhead was too far to jump to. Her voice was getting closer and annoying him more and more. Desperate for an escape, he looked inside an empty garbage bin. "Should I or shouldn't I?" he thought. "Was it worth getting into a garbage bin just to avoid an awkward conversation with someone you despised?"

"I know..." Lori said. "...We never made it to Yosemite! I haven't taken a bath in four days and then we ran out of tampons and..."

Casper quickly jumped into the garbage bin. He could hear Lori pass by the bin and then walk back. He felt nervous. "Did she see me?" He was unsure whether Lori was going to kill him, but it felt that way. He could hear every word of her conversation: "Why is she standing there?" he wondered. "Does she know I'm in here? Is she just messing with me?"

"...Totally!" Lori said. "...I came home and I had all of these old shrimp shells and chicken livers in the garbage can I forgot about and I had put some parsley in a cup of water to preserve them and that went bad...Yeah, parsley can go bad, not just bad, have you ever smelled old parsley water? Barf-o! It's like Vomit's big brother! Combine that with rotten shrimp and you have a Wikipedia of bad smells! So there's no way I'm throwing this bag away ANYWHERE near my house. I came all the way downtown to get rid of it, that's how rank it is." With that, without looking inside, Lori lifted up the garbage bin lid and tossed the bag onto Casper's head.

Rewind to last week. There was a point when Lori was shopping at Big Red Groceries and she was in the aisle where the garbage bags were. On the shelf were the extra thick two-ply, expensive "Neverbreak" bags, and the cheap "Econo" bags that break if you dared to even whisper the word "break."—guess which bags she bought?

Even the agonizing screams of disgust that Casper uttered didn't cause Lori to stop, turn around and investigate. Her colorful descriptions were very accurate, although it wasn't Vomit's big brother. It was Vomit's dad.

Casper screamed and clawed his way out of the bin. He failed to notice the female standing close by. It wasn't Lori but it was someone he knew. Darla stood on the alleyway, looking at Casper as if she had just witnessed a pig giving birth.

"Casper?" she said, staring at him and holding her nose.

"Oh, hi…Darla." He smiled.

"Everything all right, man?" she asked, looking at the shrimp shell in his hair.

"Peachy! First I got fired and now this." He tried to shake the contents off of his arms.

"Dude, you just got fired and you've already hit skid row? That was fast!"

"It's not that, I was hiding from someone."

"Wow, you must really be afraid of someone if you're willing to go in there. Was it worth it?"

Casper smelled himself and then thought of Lori. "Yes…yes, it was."

"Tell you what. My boyfriend lives near here. Why don't you come with me and take a shower, maybe he'll let you borrow some clothes."

"Don't worry, I can walk back…"

"Casper…honey." Darla interrupted. "You'll never make it home. People will set you on fire. Come with me." She grabbed a clean spot on his shirt sleeve and lead him away.

Remember when it was mentioned in jest that the Russian rocket, full of billionaires, had missed its mark and was heading into deep space? This wasn't entirely true. It was actually heading on a direct collision course with Pascal's Comet. This fact was not lost on floating oil tycoon Uri Ratbastardcoth. He looked out the porthole-type window at the ever brightening light.

"Marvin?" he called to his porn mogul friend, Marvin Lecehavitz. Marvin was busy singing *Korobein* (you know it better as that Tetris song) while his mistress bit him on the ear. Marvin unhinged the arms of his blonde mistress from his neck and floated over to Uri. "What's that you say?" he said with vodka-stained breath. Behind him, unknown to everyone else, the blonde's wig came off to reveal that she was a he. He/she/they tried to fix their wig before Marvin found out and ejected them into space.

"Shouldn't we have arrived at the space station?" Uri asked.

"Relax my friend, we have all the time in the world…unlike the people back on earth!" The two laughed heartily at Marvin's cruel joke without realizing the people on Earth were far safer than the ones in the Russian Federal Space Agency craft.

"But what is that bright light that is getting closer and closer?" Uri asked, looking at the ice and dust starting to hit the craft.

Marvin looked out the window at the approaching comet. "Perhaps it is the way the sun looks in space."

"Possible. But one thing worries me." Uri looked over at the blond(e) as he/she/they put his/her/their wig back on. He figured it was just the vodka making him see things.

"What is that, my rich friend?" Marvin asked

"When we were boarding the rocket. The ground crew, the support staff, everyone that helped us take off were so…nice."

"Yes. What is wrong with that?" Marvin floated over to the astronaut's honor bar. All drinks were in juice-box like containers.

"It doesn't make sense, my friend. I mean, we planned this trip as an emergency plan in case the United States launched a nuclear war." Uri couldn't take his eyes off the ice hitting the window with increasing frequency.

"Yes, and it went over without a hitch," Marvin said, a little loud.

"Exactly. That's my problem. Everyone helped us take off with full knowledge that they were all going to get killed. Doesn't that bother you? Not one complaint, not one person taking a gun and trying to take our place, not even an army of Chernobyl zombies trying to stop us at the last minute. It went too smoothly," Uri yelled. He started to sweat.

"Of course it went smoothly, my friend!" Marvin was starting to yell louder over the sound of ice hitting the metal shell of the space craft. "People realize it's their responsibility to let the alpha humans survive! Like the ants they are, they gladly sacrifice their lives so that we, the super humans, can carry on the…"

It is at this point that I must mention the rocket burst into a small nuclear explosion. You see, not only had the ground crew in Russia been a little peeved to be left behind, but they had armed the escape rocket with a small nuclear bomb. It was the only way they could happily work as a support crew for the billionaires' survival.

The blip in the cosmos would not go unnoticed. The light from the explosion traveled all the way from space to the telescope at the Mount Hamilton Observatory, to the eyes of Professor

Pascal, who quickly turned his head away before any damage could be done to his retinas.

"What was that?" he complained.

"What was what?" asked a young Indian woman, standing in the entrance. She was around half of Pascal's age and like him, wore a lab coat. She entered the room full of computers, telescope parts, and anything else to make it look like a place where smart people go to look up at the stars, well, perhaps it could use one of those buzzzz things you see in the Frankenstein movies.

Pascal looked at the young lady with joy. "Welcome back," he said.

"I can't believe you actually stayed here the whole time," she complained.

"Front row seats to Armageddon, are you kidding? Where have you been?"

"Same as everyone else, at the airport trying to catch a plane that never came. Every pilot would only fly to their home towns and then get off; oneway trip only. There are still thousands of people stuck in airports all over the world."

"Perhaps next time you can stay with me and have a glass of eighty-year old port."

"Sounds nice. Maybe the next apocalypse," she smiled. "So what were you complaining about?"

"Oh, I saw a bright light, like an explosion."

"Were you looking at the comet?"

"Of course."

The woman started laughing.

"Something funny?"

"Well, actually it shouldn't be funny but…I have a friend that works at the Russian Federal Space Agency. Rumor has it that the escape rocket the billionaires took to the space station was actually armed with explosives. They wanted to try your plan of nudging the craft out of the way."

"That's terrible. I can't feel solace knowing that innocent people died just to use my plan."

"Don't feel sad, Lewis…" The woman patted his back. "Winchester invented a rifle; he never killed anyone with it."

"That doesn't make me feel any better, Aarti."

Aarti turned Professor Pascal's chair around and pointed at the telescope eye piece. "Look through the telescope, see if your plan worked. If it did, you will have saved millions of lives in Africa—much more of a contribution to society than those billionaires."

Pascal did as he was told. What he saw was confusing. "No…"

"Please tell me the comet didn't speed up or break into big chunks," Aarti pleaded.

"No, neither of those."

Let us move our gaze to Antarctica. A C130 gunship was flying fast and low. For those of you unfamiliar with military aircraft, imagine a large propeller aircraft with a large back hatch. When the plane was over its drop-zone, the hatch lowered and within a few seconds eight Navy Bears poured out. You say you've never heard of the Navy Bears? Think of the Navy Seals for snow combat. This elite combat squad, all dressed in white combat fatigues, filed out of the back and deployed their parachutes. When their boots hit the snow, machine guns were cocked and ready to fire and binoculars were out, surveying the nearby compound. Within a second, two armed guards in front of the compound's entryway were dropped like hot garbage. This is where the President, Congress, some billionaires and their support staff had escaped the "Near End." Unfortunately for the President and his friends, after the now-armed support staff shot down two helicopters with a missile launcher (this was reported as engines freezing up on the news), they had taken the rest hostage.

Andre Vasquez used to be a janitor in the White House. Now he was the leader of a revolution. Less than a day had gone by when he and the rest of the staff realized that if they got into the storage locker where the guns were kept, they would be in the position of power. Inside the cafeteria of the underground complex, the President and those who used to be in the position of power knelt on the ground with their hands behind their heads. In front of them, the cook, the janitors and the housekeepers held machine guns as Andre gave a speech.

Andre poked a Southern congressman with the barrel of a handgun: "I bet you wish you hadn't voted against that immigration bill now, eh jefe? Things are going to be different around here from now on. For starters: you clean the toilets, you will do the cooking and YOU will mow the lawn!"

"There is no lawn," the President corrected him.

"Then shovel the snow! I don't care! Bottom line, you had two hundred whatever years oppressing the minorities; now it's OUR turn." The armed groups all shouted cheers of support. "That's right! Now you'll see what it's like to go into a store and some security guard follows you around!" More cheers. "You get to see what it's like to be <u>randomly</u> searched at the airport, EVERY SINGLE TIME!" More cheers. "You get to see what it's like going into a party full of White people because this cute White girl at work invited you, and you didn't want to appear mean because you're trying to get into her pants, and then you realize everyone's the same race except you and you spot someone the same race as you, and you both do that head nod thing to say 'Oh, thank God! Now nobody can tell a racist joke!'"There was no cheering this time, just confused looks. "You get to—"

At that moment, Andre and the rest of the staff noticed the tiny, red laser dots on their heads. Within seconds the muffled sound of precision machine gun fire rendered their bodies lifeless and slumped around the ground. A second later, a red dot appeared on the southern Congressman's head and one more shot shuffled off his mortal coil. The Navy Bears ran into the room from their hiding places, kicked guns out of dead hands and helped the hostages up.

"'Bout time you got here!" said the President. "My knees were killing me. Don't know how much longer I could have listened to the Castro manifesto…But why did you kill Congressman Greely? Was that friendly fire?"

"No, sir," answered the sergeant. "Some of us are gay and he said some pretty hateful stuff during his campaign."

President Jarrod shrugged his shoulders. "Fair enough. So what's the status on the comet? Has it hit us yet?"

"No, sir, the latest word is that it's going to hit Kenya and cause some climate change; possible nuclear winter there or all over the world."

"Bet those Prius-driving hippies wish they supported global warming, now," the President said, brushing off his pants.

A staff member ran over to him holding a cell phone. "Mr. President, you have a call from General Katz at NORAD."

"Where were you?" the President asked the staff member.

"I was hiding in the broom closet the whole time."

"Next time you do that I'll send you to Guantanamo–spend eight years in a broom closet!" The President snatched the phone away. "What's new, pussycat?"

There was a slight delay. Not because of the great distance between Colorado and Antarctica, but because General Katz needed time to sigh and roll his eyes. "Mr. President, we have an update on the comet."

"I already know it's going to land on Kenya, but aren't they used to that kind of thing?"

"No, sir, not Kenya. The Russians fired a missile at it in hopes the shockwave would repel it from Earth's orbit."

"And did it?"

"No, sir. Not only is it still on a crash course with Earth, but it's now headed for New Orleans!"

"What in Jesus Mary Joseph and Ringo is going on here? What kind of comet is this? Zig zags more than a Texas quarterback!"

"Unknown, sir. But since it's now a threat to us I've taken the liberty of firing a salvo of low-orbit block busters at it."

"Good, good. Keep me informed." The President hung up the phone and looked around at all of the dead staff members. "You could at least left one of them alive. Who's going to clean up this mess?"

The news of the comet's new objective had already reached the media, thanks not to the government but to the numerous astronomers like Professor Pascal, manning their telescopes. Darla, Casper and Darla's boyfriend, Gregory, watched the video footage of Louisiana: hordes of evacuees were trying to get out of town ASAP. There was chaos everywhere as grocery store shelves were stripped bare and looting set in. Even in the small town of Boutte, the news footage showed Big Goat's Electronics appliance store's window being broken. Two men entered and then ran out with a television set. There was also chaos on the bordering states. Some of them refused to accept the Louisiana refugees, using violent police force to repel them.

Casper received a phone call from Ami. "Casper!" she yelled, "You hear about the comet?"

"Yeah. Poor New Orleans, so sad. First Katrina and now this."

"Wait...poor New Orleans? What about Kenya? Wasn't that the same thing?"

"Nooo, not the same. New Orleans! The Big Easy! All of that music and good food. Those poor people. I wonder where we could send them a care package?"

Ami made a noise which sounded like growling and then hung up.

"Ahh man," said Gregory. He rubbed his short mohawk, painted green "No more gumbo."

"Meanwhile, back at Mount Hamilton Observatory," Aarti said.

"What did you say?" Pascal asked.

"Nothing, I'm just feeling like I'm in a Bruce Willis action movie. A huge comet is coming to destroy the Earth. Can two scrappy scientists stop it?"

"Unless we're wearing capes, no. But from what I can see, someone has fired a bunch of missiles at it, and they will hit in a few minutes."

"So, they've gone back to Plan A?"

"Looks like it, after my plan's spectacular failure."

"I wouldn't call it a failure, Lewis. How were you to know that this comet is behaving like no other object to come into our gravitational field?"

"It is my own faith at fault."

"Pardon?"

"Aarti, I'm refusing to believe." Pascal stood up and walked over to a computer monitor. "Lex parsimoniae."

"Occam's Razor?" Aarti asked.

"Correct. What would Occam's Razor say about what has happened so far? What do we know about the comet?"

"It has the ability to slow down even before an explosion's shockwave has affected it?"

"That's one." Pascal held up one finger.

"It changed directions when a missile was heading towards it."

"That's two." Pascal held up two fingers.

"It was hit by a rocket with passengers on it, which could appear different than a missile, meaning it knew the difference?"

"That's three…" Pascal held up three fingers. "…And four?"

"Four? Even before all of this began, this comet switched directions and instead of heading into deep space, it made a left turn and headed right for us. Like it has a cosmic GPS."

"Bingo! And guess who knew that last part and didn't want to believe it?"

Aarti walked over to Pascal and put her hand on his shoulder. "Lewis. We're scientists second and humans first. We all make mistakes."

"It wasn't a mistake, Aarti. It was my disbelief."

"In what? God? Don't get me started on you westerners and your <u>one</u> god, because we have a football team backing us up."

"No, not religion. Fantasy, science fiction; from what you know about the comet, what would Occam's Razor tell us?"

"Well…either we have a new type of comet and our instruments and missiles are all faulty or…" Aarti looked up at the domed ceiling. "…I can't believe I'm saying this…Like you, I used to believe that it wasn't possible. That if there was life out there, they would come visit, just like E.T. But, it didn't make sense. Thousands of light years away. How would they do it? Every time we discovered a new planet outside our solar system, there was always something wrong with it: not enough water, too hot, too cold, et cetera. And what about their society that makes them superior enough to come here? How did they overcome racism, the wars the environmental threats? How did they band together to overcome Einstein's theories? If what you say is true, everything— <u>everything</u> we have come to believe in will be thrown out the window."

"I know…Remember when they discovered fossilized microorganisms in pieces of rocks from Mars?"

Aarti nodded.

"And yet, even after that, religious people still believe in God. That they are the chosen descendants from Adam and Eve and the Earth is only a few thousand years old. Nothing changed for them. Nothing should change for us, either. We must soldier on, the constant skeptics and theorists. When that alien ship lands, we'll be waiting on the tarmac saying I guess Einstein was wrong, but here's a new theory."

Casper walked into his apartment. The world had changed again in his fifteen-minute walk home. Instead of Louisiana, the comet had dodged the first salvo of missiles and had chosen Yakistan as its new target de choix. Ami was glued to the TV set. When people say that, usually they mean that someone is so interested in a TV show that they can't take their eyes away from the screen for fear of missing something. This was all true, but it was also true that she had accidentally super-glued her finger to the side, a failed attempt at trying to fix the crack that's always bothered her.

"Casper!" she yelled. "Can you get me the nail polish remover?"

Casper obliged and retrieved the bottle from the bathroom cabinet. He handed it to Ami with a look of confusion. He expected to see more information on Louisiana, but instead, on the news it showed video footage of Yakistan: hordes of evacuees were trying to get out of town ASAP. There was chaos everywhere as grocery store shelves were stripped bare and looting set in, even in the small town of Wajah Almaeiz, the news footage showed Raheem's TVs & More store window being broken. Two men entered and then ran out with …a goat? There was also chaos on the bordering countries, some of them refusing to accept…Hold on a minute! I've just had the strangest feeling of…Oh, what is that feeling you have when you have done something before…It was in the movie "The Matrix"–remember, when that cat repeated itself? Of course I'll remember THAT, but I can't remember a simple word. Not very promising for a narrator eh? Anyway, while I try to rack my elderly female brain, I'll take you back to the Antarctica complex where the President is sitting down to lunch, prepared by the Navy Polar Bears.

"What is this?" The President asked the sergeant. He looked at the plate of chicken breast and some kind of red-orange jelly.

"Chicken palliard with a radish mint chutney," the sergeant answered.

The President reluctantly cut off a piece of chicken and put it into his mouth. "Mmmmm. That's better than makeup sex. Where'd you learn to cook like that, son?"

"Before I was a human weapon, capable of killing a man eight ways with a toothpick, I studied at the Cordon Bleu, sir," the sergeant answered.

The President didn't get a chance to finish the delicious chicken dish. He was interrupted by his assistant.

"Phone call, sir. It's General Katz," the assistant said.

The President took the phone away and gave the assistant a nasty look for interrupting his lunch, unconcerned that the world was in danger. "Meeow?" the President said.

There was a breathy sigh from General Katz. "Mr. President, we have a new development on the comet."

"Kitty Cat, the only three words I want to hear from you are: destroyed, yippee and party."

"Sorry to disappoint you, sir, but it's none of those."

"What is it now? Is the comet going to land on a country we hate? Because I'm totally okay with that."

"It seems, whenever we fire missiles at it, the comet actually evades them. To tell you the truth, sir, we're starting to think that this isn't really a comet."

"Baloney. Just because you throw a frog at a bunch of girls doesn't mean it's a bouquet."

"Sir?"

"It's the first comet we've ever shot missiles at; maybe this is what comets do."

"Possible." Katz answered, confused that maybe the President had a point.

"Of course I'm right. Now, what's the comet doing now?"

"It was headed to Yakistan but we took a shot at it and now it slowed down even more and switched position."

"Sneaky little S.O.B., ain't it? So where's it gonna hit now?"

"Paris."

"Paris? Well...that ain't so bad, I mean what have the es-car-gots done for us lately? Gave us a big green statue and tongue kissing, I think we should let it hit..."

"Sir?" the Navy Bear sergeant interrupted. "The Cordon Bleu is in Paris. It would make me sad to see it gone." With that statement, the President saw three red laser dots on his chest.

"Okay, okay! Put your killing sticks away! I'll save Paris, but this is it! Unless it's going to hit in the...wait a minute, did you say the comet slowed down?"

"Yes, sir."

"Okay, I may not know much about physics, but I saw this movie that had space vampires living inside a space ship that traveled around in a comet. You suppose that's what we're dealing with?"

"You seriously think it's...space vampires?"

"No! I'm talking alien, U.F.O., space ship, E.T.—me love you long time! That kind of thing."

"Sir, we've had radars monitoring space for years and telescopes combing the skies 24-7. If an alien ship ever made a peep, we would know. As far as Professor Pascal is concerned, there are no planets close enough to even consider alien life."

"Professor Pascal? Where have I heard that name before?"

"He's the comet expert, Mr. President. You hung up on him," the assistant said, eavesdropping on the conversation.

"Well, get Dr. Pepper back on the line. He's got some explaining to do," the President ordered.

Meanwhile, Dr. Pep–er, ah, I mean Professor Pascal was watching the latest direction change of the comet, caused by the newly fired missiles from NORAD.

"Oh, my Lord!" Aarti said.

"What?" Pascal asked. Before he could get an answer, the phone rang. He picked it up immediately; he knew all phone calls were important. "Hello?"

"This is the Office of the President calling. Is Professor Pascal there?" the assistant asked.

"Yes?"

"Please hold on."

The President picked up the line. "Dr. P. What's shaking?"

"Everything, soon."

"Ha, good one. Listen Doc, remember how you were trying to tell me something about the comet?"

"Yes, sir. You ignored my advice."

"Water under the bridge, Doc. Anyway, being the 'comet guy', I'm sure you have some in-fo-tainment on the comet that we may not know about."

"Believe me, I have plenty of info on the comet."

"Then why the silent treatment, Doc? You have my number, girlfriend."

"You ignored my earlier advice; I assumed it was useless."

"Doc, don't you know the old saying? You can lead a horse to water but you can't make him drink, but at least you'll have something to drink while you eat the horse?"

"I'm not sure if that's…"

"Apples and oranges, Doc—bottom line, you need to be more aggressive, like me. You think I backed down when Congress wanted to increase funding for universities?"

"Thank you for that, by the way," Pascal said sarcastically. "Thanks to you, our labs had to use jelly jars instead of test tubes."

"You're welcome. Anyway, you gotta grow a pair. We're trying to save the world here and you're letting your feelings get hurt like a five-year-old schoolgirl whose daddy didn't buy her a stuffed elephant. Man, my daughter's still steaming about that one. For crying out loud, it's been ten ye…"

"Mr. President!" Pascal interrupted. "I know what you're saying, and you're right. I let my ego as a scientist block my duty as a human."

"Good, good. Now lay it on me, Doc. What kind of comet is this?"

Pascal sighed. "Mr. President, its pattern of flight seems to suggest…intelligent life."

"U.F.O.?"

"Technically, all objects that we don't recognize are U.F.O.s, intelligent or not."

"You know what I mean, though. We're talking about the little green men in the silver jumpsuits and a big yellow lightning bolt on the front, right?"

"Sure, why not."

"You don't seem too happy, Doc. I thought this is what you scientists lived for? The Holy Grail."

"I've actually spent most of my life disproving the presence of alien visitation on the Earth. Mr President, this is like discovering that there really is a Santa Claus and the Easter Bunny. It opens the gate of fantasy: vampires, werewolves, fairies. Might as well throw them all in there."

"Buck up, little cowboy. You can't have swords and laser guns in the same movie, right?"

"What? Why not?"

"They cancel each other out. If you have swords and laser guns in a movie, it makes the fight scenes kinda stupid because you're like, 'just pick up the laser and cap that guy!' Right?"

"I guess."

"So you can't have a world with Santa Claus and Jesus. One of them has got to go. Life never allows both."

"Perhaps."

"Of course I'm right! Now let's assume we live in a world where an alien ship, disguised as a comet, may or may not be carrying vampires—not sure if those can exist in our world—either way, it's on its way here. What should we do?"

"Lewis!" Aarti called over to him.

"I'm on the phone with the President of the United States. We're trying to decide what to do about the comet," Pascal called back.

"We'll you better decide quick…I'm so sorry, Lewis. The comet's new target is Pepper Mill, California…your home town."

Chapter 3
The Goldilocks Zone

There was a large amount of mumbling, rumbling and rustling voices in the Pepper Mill town hall. There had not been this many people in the hall since they were thinking of putting a bra on the topless bronze statute in the park. Keeping the crowd in order for the moment was Sheriff Earl Taylor and his deputy, Clem Cartwright. Earl was tall of body and large of belly. Clem was average of height and skinny of body. Together, they looked like the number ten. From the back room the Mayor Renée Duncan, entered the hall. The mumbling and rustling increased in volume. Renée was a lesbian and wore a…Hold on! Why do I have to say that she's a lesbian? What does this have to do with her performance as a mayor or a character in this story? Do I have to say "that Black guy, Don" every time, or tell you about Casper's sexual preference? "Casper, the guy who likes it when the woman does all the work, came into the room?" Rubbish! Let's start again:

Mayor Duncan came into the room. She wore Gandhi glasses on her plump, suntanned face. Her red hair was cut very short and she was wearing overalls and a plaid shirt…Oh for Christ's sake! Plaid shirt? Butch hair cut? How stereotypical! I will not be party to such roughshod writing. Why don't we put an afro on Don and a yarmulke on Casper's head? There's no good reason she should look like that! Bullocks!

Renée walked over to the podium. "Earl, Clem." she greeted the officers.

"Mayor," Earl said. "What's with the hair and overalls?"

"Oh, when I heard the news, I came straight from my farm and my daughter got head lice from school so I just cut my hair short 'cause it's just easier."

Okay, she does have a good reason for her appearance. Many hands were raised and the rumbling and rustling continued. This was preventing the mayor from addressing the crowd. "Hello?" she said." Everybody?" she said louder. The audience of townspeople were full of questions. "Please, everyone," she said louder.

Earl took out his revolver, pointed it at the ceiling and fired. The whole audience flinched. A piece of the ceiling plaster hit the floor.

"Dang it, Earl!" the mayor complained. "I told you not to do that!"

"Sorry Mayor," Earl apologized. His action did have the desired effect, though. Everyone was silent and paying attention to the action in front.

The mayor regained her composure. "Hello, everyone. I'm sure you have many questions, but don't worry, I have many answers." Many hands went up. "Hold on, hold on. I'll get to your questions, but first…I got an e-mail from the head of the Federal Emergency Management Agency." The mayor unfolded a piece of paper and then cleared her throat.

"Ahem: 'People of Pepper Mill, California……Ya'll betta get your white As—'"

"Wait." Clem interrupted. "What's 'As' mean?"

"Oh, I'm sorry, she means your tushie," the mayor apologized. "She used a lot of crude, non-Biblical words I can't say because my 90-year-old grandmother is sitting in the front row; Hi, Nana." The mayor waved to an elderly woman. The woman nodded, waved back and smiled. "Anyway…" the mayor continued: "'Ya'll betta get your white As the H out of there before you get F'ed! Peace out, Bs! Signed Yolanda Iesha Washington, top W at FEMA.' And next to her name is a crude drawing of a hand flipping us off. Isn't that lovely?" the mayor said sarcastically. "So, it looks like Washington, the city and the woman, have abandoned us."

"Is she a young Black woman?" Earl asked.

"No, Earl, she's actually a 40-year-old White woman. Why do you ask?"

"No reason," Earl shrugged.

"Why would someone say that to us?" a person in the middle row asked.

"No idea, Jerry. Maybe she's trying to get fired."

To answer their question we only need to look into the office of Yolanda Iesha Washington. Imagine three hundred phones ringing at the same time, 24 hours per day, seven days per week. Each one is someone ready to complain about a horrible thing and desperate for help. These phones are covering ceiling-high paper piles of unfilled claim forms on the desk of Yolanda Iesha Washington. Now imagine Yolanda Iesha Washington grabbing the sides of her blonde-haired head and screaming in terror: "NOOOOOOOOOOOOOOOOOOOOOOOOOOOOOOOOO!"

A side stairwell door of the city hall opened. A man peered into the room. Everyone looked at him.

"Tim? Something wrong?" The mayor asked.

"I was upstairs in the cafeteria and a bullet shot up out of my soup." Tim said timidly.

"That's just Earl, Tim."

"Oh…Okay." Tim was about to leave. He waved to Earl. "Hi, Earl." Earl waved back. "We still going fishing Sunday?"

"Only if the world doesn't end," Earl joked.

"Gentlemen," the mayor said. "You can make fishing plans later, right now we have to figure out what to do about this comet. I talked to our local celeb Professor Pascal earlier, and he said there's a twenty-five percent chance that this comet is actually going to hit our town."

"Twenty-five percent?" someone yelled.

"Yes. Apparently this comet has been jumping around the globe, targeting different cities for a short time until switching to another city. So, it may or may not switch again."

"Wait a minute!" exclaimed a woman holding a sleeping baby. "What kind of comet jumps around like that?"

"I asked the professor that same question. He told me that all information regarding the comet has now been classified."

There were grumbling complaints from the audience.

The mayor held up her hands to calm the crowd. "Now, now. I agree. This is the typical Washington M.O. The professor did tell me that it is in our best interest to get at least twenty miles away from here."

"Why should we believe him?" a mailman yelled.

"Good question, Pete. He IS working with D.C. and could be deceiving us. But, I can't really imagine how anyone could have anything to gain if we abandoned town. They would, however, have a lot to lose if a comet landed on our town and everyone gets 'F'ed,' as FEMA put it, especially if they didn't warn us."

"I say we all get out of here. No matter what they're up to, I don't want to be around to see it," the woman holding the baby said. Many voices agreed with her.

"I say we stay put. If they're up to something, we should just wait and see what it is," a guy with an American flag shirt said, to more cheers.

"Well, everybody," said the mayor. "I can't really force you out of your homes—"

"I could," Earl said, patting his gun.

"…Anyway," the mayor continued. "I do think we should all go home and at the very least pack all of your things and be ready to head out of town at a moment's notice. According to Professor Pascal, we have 12 hours until impact. That's plenty of time to get two hundred miles away if you choose. But please, and I mean this from the bottom of my heart, do not wait until the last moment to leave. I don't want to see any harm come to anyone."

The meeting was adjourned. Casper, Don and Ami were standing in the back. They made their way outside to the city hall steps.

"So," Casper said. "What do you think we should do?"

"I think we should get outta here and drive up to Seattle. We can stay at my parents for a while until the smoke clears," Don suggested.

"Smoke? More like total destruction. That comet is going to obliterate everything; this town is toast!" Casper said. "I say we pack as fast as we can and leave immediately! That way, we beat the traffic jam out of town."

They started to walk. Ami was silent and deep in thought. Don noticed she had not given her opinion yet.

"Ami? What's on your mind?"

"I…I don't know if I want to leave."

"WHAT!" Casper and Don yelled at the same time.

"Are you nuts?" Don yelled. What are you gonna do, stay here?"

"Yes." Ami answered.

"Ami!" Casper said. "Like they say: 'You don't have to go home, but you can't stay here!'"

"Yes I can, and yes I will," she said.

"Is this some kind of Japanese thing?" Don asked. "Are you trying to prove how much braver you are than us?"

"Believe me, I don't have to be Japanese to be braver than you two," she said.

Casper grabbed her arm and stopped her walking. "Then what could possess you to stay here? Unless you wear a cape and want to spill the secret of your super powers, the danger is real!"

"I don't believe you," she said.

"What? Why not?" Casper asked

"First the world was going to be destroyed, then it wasn't. Then a comet was heading towards Kenya, then Louisiana, Yakistan, Paris and now Pepper Mill? C'mon Casper, this has bovine scatology written all over it!"

"To what end?" Don asked. "Like the mayor said, there is nothing to gain by us abandoning our houses and getting out of danger. You know what happen to those poor people who couldn't abandon their homes during Katrina? That's why we take every threat of disaster seriously!"

"If Hurricane Katrina suddenly popped from Louisiana to Kenya to Paris to here, don't you think someone would have said, 'Wait a minute, that's not how hurricanes act, what's going on here?'"

"Of course they would," Casper said. "But we know a lot more about hurricanes than comets."

"Detarame!" Ami yelled. "We know enough about comets that they don't slow down and switch directions! I know you don't believe that aliens would make a journey to Earth, Casper, but maybe you should open your mind to it."

"Ami, it's not an alien ship! Do you know what the Goldilocks zone is?"

"Not really into strip clubs, Casper," Ami said.

"It's not a strip—it's the location where a habitable planet could be in a solar system. Like the Earth compared to Mars and Venus. Too hot like Venus, no life. Too cold like Mars, no life. The Earth is just right because we have liquid water and all that. The Kepler space mission discovered a planet in that perfect area, the first ever discovered. That's probably the closest place an alien could come from, if the weather conditions are right, life evolved and they have a space program!" Casper started yelling.

"It happened to us, why not them?" Ami yelled/asked.

"Because, even with all the right conditions, that planet is six hundred light years away! Six hundred! Nothing and nobody travels faster than light! Nobody makes a six hundred-year journey just to visit us! Nobody out there cares about us! There is no life in outer space! WE ARE ALL ALONE!" Ami and Don stared at him with concern.

"Casper?" Ami said. "I don't know what's going on with you, but I'm not leaving. I mean, seriously. If this were a real emergency, isn't this the part where the government sends in helicopters and army guys to evacuate people? Do you see any government people taking this seriously enough to send trucks and stuff to get us out of here? The governor hasn't even declared a state of emergency!"

"Well…" Don said. "The head of FEMA did sound like she just fell off a nut harvester."

"And yet…" Ami said. "Evacuating us ain't important enough to appoint someone else? This has conspiracy written all over it. I'm not going anywhere until I find out the truth."

"Then you can stay and die here, Agent Mulder!" Casper stormed off.

It's Christmas time. A little boy came downstairs and saw a huge box, decorated with golden wrapping paper and a big red ribbon on it. He joyously squealed with delight and opened the present as fast as he could. Suddenly, out came five golden retriever puppies all barking and yapping with enthusiasm. "This is the best Christmas, ever!" he yelled. Okay, it's not Christmas, and this scenario has absolutely nothing to do with the story. I just found that last scene a little stressful and thought you'd like something cheerier. Moving right along, there is a person who is even more stressed than he was during the election. The U.S. president looked out of a window of the Oval Office—well, not really the Oval Office. It's a replica built at the Antarctica base. He is stressed out because he has to make a decision: Is he going to allow a comet to land on an American town and destroy it or is he going to trust a bunch of godless scientists that this is actually a space ship that will land softly. Even if it is a space ship, looking at evidence from past science fiction movies, there is no way to tell if these aliens would be friendly. If they are anything like us, the only reason to travel to another country is to find resources to exploit. Columbus, the Pilgrims, Magellan, all had an agenda that had nothing to do with the natives' best interests. Sure E.T. was cute, but what was he doing here, really? Why didn't his people contact the humans before landing? And what was with all the plant stealing? We might have the ability to put him on a table and dissect him like a green turkey, but he could bring things to life and levitate middle-school kids on bicycles, weighing God knows how much! This explains why there has yet to be a sequel to E.T., because we know what happens when he comes back with his army, screaming: "Okay humans, grab your ankles and put on your 3D glasses!"

The door to the Oval Office slammed open and in stumbled Jarrod's daughter Megan and the assistant who really needs a name because he's been in like a billion scenes already. They giggled and hung onto one another, oblivious to the presence of the leader of the free world watching their every action. It appeared that their presence is going to change the meaning of the word 'Oval Office'. As Megan looked around for the liquor cabinet (there wasn't one), she became aware of her father. "Oh! Daddy, hi?" she said, trying to smile the entire situation away.

"Mr. President," said Barry, finally getting his name. Barry tried to button up his shirt which Megan had used her teeth to unbutton moments earlier. "I can't find my button."

"Here." Megan said, spitting a button into his hand.

The President walked over to them. There was no expression of anger on his stone cold face. He put his right hand on Barry's shoulder. He then put his left hand in the position used to shake a person's hand. Barry was wise enough not to shake the President's hand because that was not the reason his hand was in that position.

"Barry…" the President said. "…Imagine, if you will, that this hand represents my nerves." He shook his left hand up and down as if shaking the hand of an invisible person. "Now, this hand…" He took his right hand off of Barry's shoulder and turned it upside down to form an upside down peace sign, or a little man with two legs, if you will. "This hand represents you." He put his right hand on top of the shaking left hand to simulate someone riding a horse. "This is you, and these are my nerves. DO you understand what I'm saying?" Barry nodded. The President shook his hand, representing the horse jumping around. "Do you see what you're doing, Barry? See how my nerves are bucking around and look at you, riding them like a rodeo clown dipped in super glue? Look at you go, Barry! Yee-haw! Ride those nerves, Barry, ride 'em!"

"Dad-D!" Megan yelled to get her father to stop torturing Barry.

"All right, you get my message, right, Barry boy?"

Barry was sweating. He nodded.

"Now then," the President said. "Why don't you go get things ready for the teleconference—and you!" The President pointed to Megan. "Do you know how many favors I owe the Murdock family for keeping your nipple slips and 'oops, no underwear!' shots out of the tabloids?"

"I'm bored, daddy!"

"Sweetheart, this complex has a tennis court, a swimming pool, a bowling alley and a movie theater that shows banned movies. How can you get bored?"

"I want to go back home!"

"Texas? Why would anyone want to go back to Texas?"

"Not Texas! The White house!"

"Oh, darl'n. We have to stay here until that comet thing is over. If it zombifies the entire human race, we're gonna have to wheel you down to the sperm bank to reboot the human race."

His daughter had the same look on her face you would have if you had discovered your bathtub was full of pine cones.

"Don't give me that look, sweetie. We have some celebrities down there. You ever hear of Andy Kaufman?"

Thousands of miles away, the professor and his assistant, Aarti, were also struggling with stress. They were sitting on top of an amazing scientific discovery and yet, due to a presidential gag order, couldn't talk to the press or anyone else about it. The professor was trying his best to look inside the comet's nucleus; there was nothing unusual about the comet's makeup. There was no hidden alien ship, only a mixture of dry ice, sand, methane and ammonia, leaving a spectacular trail in its wake. Pascal sighed.

"Did you find anything in the center?" he asked Aarti. She was checking her data on a computer.

"Sorry, Lewis. It's just a normal comet."

"How is it doing it?"

A beeping noise went off on Aarti's tablet computer. She pressed a button and the screen presented her with multiple views of different locations: 1) the President in Antarctica, 2) General Katz at NORAD, 3) the Governor of California (who's not going to have a speaking role, so let's skip his name) and 4) a YouTube video of kittens playing in a box with the word 'FEMA on it.

"Gentlemen," the President said.

Aarti cleared her throat.

"Gentlemen," the President repeated. "We are on a precipice of a decision which will effect MANKIND for some time to come: Do we continue shooting rockets at an object which has shown itself to be wily, if not cunning, in its ability to avoid such rockets, and risk the target being shifted to somewhere that's worth a post card? Or do we trust our big brained Bronies at the observatory and set up a landing strip in…in, where is it? Pepper Mill, California? General Kitty, your thoughts."

General Katz closed his eyes for two seconds. "Mr. President. I think that whether it's a comet or E.T. is irrelevant. The most important thing we need to do is get those civilians out of there, first. Then set up a forward base."

"If you put a base there, General…" Pascal said, "…then a lot of soldiers might get killed if it's just a hunk of space dust."

"You've been studying that thing for hours, Doc. Any evidence to suggest that it's more than space dust?" the President asked.

"No sir," the professor said. "There is no evidence that there is any kind of space craft inside the comet."

"Doesn't make sense, Doc. Not giving me much to go on. What am I supposed to do? Split the baby in two and put half of it in the fridge for baby pops? Can't set up a landing strip for a comet. If it walks like a duck and quacks like a duck, what is it, Doc?"

"…A duck?" Pascal answered.

"Platypus!" Aarti yelled.

"What?" the President asked.

"Platypus!" Aarti said again.

"Platypus to you too," the President said. "Is that a cuss word in your country?

"No, sir. A platypus looks a little like a duck but it's not."

"Course not," the President said. "Platypus got that fur and that flat beaver tail thing."

"It has a duck bill, webbed feet and lays eggs," Aarti argued.

"Professor Pascal, can you tell me what in Sam Hill your man Friday is talking about?"

Professor Pascal looked at Aarti. "I have to say I'm a little confused myself, Aarti?"

"Perception, Lewis! Remember that tribe in the Amazon that never had contact with other humans and no one knew about them until they filmed them from a helicopter?"

"I guess," Pascal answered.

"What was going through the minds of those natives as they watched that big flying thing overhead? God? Giant dragonfly? Evil spirit?"

"Most likely, all of those."

"But nothing like, 'Oh look, a craft that uses propellors to create lower air pressure above it and therefore creates lift.'"

Pascal thought for a second. "Technology."

"Right." Aarti said.

"Hell-lo! People that didn't finish college here!" the President complained.

"I did," General Katz said.

"What's she means, sir, is that we are dealing with an advanced civilization that has traveled millions of light years to get here and we have no idea how they did it because we're as unaware of them as natives seeing a flying machine for the first time."

"So that's two votes for U.F.O. landing strip," the President said.

"Sir, it could be a weapon <u>disguised</u> as a comet," General Katz said.

"And launched by whom?" Pascal asked.

"Space terrorists?" the general answered.

"I never thought of that," the President said. "Way to stir the pot of paranoia, Kit Katt."

"Mr. President," Aarti said. "In sci-fi invasion movies, they all make the same mistake. Before attacking, you have to have to have a scout mission where you gather intelligence <u>first</u>. Learn the enemy's weakness and then invade later. I'm surprised the general doesn't know that."

"Whoa, General Tabby, she schooled you!" the President teased. "Tell you what—we'll do a combo meal. First, move the townsfolk to the nearest campsite or whatever, then we put a base slash landing site in the town. It'll be up to the aliens if they come in peace or leave in pieces." The group agreed on the plan. "Now, I just need to find the head of FEMA and let her lead the evacuation plan. She was supposed to be in on this meeting but said she had something more important to do. What could be more important than this?"

In a rich suburb of Washington, D.C., Yolanda Iesha Washington is busy doing a drive-by shooting on a rival soccer mom's house, while yelling, "Westside PTA rules!" from her minivan window.

Her actions have caused an inaction on the part of the people of Pepper Mill to evacuate to anywhere else, except Casper who had gone home and packed yet again. This time there was no reason for the camping equipment; this was going to be a one-way trip. He packed the most important things he could think of: photos, laptop, important paperwork and the watch his dad had given him. He had yet to replace the battery; not many people wore watches nowadays. He wondered if it were really smart to be leaving his friends behind to save his own skin. He still had 10 hours to turn around, find his friends and convince them that it was foolish not to evacuate. "No," he thought. "They'll figure it out. They'll come to their senses and leave on their own. Once I'm gone they'll leave also. But, what if they don't?" He shuddered with this thought and tried to push it out of his head.

There was far less traffic heading out of town this time, but he noticed the cars leaving all had something in common, they were all SUVs. He stopped walking down Main Street to look at the caravans of utility vehicles racing past, overflowing with stuff: TVs, workout equipment, and yoga mats.

Also staring at the caravan, leaning against the doorframe of his bar, was Baboosh. He saw Casper and called out. "Ahh, Casper, my friend. You are still here."

"Sure, but not for long."

"Right, soon the invisible comet will come to smash us all."

"I don't think it's…"

"Look at that, Casper my friend." Baboosh had a habit of ignoring what you were saying and replacing it with what he wants you to say. He gestured to the SUV parade. "All of the Newbies are leaving town like rats leaving a sinking toilet."

It was true, as far as he could tell, the regulars were holding their ground. He couldn't look around without spotting someone that he didn't recognized. He kept his escape plan to himself and continued his walk to the bus stop. If he took the bus to the mall, he could transfer to another bus which would take him to the airport. He received a text from his mom:

r u lEvN twn?

"Are you leaving town?" he answered: "Of course I am." She texted that she thought he should come to Florida where she was. He texted that he would think about it. He had no real plan about what he would do, once he left town. If he moved in with his mom he would be nothing more than a live-in maid, chauffeur and butler rolled into one. It wasn't her fault for treating him this way. It was because there was nothing to do in her condo: his friends were not there, there were no interesting hangouts; not even a mall nearby. On visits, he always ended up depending on her as if he were a little child again. He couldn't even have a meal unless she was somehow involved. Casper arrived at the bus stop, he wanted to turn around. He looked around for any sight of his friends coming to join him—no such luck.

Let's talk about quantum physics. When the Big Bang occurred, 4.5 billion years ago, not only was our universe created, an infinite number of universes were created with an infinite amount of variations. It stands to reason that another YOU can be walking around doing things the same way or perhaps a little differently than yourself. Sometimes the decisions you make are minuscule and the results are virtually undetectable, but sometimes even the most insignificant occurrences can have the most grandiose repercussions: If only Hitler's mom had a headache and said "no" the night he was conceived; if only Abe Lincoln had stayed home instead of seeing that awful play. And now for Casper; if only he'd picked up that penny.

He saw it, right on the sidewalk, next to a cigarette butt, Staring at him like a shiny anomaly. He refused to bend over to pick it up. It was beyond his Profit Bend Tolerance. The PBT is the amount of energy you are willing to spend on picking up an amount of currency, either off the ground or in an extreme case, out of a toilet. To find out yours, just start throwing money on the ground or into a toilet until you can't take it anymore and pick it up. That's your PBT. Now, if you have anything revolting inside the toilet, that can raise your PBT to several hundred dollars for most, unless you're used to that kind of thing. Casper's PBT for a non-toilet situation was around ten cents; therefore, he ignored the penny and instead kicked at it until it rolled out of sight. In another universe he picked the penny up, boarded the bus, moved to Florida and lived a quiet boring life, taking care of his mom. In yet another universe, he picked it up, moved to Los Angeles, met a girl name Stacey (spelled: X-S-A-Q—C-E-A-E). They opened up a surf shop, had terrific sex and lived happily ever after.

In this universe, he of course ignored the penny, and so…

The outbound bus crept to a stop. No one got off. Casper climbed on and put his money into the meter. He then headed to the back to find a seat until the bus driver stopped him.

"Hey!" the gum-chewing, unshaven, bald driver said. "You're a penny short!"

"Pardon?" Casper says.

"You're short a penny, my man." the driver repeated.

"Oh, sorry," Casper said. He started to fumble through his pockets: gum wrapper, paper clip, lint, Pokemon card–Pokemon card? Everything but money. "Uhh, I don't have a penny. Can I just go on?"

"NO!" the driver yelled. "Exact change!"

Casper looked to the other riders, hoping someone would spot him a penny. They looked at him as if he were a urine-filled sponge, covered in used hypodermic needles. "But...it's only a penny," Casper pleaded.

"Only a penny?" The driver raised his voice. "Then why don't you have 'only a penny?'"

"Because it's..." Casper began to explain.

"If a penny is so insignificant," the driver turned and looked at Casper. "Why does the U.S. government waste 1.50 cents making each one? Are there people making that penny? Is there a town that feeds its people on 'just a penny?' Can little Johnny not go to a good public school in that town that makes 'just a penny?'"

"Little Johnny—what?" Casper asked.

"EXACTLY! Unless you can come up with 'just a penny,' my friend, you must vacate the bus until you can show some respect to the United States of America and its currency."

"What the f—"

"Good day to you, sir!"

"All I want to—"

Before Casper could finish his sentence, the driver got out of his seat, grabbed Casper by the shirt collar and forced him off the bus. "I said, 'good day!'"

The driver spat his gum at Casper's feet. The door of the bus closed and the driver screeched off, nearly running over an old lady in the cross walk.

"A little <u>stressed</u>, are we?" Casper yelled.

Casper returned home to get some change. If he hurried, he could catch the last bus to the mall, which left in thirty minutes. Opening the door, he was greeted by Ami and Don. Ami ran up and hugged him. "Casper!" she yelled.

Casper was taken aback. "Are you drunk?"

"No! Baka boy! You came back!"

"Huh, well yeah, but..."

"I told you, Don!" Ami turned to Don.

"Yeah, yeah." Don complained.

"You owe me ten dollars!"

"Fine, I'll pay you later." Don complained. "Casper, my man. I knew you'd come back."

"No, you didn't!" said Ami. "You said he was a coward and would run faster than Superman with diarrhe—"

"Ami!" Don interrupted and glared at Ami. "Casper came back! That's all that's important! So…Casper, I'm so glad you came back. When me and Ami were watching TV we saw the ultimate evidence that something weird is going on."

Don walked over to the television and turned up the volume. It was on the local news channel. The story concerned the comet but there was a new development which made Casper's eyebrows rise.

The female newscaster read the story: "…scientist are now saying that Pascal's Comet, which has terrorized mankind for the past two weeks, will cause an impact event in the Pacific Ocean, somewhere near the Bering Straight."

"WHAT!" Casper yelled.

The newscaster continued. "I'm going to speak to Professor Pascal, renowned astronomer and expert on the comet. Professor Pascal, how is it possible for a comet's trajectory to jump from Kenya to Louisiana to Yakistan to Paris to Pepper Mill, and now the Arctic?"

Professor Pascal appeared on TV. He looked tired and a little pale. "It's simple, Joanne. This is no ordinary comet. This is a special comet we are calling a charged iron core comet, meaning instead of ice and sand, it's actually made up of magnetic metals. When these metals come into contact with a large magnetic source, they act unpredictably, in this case, jumping around from location to location."

"If that's true, then what makes you believe it will crash into the Bering Straight? Can't it switch locations again?"

"We're pretty sure this will be the final course adjustment. It's already past the influence of the Earth's gravitational field, responsible for all of the course corrections."

"So you're saying, Professor, that after all we've been through the comet will land safely in the water?"

"Yes, Joanne." When the professor said this, he looked at the ground.

"But won't that cause a tidal wave?"

"Under normal circumstances. But the location of the impact will cause no more high waves than a tropical storm. Damage to the coastline won't even be noticed."

"You've heard it here first on Channel 11 Action News," the newscaster said happily. "Looks like we avoided a national dis—"

The newscaster didn't finish her sentence, not because anything bad happened to her, something bad happened to the television. Casper threw a boot at it and sent it flying off its stand with a crackling, sparking crash.

"My TV!" yelled Don.

"My boot!" yelled Ami.

"Okay, first of all," Casper said. "It's not your TV, it's mine."

"Yeah, but…I watch it." Don complained. He walked over to the table and cut on the transistor radio.

"Second of all," Casper continued. "WHAT A SUPER LOAD OF OLD CRAP!"

"Now do you believe us?" Ami asked.

"I don't know who to believe–charged iron core comet–what the heck is that? Even if an object had a gigantic magnet on top of it, it doesn't cause it to switch trajectories like that! Do you know how many satellites there are in space? AROUND thirteen hundred! Thirteen hundred! Do you see those large metal objects switching orbits from Kenya to Pepper Mill?"

"Exactly why we should stay here," Ami said.

"I don't know about that," Casper said. "I said that everything sounds like crap. I didn't say we were not in any danger."

"Oh yeah?" Don asked. "Check this out." He turned up the volume on the radio. DJ Skip Recordson was interviewing a representative from NASA.

"Yes, Skip," the man said. "The comet is going to crash into the Baltic Sea. There will be no tidal waves or any evidence along the West Coast of it ever hitting—"

"WHAT!" Casper yelled very close to Ami's ear. She flinched. "Is this a conspiracy?"

"Bingo!" Don said. "Suddenly there's going to be no evidence of a comet hitting? What did you say that thing was five miles long? Surely there would be a few ripples on the beach in California."

"I don't get it," Casper said. "Why would they do this? What do they have to gain…" He thought for a few seconds. "Unless they screwed up."

"Come again?" Don asked.

"What if they screwed up and the comet is going to hit us, when it wasn't before. Like, what if they did something to knock it off course and they don't want to be responsible."

"Doesn't make sense, Cap. Everyone is going to realize the mistake, once it takes out Pepper Mill."

"But you know how the US government is: one coverup at a time."

"Whatever," Ami said. "Either way, they're lying and we shouldn't believe a word that's coming out of their mouths."

"AND, we should get out of here," Don said.

"OR, we should stay here and find out what the cover-up is," Ami said.

Ami and Don looked at Casper as if he was the tie-breaker. "What?" Casper said. "Why are you looking at me? I'm between leave and get out of here."

"How about a compromise?" Ami said.

"Such as?" Casper asked. "We stay and get half killed?"

"We wait around until we see clear evidence that there is danger," Ami answered.

"What?" Casper said. "We can't wait around until we see the comet about to hit. We'll never have enough time to escape."

"If this is a real emergency, the government will send the Army or National Guard to get us out of here, waaay before then, right?" Don asked.

"Probably," Casper said.

"Then it's settled," Ami said. "We stay until they come and get us out."

They each nodded in agreement.

The plan of waiting until help arrived was an ill conceived one. If everyone was waiting on the head of FEMA to come to the rescue, they were just setting themselves up for disappointment. At that moment, Yolanda Iesha Washington was outside a Las Vegas Casino doing a doughnut in her car in front of a police car, which ironically had two police officers in it eating doughnuts. As if that wasn't enough to get their attention, she was waving her middle finger out of her window in a defiant salute.

Meanwhile, and I hate to use the word "meanwhile" as a transition between scenes, but there's really nothing else going on in between the previous scene and this next one except Casper goes to use the toilet, and nobody wants to see that—well, I'm sure someone does but they're rather insane and should seek psychiatric help immediately! So, meanwhile in the observatory—tell you what, if you want the transition to be more interesting, you can imagine the Batman logo spinning and a jaunty trumpet playing after I say: "meanwhile." So, MEANWHILE (spinning logo, trumpet), Professor Pascal was finally taking a moment to go through his email in-box and sort through the hundred-plus messages from Casper.

He ignored Aarti when she said, "I don't believe it." She was referring to more data on the comet which showed that it was still no different than a regular one. She looked over at Professor Pascal. "Lewis?" she asked. He ignored her. She repeated it again. "Lewis, are you listening?"

"Oh, sorry Aarti, I was just poring through tons of e-mails from one of my students—he lives in Pepper Mill."

"What does he say?"

"At first he asks me about the comet and all that stuff, but then he says something I don't understand."

"What's that?"

"The only order for evacuation came from the mayor."

"As it should."

"No, you don't understand. There's no National Guard or anyone else telling the citizens to get out of town."

"What are you talking about?"

"I'm saying that half of the citizens in Pepper Mill are still in town and are refusing to leave because they don't believe that the comet is a danger to them."

Aarti stood up. "Holy sucking fit! Lewis? Why are they still— they're in great danger!"

"My question is, why hasn't the government evacuated them yet?"

"Call the governor!" Aarti opened the app on her computer for video conferencing. She was presented with a YouTube video of kittens playing in a box with the word 'Governor' on it. She closed the window. "Call the President! Call someone! Those people can't be in that town when that thing lands, extraterrestrial or not! Just send him an e-mail and tell him to leave!"

"We both know why I can't do that," Pascal said sadly.

"The President's gag order?"

"Correct. If I tell him to leave he's going to drill me about why I haven't answered his e-mails and then we'll get into a back and forth comet data conversation. Next thing you know, he spreads the word and people will be flocking TO the comet instead of evacuating."

"Well, we can't let them hanging out there."

"Don't worry about it, the military are heading there right now to set up the landing strip. I'm sure they'll have no interest in having the townspeople hanging out there and they'll evacuate them."

"Or they'll just shoot them all to keep it a secret."

"Please, Aarti, this isn't some third world dictatorship. This is the land of upload video democracy. Nothing happens in America without viral video evidence."

"It's also the land of fake news, PhotoShop, After Effects and video EDITING."

Pascal thought for a second. "Perhaps you're right. I'll send him a short message that lets him know to get out without engaging him."

Casper looked at his smart phone displaying the message:

Great Evil Took Our Universe Today. do not reply, pascal.

"Okay, it looks like Professor Pascal has lost his freaking mind. Guess the comet stress has gotten to him," Casper said to himself. He picked up his cup of coffee from Jack's Magic Beans Café, took a sip and then turned his phone to show it to Ami, who was sitting across from him.

"What's that?"she asked.

"It's a message from my professor."

"Oh, good, finally! What does he have to say?" She read the screen. "What? What is he talking about? Has he lost his marbles, and the bag they came in?"

"I know. Maybe he's stressed out. Look, he even spelled his name with lower case and everything else is capitalized."

Ami grabbed his phone and took a close look at the screen.

"What is it?"Casper asked."

Ami read the message. "Great Evil Took Our Universe Today. do not reply, pascal."

"Yeah? So? It makes no sense."

"Everything is capitalized except for the last part."

"Exactly, He sucks at the text messaging."

"No, it's an embedded message–the first part: Great Evil Took Our Universe Today. G-E-T-O-U-T are capitalized. Get it? Get out!"

"What!" He looked at the screen. "What about the second part?"

"'do not reply, pascal', were all lower case, meaning he didn't want that to be part of the secret message. Most likely he's being monitored by the government and can't contact you!"

"Holy sucking fit!" Casper yelled. This got the attention of the other three Pepper Mill locals in the café who had refused to leave town, as well as Don, who was working behind the counter.

"Cap?" Don asked.

"I got a message from the professor! He said we have to get out of town! It's a cover up! The comet is heading here and the government isn't telling us!"

There was a collective gasp from the other customers.

"I knew it!" Don yelled. He attempted to jump over the counter to join Casper and Ami. I say "attempted" because it was an unsuccessful leap that knocked over a tea display and sent an empty tip jar to the floor with smashing excitement. For a few moments, Don occupied himself with cleaning up the mess and then ran over to Casper and Ami's table.

"You know," Caper commented. "If you hadn't knocked over all that stuff, that would've been really cool."

"I know, right?" Don said. "I've been practicing that move after work for <u>weeks</u>, in case some hottie came in and I had to get her a napkin or something."

"Sweet!"

"Yeah, I don't know what happened."

"I think you caught the tea display on your right foot. Perhaps you could have lifted it a bit more."

"Usually I do. I think they must have moved it a little since the last time—"

"HELL-LO!" Ami yelled. "Talk baka gymnastics later! We got to get out of town—we gotta tell everybody to get out of town!"

After some intensive packing, Casper, Ami and Don piled into Casper's car, along with multiple boxes of stuff. Inside the car and on every available spot on the roof, it looked like the truck from the opening of the Beverly Hillbillies sitcom. Casper and Don were in the front, while poor Ami sat in the over-packed back seat with a box of comic books smashed against her cheek. Unlike the first evacuation, a car was now an option. The entire population of the United States was not on the road and half of the city's population had already evacuated with the first warning. Don had a megaphone which he bought for love. It wasn't a love of protesting or yelling at people who he found idiotic, but for the girl he called the 'love of his life.'

Before he, Ami and Casper lived together, Don fell in love with Consuela Ramona. Consuela was half Brazilian and half Asian. On the beauty scale, she was quite easy on the eyes, as if actors Selma Hayek and Penelope Cruise had somehow managed to have a baby together. This baby was then raised by an aerobics instructor, a super model's makeup artist and a porn star. It was uncertain what she saw in Don. To say she was out of his league was an understatement. Every waking moment of their three week relationship, he questioned this fact as did the countless men that wondered, "What does she see in him?"whenever the couple walked into a public space. Don's jealousy grew and grew as did his lack of confidence in his ability to keep a girl like her. He started to question her motives and eventually questioned her out of the relationship. Realizing how jealous and insecure he was, he ran to the local Radio Shack™, bought a megaphone, ran back, bought some batteries, ran back again because he bought the wrong size batteries–why do they make C size batteries anyway? No one ever uses them? Ran to her apartment and started broadcasting how much he loved her, how he was sorry and all of the other cliché stuff a guy has said under a balcony since Romeo started Juliet on that murder suicide thing. Unfortunately, during their hiatus, Consuela had hooked up with another African American nerd with glasses. It was then Don realized she liked him, just because he really was her type and he had blown it, big time.

Anyway...Don had a megaphone. As Casper drove the car, Ami yelled out of the window: "Get out of town! Now! The comet is real! We got a call from Pascal! It's all true!" Those that looked at her received her message the same way anyone would receive an unsubstantiated message from a doomsday sayer yelling out of the window of a 1985 Yugo GV, a beat up car imported from Yugoslavia, voted as one of the top worst cars of all time. After a while of this, Ami withdrew to the inside of the car. "It's not working, no one believes us!" she complained.

Baboosh was walking down the street, carrying a case of beer for his bar. "Baboosh!" Ami yelled. "Get out of town! The comet is real!"

"Yeah, right, Ami, that funny joke." Baboosh laughed. "You funny Asian joke girl, like Margaret Cho."

'I'm Japanese, not Korean!"

"I know, that's why I said Asian. It's a generally accepted all-encompassing stereotype."

"That's like me calling you an Arab."

"What!" Baboosh yelled angrily, dropping the case of beer. There was the sound of a bottle breaking. Baboosh picked up the box and continued on his way.

"Guys!" Don interrupted. "This is getting us nowhere! We have to get everyone out of here! Cap, how long do we have?"

Casper looked at his smart phone. He had calculated the comets progress and had set a stop-watch timer to match the time of impact. "It looks like we have an hour to spare, If we wait, after that, we'll have to floor it." As if on cue, the Yugo backfired.

"Floor it? In this thing?" Don asked.

"Oh, hi," Casper responded, "You must be Funny's cousin— Un-Funny. Tell you what, we'll drive by the police station and tell them what's going on. If they don't take action, then there's really nothing we can do." The three looked sad at the prospect of giving up and abandoning the rest of their town's folk to die in a comet impact.

Meanwhile (spinning Batman logo and trumpet music). The President of the United States was sitting down to a cabinet meeting in his Antarctica compound. The room was surrounded by the latest in over-charged, government technology: Monitors, computers, radio transmitters, all showing the coming and goings of the world they were hiding from. Of most interest was the satellite view of the town of Pepper Mill. From what they could tell, with the billion dollar satellite that can see a dictator pick his nose from space, the town looked perfectly normal. Cars were moving around like ants, little dot-looking people were doing their routine little-dot activities. This was not what they were supposed to be seeing. The President made this observation apparent to the rest of the cabinet members.

"Can someone please tell me, what in the name of funky Jesus are all of those towns people STILL doing in that town?" he asked.

A glasses wearing member of the Homeland Security team squinted at the monitor. "Well sir, it appears they didn't heed the warning about the evacuation and are staying."

"I know that, Poindexter-stein, I'm asking, why haven't they been evacuated hours ago like they should have? Where's that woman in charge of FEMA, what's her name, the Black chick?"

"Yolanda Iesha Washington, sir," Barry the aide answered. "She's not Black, sir, and she hasn't been seen in hours; nor is she answering her phone."

"And when was I was supposed to be made aware of the fact that the person responsible for getting the people out of Dodge is nowhere to be seen?"

"I sent you several text messages sir. "

The President looked at Barry as if Barry had walked in on the President's grandmother eating a sub sandwich while she sat on the toilet. "Text messages? Text message! As in those things my daughter gets about how someone just ate a good sub sandwich with a little smily face? Did you attach a smily face with the message that the head of FEMA is nowhere to be seen and as a result THOUSANDS of people are about to die? What kind of e-mo-gee do you use for that, Barry? Cartoon meteorite hitting the vomiting guy? Old school emoticon of I=3? So it looks like a nuclear bomb?"

Barry, wisely kept his mouth shut. The President turned to the head of the Department of Agriculture. "Congratulations, Tim, you've just been appointed the head of FEMA, too." Tim did a fist pump and silently yelled: "Yes!" as if this was a good thing. He was perhaps happy to actually be doing something, because, let's face it, there's no job for the Department of Agriculture in a post apocalyptic bomb shelter. He knew his only purpose was going be emergency cannibal food ration or zombie escape bait.

But where is Yolanda Iesha Washington? You may ask, or you may not ask—whichever. Let's talk about her anyway because I'm the narrator and you'll go where I want you to go. As you read this sentence, Yolanda Iesha Washington is actually doing her job. She has assembled a flotilla of helicopters, all terrain vehicles and a C-140 aircraft, full of redirected wooden food crates stamped with the words:

"TO KENYA, WARNING, MAY CONTAIN 15% RODENT HAIR AND FECAL MATTER. FDA APPROVED. DO NOT GIVE TO AMERICANS, (EXCEPT BLUE STATES, BUT CALL IT

ORGANIC OR SOMETHING LIKE THAT), WHAT DOES IT
MATTER...THIS IS GOING TO AFRICA, THEY'RE USED TO
THAT KIND OF THING."

There is also another large group of military aircraft as well;
tanks, trucks or anything else needed to secure a perimeter, on their
way to Pepper Mill. It is not another federal relief agency but a
force lead by one of the leaders or NORAD, General Flint Katz
AKA, Kitty Cat, Kit Kat or whatever moniker the President of the
United States can give him. The general was on his way to Pepper
Mill, even before the President had realized that there was no one
on their way to aid the citizens. It was his own decision. You see,
General Katz has a personal interest in evacuating the citizens of
Pepper Mill–actually he only wanted to evacuate one citizen of
Pepper Mill, his daughter.

A long time ago, his grown-up daughter was a little girl (as it
goes). Being little made it easier to sit on her dad's knee where he
would pretend to be a pony, bouncing her up and down with
laughing glee. Those where good days, full of "I love you daddy!"
moments and gave him the false sense of security that these days
were going to last forever. Alas, one day, she turned into a teenager.
Actor Alec Baldwin once said: "My daughter is 13 and I see now
why, in these films, whenever they represent a Mayan culture, or
any tribal culture, or a Hawaiian culture, they always throw a
teenage girl into the volcano as a sacrifice."

General Katz agreed that raising this hell-fire teenager was
harder than the time he was bogged down by machine gun fire in
Afghanistan, while knife fighting three members of the Taliban,
armed only with a spork. (FYI, he killed all of the the above, using
the spork.) Like a good soldier, he tried his best to raise a polite,
respectable child and all was going relatively well until one day:
Lollapalooza. If you say that word: Lollapalooza out-loud to
General Katz, he will ask someone to throw something heavy and
sharp at your head. It was unlikely that this will ever happen,
because how often does the word Lollapalooza come up in
conversation? "Hey Charley, check out the Lollapaloozas on that
one" might work, but that person would sound like an idiot. You
see, at that rock concert, his daughter was introduced to several
things that started her on a course to downward mobility: Drugs,
sex and rock n' roll, which she didn't really listen too because she
was too busy with the sex and drug stuff. By the time she had

sobered up (temporarily) she found herself moved into a one bedroom apartment, shared by six other people in the small town of Pepper Mill, California. Eventually, the six became two, because four had discovered Jesus–well, they discovered the teachings of Jesus, not the actual man hiding somewhere like a biblical Where's Waldo.

His daughter got a job and seemed to be on her way out of teenage rebellion woods. But the rift between the two, created during those years, remains to this day. He knows where she lives but refuses to visit. She knows where he is (NORAD HQ) and has made it part of her life to protest and rebel against the military industrial complex. Their social stalemate seemed to be on a path to eternal separation, until he learned about the latest target of Pascal's comet. He is now on an important mission, not the one assigned by the President, but the one every father takes when they have a child—a mission of love, to heal the wounds created by himself, and his daughter, Lori.

"Watch where you're going, lame brain!" Lori yelled at Don. Don was not driving but he and Ami were the only ones Lori could see in the car that almost ran over her in the intersection. Casper had been looking at his doomsday calculator app and almost ran over her. Before she could look at him, he had ducked down in his seat and out of site, causing Don to get the brunt of the insult. This was odd because Don was on the right side of the car and would have to be in London for him to be the driver. This thought never crossed Lori's mind and didn't keep her from using the "lame brain" comment.

"Hey!" Don yelled back with the megaphone, "Who are you calling lame brain, you, you…" Don couldn't think of an insult. He turned around to Ami: "I need an insult for a girl that's not sexist or uses the B word—and Casper, get your head off my lap before people think we're married!"

Ami completely ignored Don's request and asked Casper a question: "How much time do we have?"

"30 minutes until we have to hit the road, and then we need to drive…at 75 miles per hour for at least two hours to get to a safe distance." Don and Ami looked at each other with genuine confusion.

"Wait!" Ami said. "We have to drive at 75? Constantly? For two hours, in THIS thing? That's loaded up with all of our stuff! Please tell me you mean't kilometers!"

The reality of the situation hit Casper. "Uhh…Yeah. I guess that's gonna be hard, huh?"

"Casper, you lame brain!" Don yelled. "Why didn't you mention this, earlier? We could have been on the road, hours ago! We can't get this thing up to 45! Miles or kilometers! The only horse power this thing has is the glue holding it together!"

Casper patted the steering wheel. "Don't listen to him Betsy." He looked at Don. "I'm sorry, I miscalculated. I never could solve those travel equations in algebra. I'm an astronomer not a mathematician. I mean seriously: A train is going 50 miles per hour and another train is going 50, they're 100 miles a part, when do they meet?"

"ONE HOUR!" Don and Ami yelled.

"Exactly, useless algebra!" Casper complained.

"Yeah," said Ami. "Heaven forbid if you ever have to use math in Astronomy!"

"Floor it!" Don yelled.

"What?" Casper asked.

"Floor it! Floor it! Floor it! Floor it! Floor it! Floor it!"

"Should I floor it?" Casper asked

Don tried to put his foot on Casper's foot to try to force the car into a higher speed. He missed and only managed to put a hole in the floorboard, large enough to see the street, sadly passing underneath the car.

"Dude! You wrecked my car!" Casper complained.

"Casper, a cat on the hood can damage this car!" Don complained.

"For the record, that was a large cat!"

"You guys stop arguing and figure out how we can make this car go faster! I just saw a guy in a wheelchair challenging us to a race." Ami looked at one of those lighted signs that warn you when you are driving too fast in a school zone. Whenever you go over 25 miles per hour, they usually flash: "SLOW DOWN!" this time it said: 'NO NEED TO BE SARCASTIC'.

No amount of comments from Don, Ami, or the town of Pepper Mill could make 'Betsy' as Casper called her, go any faster than she could. When the guy in the wheelchair circled around the car for the second time. Casper devised a better plan of escape: "Okay, this is what we do. If we make it across the South Bridge we can make it to Highway 101. Once there, we hitch a ride with anything that can gun it up to 100 miles per hour, and maybe, just maybe, the worst thing that'll happen will be a massive shockwave that'll toss us around like a hot wheels car in a dryer, but we'll still have a better chance of living than if we stay in this town."

"Whatever, just do it!" Don complained.

Ami let out a weird sound, like a whimper and scream at the same time. "What is it?" Casper asked.

"This sucks!" she answered. "I actually felt calmer when the whole world was going to be destroyed. Now, that it's just us—I can't take it! It's like when it's just you and you know that if you can do the right thing and escape—it's like you have all of this hope suddenly and the minute something comes up that ruins everything you feel like it's so unfair, you know? Like why me? Why does a comet have to land on MY town? Thousands of people in this world committing genocide, polluting the planet, driving around in black vans, kidnapping cheerleaders, chopping them up and selling their body parts in psychotic vending machines and—"

"Okay! Okay, Ami!" Don interrupted.

"Anyway…" she continued. "It's not fair. What did we do? What did any of these people do?"

They all thought for a moment as Casper made a couple of turns which will take them to the South bridge.

"Well…" Casper said. "…you're a Buddhist. What does Buddha say about a situation like this?"

Ami thought for a second. "I don't know, Casper. I'm a terrible Buddhist. I know the thought of being obliterated shouldn't bother me if I've found inner peace and all that, but I haven't found inner peace and in an hour I'm gonna be outer pieces. What about you, Don, you ready to die? Again?"

"Strangely enough, I'm feeling more peaceful this time." Don answered.

"Really?" Casper asked.

"Yeah, I mean, when we were about to die the first time, I felt that I've made my peace with God."

"But you seem just as freaked out right now." Ami added.

"I know. But you know what, it has nothing to do with me or my life. I'm actually more worried about YOU two. I want to see you guys survive. That's the part I'm worried about. I don't want to see my friends die. Who wants to see their friends die?"

The three were silent in contemplation. The silence was broken by a rumbling noise.

"Sweet Jesus in a candy store! What's that, the comet?" Ami asked.

"No, Casper answered. The sound is too choppy, like a…"

Casper's explanation would have been correct. The word "helicopter" was what he was going to say. The object of conversation was a UH-60L Blackhawk copter. It wasn't part of the military. Apparently, FEMA had beat the military to the scene. The giant, black bird flew into view in front of their car. It wasn't that much higher than the telephone poles. The wind and turbulence of it's rotors, thumped through the car's passengers like a bass drum at a rock concert. Casper slammed on the breaks in fear the copter was going to run into them. He could see the face of the passenger, it was Yolanda Iesha Washington. She was wearing a white cowboy hat and sunglasses, almost reminiscent of Robert De Nero in Apocalypse Now, except the music she was playing, instead of Wagner's *Flight ofthe Valkyrie*, was *Fight the Power* by Public Enemy. Yolanda Iesha Washington took out a Megaphone, very similar to Don's and yelled out of the window: "Attention mofos of Pepper Mill! Evacuate the area, immediately! You have one foot in the grave and the other one in a hearse! All citizens head towards the Northside bridge, now!"

Casper stopped the car. "Why in the world is she blocking our way? We're almost to the Southside bridge?" he asked.

"That's why," Ami said pointing to the direction of the Southside bridge. Trucks, RVs, a High Mobility Multipurpose Wheeled Vehicle (AKA a humvee) and something that looked like a tank with the word FEMA, hastily painted on it, rolled across both lanes of the Southside bridge, preventing any car from leaving in that direction. Casper made a U-turn and as if he had become the leader of the FEMA evacuation parade, made a relatively hasty retreat in the other direction.

"What are we supposed to do even if we get across the bridge?" Casper asked.

"Well, now that FEMA is here, maybe they got some helicopters or something on the other side of the bridge," Don said. "Look, I think I do see some helicopters and stuff on the other side of town." He pointed in the direction of the Northside bridge. There was some type of movement, similar to the FEMA activity on the other side of the bridge. As if awakened to the seriousness of the situation, the remaining citizens of Pepper Mill, started to scramble like a flaming ant hill. Even those that said they'd rather die than leave the home their parents lived in, ran to their houses and started packing as fast as they could. Mayor Duncan and officers Earl and Clem were among the holdouts. As Clem was trying to direct traffic in the direction of the Northside Bridge, Earl was on the opposite side of the street, directing people in the direction of the Southside bridge. The mayor, spotting this conflicting event from her office window and ran outside to Earl.

"Earl!" she yelled. "Why are you and Clem sending people in opposite directions?"

"Cause, I'm taking my orders from the United States Army."

"Earl! That isn't the army, it's FEMA! Look at the letters on the side of the trucks!" The mayor pointed to an RV passing by with the letters on it.

"I'm not paying any attention to them, I'm taking orders from General Katz, himself." Earl handed the mayor his police radio.

"Hello?" The mayor yelled into the radio. "Who is this?"

"This is General Flint Katz, leader of NORAD, who is this?"

"This is Mayor Renée Duncan!"

"Mayor, we gave you citizens hours, if not days to evacuate the town of Pepper Mill, now I need you people to move faster than you've ever moved before! Your lives depend on it!"

"General, I don't know what's going on here, but first the comet is going to land on us and then the comet is going to land in the Bering Strait which is millions of miles away from this town. From what I can tell, the only emergency is your lack of credibility!"

"Mayor, this is the <u>real</u> information! The other stuff was for security reasons! We need you and every living thing OUT of town, NOW!"

"Then why are you and FEMA asking us to evacuate in two different directions—at the same time?"

"Wait, what? FEMA is there?...For crying out..."

"See what I mean, General. You don't know what your left hand is doing! Like my Nana says, you're eating a sub sandwich while sitting on the toilet!"

"That's disgusting!"

"True, but accurate. You can see my position though."

"Okay, here's what's going to happen: The U.S. Army is in charge, ignore anything coming out of the mouth of the squirrel-filled head of FEMA; she's rather insane!"

Unfortunately, Casper and most of the towns-people were being mislead by the squirrel headed, Yolanda Iesha Washington. In her defense, if they had listened to her, they all would have escaped across the Northside bridge. Unfortunately, due to the large numbers of tanks, humvees and other U.S. Army vehicles coming across the bridge, the civilians were stopped in their track and forced to retreat back to the center of town.

"What is going on here? I feel like we're being herded!" Casper complained. All around them, towns people were carrying everything that they could: boxes of prized possessions, filled fish tanks, stuffed moose heads, wooden cigar store Indians and a theremin. Adding to the panic, overhead, army helicopters were nearly hitting FEMA helicopters. This drew the attention of most people on the ground except Ami. She was looking at the army guys setting up a tent in the park near a statue of Sacajawea, holding a baby in one right arm and an upheld sword in the left hand.

"Why are they setting up a tent when we're supposed to be getting us out of here?" she asked.

"No idea," Don said. "I'm wondering how we're going to get out of here when they're blocking <u>both</u> bridges?"

On the Southside bridge, the FEMA vehicles and the army vehicles had met in the middle and refused to give way to the other. It had created a classic North-and-South-Going-Zax standoff. To make matters worse, the army tank began to push a FEMA RV off to the side with dramatic effect. Instead of sliding to the side like a puck on an air hockey table as they had wanted, the contact caused a horrible crunching screeching, slow motion collision. If that wasn't enough, the gas tank on the RV ruptured and burst into flames. This ignited the emergency re-fuel vehicle that the tank ignored in its ill-planned solution to the gridlock. The tank tried to back up; I say tried because by this time, other army vehicles were blocking its rear path. The tank rolled over some of the vehicles, ending the lives of two soldiers. When the gas tank exploded, four FEMA workers in a truck joined the soldiers in grunt heaven, which I'm sure looks a lot like an eternal beer commercial.

"God's beard! What is happening over there, Captain?" General Katz yelled into the walkie talkie after witnessing the huge fireball coming from the direction of the bridge. The captain's answer was not heard by the general because at that moment, a loud crashing twisting metal sound was coming from the direction of the other bridge.

Constructed in the 1800s, the Northside bridge was built across the Sierra River in order to get horses and prostitutes into town. Years later, after many renovations and upgrades (and less prostitutes), the bridge had evolved to match one of the modern, single lane, steel bridges you would see in most small towns. It was capable of withstanding storms, tractor trailers and other daily usages. It was not prepared to withstand the weight of four tanks and two tractor trailers at the same time; pieces of their flaming wreckage dammed the river below; escape in that direction of town was not an option.

Casper's car was going no where. Truth be known, it would have died 1.7 miles after they crossed the bridge, but that's a scenario in another universe. There were so many cars, trucks and people in the center of town that it was impossible to go in any direction. "What now?" he asked.

"I'm going to ask somebody," Don said. Ami didn't speak, she was too busy looking at the soldiers setting up infantry cannons in the street. "Are they going to blow the comet up?" she asked Casper.

"That would be stupid, especially with cannons," he answered. "Like throwing a needle at a snowball."

"Then why are they setting up shop?" She pointed to the cannon and then the soldiers coming out of the coffee shop, sipping lattes.

"I have no idea what's going on Ami, But I do know we have to find a way to get out of here," Casper said while rolling down the car window. He blew the car's horn to get the attention of a soldier. "Excuse me, sir!" he said to the guy who was probably younger than he was.

The soldier, like the others was, dressed in a strange, camouflage patterned uniform. Instead of the usual swirly jungle or desert colors, it was more blocky in urban colors: black, grey, blue and brown. He was holding a large machine gun which made it unnerving when he walked over to their car. Before Casper could ask him a question, it was answered: "Sir, I need you and your passengers to make your way over to that big grassy field in the park for an air EVAC, ASAP!" He pointed in the direction of a large hill in the middle of the park, near a statute of General

Custer holding a baby in his right arm and a lion's head in his left hand.

Hundreds of people had already started making their way over to the field. Helicopters from multiple directions were landing, picking up passengers and taking off with the swiftness of hungry sea gulls at a garbage dump. Now, at this point, you may or may not be asking: If the exit out of town to the North is blocked and the exit to the South is blocked, what about the East and West? Perhaps this never occurred to you at all and you were quite happy to blindly go along with a bad plot, full of holes, like watching a TV show featuring a talking, crime solving helicopter. Or perhaps you were waiting until the end of the book, so you could ambush the author at a bookstore signing, shoving the book into his face with righteous indignation while yelling: "You were wrong and I am right!?" Thrusting your pelvis in the author's direction, over and over, creating the proudest moment of your sad, sad life—the day you bested the <u>smartest and best looking writer in the world</u>! Sorry to burst your bubble, but, as for the West, they had something called Nowhere Mountain. Nowhere Mountain does have a dirt road that goes in the direction of a major highway as well as the ocean. If you take this road, it will lead you straight up the mountain to an observation deck and that would be as far as you could get in an automobile. On foot, you could get even further, provided you like rolling around in a forest full of poison oak, rabid raccoons, skunks or anything else which will attack you on your journey. If you go towards the East, you will run into Big Lake. Big Lake is a…Big Lake which does lead to another town and a major highway if you can get across it. Some towns people that were lucky enough to be on their boats during the evacuation have managed to get across Big Lake. As for people like Casper, to get across Big Lake, you must fight your way out of town, find a boat which can carry you, all of your friends and your tons of stuff, fight off the other people that want the same boat, figure out how to drive a boat, pray to your god that the boat isn't locked up and then get across the lake at a puttering speed, just in time to be obliterated by the comet. Bottom line, a helicopter is a good alternative to rabid animals and slow pleasure cruises.

Casper and his comrades had abandoned their car and most of the things which were unimportant to them. They all had their laptops (the computers, not the things above your knees that disappear when you stand up), they all had their favorite clothes and knick knacks tucked away in their backpacks. The helicopters continued to land and take off. Casper and his friends were getting closer and loser to the front of the pick-up line but still moving at a slower pace than Ami was comfortable with. "Casper, how long do we have?" she asked.

Casper looked at his clock. "Well, if we go really fast for 30 minutes, we'll only get killed by a shockwave."

"Do I want to know how fast?"

"No."

"How fast do those helicopters go?"

Don interrupted. "I actually know the answer to that; 160 miles per hour."

"How do you know that?" Casper asked.

"Remember that show: Night Copter?"

"No."

" 'Bout the talking helicopter that solves crimes?"

"No."

"Played one episode at 1AM on a Monday and then got cancelled?"

"Of course." Casper rolled his eyes.

Ami was feeling worried and confused, more than she had ever been in her life. Surely, the army and FEMA knew that there was no way they were going to evacuate anyone to safety in the short window they had. Also, in a spot near a corner of the park, a tent of some sort was being set up. A CV-22 Osprey flew into view. The best way to describe this army aircraft is simple. A propeller airplane, whose wings can rotate to let it take off and land like a helicopter. The Osprey landed and soldiers started carrying boxes of equipment off of it.

"This is crazy…"Ami said.

"What?'Casper asked.

"This whole thing–they're not evacuating, they're evicting!"

Casper looked around. "It is weird, it's like they could give a crap if they're killed or not."

"I don't like it. Maybe we should stay?"

Don grabbed both of Ami's shoulders. "I don't know what you're thinking, Ami, but we're getting out of here!"

"But…"

"No buts!" he yelled.

Ami had only seen Don so forceful and serious once before. The last time he had shown such emotion on her behalf was during the "Mark" days.

Mark Summers was Don's high school friend. When they graduated from high school, they both went to Pepper Mill University to get their degrees in computer engineering. Their dream was to start a company that specialized in jet packs, android butlers and sex bots. They rented an apartment on Main Street, near the coffee house and the book store and they lived the perfect bachelor lifestyle. Ami Nakajima was a classmate of Mark. She was undeclared at this point in school majors and boyfriends. She and Mark started dating and, under the objections of Don, she moved in with the two amigos within three months. Things seem to be rolling right on track for Ami. She was dating a handsome, blond-haired, blue-eyed gaijin, she was far away from the influence of her parents and their conservative ways and she was living with a real live, Black guy. Unfortunately, the Black guy was not as cool or knew how to dance like the American media made them out to be. At one point, the handsome gaijin cheated on her with some blond girl that worked at a record store. Mark said that it was a one night stand, but then he also had another one night stand with another girl that worked as a supervisor at Big Red groceries. The Buddhist in Ami tried to forgive him for the first mistake, but the second lead to a heated argument and Mark proclaiming that Ami needed to go because she was 'cramping his style'. Ami ran into the bedroom and started to pack. A knock came on the door. After yelling "Jigoku e ike!" through the door, Don came inside the room. Ami was crying. He came very close to putting his arms around her but stopped himself at the last moment. "Ami?" he said. "I'm sorry about what happened between you guys. The lease is in my name so, you don't have to leave until you find a place to live."

"No freak'n way that's happening!" Mark yelled, ease dropping on the conversation. "I don't want her living here, getting in the way. What if I want to bring someone back here?"

There was an expression on Don's face. Like he had just seen his best friend rip off a mask to reveal a hideous beast. It was what Ami called: 'Serious Don.'

"We can't kick her out, Mark, she needs to find a place to live."

"Who cares? We were here first!"

"The lease is in my name, Mark. I say for now, she should stay."

"Dude! Let me put it to you this way. Either she goes or I go!"

Don thought for a long time. He had to make a choice between his best friend who he's known for four years and a girl he's known for only four months. Don walked over to Ami. "Ami...I'm sorry." Mark smiled. Ami looked down sadly and started to pack. Don stopped her."...But you and I have to find a new roommate."

That was almost four years ago. Ami will never forget that day. Don caught her looking at him. "What?" he asked.

"Nothing. I was thinking about Mark."

"That jerk? I heard he sells his body for crack sandwiches."

"That's a lovely story," Casper interrupted. "Get ready, our chopper is next." Sure enough, they were going to be in the group that got loaded onto the next Black Hawk.

Casper had never been in a helicopter before. Under different circumstances, this would be a pleasant activity. To suck the enjoyment out of the scene, behind him he saw hundreds of locals, all scurrying to get on the next ride to salvation. Even with the best miracle, there was no way all of them were going to make it out of town. Looking at the back of the line was like seeing a bunch of victims, minutes before they all died. He didn't bother to look at his timer anymore. "Either we make it or don't," he thought.

"I still don't think this is real," Casper heard someone behind them say. "There's no comet. This is all some plot by the bank to take our land or something. None of this is real!"

Suddenly, things just got real.

Casper had studied enough physics to know why things do the things they do and when they do it. He knew why they had just heard a sonic boom but he had no idea why a flash of light and then cloud rings appeared from the flash point and spread out as if the clouds were behaving like the waves on a surface of water when you drop a pebble on it. Everyone shuddered, some screamed.

"Casper! What was that?" Don asked

"I...I...I don't know."

"It's our cue to get out of here!" said a guy they were in line with. Luckily for them, their helicopter was just landing at that point. Instead of the orderly helicopter embarking by the townspeople from earlier, there was pushing and shoving as the ones in the back of the line realized they were going to be the recipients of the Presidents "thoughts and prayers" speech that they give when a bunch of people die. Casper never liked guns except in video games, but at that moment, when the Soldier fired in the air and yelled for people to remain calm and proceed in an orderly fashion or he would end their life's sentences with a 'period' between their eyes, Casper wished he had a machine gun to use for everyday use.

Casper and Don got onboard the helicopter; there were no seats left. Don guided Ami inside the copter until she was in front of him. She was not comfortable with Don and Casper being almost outside the copter. It reminded her of her train commute to school everyday in Japan. The trains were so packed that there were men whose job it was to pack you into the cars using shoving if not sticks. Once on board the train, you were sometimes treated to groping by creepy businessmen. It could be called packed like sardines, except with sardines the can was completely closed. With the helicopter, the door was going to remain open and Casper and Don will have to hang on for dear life while the copter sprinted at 160 miles per hour. An optimistic soldier was trying to fit a 200 pound guy behind Casper to much avail. Ami decided to ask another soldier inside where they were going.

"For you? We're going to house you in a temporary facility in Manzanar," he answered. This was one of those "pick up the penny" quantum reality moments for Ami. If the soldier had said "Lone Pine" like they were really headed instead of making an obscure racist joke at the Japanese girl, then she would have escaped the fate that awaited them, moved back to Japan, got married to a Japanese salary man that probably gropes school girls on the train, had a kid, got a divorce and spent the rest of her hard working life wishing she had stayed in Pepper Mill. Alas, the racist joke from the soldier's mouth was received and processed by someone that was very good at American history, trivia and conspiracy theories. What is Manzanar, You ask? In 1942, during World War II, the United States Government ordered more than 110,000 Japanese men, women and children to leave their homes and detained them in remote, military-style camps. Manzanar was one of these camps. So when the racist soldier's said: "Manzanar" and then added a little smile as if he had got one over on her, like saying "Auschwitz" to a Jewish person and thinking you're smarter than them, he was sadly and intellectually mistaken.

"Let me out!" Ami yelled.

"What?" Don said.

"Out!" she yelled

"Ami! Are you crazy, we're about to take off, why would…" This question went unanswered as Ami pushed into Don, who pushed into Casper, who pushed into the soldier trying to get the fat guy inside. Lots of yelling and commotion from inside and out were heard.

"Out, now!" Ami yelled. And with super human strength or, rather, the adrenaline one would use if someone was sending you to a place you didn't want to go, she shoved as hard as she could and sent Casper, Don and the non-racist soldier plummeting onto the ground just as the helicopter lifted up.

"Ami! What the f—" Casper's curse was unfinished as Ami got off of him and started running across the field, away from the crowds and the landing site.

"Ami!" Don yelled. He started chasing after her.

"Guys!" Casper yelled chasing after them.

"Hey! Come back here!" yelled the soldier, also giving chase. "You're not allowed to stay here!" he yelled. The helicopter flew away to make room for the next copter to land and rescue those who actually wanted to leave. The train of chasing made it onto the baseball field. Don called after Ami and was amazed at her speed. But he had a lot more stamina than her. A Jamaican track coach once said: "Have you ever seen a track race, and you see one racer suddenly speed up and break away from the pack? The truth is, he's not speeding up and breaking away from the pack, it's just the other racers around him are giving up." Ami gave up running and Don was able to catch up to her. He grabbed her shoulder and prevented her from running any further.

"What the heck are you doing? We were about to get out of here and you've doomed us all!" he yelled.

"You didn't have to follow me!" she yelled back.

"What the heck! You guys!" Casper yelled

"You three need to come with me, now! You are not allowed to stay in this town!" yelled the soldier.

"I told you, I'm not leaving without my friends!" Don yelled back.

"Ami! What would possess you to do that?" Casper asked.

"Manzanar!" she yelled.

"Manza-what?" Don asked.

"Manzanar! The place they were taking us to was Manzanar! And the guy that said it gave me this weird evil grin after he said it!" she explained.

"We're not taking you to Manzanar..." the out of breath soldier said. "...We're going to Lone Pine."

"Sure, like I'd believe you!" Ami said angrily.

"Wait, what's Manzanar?" Casper asked.

"It's where they housed Japanese people in interment camps during the war," Don answered." Ami looked at him with surprise and admiration, unsure of how he knew that. "What?" he asked. "If it's racist history, I know it."

"What? You think they're sending us to a concentration camp?" Casper asked.

"Why not?" she answered."

"They wouldn't do that? That would be stupid. What purpose could that possibly serve?" Casper asked.

"I don't know, but comet moving from place to place, news that it's hitting Alaska, soldiers drinking lattés instead of getting out of here and then a Japanese interment camp? How am I supposed to believe anything that comes out of their mouths?" She pointed at the soldier.

"Ami, I don't know what's going on—maybe it's a secret government project or they want to build a huge strip mall here. The only thing I know is we have to get out of here before that comet hits our town...and according to my app...we have..." Casper looked at the count down. "...Oh Crap!"

"How long?" The soldier asked. "O-Crap? How long is o-crap?"

Instead of answering, Casper just looked up. Overhead, about 100 miles up, in the broad day light there was a second sun getting closer and closer to them. The rest followed his example and looked up.

"Oh God!" Don said. "It's too late." He looked at Ami. She had a sad and fearful expression.

"I...I was wrong," Ami said. She turned to Don and Casper. "I'm so sorry guys, I thought for sure this was some kind of cover up."

"Whelp, in all honesty, I wish you were right, Ami," Casper said.

When someone is about to die, they always use the expression: 'Your life flashes before your eyes' as if your life has been one big movie and at the end of the series, there is this huge montage, highlighting the best scenes. For Casper, all he could think of was the rapidly approaching bright object and how death was going to feel. There was an urge to run, but where? Only a jet-pack wearing, diarrheic Superman on methamphetamine could run fast enough from it. No, he would stay there, in the field with his friends and the soldier. He could hear screams and could see some people were running for their lives while others were trying to get on what was going to be the last copter out of town. There was pushing and shoving from the civilians. The military personnel held their ground and looked up as if they were watching fireworks on the 4th of July. Casper thought about Ami's conspiracy. "Ami, I think you're right. The military aren't panicking" They all looked at the soldier standing next to them. He was looking at a photo of a blonde girl and crying.

"We were supposed to get married," he sobbed.

"Ooookay, maybe only higher level military personnel know the truth." Casper added.

There was a deep rumbling noise from the sky getting louder and louder.

"Sorry Ami," Don said.

"For what?"

"Remember that time I said I ran into Mark, and I said he was poor, covered in sores, had a hypodermic needle in his arm and begging me for money and to have you back?"

"Yeah?" Ami raised her eyebrows.

"That was a lie. He was actually working in Silicon Valley, running a company that specialized in jet packs, android butlers and sex bots. He was making more money in an hour than you make in a year and he was engaged to a part-time model."

"What? Don! You lied to me?" Ami pushed Don.

"I'm sorry Ami, but I didn't want you to feel bad."

"Feel bad? Why would I feel bad? That the man I despise the most out of anyone in my life, didn't end up getting a divorce and become a homeless meth addict who liked wearing underwear on this head!" she yelled.

"Well, excuse me for trying to make you feel better!" Don yelled. Ami and Don began to argue a little until Casper broke them up.

"You guys! Now is not the time. Do you want to go into the afterlife arguing? Oh, and Don…Remember that month you tried to be a vegetarian?"

"Y-yeah?" Don said raising his eyebrow.

"Well, when it was my time to cook, I would stick chicken broth in <u>everything</u>."

"What! For snake's sake, Cap! Why?"

"I was worried you weren't getting enough protein."

"Casper! Who are you my mother?"

"Well…" Ami interrupted. "When you tried to become a vegan…I repackaged all of your vegan sausages with pork ones, for that reason."

"Arrgh!" Don yelled.

"What's the big deal?" Casper asked "You gave it up, anyway."

"Waay besides the point!" Don yelled.

"What about you?" The soldier said to Ami. "You got anything else to confess?"

Ami gave him a look that asked: "Who are you, again?" She looked down at her shoes then looked at Casper. "Casper, I want you to know that I've always thought of you as the brother that I wished I had."

Casper smiled and gave her a quick hug. Ami turned to Don.

"…And Don." Don smiled and hugged her.

"I know, your Black brother, right?" he joked.

"No," she pulled away from him and looked him in the eyes. "I…I"

"What is it Ami?"

There was a look in her eyes that Don had never seen before. A look of admiration or was it respect? He was unsure. "Ami?" She kept looking at him. Suddenly, within a second, everything got bright. It was like someone had turned up the exposure setting of the sun, without increasing the heat. And speaking of the sounds of blue whales and terrible segues, there are sounds you'll hear, according to the Cornell Lab of Ornithology website (which should have more to do with birds than sea life): The constant frequency (CF) moans, long, frequency-modulated (FM) moans, and long amplitude modulated purrs. Now we all know that high pitched whiney sound the whale makes but I want you to imagine, if not research, the really, really low guttural, bass sound the whale makes, like a burping, underwater lion slowed down. A sound that reverberates through your chest and bones, and played so loud that you couldn't yell over it. That is the sound everyone on the entire planet heard as the light bathed the town of Pepper Mill, California in white.

Casper texted his mother:

SRY I WONT B HOM 4 HANUKAH. LUV U 4 EVR.

He grabbed onto his friends, the soldier grabbed onto Casper, and Ami, without taking her eyes off Don, yelled as loud as she could:

"I L_____!!!!!!!!!

Chapter 4
Schrodinger's Katz

In order to survive a direct hit from a nuclear bomb, or in this case a five mile long object from outer space, you would have to be in a bomb shelter, many miles down. Not only that, but all of your little escape gofer tunnels would also have to be many miles down and the exit, many miles away, or else it would all collapse. Even NORAD has about a 70% chance of surviving a hit from a nuclear bomb and they are more prepared than a bunch of people standing outside. The chance for anything is never zero because we live in a universe of infinite possibilities. The chance of you wining the California Lottery are one in 18 million or, to put that into perspective, you would have to look at every ticket, 24 hours per day for 34 years until you find the winning ticket. OR to increase your odds, you could track down the winner, kill them, steal their money and take your chances in the court system. You have a better chance of being proven innocent and released (please don't do that). But, people DO win the lottery, do they not? It is also possible for people to shoot politicians and get out of jail time by blaming it on twinkles. People have fallen out of airplanes without a parachute and survived, in spite of their new nicknames related to pancakes. Babies and toddlers survive falling from hotel balconies all the time–well, perhaps not all of the time. If it happened ALL of the time then it becomes so normal, hotels would advertise: "Easy access balconies for drunken parents, toddler neglect!" So yes, you could survive a direct impact from a comet. The math to calculate your chances would be too large to fit on this page, but you could survive...Mr. Superman...Incredible Hulk or whatever your super powers are.

Casper was not feeling super–actually, he wasn't feeling anything. He was seeing something though. A beautiful theater; huge and opulent, with red velvet seats and at least four levels of seating that went up to a golden lighted ceiling. He was on the ground floor, facing the stage. All of the seats were empty except one near the center front. He could see what looked like a man, eating something. Casper walked towards the row of seats and made his way over to the person. It didn't take long for him to recognize the man. It was his father, the late Dr. Hershel

Cornbregger, sitting in this mysterious theater, eating popcorn. Casper's dad looked much better than the last time Casper had seen him in the hospital. His salt and pepper beard was more black. He weighed a lot more, had more hair on his head and looked like he did when Casper was in high school. Casper looked around again, as if this were a practical joke and he was being filmed. Joke or not, the emotional toll of seeing a dead relative alive and apparently enjoying a carb-filled snack, could only put so much pressure on Casper's heart. "PAPA?" Casper yelled and he started to rush towards the man, his arms ready to hug his father. Dr. Cornbregger held his arms out, not to hug Casper but to prevent Casper from hugging him. This of course confused Casper and hurt at the same time. "Papa? Wh…"

Dr. Cornbregger used his finger to make the "shush" sign. Then, putting his hands over his mouth to muzzle and deepen his voice he said: "I am NOT your father."

Casper immediately got the Star Wars reference and he also realized he had been hit with a comet and anything that was going on after this point is worth questioning. "You're not? Where am I?"

"Carnegie Hall," Dr. Cornbregger answered.

"Carnegie Hall? How did I get here?"

"Practice, practice practice," Dr. Cornbregger said. There was the sound of rim shot on a drum, heard from the orchestra pit.

Casper looked, but he could not see a band or orchestra.

"Have a seat" Dr. Cornbregger gestured to the seat next to his.

Casper slowly sat down and studied the face of his dad. "You're not my dad. Who are you then?"

"What do you think?"

"Am I dead?"

"I asked, what do you think, not, let's play 20 questions."

This was freaking Casper out. His dad always used to say those type of things to him, forcing Casper to work problems out by himself. "What do I think?"Casper looked around, once again. "I think I'm probably dead, and this is Olam Ha-Ba, perhaps?"

Dr. Cornbregger looked at the ceiling "The world to come? Interesting."

"Gehenna?"

"Hell? Even more interesting."

"Then where? If it's not Heaven or Hell, I can't think of anywhere else it could be."

Dr. Cornbregger pointed to his own head.

"In my head?" Casper almost laughed. "Are you kidding? Is that what happens when you die? You go into your own head?"

"Why do you have to be dead to go into your own head?"

"You don't, but being hit by a comet is kind of a game ender."

"And if you're not dead?"

"If 'm not dead then…this has all been a dream, or I'm crazy."

"Or..?" Dr. Cornbregger rotated his hand to indicate Casper should keep guessing.

"Or, the comet was not a comet but something else that didn't kill us…and this is me knocked out or something like that."

"Oh look, the show's starting." Dr. Cornbregger looked towards the stage. A very rotund woman in a Las Vegas style, red chorus girl's outfit came onto the stage.

"And now, Ladies and gentlemen, the great Cosmos," she said in a heavy New Jersey accent. Seconds later a gentleman, weighing the same as her, dressed like a magician (top hat, cane, shoes with spats) spun onto the stage. There was brief music, just enough to do that "taa-daa!" song. The magician started to do some standard tricks, pulling endless, colored handkerchiefs from his hat or making a deck of cards levitate. They all ended is disaster: the handkerchiefs got stuck when he pulled and the deck of cards went flying in all directions, some hitting the magician in the face.

"This sucks," Casper complained. He reached over to try to take some popcorn. Dr. Cornbregger pulled the popcorn away. "Selfish figment of my imagination, aren't you?"

Dr. Cornbregger hushed Casper. The magician's assistant was wheeling a large red box with a lid, onto the stage. Badly painted on the side of the box, were the words:" "The Hyper Cube."

"This is my favorite trick," Dr. Cornbregger said. The Magician went offstage and returned with a white cat. He placed the cat into the box. Casper didn't know what the trick was but because of the lack of success of the other tricks, he knew this was going to end in failure. The assistant handed the magician a sealed bottle with a skull and cross bones on its side.

"What's that?" Casper asked.

"Poisonous gas," his dad answered.

The bottle was placed inside the box. "Wait! What is he doing?" Casper complained.

"Don't worry, the bottle is sealed," Dr. Cornbregger assured Casper.

"But what if the cat opens it somehow?"

"Hmmm, I never thought of that," Dr. Cornbregger said rubbing his chin.

The assistant handed the magician a cylindrical silver tube. On the side was the warning symbol for radioactivity.

"Now what? What's that?" Casper asked.

"That's a radioactive substance."

"Huh? Poisonous gas? Radioactive tubes? What the heck? Where's the Humane Society when you need them?"

"Don't worry, it's only a small bit."

The magician closed the box and stood back. The assistant stood still and gestured to the box. Nothing else was going on for at least a minute. The sound of a drum roll was heard.

"Now what happens?" Casper asked, getting impatient.

"What do you think?" Dr. Cornbregger asked, looking at Casper.

"What do I think? What do I think? I think that cat's in danger if something happens with that poisons gas or the radioactive tube."

"The radioactive substance won't harm the cat... Unless it leaks and causes the bottle of gas to also leak."

"What are the chances of that happening?"

Dr. Cornbregger smiled.

"Why won't you answer me!" Casper yelled.

Everything went black except a lone spotlight on the red box. Casper felt as if he were being drawn towards the box, almost as if he were floating towards it; the closer he got towards it, the brighter everything got until all he could see was white.

All was quiet...

There was a sound of someone's muffled voice saying a word over and over. Casper could feel his body. He knew he was lying on his back and he could feel grass under his arms.

The muffled voice continued to say the same thing over and over.

'Surf...Surf?" it sounded like to Casper. As though his ears had experienced high altitude pressure and were clogged, they popped and sounds started to slowly filter through: other voices calling other words, a helicopter and a walkie talkie. The voice was now understood to be yelling "Sir!...Sir!"

Casper opened his eyes. Everything was blurry but quickly came into focus in time with his returning hearing.

He was on the ground and there was a soldier standing over him. "Sir! Can you hear me Sir?"

Before Casper could think about it, he had nodded yes. "Well, at least I'm not completely paralyzed," he thought.

"Sir! What's your name?" The soldier yelled a little.

"Casper Cornbregger."

"Okay Mr Cornbread, can you stand?"

"Cornbregger!" Casper corrected, reliving high school hazing. He allowed the soldier to help him up. A quick look around revealed others being helped up and quizzed about their identity. They were still on the field. The sight of the field was amazing to him. There was nothing interesting about it that wasn't there before the bright light, but the fact that it was still there was the amazing thing. After what had happened, there should be a large crater, the size of a city. As fas as he could tell, not one blade of grass had been disturbed and not one life had been taken. Non-the-less, the army seemed to still be in emergency mode. They were helping people get out of the park as fast as possible. "Sir, do you live in this town?" the soldier asked. Casper

"Yes."

"Sir, I need you to return to your residence now, and await further instructions." Casper was about to head back home, when he realized he hadn't checked on Don and Ami. A look around produced neither of his friends. "Don! Ami?" he yelled. He navigated his way through crowds of confused locals. Some of them were looking up. Casper assumed they were glad to see the sun again or the blue sky. The army was giving everyone the same instructions to shelter in place. Casper headed in the direction of home, perhaps his friends were just ahead of him. Hearing his name being called, shook him awake even more. A quick scan revealed Don, standing near an army humvee. Casper ran over to him and gave him the best hug a guy could give another guy that were not dating. "Don! You're alive! We're alive!"

"I know! I know! Can you believe it? A comet landed on us and we survived! I'm like, where's my freak'n T-shirt that says I survived getting hit with a comet!"

"Where's Ami?"

"She's not with you?"

"No, I just woke up. Oh crap, I hope she's not…"

"Excuse me, sir," the soldier that woke him up interrupted. "If you're looking for the Asian woman, she said to meet her on the roof of your building."

Casper and Don looked at each other before starting to hurry home.

The jog home shown more people looking up. Casper looked up but all he saw were the two to four story buildings. "What are people looking at?" he asked Don.

"I was wondering that, too. Maybe they're seeing if that was really it, like we haven't seen the real comet hit. Or thinking that this was a miracle and any minute now, Jesus is going to show up and say, 'Rapture time! Everybody out of the pool!'"

Casper tried to call Ami on his cell phone; she didn't pick up, so he left a short message. He got a text from his mom saying:

RU OK?

He responded that he was fine and would give more details later. He looked over at Don.

Don was telling his parents the same thing. It was hard to describe what was going on in a short conversation. He also said he would call later with more information, once they find out what had happened to them.

From what Casper could tell, not one leaf or telephone pole was out of place in the town. As bright as the light had been, he thought there would at least be burn marks or evidence that something weird had just happened. It was a little disappointing. When the army guys left, what would he have then? He'd go back to his normal existence before this started. He'd be just another student at Pepper Mill University. He'd be unemployed, lacking lots of his stuff, dateless, fatherless and now hopeless that he could ever trust anyone ever again.

Don ran on ahead and reached the apartment before Casper. Casper bounded up the many flights of stairs. Before he continued on, to join Ami and Don on the roof, he noticed his apartment door was open. He went to close the door and to see if the landlord had broken in and stolen any thing else. The apartment was the same as they had left it. He heard the radio, he could have sworn that Ami took it with her on their attempted escape out of town. The radio was loud and broadcasting some type of news story. Casper went to turn it off before he ran up to the roof. The female newscaster was very excited and talking about Pepper Mill. Of course she would be—their town just survived a comet hitting it. The broadcaster was describing the events:

"…This small California town used to be known for the old Pepper Mill and brothels, until the businesses moved to China as did the prostitutes, Now, it's home to a college which boasts an award winning astronomer who ironically is the one that discovered the comet which according to NASA, apparently hit somewhere in the Bering straight. And now, as if things couldn't get much more, shall we say, amazing for this small hamlet—"

"Diane," a male newscaster interrupted. "How big are we talking about?"

"Oh, it's big, Carl. Early reports are saying as big as the entire town, that would put it at least five to six miles wide. And it's just sitting there."

Casper ran out the door to join Don and Ami on the roof. "Was there something sitting on the ground that was carried by the comet?" He thought about some type of comet residue or a strange crater that surrounds the town. He slammed the roof door open. Don and Ami sat upright in the lawn chairs that Casper had set up on the roof for doing illegal barbecues and roof parties. Seeing Ami, Casper forgot about the crater and hugged her. "Ami-chan! You're alive!" Ami was stiff as if all life had been sucked out of her. "Ami! Are you okay?" She didn't respond with words. She slowly pointed up at the sky. "What? The comet? I know. Don wants to make a I survived the comet shir…"

"Casper?" she asked, pointing higher. He followed the direction of where her finger was pointing. It took him a second to figure out what she was gesturing to.

There was something in the sky—a curved line—not a line, an arc? The arc didn't seem to have an end. It was big. So big it looked a little blue and far away. "A weird upside down rainbow? An illusion?" he thought. The words of the female newscaster came to mind: 'big as the whole town.' Casper followed the arc with his eyes which kept going and going all around them. It was then he realized it wasn't an arc, it was a large ring, so large it surrounded the sky all around the town's edge. He did a 360 degree turn, again and again until he collapsed, dizzy, into one of the lawn chairs. "What is that?" he asked

Ami was smiling and looked a little teary. "I think we know what that is." She laughed a little.

"But…" Casper noticed the slight pattern on the ring. Not only that, but he realized the ring was actually rotating, counter clockwise, very slowly. This put to doubt any chance this was not an alien space craft. He felt like crying. Not from sadness but for loss of scientific innocence. Don had his hands up to his mouth and kept saying "Oh wow…" over and over. Casper reached out his hands and grabbed Ami's and Don's. "Is this real? Am I dreaming? Am I really here?"

"I thought the same thing," said Don. "I'm still waiting until I wake up. Maybe I should just jump off this roof and see if I wake up."

"Please don't," Ami said.

"Why not?"

"Because this is not a dream."

"How do you know?"

"Ask me to do something inappropriate."

"What?"

"Ask me to do something inappropriate."

"Like what?"

"It's your dream, anything you want is possible. Any-thing!" She winked and moved closer to him.

"Hmm. Okay. Ami, I want to see you in a sexy French maid outfit, singing 'I know What Boys Want.'"

"16 plus 16 equals 32!" she yelled and then reached over and slapped his face.

"Ow, what the heck! Ami! Why did you do that?"

"Math skills, pain and lack of cooperation from your dream's cast members. Perfect sign that this is not a dream."

"You know, just the math test would have been enough!" Don complained.

Ami had also helped Casper realize this was not a dream. He pressed his back into the lawn chair and exhaled. "This is really happening," he said quietly.

There were many eyes on the huge floating ring. Even though the army was able to keep people at least 10 miles away from the town of Pepper Mill, they couldn't keep people from seeing something so large.

The President and his cabinet, like most of the world, was watching the report on the major news channels. The blonde-haired Diane (the same reporter Caper heard on the radio), stood in the street of a town right outside the army perimeter. The camera had a clear view of the entire ring.

"As you can see, the ring is hovering less than 1000 feet above the town, or about the height that a commercial airliner flies. It's apparently rotating counter clockwise; unknown if that has anything to do with it being able to levitate. The size of this ring is quite massive. Rough estimates are putting it at least five miles around—about the size of Pepper Mill and some of its surrounding area." There was a roaring sound overhead. The camera panned up to capture four F-15 fighter jets screaming overhead in the direction of the ring. "It looks like the military are sending in even more support for the ground troops in and around the area where the ring is."

"Dianne," Carl asked from the TV studio, "I understand we obtained some footage of the explosion that happened in Pepper Mill a few hours before the ring appeared, is that true?"

"That's right, Carl. The video was recorded by a father capturing his son's little league game, in a nearby town."

"Let's take a look at that footage."

The video was played. On screen was a standard little league game involving kids between the ages of six and nine. A father's voice was heard giving the play by play of his son's effort to hit one out of the park. The whale-like sound was heard and the camera quickly shifted from filming little Johnny on the home plate, to the sky. The comet resembling a standard large destructive object from space, long smoky trail and a fiery head, plummeted down towards the town. Suddenly, as if it hit an invisible ceiling over the town, it exploded into a brilliant white ball. The camera action became very chaotic and jumbled as the father ran towards his son. All of the other parents ran towards their own children. Upon reaching his kid and grabbing him to get out of there, the father turned the camera back towards the explosion. Instead of seeing a big flaming fireball, everyone saw the ring slowly materialize out of nothingness, as if it were being created from the pieces of the explosion itself into a solid object; it was like watching the ring explode in reverse. The rest of the footage was the reaction of the parents to what they had just seen.

The President turned his attention away from the monitor playing the newscast, to the one showing General Katz.

"Big C! How are things from inside the devil's mouth?"

General Katz sipped a latté. "So far we appear to be unharmed. The only casualties were the ones on the fallen bridge and the traffic jam on the other bridge."

"So what's the story on the UFO?"

"The rough estimates from ground sightings put the object at two foot thick, height of around 100 feet and five mile diameter."

"Two foot thick? Not very much room for E.T. to walk around in."

"When viewed from the ground the object is also rotating counter clockwise, at around one revolution every 42.7 minutes."

"And what's keeping it in the sky? Do you see any propellers or rockets?"

"No sir. It's beyond my understanding for how this thing is even in the sky at all."

"Well General Whiskers, let me ask our esteemed experts" As the President spoke, multiple video windows opened on the big screen: "Dr. Julius Colby from the NASA Ames Research Center, Dr. Sal Roselli from M.I.T; Mr. Theodore Larson from the Jet Propulsion Laboratory; astrophysicist, Dr. Julius Xiang, actual medical doctor, Parker Wright, MD, MPH, PhD LMNOP; and our esteemed space—the final frontier experts; Professor Pascal and his lovely Bollywood posse, Dr. Aarti Panjwani."

Aarti started to complained about the "Bollywood" comment but the President cut her off. "Look at that, I got the biggest bucket of brains in the country at my disposal. I feel like Professor X."

"Who is Professor X?" Dr. Xiang asked.

"From the X-Men?" the President answered.

"Is that a rock group or something?" asked Dr. Xiang.

"Need to get out of the lab more, Doc." the President answered. "Professor Pascal, sounds like you're in a wind tunnel. What's that sound?"

"You'll have to excuse me, Mr. President. Dr. Panjwani and I are in my car driving to Pepper Mill."

"Got news for you, Doc…" the President said. "…Your home in Kansas just got picked up and thrown smack dab in the middle of Oz. The good news is, looks like I have the biggest smarties in American here to drop some munchkin knowledge on us. Gentlemen…" Aarti cleared her throat, "…Fellas, instead of silently slipping in like you would expect a UFO to do, this Some-B announced to the whole wide world and the media, "look at me, over here! Hey boys! Check out these!" The town of Pepper Mill is ground zero, we're are at Def-con two and the UFO just caused everyone to go number one."

"About that," Dr Wright interrupted. "…The news is showing what looks like a devastating implosion of some sort before the ring appeared. Are the town's people all right? Are there any radiation burns, hearing lost, or anything requiring medical attention?"

"How's 'bout that, General Scratching Post? You seem okay, how are the towns people?"

"As I was telling the President…" General Katz explained. "…The only casualties were caused during the evacuation. As for me…I"

"Something wrong, General?" the President asked. "Cat got your tongue?"

General Katz sighed. "…I have this injury I sustained during a tour in Africa…No, it's a long story."

"Please go on General," Dr. Wright asked.

"When I was with Adventurer Squadron on a hostage rescue mission in Somalia, we managed to get into a fire fight with some Somali pirates in the Gulf of Aden. Bullets were flying back and forth. We had them completely out gunned, so eventually they even ran out of bullets. So we thought it was over. Next thing you know, they started firing arrows at us."

"Wait, arrows?" asked Dr. Colby.

"Yes, arrows," the general answered.

"Call me wrong, General Furry…" said the President. "But to be correct in my political incorrectness. if a bunch of Africans are going to run out of bullets, shouldn't we expect to at least see a spear being thrown at you?"

"You're preaching to the choir Mr. President" the general answered. "We were caught off guard as much as you are, and we were laughing and joking about it. I stood up to tell them that they had to be kidding. We were having having fun. And then…"

"And then, what? Mr. Larson asked."

"I was an Adventurer, until I took an arrow in the knee."

"Ow," the President said.

"Ow is right. Ever since then, I had to take desk jobs because that knee has always bothered me if I'm on my feet for more than an hour."

"So, did the stress of the ring's appearance exacerbate your injury?" Dr. Wright asked.

"Doctor!" the President said, "Watch the sex talk, we got a lady present."

"Exacerbate!" The doctor said. "Has your leg gotten worst?"

"Doctor...it's gone!"

"Your leg? Holy crap!"

"No, no, the pain! Not just the pain, Doctor, that scar is gone —like it's never been there—completely healed over...And I feel... I feel great! Almost younger."

"Doctor Wright? Any explanation?" the President asked.

"Well, I can't explain the cellular regeneration thing but I do know when people get exposed to certain chemicals they can sometimes feel a rush of euphoria. Have you seen the ring put out any type of spray or gas?" Dr. Wright asked.

"Not unless it's radiation," explained Dr. Roselli. "If the ring was putting out anything like that, we would see evidence outside the ring as well as inside."

" General..." said Dr. Wright. "I have to ask you to get your medical personnel to collect some blood samples from yourselves and a couple of townspeople. Make sure you test peoples' thyroids for radiation exposure as well as extra levels of steroids which would explain the rapid healing."

"You get all that General C?" the President asked. "Go out and poke everyone."

"Yes, Mr.President, we'll get right on it."

"Also..." Dr Xiang added. "Please keep us informed if any other people experience any physical changes."

"HOLY CRAP!" Ami yelled. This startled Casper and Don because they were still on the roof, lying in lawn chairs and looking up at the ring, and Ami was downstairs in their apartment taking a shower. After all of the drama they had gone through, it was supposed to be a quiet, meditative experience, But whatever she had yelled 'HOLY CRAP' at caused her to abandon the shower, run up two flights of stairs while wearing nothing but flip flops and a towel and re-join the other two on the roof,

Casper and Don had seen her in this state of dress many times, but not outside the apartment. She ran up to Casper and yelled: "It's gone!" Her hair dripped water on his hand that was holding a bottle of beer.

"Whoa! Crazy lady outside!" Casper yelled.

"What's gone?" Don asked.

"Please tell me your lady parts didn't just fall off." Casper pleaded.

"No! Urusai Baka! It's gone!"

"WHAT?" Casper and Don yelled.

"My tattoo!"

Casper and Don looked at each other.

"What tattoo?" Casper asked.

"I had a tattoo, and now it's gone!"

"Ami, you don't have a tattoo," Don informed.

"Yes I do…did. And it's just disappeared!"

"Ami, I've known you for four years, and I've never seen a tattoo on you…" Don said. "Unless…"

Ami blushed red.

"Did you have a secret tramp stamp somewhere that you never told us about?" Casper asked.

"I've definitely never seen it," Don smiled and nudged Casper's elbow.

"Thank God for that." Casper and Don clinked beer bottles."

"BAKA!" Ami yelled. "It disappeared!"

As if they finally understood what she was complaining about, Don and Casper stopped joking around.

"Wait," Casper said. "You had a tattoo, that's not a lick-and-stick, on a rated R or X rated part of your body, and now it's gone?"

"YES!" she yelled.

"Bid deal."Don said. "You got ripped off. They probably used cheap ink."

"No! I've had that tattoo for three years. It would have faded a long time ago. This thing disappeared,—like, overnight!"

"Can…we see?" Casper asked.

"No, you pervert!"

"I agree," said Don. "If you want us to believe you, you have to show us the scene of the crime."

"No way! Just take my word for it. It's gone, as if I never had a tattoo there!"

"Hmm," Casper said looking at Don for an answer. "Don?"

Don shrugged. "Beats me, I don't know anything about tattoos and how long they last."

"I've seen old people with tattoos, Don!" Ami said.

"I still want to see where it was," Casper said.

Ami hit him in the back of his head with her hand. "Concentrate! What would make a tattoo disappear?"

"Ow!" Casper complained. "I don't know, what was it of? A Pokemon peeing on a Chevy logo?"

"Yeah, Ami, what was it?" Don asked. "An eagle grabbing a snake while holding the Japanese flag? A sumo wrestler with a fish in his mouth, holding a Japanese flag?"

"Never mind about that!" Ami said frustrated. "Let's focus on the disappearing?" She crossed her arms.

"But all evidence is retaliative," Don countered.

"Agreed," Casper said. "Tell us what it was and maybe it will offer some evidence of the mysterious disappearing tattoo."

"Fine…" Ami said. She sat on her own lawn chair and buried her head into her hands. "It…it was Mark."

"Mark?" Casper asked. "As in Mark of Zorro? Because that would be cool."

"No!" Ami said. "It was the name 'Mark, with half a heart around it."

"As in ex-boyfriend, Mark?" Don asked.

"Yes," Ami mumbled.

Don raised an eyebrow. "You had Mark's name tattooed on your hoo-ha?"

"Not ON my hoo-ha!" Ami complained.

"What's a hoo-ha?" Casper asked.

"When did you get that?" Don Asked.

"It was right after he cheated on me…the first time. We were trying to do the reconciliation thing. It was stupid. He said we should get each others' names tattooed, so that when we did it, our names would meet and…"

"Arrgh! La-la-la-la-la!" Casper yelled, while covering his ears. "TOO MUCH INFORMATION! Must-burn-my-ears-off, now!"

"So you're saying he has your name on his hoo-ha, also?" Don asked.

"Yes." Ami asked.

"Ha! So that's why his new girlfriend is named Amy, A-M-Y. Easier to change the tattoo." Don added.

"I didn't need to know that," Ami complained. "Getting back to my original concern; My tattoo is gone!"

"Well, I have no idea what can happen to make a tattoo fall off," Casper said.

"Except maybe a UFO the size of our town suddenly appearing with a flash of light!" Ami said.

"Oh yeah, that," Casper said looking up. "I guess that could be a sign that we've been zapped by something."

"An alien race that hates tattoos?" Don suggested.

"What other horrible effects have we also been exposed to?" Ami asked worried.

"Technically speaking…" Casper added. "Removing a tattoo of a cheating ex-boyfriend is actually a good thing. Maybe the aliens are doing you a favor?"

"Hmm," Ami thought. "Perhaps. You guys have any tattoos or anything that's gone?"

"Nope," Don said. "Never liked sticking needles in my arm." He lifted up his shirt sleeve to indicate getting a needle in his arm. He realized that something was missing. "Wait one darn minute– what the? My scar!"

"What Scar?" Casper asked.

"I had a scar on my left arm from a time I scraped my arm on a nail at summer camp. It's always been there and now it's gone!" Don explained rubbing his arm as if the scar would reappear.

"Ooh! That's freaky," Casper said. "Wait, I have a scar on my hand I got when my Aunt Fay's toy poodle attacked me." He looked at the top of his right hand. Sure enough, just like Ami's 'hoo-ha' tattoo and Don's nail scratch, the scar had been removed. "Okay, freaking out–again! Aliens travel all the way here to abduct bad tattoos and scars?"

"I'll allow that," Don said. "Maybe they'll give me perfect vision as well."

"No, that would mean we're dead," Casper said.

"Pardon?" Don asked

"Dead," Casper explained.

"If we were dead and this was like heaven or something, having perfect eyes and tattoos removed would make sense."

"You think we're dead?" Ami asked.

"Well, I have been thinking about it—I mean really bright light, giant halo in the sky, perfect skin, I feel like the air is a lot cleaner."

"Perhaps," Don said."But it doesn't mean we're dead."

"How do you know?" Casper asked.

"Well, Ami's all Buddhist, you're Jewish, I'm Catholic. Surely we wouldn't be in the same place."

"Holy super-sized bucket of crap, Don!" Casper yelled. "You think heaven is all segregated? Gee wiz, man. You're the last person I'd expect to believe in apartheid heaven."

"That didn't come out the way I meant," Don said, embarrassed.

"Yeah Don," Ami said putting her face close to his. "What's Black people heaven like? Apparently there are no Whites and Asians there. What about Michael Jackson? Does he get a travel visa?"

Don sighed. "What I mean is that heaven, to me, is what you imagine it to be. If heaven is fluffy clouds, harps and holy-holy-holy, that's what you get. If heaven is girls in bikinis and all-you-can eat fried onion rings, so be it. That's what you get."

"So, why can't this be heaven?" Ami asked.

"Sorry Ami," Don said. "Sitting on this roof and drinking a beer is pretty nice but it could use a bikini girl or two."

"You do have a girl in a towel…" Casper gestured to Ami. "…a towel stolen from Holiday Inn—I guess this ain't heaven. I'm pretty sure God frowns on hotel theft."

"You guys are freaking me out," Ami said. "Now I'm starting to think I'm dead!"

"You're not dead," Don said. "Remember the pain you gave me? Why would there be pain in heaven?"

"Good point," Casper said. "But I'm still worried about what other things the aliens have done to us."

Don stood up and started walking towards the exit.

"Where are you going?" Ami asked.

"To give myself a complete check up. I don't want to have a third nipple or something."

As Don entered the exit heading downstairs, Ami pulled the top of her towel forwards and peered at her breast.

"What's on your mind, Lewis?" Aarti asked Professor Pascal. He had been silent for almost an hour of driving. She knew it was all about the UFO but she wondered which part: The scientific, theological, or the social.

He sighed. "It's something the President said, Aarti."

"OUR president? That bumbling buffoon?"

"Not your favorite person, I know. But, he said something earlier when we were discussing the fact that I've spent my entire life disproving the existence of UFOs visiting Earth. He said to me that Santa Claus and Jesus can't exist in the same universe."

"What does that mean?"

"Well, he was saying that as soon as the UFO showed up, it changed things"

"Of course it did, that's obvious."

"No, not in the way you think. He's talking about on a level to finding out for religious people that Santa Claus is the real deal and Jesus is the one that should be in shopping malls letting screaming kids sit on his lap and throw up on him."

"You're upset that you were wrong about the greatest scientific discovery in history?"

"I'm upset that a bunch of really bad TV shows, hack writers and cults were right about UFOs. If they can visit us, maybe they've always visited us–maybe the Scientologists were right about them? Everything is on the table now. Let's bring in the Loch Ness Monster and vampires, why not? It's all on the table. The President, as idiotic as he can be, was more open to this thing being a UFO than I was. Me, the expert! I don't know what I'm supposed to do, Aarti. As soon as that thing entered the atmosphere, my job became obsolete. What do they need an astronomer for? If they want to see it, all they have to do is watch the news. They don't need the opinion of a skeptical scientist who can't figure out how or why an alien race, 500 light years away, would make a journey to an insignificant, one-in-a-billion planet. But, what do I know? I'm just a scientist. The real experts are the science fiction writers, the comic book artists and our bumbling buffoon President!"

There was a moment of silence until Aarti spoke. "I like fairies."

"What?" Pascal asked, confused.

"I said, I like fairies."

"That's nice, Aarti, but what does that have to do with me?"

"I like fairies, I hope they're real. Do you think they're real?"

"No, of course not."

"Santa Claus, UFO, Jesus but no fairies?"

"No, well, I don't know, I guess anything is possible, now."

"You know that's not true. You immediately said no. The scientist in you said no because the scientist in you wants to take things one theory at a time. Yes, there is a UFO over Pepper Mill. UFO stands for Unidentified Flying Object. Identify it first and then tell me it has aliens in it from 500 light years away. If you see Santa, find out how fast he has to travel to bring every kid on Earth a present. It's what you do, Lewis. It's what you are. Don't let the buffoons push your beliefs further than they need to go. You believe in what you want at your own speed. You don't believe in Santa? Millions of kids do. Be the adult, but let them believe in Santa if it lets them sleep like little angels on Christmas Eve."

There was another moment of silence.

"650 miles per second." Pascal said.

"What?"

"650 miles per second. That's how fast Santa's sleigh would have to be traveling, assuming he only delivers to good Christian kids"

"Really? How do you know that?"

"Because, I'm a scientist."

Dianne Chanowitz, the news reporter for Channel 2 Action news, stood on the access highway that leads to the Pepper Mill Southside bridge. She quickly fixed her hair and told the camera man she was ready. "This is Dianne Chanowitz, reporting live near the town of Pepper Mill. As you can see, there seems to be some sort of traffic jam of military vehicles leading into the town." The camera paned over to reveal the numerous trucks, tanks and other army vehicles, stalled in a traffic jam. "We found out through inside sources that there was an accident on both bridges leading into town earlier and there may have been some casualties, but we were also told that the wreckage from the accident on the Southside bridge was already cleaned up, hours ago. Now, why these vehicles are not entering the town is a mystery. It could be a strategic issue or maybe they need more time to study the ring."

There were the sounds of distress from people on the ground as if they had seen something horrible. The camera panned up to the sky to where the ring was. A squadron of Blackhawk helicopters were trying to fly over and under the ring. The helicopter that flew over the ring did so without incident, but the ones that tried to fly under, slowly came to a complete standstill and were then thrown backwards. One copter regained it's composure and turned around, the other seemed to spin for a while in confusion and then wobbled downwards. At the last moment, it pulled up a little but still managed to hit the ground. "Did you see that?" Dianne said to the camera operator.

"Did you just see that?" General Katz said to a lieutenant. The lieutenant was silent and confused from what he had just seen. General Katz picked up a walkie talkie: "Captain Phillips, what happen to your choppers?"

"General, they claimed they were going to fly underneath the ring to get some surveillance of the bottom, when it felt like something just grabbed their airship and slingshot them backwards," Captain Phillips answered.

"Check on the men in the downed copter and then fly another one around it, and this time approach with extreme caution and not so fast?"

In no time, another helicopter approached the ring. It slowly flew over it without any change in its speed or trajectory.

"No problems experienced, general," Captain Phillips broadcasted.

"Fly underneath it," the general ordered.

The copter tried to fly under and up through the ring. As before with the other helicopters, if was stopped and pushed back with opposite and equal force. Because of its slow speed, it was able to correct itself easily and remain in the air.

"Something is prevented them from flying through the center, Sir." Captain Phillips reported.

"Fly over the top and then enter from the outside of the ring."

The Blackhawk flew to the outer city limits, turned around and returned.

It dipped down to fly underneath the ring. The air craft was pushed back to the outside of the ring.

"Oh no," General Katz whispered.

Mayor Duncan approached the general. "General! I need to have a word with you!" she yelled.

"Not now, Mayor!" The general started walking really fast to a humvee. He wished he could feel good about how his knee was not bothering him as he kept a fast pace.

"General! Why haven't we've been evacuated? I heard the mess on the Southside bridge was cleared away and yet we're still in shelter-in-place mode."

"Mayor, I really don't have time to talk to you right now, we have more pressing problems than that bridge." The mayor hesitated for a second and then hopped in the humvee next to the general. "General! I know that there's a UFO over our heads, and I'm pretty sure none of us were even supposed to be here when it arrived, so it makes no sense that you would still keep us here! I'm responsible for the lives of thousands of people and if there's any danger to us I think—"

General Katz cut her of with a wave of his hand. "Mayor, right now we have a problem which may prevent EVERYBODY from evacuating!" The humvee sped to the Southside bridge. In their sight they could see the bridge. In the middle of the bridge, a battalion of soldiers, humvees, trucks and tanks were stopped halfway across the bridge.

"What the?" Mayor Duncan said.

The humvee slowed down to a crawling speed. On the other side of the bridge, a tank was trying to move forwards. It stood in one spot as its treads spun in place, kicking up dust and sparks. It appeared as if it were stuck on something. It couldn't move forwards one inch, but in an instant, it reversed itself and moved back to the other side of the bridge. The place where the tank once stood was replaced by two members of the U.S. Army 42nd Infantry Division, holding really large machine guns. Seeing soldiers with guns was something Mayor Duncan was getting used to. Seeing them point the guns at them was not. The soldiers opened fire, the mayor closed her eyes, thought about her daughter and her wife, Kathy and prepared for death. She heard the general yell, "No wait!" She opened her eyes when the shooting ended as fast as it had started. She was alive. She had survived a UFO landing and now machine gun fire. She checked herself for bullet holes, then the humvee. The general had gotten out of the vehicle and was walking towards the middle of the bridge. He had his hands up and yelled: "Hold your fire!" On the middle of the bridge, lay the two soldiers, dead. Some of their comrades ran to their aid but it was too late. The general continued to approach the middle of the bridge. He was walking slowly. Mayor Duncan assumed it was all related to the forces on the other side opening fire on them, but when the general came to the middle of the bridge, about five feet in front of the dead bodies, he stopped. His hands were still up. He walked forwards and then stopped again. His hands were resting on something. Something that wasn't there.

Mayor Duncan got out of the humvee and walked towards the general. "Ma'am!" the driver called out. She ignored him and walked to where the general was standing. His hands moved along like he was mime trapped on the side of an invisible wall. She lifted her hands and placed them beside his. There wasn't anything there, just air. When she moved her hands forwards, it was like the air became more and more solid until it felt as hard as one foot thick glass. When she pulled her hands back, the air became thinner and thinner. She repeated this experiment over and over. "What is that?" she asked.

"It's a problem," The general responded.

Chapter 5
Language Barrier

In an auto repair shop in Pepper Mill, a man named Manny had finally tracked down a front window for his 1929 Stutz M-22. It was a rare car, so finding the glass was even more of a rarity. "Be careful with that, Manny, the auto repairman said as Manny and his assistant started walking away with the glass. "If that get's broken, that's it, I can't get you another one!"

"Don't worry, Sal," Manny said. "I'm going to slowly walk this baby home, even if it takes a week!"

Back in the regular story, in Ami, Don and Casper's apartment, they were dealing with another problem: getting a TV to work after you've thrown a boot at it. The radio had proved to be limited in the information department. When the story of a helicopter crash was reported, no information about it bouncing back was added. When they tried to look up information on the internet, there were so many rumors and internet hoaxes it was hard to figure out which information about the town was true. Apparently, they were all dead, the government had hit the town with a nuclear bomb, and if they gave a guy in Africa $1000 he could claim his fortune as leader of an obscure country.

In spite of the big crack in the TV, they did manage to pick up a station. Its news reporting was fading in and out of a TV static snow storm of jumbled signal waves. The voice of the female reporter told them things they already knew: a large object was now hovering over the town, a helicopter had crashed and no one was able to get into town because of the earlier bridge accident.

"So that's why they won't let us leave, yet," Casper said.

"They can still fly us out, or use boats on the lake," Ami suggested.

"How long they gonna force us to stay inside?" Don asked. Earlier, a helicopter had flown really close to their rooftop patio and had broadcast the message that all civilians were to shelter in place, inside their homes, and to await further instructions.

"They probably want to find out if we've been exposed to some weird, freaky alien ray or something. We could actually be quarantined," Ami said trying to find an internet site that didn't claim Pepper Mill was destroyed.

The news reporter continued to give more information on the exact same thing she had reported earlier. At one point, the picture became crystal clear. The news show paused for a commercial break with mariachi music and the words "Spanish Television One will return after these messages from our sponsors." A soccer commercial came on; two men were facing each other as if they were going to fight instead of playing soccer. "Join us on Saturday as Brazil takes on Portugal in a match to the death! Here, only on Spanish Television One!" the announcer yelled.

"Why do they call this Spanish TV, when they keep speaking English?" Casper asked

"I don't know. Maybe it's a special English version," Don answered.

Another commercial came on. Two women wearing evening gowns were choking each other. They both ended up falling into a swimming pool. "Next on Savage Hearts!" The announcer said. "That is weird," Don said. "I remember that commercial in Spanish. Remember when we used to make fun of it?"

"Even TV has gone coo coo," Casper complained. It doesn't look like they have any more info than us." He looked at his phone to see if there were any messages from his mom. His phone was dead. He looked around for a charger. "Ami, did you see my charger?" he asked

"In the box marked; electronics," she answered.

He found two boxes marked the same way. "Which one? There are two marked; electronics."

"Why don't you open them?"

"Just tell me which one."

"Casper! Open them and see!"

"I don't feel like rummaging through boxes!"

"Fuzakeru na!" she yelled

"Hey!" Casper yelled. "...I'm not acting stupid!" he yelled back. He started rummaging through one of the boxes. Ami stuck her head into the room.

"What?" she asked.

"I told you I'm not acting stupid."

"How do you know I said that?"

"You said, 'stop acting stupid!'"

"Ha!" Don said. "Gotta stop cussing us out in Japanese, Ami, we're figuring out what you're saying."

"Don, I've never said that to you guys before," Ami said slowly.

"Bull," Casper said. "You've called us every name in the book."

"Except smart." Don added.

"You mean: 'Smart'?" Ami said.

"Yes, smart…but in Japanese," Casper complained

"I just said it in Japanese."

"Really? Smart is the same in English?" Don asked

"Casper, I <u>said</u> the word in Japanese…It's not the same word."

"Ami, you just repeated the word 'smart' in English. You didn't say anything in Japanese," Casper answered

"Stop messing around, you idiots!" Ami put her hands on her head. "It's been a long day. I'm stressed out and already on edge. I swear, if one more thing happens, I'm going to explode!"

"Please, no exploding," Casper said patting her shoulder. Ami lifted her head and had an expression on her face as though Casper's hand was electric. "We're all stressed out, we've had a long day too…Ami? What's wrong?"

Ami's face was one of shock and awe. "Casper, what I just said to you and what I'm saying to you right now, is all in Japanese."

"No it's not, it's English," Caper said.

"Yeah, Ami, you're speaking English," Don agreed.

Ami left the room. She returned with a book and handed it to Casper. "Here, read the cover of this!"

"Why?" he asked.

"Just do it!" Ami yelled.

Caper read the book cover. "Kafka on the Shore by Haruki Murakami. Yeah, so?"

Ami put her hands on her mouth. "Casper, this book is completely in Japanese, including the cover!"

"Sooo, you're saying not only did you loose a tattoo, you lost your Japanese as well?"

"It's not just her, Cap," Don said. "Remember the Spanish channel? The one that's suddenly in English?"

"Oh crap! We've lost our different languages!" Casper said.

"Wait, let me try something," Ami said. "Hello, hello, hello. What did I just say?"

"You said 'hello, hello, hello' in English," Don answered.

"No, I said hello in Japanese, Mandarin and French! You heard all of them in English! I didn't loose my Japanese, we just understand <u>all</u> languages!"

"All languages?" Casper asked.

"Probably," Ami said.

Don and Caper looked at each other and yelled: "MR. FUNG'S!" They put their jackets on and ran out the door, much to Ami's confusion.

A little while later. Casper Don and Ami hid in an alleyway to avoid detection by an army truck. It passed by the ally and headed towards the Southside bridge.

"Why are you guys risking being out here when they told us to shelter in place?" Ami asked.

'Why are you risking the same thing following us?" Casper responded.

"Are you kidding? You yell Mr Fung's and run out the door? Who wouldn't investigate that?"

After checking to make sure the way was clear, Casper and Don darted across the abandoned street. Ami timidly lagged behind. After looking around one last time, Casper turned his attention to a sign over a restaurant's window "Check it out!" he said to Don. There was nothing special about the sign, but Don immediately got what Casper found so interesting. It read: 'Mr. Fung's Chinese Food' and underneath that, smaller letters read: 'Lotus Blossom Chinese Food.'

"What's the big deal?" Ami said. "You guys ran out of the apartment to get some Chinese food? It's not even open; everyone's on lockdown."

"You don't get it, do you?" Don explained. "Casper and I have always had a bet about this place. We know it as Mr. Fung's, but the words Lotus Blossom are actually in Chinese. We're reading the REAL name of the restaurant!"

"And…that's worth getting caught by the army?"

"Oh, the bet goes beyond that," Don continued to explain. "You see, I've always thought that this restaurant had two menus, one in English and one in Chinese."

"So, lots of restaurants do that."

"True but I also believe that they have two price tiers. One for Chinese people, who can read Chinese, and everyone else gets ripped off by paying the non-Chinese prices."

"On Don, you're so…" Ami was about to say paranoid until she read the posted menu in the window. The price for Honey Walnut Prawns was priced at $6.95 and written underneath, the words Honey Walnut Prawns: $4. "Son of a…"

"I won!" Don yelled before doing a little dance.

"Great," Casper said sarcastically. He reached into his pocket and pulled out his wallet. "Here's your dollar, you've proven that human ethics is doomed to extinction."

"IdiotsYou guys get super powers and you waste it on Chinese menus," Ami complained.

"That, and finally hearing you call us idiots in English." Casper added.

"Yeah Ami, you better check yo' self before you insult us from now on," Don warned.

When the three of them turn around to go back to their apartment, they were startled by the appearance of a soldier pointing a gun at them. They all did that startled action you do when you turn around and someone is pointing a gun at you or, when one acts when a gun is pointed at them, after they turn around.

"What are you three doing on the street, you're supposed to be inside?" The soldier said. He looked at them closer and lowered his gun, much to the other's relief. "Hey! I know you," he said. They recognized him also. He was the soldier they were with when they thought they were all going to die. "Hello again."

"Oh, it's you,"Ami said trying to catch her breath.

"What are you guys doing out here? You should be inside." The soldier repeated.

"I'm sorry." Ami apologized. "My friends and I discovered that we can understand any language. We came down here to try it out on this Chinese restaurant." Ami pointed to the sign. The soldier looked at the sign and read it out loud.

"I don't get it. It's all in English."

"It's not, actually." Casper explained. "The words on the bottom are actually written in Chinese, you can now read them."

The soldier turned his head in disbelief. "Say what?"

"Trust us, it's real. It's probably an effect of the UFO," said Casper

"Probably?"Ami asked in sarcasm. "You think?"

"So you guys are saying that I can understand Chinese now?" the soldier asked finally getting it. He's rather slow to reality isn't he?

"Not just Chinese, we think it's all languages," Ami said. "Why, even now, I'm speaking Japanese to you. Matter of fact, since we discovered this, I've been speaking Japanese the whole time."

"What?" Don yelled. "You've been speaking Japanese! All this time?"

"Yeah, so?"

"Has it always bothered you that you have to speak English?"

"It gets tiring, thinking in English, Don. This is like a vacation."

"Wow! I can speak any language? Cool! Now I can order French fries in a French restaurant," the Soldier said.

Casper looked confused. Not just from what the soldier said but by the sight of something he recognized—it was his bike. He knew it was his bike because he had painted it bright orange with black stripes on the chance that no one would steal a bike with such distinguishing markings. The bike was not going down the street by itself because that would completely change this to a ghost story and having a ghost story with a guy named Casper would be ridiculous. The bike was being ridden by a familiar face, and a familiar face of someone who had developed a bit of a reputation for stealing things lately–their landlord, Mr. Campbell.

"Son of a Bike! Mr. Campbell stole my bike!" Casper yelled and pointed.

The group looked as Mr. Campbell continued to ride down the street and away from them.

"After him!" Casper yelled. No one moved. "He's got my bike!" Casper poked the soldier" Quick! Gomer Pyle, fire!"

"You want me to shoot a guy that stole your bike?"

"For crying out loud! Aren't you supposed to be policing the streets? Do some policing, shoot someone! Isn't that what the army does?" Casper yelled.

Before the soldier could say: "I'm not shooting anyone." Casper was already running down the street after Mr. Campbell.

"Hey! You have to go back to your home!" the soldier yelled. He started chasing after Casper. Ami and Don ran after them both.

In a more serene location, a hillside overlooking the town of Pepper Mill and the ring hovering above it, Dr Lewis Pascal and his assistant Dr. Aarti Panjwani sat on a blanket, set on the grass. They had pulled over the minute they were able to get a good view of the entire remarkable scene. Professor Pascal had a pair of binoculars in the trunk he usually used for quick astronomical observations. This was not a quick observation. Pascal gazed longingly and intensely at everything he saw. The news had reported accurately about the ring: it's size, it's rotation and it's light gridded pattern. What they did not report was the quietness. With something so large, hovering over the town, you would expect to hear some kind of humming or roaring. This would better explain the simple question, how was this thing staying up in the air?

Pascal posed this question out loud: "How in the world is that thing staying up there? Look at it Aarti, sitting up there, not wobbling or drifting one inch. It's like it's laughing at us—mocking our inferior technology. How did they do it? I wonder, how did they work through their differences and come together to advance their technology? We had the Russians and John F. Kennedy, pushing us towards the moon, who did they have?"

Aarti took the binoculars from Professor Pascal. Instead of looking up at the UFO, she pointed it at the ground underneath it. "No movement on the ground. I guess it's not creating a downward force like an engine would. They surely have something we don't have."

"It's so beautiful...so beautiful. I feel so lucky. I thought this was impossible, but I'm lucky enough to be alive right now...at this moment. I feel like one of the Wright brothers watching the Space Shuttle take off."

Aarti gave the binoculars back to Professor Pascal. "'Lead me from the unreal to the real, Lead me from darkness unto light, lead me from death to immortality.'"

"That's nice, what's that from?"

"The Brihadaranyaka Upanishad."

"Now I know even less than I did before." Pascal looked at the ground as Aarti did. He could see across the stream the Southside bridge ran across. He panned over to the bridge; the traffic jam held steadfast. On one side the incoming army, on the other side the forces of General Katz. "Why are they all just standing there?" He saw something rapidly approaching General Katz forces. It was a man on a bike being chased by four individuals. "Looks like a little drama is approaching the bridge."

Aarti took the binoculars and peered at the scene. "Maybe they're making a break for the bridge. I hope they make it. Those tanks and things aren't moving at all."

Mr. Campbell looked back at Casper and the others running after him. He was not in the best of shape but surprisingly, he felt energized enough not to slow down in his escape from town.

Casper was also surprised at himself. Usually he would become winded after running for five blocks but he was able to keep Campbell within his sight at all times. His calls of: "Stop! Thief!" had no moral or legal effect on Campbell's velocity. Ami, Don and the soldier bought up the rear of the chase train. Campbell turned the corner and was on the main road leading out of town. There were lots of army vehicles in both lanes leading to the Southside bridge, responding to the invisible wall. There weren't many soldiers on foot on the road; their backs were turned to Campbell and he was able to easily pass them without incident. Casper and his friends drew more attention with his yelling and the soldier yelling stop. Two foot soldiers jumped in Casper's way right after Campbell zipped pass them. "Hold it right there!" One of them yelled, blocking Casper with a large gun.

"He stole my bike!" Casper yelled. This did nothing to stop Campbell from making it all the way to where the general, the mayor and the others were standing, still trying to figure out the invisible wall that was blocking their path. Campbell saw there was an opening of vehicles and people on the bridge he could navigate through. He looked behind to make sure Casper and the others had stopped following him. Assured of his freedom, he laughed, smiled, waved and yelled: "So long, suck…" The last word he wanted to yell was "suckers!" but he didn't finish. At the moment he spoke, he hit the exact same spot on the bridge where tanks and bullets were stopped dead in their tracks. When he hit the invisible wall, it would best be described as watching a speeding bicycle, ridden by a sack of wet potatoes, hitting a brick wall. First, he hit the wall and then the bike flipped up and smashed him against the wall. Like a frog on a windshield, he slowly slid down to the ground, his face creating a loud squeaking sound the whole time.

At first, Casper was very annoyed that he couldn't get pass the members of the infantry, when he saw what had happened to Campbell, he backed away in shock. Don and Ami had also witnessed Campbell's accident and stopped running.

"Did he just run into something?" Ami asked.

"They must have some kind of tripwire thing running across the road," Don said.

"Why would they do that? Why is the army trying to keep us here?" Casper asked.

"All right you three, back to your homes, now!" yelled an army sergeant. "The next time I catch you in this area, we'll have you arrested and thrown in jail, so move it!"

"I got them, sir" (the soldier, who keeps chasing them, and who I hope gets a name soon so I can stop calling him 'the soldier') said.

General Katz pointed to Campbell, "Pick him up and take him to the infirmary, when he comes to, put him in a jail cell," some men went over and picked up Campbell and Casper's bent up bike.

"General!" Mayor Duncan said. "Why is he going to jail? Are you going to lock up everyone that see this thing?"

"Mayor, he's going to jail because those people chasing him were yelling 'he stole my bike' and 'stop thief!' The last thing we need in this situation is a crook running around stealing stuff and throwing a monkey wrench in the works. And as for this—thing, it's only a matter of time before the townsfolk see this. We have to take this nice and slow so we don't start a panic."

"You seem like you have experience with this kind of thing," the mayor said, pressing on the invisible wall.

The general took her hand away from the wall. "I do. We tried to open a Disneyland in Iraq. You talk about too much information getting out too fast! Ever seen a guy in a Micky Mouse suit pelted to death by sandals? I have."

The mayor sighed. "You guys are going to cover this all up, aren't you?"

"Mayor, in America, the truth is nothing more than a cover-up done the right way."

On the hill nearby, Aarti handed the binoculars back to Professor Pascal. "I saw it but I don't believe it. It's like there's nothing there blocking them, yet it stopped a guy on a bike."

"And apparently tanks and anything else trying to get in and out of town. Incredible, simply incredible! I think we need to get Dr. Roselli and the others in on this because I have no idea how an invisible force field is possible" Pascal started packing up their things. Aarti started folded up the blanket they were sitting on.

"Lewis?"

"Yes?"

"Have you considered the fact that perhaps none of this is real?"

"What do you mean, Aarti?"

"Dream state, stuck in the Matrix, or death? Perhaps the reason we are seeing an alien space craft, a force field and whatever else is going to show up is because we're dead or even on drugs?"

"That would make things easier, wouldn't it? I wish I were on drugs because it's going to take super-crack to explain how that eight kilometer long ring is staying up there, projecting a Star Trek like force field."

When Casper and his group were forced back into his apartment; he didn't expect there to be an armed guard guarding their door. The unnamed soldier was somehow punished for letting them get too close to the bridge and was ordered to watch guard over their apartment building to prevent any more excursions. Don cut on the television. This time, the only channel he could pick up clearly was the China News Network (not to be confused with CNN). They didn't report anything new: the size of the ring, military keeping everyone at bay, the footage of the baseball game where the comet transforms into the ring. They didn't mention the helicopter crash caused by the force field; that story was reported as a mid air collision or engine failure and the footage was never shown. Also, for the first time, the words "American Military Experimental Weapon" were used.

"What the?" Don said.

Casper came out of the kitchen holding a plate with a turkey sandwich on it. "What's the matter? Your Chinese is a little rusty?"

"They just called what's going on a 'military experiment.'"

"Oh-oh."

"O-oh is correct. They're doing the cover up thing, again!"

Casper sighed. "How can they expect to cover something like this up? People from miles away can see that big floating ring!"

The Chinese news reporters started describing the ring as a new type of power source that operates on magnetism and the Earth's gravity. As for those that claimed to see the explosion, it was an accident when the invention was activated. It was also the cause of the reported casualties.

"That's it!" Don said. "I'm calling the newspaper." Don picked up his cell phone and tried to do a web search. There was no signal. "Crap! No signal, I'll use the regular phone." He picked up the LAN line phone. "Double crap! No signals anywhere. Ami! Do we still have internet?"

"Nope! It just died!" she yelled from her room. "Right when I was going to e-mail my mom about the ring."

"They're blocking our signal!" Don complained.

"The UFO or the military?"

"My guess is the military, aliens don't care who you talk to!"

"How can they cut our cel lines?" Casper asked.

"Easy—you call the phone company and say, stop all calls in and out of Pepper Mill. Remember when the San Francisco Police stopped cel service for protesters in the subway?"

Ami came into the room. "Nuke this! I say we make a break for it!"

"Again, how?" Casper asked.

"We can't use the bridges, but if we sneak out at night, we can go down to the lake. If we find an inflatable raft we can…"

"Enough! Don yelled."

"What? What's wrong?" Ami asked.

"Why do we have to sneak out of here?"

"Hell-lo. Because the military is trying to keep us here?"

"Big F-D. They don't want us to leave. Maybe they have a good reason for it."

"Don't be so trusting. You heard the reports, They're covering this up as a military test—and the phones? We have to get out of here!"

"But, why?" Casper asked.

"WHY? before they kill us, you idiot!"

Casper walked over to Ami. "Ami, if they wanted to kill us, they've pointed guns at us many times and had many opportunities. And as for the other stuff, of course they want to cover this up. There's a UFO over our heads, our skin has been updated and we can understand every language. If they tell everyone about this, they're gonna be coming in buses. It'll be like Woodstock meets Burning Man, 24-7."

"So you're okay with staying?" she asked Casper.

"Of course. I want to study space, this is a dream come true. The only thing that'll make me leave is if that thing started turning people into burnt skeletons."

"And by then, it'll be too late!"

"Probably. But so far, good skin and cleaner air aren't close to the skeleton ray."

"What about you?" She turned to Don. "You said your goal was to keep us alive."

"It is." Don answered. "We're alive and from what I can tell, not in harm's way. Like Cap said, we're at ground zero of the most important discovery since marshmallow met fire. Why would I leave this?"

Ami sighed. "I...I just feel like an idiot. For getting you guys into this mess."

Don put his hand on her shoulder. "Don't worry about it Ami-chan?... Hey! check that out, the word 'chan' didn't translate. Are we losing our powers?"

"No," Ami said.

"How do you know?" Casper asked.

"Because I'm still speaking Japanese to you, idiot."

"Oh right—enough with the idiot!" Casper said. "So don't worry, Ami-chan. Before, we were trying to escape death, now we're going to discover new life. Hey, does this thing translate Klingon?"

"Ta' Soh jatlh tlhIngan?" Don asked. "I guess not."

Casper and Ami looked at Don with confusion.

On the Southside bridge, being illuminated by spot lights in the night air, Professor Pascal and Dr. Panjwani were conducting short experiments on the two foot thick force field. Professor Pascal seemed very fond of the one where he leaned against it and was suspended in air. The voice of Dr. Xiang, broadcasting from Aarti's video tablet device, reminded him that the force field could be radioactive and it was best to limit contact with it.

Aarti pointed the camera at the body bags containing the soldiers that had shot at the field earlier with deadly results. "So, Dr. Xiang, is that what happened to these two?"

"No," Xiang answered "They are the result of Newton's third law: for every action there is an opposite and equal reaction. They were shot by their own bullets."

"So, it's not a force field, if a reflection field." Pascal asked.

"Something like that. Any force exerted on it is met with equal force," Xiang responded.

The President's voice chimed in on the video tablet. "So we need three questions answered: How does it work, and can we get through it?"

"That's two questions," General Katz pointed out.

"I know, I always leave room for a follow-up question," said the President. "

Dr. Xiang scratched his chin. "To be honest, it's really impossible for this thing to work, just like it's impossible for a large metal ring to be floating without any sign of propulsion."

"They don't call it advanced technology for nothing, Doc," the President said.

"I know, I know, and that's basically going to be my answer for many things. You see, there are four forces we know about: gravity, which can hold things to a planet, but can't stop bullets and apparently has no effect on a floating ring, there's electromagnetism which could repel metal bullets and tanks, but people and their clothes aren't made of metal, and then there are the strong and weak forces that keep our electrons and atoms together. Unless they're solid objects like a wall, I can't imagine anything else creating such a force to repel matter. Being that this thing is virtually invisible, like air, it could work if it were a super powerful wind or something like that, but you said this thing doesn't exert any force until you push against it."

"So no dice, Doc?" the President asked.

"Not yet, Mr. President. For now we can only say they've discovered a 5th force we don't know about, just like they found a way to defy gravity."

"And my third question—see, I told you I had a follow-up question; Why is there a force field in the first place? Why are they trying to keep us out of the town?"

"Actually, Mr. President…" Dr. Larson said. "…Are they trying to keep us out or keep the townspeople in?"

"That is possible," Dr. Wright said. "The townspeople have obviously been affected with something that heals lifetime wounds and removes tattoos, God only knows what other changes are coming their way. We'll only know once we get the blood sample data the army has."

"About that, Dr. Larson," General Katz said. "We aren't set up to do lab work on the fly. We did send the blood samples to the lab at the Medical Center but they don't have any lab technicians that know how to run the tests. They evacuated with the first round of refugees."

"What about medical students? Find out if any of them got any training in lab work."

There was a knock on the door of Ami, Don and Casper's apartment.

"Visitors? Now?" Casper complained getting off the living room couch to answer the door. Ami peeked out of her bedroom. Don was so exhausted he refused to even get up. Casper opened the door. It was the unnamed soldier and another foot soldier.

"Oh, it's you," Casper said.

"Hello again," the soldier said, embarrassed. "Sorry to wake you guys up."

"That's okay. I was up watching a Communist Chinese blooper show."

"Really? How is it?"

"Tragic and unfunny."

"Oh, sorry. So anyway, the reason I'm here is I have to round up anybody with any medical training whatsoever. Anybody like that here?"

"Why? Are we all gonna die?"

"I don't know. I think they want to make sure we aren't dying."

Casper turned to Ami. "Ami? What do you think?"

Ami thought for a second. "I have a little bit of training: I have CPR, phlebotomy, EMT, medical lab technology, Philosophy 101, Computer 1A and 1B, sociology, Drama 2B or was it not 2B? And Jazz dancing."

"She's a little all over the place, isn't she?" Casper asked.

"We can use the medical stuff, but not the other things," the soldier said. "Can you come with us to the medical center?"

"Sure," Ami said. "Let me get my things."

"You sure, Ami?" Casper said. "Remember what you said about the military, earlier?"

"It's okay, Casper. I'm curious about what's happening to us, too. Besides if they need me, they won't kill me."

"Kill you?" The soldier said, insulted. "Why would we want to kill you? We're stuck in this town—er-ah, we need everyone's help."

"What do you mean, stuck?" Don asked, coming out of his room.

"Nothing—er-ah—figure of speech," the soldier said before giving a demonstration of the world's worst, fake laugh. "We have to go, Miss...?"

"Nakajima...Nakajima Ami." She smiled at him

"Private First Class, Tommy Finn, Ma'am." He smiled back. (He has a name, thank God for that.)

Ami went into her room to change out of her embarrassing Sailor Moon punching Pikachu night shirt. In a short time, Ami had her clothes on and her backpack full of medical reference books. She, Private Finn and the other soldier (who's not going to get a name because you will never see him again) left and headed downstairs to an awaiting humvee.

Casper turned to Don. Don had a worried look on his face. "So, you think she's in any danger?"

"N-naw. Like she says, they need her for something."

"So why the concerned look?"

"It's nothing…it's…"

"What"

"It's…Remember when we were all going to die?"

"Which time? Is it weird it's happened more than once?"

"Second time, baseball field, bright light."

"Rings a bell."

"Do you remember, something Ami was trying to tell me? She yelled something."

"All I remember is I was about to die, I wasn't paying much attention to other people's screaming, only my own."

"I could have sworn it was like, I'll… something"

"I'll miss you? I'll bake you a pie? I'll see you in the next life? I'll be home for Christmas?"

"Maybe…Just maybe."

"What else would she say?"

"I don't know…I guess 'I'll miss you' was probably it. Good night." Don went back into his room. Casper went back to the Chinese blooper show. They were showing a man in a gorilla suit on the street in Beijing, blocking a tank while goofy music was playing.

"This is going to end badly," Casper said.

Most of the townspeople were going to sleep that night, Ami was not one of them. In the humvee, she looked out the side window to see the ring. She expected it to be glowing like any generic UFO from the movies but it wasn't. The only way you were able to see it was the way it blocked some of the starry night sky.

"Where you from, Miss Ami?" Private Finn asked her.

"Nakajima."

"You're from Nakajima, AND it's your first name, whoa!"

"No my name is…never mind, I'm from Osaka."

"That in Arkansas?"

"Osaka, Japan?"

"Oh, you're from Japan?"

"Yep."

"Japan, Japan?"

"Yes, the real one...unlike Mecha-Japan."

"Wow, that's great! How do you say 'hello' in Japanese?"

"Uh, well, I can't say it because of the instant translation thing."

"Pardon?"

"I...you keep forgetting that I'm speaking to you in Japanese, right now. If I tell you how to say hello, It's going to come out as 'hello'. See, I just did it. See what I did just now?"

"Did what?"

"Ami sighed. Tell you what; it's spelled: K-O-N-I-C-H-I-W-A."

"How do you say that?"

"If I say it...Hey driver! How long until we reach the medical center?"

The humvee continued on its short but, for Ami, long journey. At the bridge, the army on the outside were setting up a little camp, near the hillside where Pascal and Aarti had first observed the ring. Tents of all sorts were being erected as well as anti-everything weaponry in case something happened in the realm of burnt skeleton ray. Aarti was turning in to her tent. She came out, while brushing her teeth, to look at the ring's silhouette, one last time. Pascal was standing on a cliff, on the river's edge. He was leaning on the force field, suspended in air and looking down at the rushing river's water below, it's was an unnerving site.

"Lewis!" Aarti yelled. Pascal pushed away from the invisible wall and stood upright. Aarti walked over to him. "That's not safe."

"It's following the path of the ring," he said looking up and pointing where the ring hovered overhead. "It must go all the way around the city."

"Maybe."

"They're trapped."

"For now."

"Yet, the river...."

Aarti walked over and put her hand on his shoulder. "Get some sleep, Lewis. It's been a long day." She lead him back to the camp site.

In his tent on the Pepper Mill side of the bridge, General Katz was dealing with something much more important than force fields and alien visitors.

A lieutenant rushed into the tent." Sorry sir, we lost her."

"You lost her? Does that mean she's in here with us?"

"Yes, sir. We tracked her down and told her you wanted to see her but she gave us the slip. I think she's moving from house to house and staying with friends. If you want, we can do a major house to house sweep and bring her in by force."

"No, that won't be necessary. The more you chase after her, the more she runs. We'll take the pressure off for now. She'll come out in the open eventually."

"Yes, sir. And what do you want to do with her once she's captured?"

"Bring her directly to me. I don't care what's going on."

"Yes, sir."

"Dismissed."

The lieutenant turned around and made it to the tent entrance before the general stopped him.

"Lieutenant!"

"Sir?"

General Katz looked at an old photo of Lori when she was 5. She was saluting while holding an American flag. "Don't ever have kids."

"Yes sir."

Thousands of miles away, an American leader was having trouble sleeping. It had nothing to do with the constant days of light outside in the Antarctica landscape. It was the weight of the world weighing on his shoulders. To ease the tension in his shoulders, his wife, Betty was massaging said shoulders and offering words of comfort.

"Poor J.J.," she cooed "So much pressure keeping the world safe for democracy and comets."

"Thanks B. But it's not just that, it's Megan. I caught her making out with my assistant, Barry."

"Barry? Is he the one that looks like Rob Lowe or the other one?"

"The other one."

The First Lady scrunched up her face. "She can do better than that."

"I know. It's this darn base. There are slim pickings in here."

"Then why are we here? The comet didn't destroy the Earth; what happen to that anyway? Did it really land in the Bering Straight?"

"I can't tell you the truth right now, darl'n otherwise I'll have to have you shot."

"This is related to that military weapon being tested in California, isn't it?"

"Can't talk about it, Betty."

"J.J., is this whole thing a big cover-up for that thing flying over California? You been lying to us the whole time?"

"Seriously, Betty. Shot-in-the-head kind of secret. They don't call you the First Lady for nothing. Second ones in that closet, wait'n to be activated."

The First Lady looked at the closet before realizing he was kidding. "All right, all right." She massaged the President's shoulder a little while longer. "But we can't expect Megan to be cooped up in this base for too much longer. She's getting cabin fever. Girl her age is like containing a fire in a tampon factory."

"Ew-uck!"

"Point is, if the emergency is over. You can at least send us to Camp David or some place normal"

"The emergency is still here, Butter Cups. Until we find out more about the...stuff I can't tell you about, nobody important is going to be put in harm's way."

"And how long are you planning on keeping us here?"

"I don't know, Betty. Before, when I thought the world was going to end, it was much easier to know where things were going: Nuclear winter, zombie apocalypse,...eating Barry. But now, it's like the future just got split into two or three possibilities. It's like the town of Pepper Mill is inside a box and we can't see what's happening in the box so we have to guess what's going on."

"Pepper Mill? Is that the town where the stuff you can't talk about are happening?"

"Methinks I saith too much."

"Is it?"

"Bullet in the head, Betty, bullet in the head." The President turned his back to her, lay down and pretended that he wanted to sleep.

The First Lady kissed him on the back of head. "Fine, don't talk about it. You do what you think is right for the country and the world. Just make sure you do what's right for your family first. I'm pretty sure there's no 'Second family' in that closet."

Casper was awakened by the sound of roosters crowing. Considering how far away he lived from the farms and ranches near Baker's Field, this was an odd sound to hear. He got out of bed to investigate. The golden California sun was up. He guessed the time at around 7:30. After putting on some pants, he walked by Ami's room to see if she had returned. The door was open and there was no sign she had occupied her bed. Someone else was up. Don stood at the living room window, gazing out unto the street. "Hey, Don Juan. What time did you get up?"

"I couldn't sleep. Been up waiting for Ami to come back."

"Huh? Why?"

"In case something happened to her?"

"Like what? She went to the campus, protected by army dudes."

"Army dude, exactly," Don said with an angry tone.

Casper walked over to the window to see what he was looking at. On the street, the army humvee had returned with Ami and Finn in it. They were talking. She laughed at something he said, patted his shoulder and then exited the vehicle. Finn drove on with a double toot of the horn.

Don and Casper left the window. "Wow, she must have been busy."

"Whatever," Don said heading to his room.

"Hey, aren't you curious to hear what she was up to?"

"Whatever. I'm going to bed." Don went into his room and closed the door.

"What's his problem?"

Ami, not realizing Casper and Don were awake, tried to sneak into the Apartment.

"Young lady!" Casper said startling her. "When I told you to be back at ten, I mean't PM!" he joked, putting his hands on his hips.

"Sorry, Dad," Ami said, putting her backpack down.

"Busy day at the hospital?"

"Omigod! It was insane! I did like 1000 blood draws and processed gallons of blood!"

"Ew-uck."

"Well, not really, but there was a lot of poking and processing."

"And what did you find out?"

"They wouldn't tell us."

"Huh?"

"Well, me and a couple of students were doing the draws and running the centrifuges but the lab techs were the ones with the microscopes, getting the results."

"That sucks, at least they could've shared some information with you."

"Well, to be honest with you. I could tell some things that they were looking for."

"How's that?"

"Tube colors."

As in tops?"

"No, idiot. The test tubes. Whenever you do blood draws, they always put the blood in different types of test tubes with certain color tops and chemicals to preserve the samples or to keep the blood from clotting. That way the lab knows what to do with it or how to store the tubes so that the samples don't get contaminated. Different test tubes for different test: like red with gold stripes is for testing the kidneys and for HIV, gray tops for blood alcohol–that kind of thing.

"So what were they testing for?"

"From what I could tell, drugs, thyroids and a blood culture for testing bacteria."

"Thyroid?"

"They were probably looking for radiation type things or something to explain the scar removals."

"Alcohol and drugs?"

"Not sure. Make sure we're not all high? We also did some sticks to check peoples blood oxygen levels. Maybe that was related to how clean the air feels around here."

"Wow, well done, Detective Nakajima."

"Thanks. Where's Don?"

"He went to bed right when you and lover boy came home."

"Lover boy?"

"Private Parts?"

"I don't get…oh wait, Finn? He was just giving me a ride home."

"I saw your little giggle-talk down there." Casper nudged her shoulder.

"He was just dropping me off."

"That's what SHE said!"

"Huh?"

"Never mind. I was trying to make a sex joke out of what you said, It failed–I'm tired. I haven't had breakfast yet. You hungry?" Casper walked over to the refrigerator.

"No. they fed us army breakfast."

"Eggs and bayonets?" He opened the fridge. He shook the empty milk container. There were no eggs or bayonets to eat. "Darn it! I hate it when you guys put an empty milk container in the fridge."

"It's YOU, Casper that does that."

"Oh right, you're the one that leaves the toilet seat down. Man, this fridge is empty. We have to go shopping. —how are we going to go shopping? Can't go shopping on lockdown."

"Casper, do we need to go shopping?"

"We need to go shopping!"

"Well, maybe I can talk Finn into picking up some stuff for us."

"Ah-Ha!" Casper yelled.

"Ah-ha yourself. There's nothing going on! He told me to call him if I needed any favors. Might as well take him up on it."

"Whatever it takes; we need food! They can't have us locked inside all the time. I can't watch anymore Chinese cable TV! Did you know they eat bear paws?"

"I love bear claws."

"Not the dessert thing, paws!"

"Oh."

"Now I'm hungry for bear claws. Ami, talk to your boyfriend about letting us go shopping."

"He's-not-my- boyfriend!"

"Talk to someone then, before we run out of toilet paper."

"Out of toilet paper! Oh-no-no-no-no! That's not an option!"

"Exactly! Talk to someone."

"Funny thing is, I did get to do a blood draw on the head of the army forces."

"Who is it?"

"His name was General Cat, I think."

"As in meow?"

"Not sure—anyway, he was real chatty. Told me how he has a daughter my age."

"Did he give a clue about what that thing is?" Casper pointed upwards.

"No, we mostly talked about the effects it's having on us. He didn't even know about the language thing."

"Really?"

"Well, if you think about it, unless they're in a foreign country, everyone in the army speaks English to each other."

"True. So why don't you get General Cat to throw some mice our way?"

"I have no influence over him, no more than I have over the mayor."

The mayor at this time had some of the same concerns as Casper and Ami. Unlike the rest of the citizens, she had easier access to General Katz but just as much access to the truth. She entered the mess hall tent right when he was finishing his breakfast.

"Morning, Madam Mayor. Care for some scones?"

"No thanks, I already ate. Matter of fact, I'm here to talk to you about food."

"Sure, what's on your mind?" Katz gestured for her to sit across from him. She obliged and sat down.

"How long do the citizens have to be on lockdown?"

"Unknown at this time, we haven't got all of the blood test back."

"About that. Why didn't they do any citizens?"

"First line of defense, Mayor. Gotta do health care workers and military. If they go down, the citizens don't stand a chance."

"Okay, I'll let that slide. But about the lockdown, we can't be inside forever. We need to go to work or food shopping before we run out of money or food."

"The money thing is the least of your worries. Some jobs can be done inside with computers. Anything else like retail aren't going to suffer. Clothes aren't going to rot."

"But food in the grocery store will."

"Hmm, I guess." The general thought for a brief moment. "Tell you what. We really don't know how long that force field thing is going to be up. I think we should prepare for the long haul. I'll allow all of the people in the restaurants, convenience stores and grocery stores to do an inventory. This will be an order, not voluntary. Once we have an idea of what we have, I'll allow a short window for towns people to pick up rationed supplies. That work for you?"

"Yes…Thank you." The mayor was surprised at how easy it was working this out with the general. She had expected more of a fight. "I'll get a list of all of the restaurant and grocery store workers still left in town."

"You do that. If you need any extra man power, you can use a couple of my boys for security and those FEMA workers that got trapped in here."

"All right. Thanks again." The mayor left the tent.

The general turned to his lieutenant. "Didn't you say my daughter works in a grocery store?"

"No sir, a record store."

"Blast it! I was hoping to smoke her out and put her to work."

Across the bridge, Professor Pascal emerged from his tent. Before he could go to Aarti's tent to ask her if she wanted to drive somewhere for breakfast, he saw her. She was recreating the stunt that he was doing last night. She was leaning against the invisible wall, preventing her from falling into the rushing water below. He now understood how unnerving it looked to an observer. Pascal walked over to her, grabbed the back of her belt and pulled her back to the cliff's edge. "I thought you said that was dangerous?"

Aarti smiled. "Dangerous…but really cool."

"Did you notice the same thing I did?"

"No, what?"

"The water."

"Pardon?"

"Come here." Pascal grabbed her hand and led her to a spot on the cliff where they could get a good view of the river. "Where do you think the force field is?"

Aarti picked up a rock and threw it at the force field. It bounced off and was thrown right back at them. It hit her on the knee. "Ow!" she complained, rubbing her leg.

"Watch out for Newton's law. So where is it?"

"At this point, it looks like it's cutting dead center."

"At this point, would you say, it's cutting the river in half?"

"Sounds accurate."

"So what's wrong with what you're seeing?"

Aarti looked at him and then at the river below. There was nothing strange about the water. A stick flowed downstream without doing anything weird. It bobbed and spun in the water just like it would do in any other situation.

"Wait! Holy bungalow!"

"You see it?"

She picked up a stick and tossed it at the field. It bounced back and almost hit her shoulder. "It's us!"

"It is. We better contact the group."

Ami, like Don, had gone to bed to catch up on lost sleep. Casper had spent his morning trying to get more channels on the television. He was able to add a Spanish channel and a right wing news channel. A male reporter wearing an American flag on his lapel was reporting about the ring. He was calling it an American Military balloon experiment, involving a new type of power source. According to their channel, anyone calling the ring a UFO or an object from space are nothing more than biased latte liberal media types trying to discredit the existence of God and looking for an excuse to blame the President for a cover up. There were no mentions of the citizens; it was like they didn't exist anymore. They, like the ring were being covered-up by lies, speculation and emotional, couch potato science. Casper rolled his eyes and wished he could un-pick up the channel. When he fiddled with the TV, the channel came in even clearer. He would have spent the rest of his afternoon working on the TV if he had not heard the ruckus outside. He went to the window.

A white, FEMA SUV slowly drove by. The passenger had a mega phone and was repeating a message over and over: "Attention citizens. If anyone was working in a restaurant, grocery store or anywhere else that provided food and supplies or even if you have experience doing inventory, please report to the town center near that statute of Sammy Hagar..." There was some mumbling of conversation inside the car. "...Sorry, I was just informed that it's General Custer. Please report to the statute of Custer killing a Native American baby..." More mumbling. "...Sorry, holding a baby...And a sword...Even though he used a rifle...And didn't like Native Americans...babies...You can see how I got confused.... What? He's holding a lion's head?...For Christ Sa—Please report to that statute! This is an order."

"Well," Casper thought. "They fired me but I do have experience and it'll get me out of the house—why not?" He went to wake up Don.

During their video conference, no one expected Dr. Colby, Dr. Roselli and Mr. Theodore Larson not to have any answers for how the force field worked, no one also expected Dr. Wright to say he saw no anomalies in the blood work collected, scanned and e-mailed to the best labs in the world. All samples produced perfect, healthy blood which was the only thing odd. General Katz informed them all that the people in the town knew how to speak all languages.

Aarti asked him, in Hindi, if he understood what she was saying. She told him what she had eaten for breakfast. Although he couldn't speak it back in Hindi, he was able to repeat her words back, in English.

Professor Pascal felt a little superior to his fellow scientist. He knew something that they didn't. He tried not to let it go to his head. "Gentlemen," he said. "I don't know how the force field works, why people are losing scars and can speak every language but I do know what the force field is doing."

"What ya got, Doc?" the President asked.

"The force field is to keep us out."

"Uhh, Doc, even I could have said that."

"No, Mr. President. The force field is to keep US out."

"Not earning your degree today, Doc."

"You don't understand. The field is only active when WE try to cross it or WE throw something at it, or drive across it."

"Are you saying it's intelligent?" Dr. Xiang asked.

"I'm not going to speculate about how its brain works, but I do know that air, water, wind, electricity, radio and TV signals, phone and internet signals—at least before you guys cut them off—insects, I even saw a bird fly in and out of the field, everything flows through without any interference. Everything but us."

"We're being targeted?" Mr. Theodore asked.

"Down to the atom. They don't want the general and the enhanced towns people to leave and they don't want us to go in. It even treats us differently than a projectile. Projectiles bounce off, but we just come to a dead stop. My guess is to keep us from trying to fire weapons at it, while trying not to harm us at the same time."

"Professor, you said you saw a bird fly in and out of the field? Did you think of doing an experiment, like putting an animal through it on a string and pull it out so we can analyze it?" Dr. Wright asked.

"I can answer that," Aarti said. "I found a beetle. I put it down on the bridge near the edge of the field and waited for it to crawl across; it was blocked just like us."

"But you said it's blocking us, not bugs and stuff," the general said.

"It's blocking us AND our influence." Pascal answered. "It seems to know what we're up to. Even if you tried to drive a remote control car across, I bet you it'll block it; it knows you have something to do with it."

There were lots of mumbles and words like "amazing" and "remarkable" being said.

"Gentlemen…" the President said. Aarti cleared her throat. "…Gentlemen, this complicates any type of evacuation or sending supplies into town. I think priority number one should be finding a way in, around, over or under that force field."

The meeting was adjourned. Those on the outside of the field went to work trying to figure out how to get in and the ones inside went to work, planning on what to do if they were stuck inside forever.

Near the statute of Sammy Hagar-er-ah I mean General Custard–the service industry employees of Pepper Mill gathered to hear the current field leader of FEMA explain their mission. They stared at the ring for a moment until they were content it had not changed since it landed. Casper and Don took their places behind a couple of people he recognized: his friend Darla from Big Red Groceries, and Baboosh the bar owner.

"Darla!" Casper yelled. They hugged. "I'm glad to see you and sad at the same time."

"I know, me too. I almost made it out, but Gregory took off without me."

"Wait, he left you here? To die"

"Sure did."

"Wow…sorry."

"That's okay. Once they let us leave, I'm going to track him down and turn his skin into an awesome drum."

"It's nice to have goals." Casper looked over and saw Sue, the supervisor from Big Red Groceries. She gave him a "what are you doing here?" sneer.

The FEMA leader spoke once everyone had gathered. "Listen up, everybody. My name is Ty Lithgow. I'm the current field officer of FEMA. Our former leader went AOL and we can't find her. So for now, I'm going to be handing out assignments to help manage our civilian task force–that's you. The situation is this: We are under a state of quarantine. As far as I know, the ring has affected us all and until we are rendered safe to re-enter the public realm, we have to remain in this town indefinitely." There were sounds of concern from the crowd. Ty raised his hands to quiet the crowd. "Calm down everyone. Just keep in mind; we're safe, we're protected and we're together. Now, until we get out of here, we have to inventory all of our resources, that way no matter how long we're here, we won't run out of food, medical supplies and all the kinds of things we need. Your jobs are going to be to return to wherever you were working before the ring appeared and inventory everything there. Box what you can and freeze what can be frozen for later. You will be paid for your work, whatever you used to make. We will be issuing you some forms to…" Ty's speech was interrupted by Sue raising her hand. "Uh yes?"

"Yes, Hi. Sue Zelinka, Big Red Groceries, store number 1926, Team Leader."

"Yes, Sue, what can I do for you?"

"Ms…Zelinka. Anyway I only see two other employees that used to work at MY store—"

"That's great…Ms Zelinka, You won't need more than four employees. We can round up—" Ty was interrupted by Sue's hand raising, again.

"The problem is, one of them was not really a 'team player.'"

Sue made air quotes with her fingers.

Casper nudged Darla. "That's you."

"And the other one…" Sue said looking at Casper. "Was fired for being undisciplined, uncooperative and generally NOT Big Red Groceries material."

"What do you want me to do, Ms Zelinka?"

"I was wondering if I can train some new employees to—"

This time, Ty stopped her from talking with his hand up. "Let me stop you there, Sue."

"Ms Zelinka."

"Whatever, Sue. We really don't have the time or the manpower for personal squabbles or conflicts—"

"But I…" Sue tried to interrupt again.

"But, nothing. Whomever you were working with before the ring, fired or not you're going to have to buck it up and work with them again. We need <u>everyone</u> pulling together here, this is an emergency situation."

"But what if they act bad?"

"I don't care if they come in drunk and naked…"

"Woo-hoo!" Casper and Darla yelled.

"…As long as they can lift and count to 10, deal with them, Sue. And if you can't, I'll put THEM in charge."

Don rose his hand and was acknowledged. "Speaking of which, I worked at Jack's Magic Beans Café, but Jack and all other employees managed to escape. What am I supposed to do?"

"What's your name?" Ty asked.

"Donald Byrd—Don."

"Congratulations, Mr. Byrd, you're now the proud owner of Don's Magic Beans Café."

Don smiled and raised his eyebrows. "Awesome…Awesome day."

Ty finished his speech and the crowd started to disperse. Casper walked over to Sue. "So, Fat Butt, what time should I be at work?"

Sue narrowed her eyes and gritted her teeth. "6 O'clock and don't be late!"

"I'll be there at 9," Casper said walking away.

"I'll be there at 6," Darla said. "But I'll be drunk and naked."

To explain the events of the rest of the week, imagine there is an 80's montage of tom foolery. If you are unfamiliar with an 80's montage, I suggest you watch a *Rocky* movie, *Karate Kid* or some other film where the main character has to get in shape to beat the big bad Russian or school bully, while a blaring soundtrack by *Journey*, *Lover Boy* or another 80s pop band is playing in the background. The blaring sound track is true because of the way Darla would blast the music all over the store but the workouts were usually replaced with hijinks, perpetuated by Casper and Darla against Sue such as: covering her office doorway with clear packing tape, so she runs into it like a spider web; spray painting "Fat Butt" on her office wall; placing the entire contents of her office into the ladies room and filling her office with toys and stuffed animals that avalanched out when she opened the door. No one was gladder to see the weekend more than Sue. Formerly, Casper and Darla would work on the weekend but they created their own fluid schedule as well as a flexible dress code. Casper developed a fondness for wearing Hawaiian shirts and flip flops and Darla dressed like a vampire dipped in Goth paint.

Darla was just finishing boxing up the alcohol section. She unlocked a glass cabinet and took out a bottle of Jose Cuervo 250 Aniversario. "Hey Assistant Manager, Casper. I want to buy this for myself. How much should I charge?"

"How much are they selling it for, Assistant Manager, Darla?"

"$2,250"

"$19.99?"

"Thanks Assistant Manager, Casper."

"Well, Assistant Manager, Darla. It's dark outside so I'm going to take off and go to The Pepper Grind."

"Oh, Baboosh is re-opening it? Cool!"

"Yeah. Me and my roomies are meeting there, you wanna hang out with us?"

"I'll check in later. First I'm going to sell myself this $700 bottle of gin for $10."

"Hey! That's stealing."

"$19.99?"

"Sold! See you later." Casper waved goodbye and made his way to Sue's office to tell her he was leaving 30 minutes early. It wasn't a courtesy thing, he was going to rub it in her face. She was in her office, siting at her desk with her head in her hands. He knocked on the wall because they had removed her door earlier in the day. "Hey, Fat Butt, I'm leaving early." He was about to leave but noticed the lack of response from her. "F.B.? You hear me?" There was a whimpering sound. Casper started to leave again but came back. "Sue?" More whimpering. "Sue? Are you…Crying?"

"Go away!" she yelled.

"Ooo-kay." Casper again attempted to leave but was drawn back. "Is it something I did?"

Sue lifted her head from her hands. "Do you think— Einstein?"

"Hey we're just having some fun."

"Fun? You super glued my office supplies to the ceiling!"

Casper looked up at the stapler and other small office items on the ceiling. He laughed.

"Yeah, laugh it up, fuzz ball! You aren't the one getting victimized here."

"Whoa-whoa-whoa here! You were victimizing us waaaay before we went after you!"

"What? By making you do your jobs? How dare I!"

"Doing our job is one thing Sue, but if this were the Matrix, you swallowed a big bottle of those blue pills."

"Is that the one that keeps you in the Matrix or gets you out?"

"I think it keeps you in?"

"I think that was the red pill?"

"No, that gets you out."

"That doesn't make sense, the red one should have the negative consequence—whatever, you guys were terrible workers! Of course I'm going to come down hard on you!"

"Totally get that, Sue. But working here…Well it sucked. Retail sucks. Working retail sucks like those giant pipes you see city workers sticking in man holes to suck out the sewage, except the truck that's collecting it explodes at the end."

"Then why didn't you quit?"

"I was going to, once I finished school. What? Do you think I was going to retire here? Was that going to be your plan?"

"Maybe…They have a 401K plan and stuff."

"Oh Sue," Casper said sadly.

"Don't 'Sue' me."

"Ha!" Casper laughed. "Sue me, that's funny."

"I'm glad I could provide such entertainment for you and your partner." She started to cry a little."

"There, there," Casper said walking over. He was going to put his hand on her back but the thought of touching her made him queasy, he poked her with one finger instead. "Cheer up, we were only kidding you."

"But, I can't work in this environment! I'm already stressed out as it is! My boyfriend was supposed to drive up and rescue me during the evacuation but he never made it in time."

"You have a boyfriend?"

Sue lifted her head. "Is something wrong with that?" she said angrily.

"No, no. Just I figured you had your heart removed so you could work more hours."

"Well I do…did. We were going to get married…as soon as his divorce went through."

"Divorce? A married man? Sue! You little vixen! I had no idea you were so scandalous."

"Exactly. You know nothing about me!"

146

"Kinda hard to cross that line when you keep up the great wall of Big Red Groceries operations manuals."

"I was trying to get ahead, you moron! Unlike you guys and your college (air quotes) and your rock n' roll band (more air quotes), this is all I have! And now, you guys are taking it away from me!" She was about to cry again.

"There, there, don't cry." Casper jumped up and pulled a tissue out of a box, super glued to the ceiling and gave it to her. After a couple of loud, honking nose blows, she looked for the garbage can. Casper pointed to the ceiling.

"See, I can't work in this, no one could!" she started whimpering.

Casper sighed. "Okay, Fine, we'll call a truce. But things are going to be different around here."

"As long as the pranks stop and you guys do the actual work, I'll be happy."

"Good, so stop your blubbering. We'll cut the pranks and do the work. But, no more stick without the carrot."

"Huh?"

"Carrot and stick? Motivation? You can't beat us with a stick all the time without offering a carrot."

"What are you talking about?"

"It's a metaphor for motivation. I see that word never made it into the Big Red manifesto—we'll work on it later. Just learn to chill out once in a while. Like, if we're standing around talking to each other it's not because we're goofing off, it's because we're friends. Isn't it much better to work with people you like than those you're afraid of?"

"I guess."

"And if we get a 15 minute break, is it fair to include the time to walk back and forth from the break room?"

"Probably not. I always had to wolf down my lunch because of that."

"Exactly! See, we have common ground! Comrades, proletariats against the aristocracy…"

Sue held up her hand. "I swear to God, if you mention the word 'union' I will end you."

"Fine, one step at a time. Speaking of rights. I'm off, as it is my right to leave when I want to."

"But Ca…'

Casper held up his hand. "But I'll try to set a permanent schedule. But no Saturdays."

"Jewish sabbath?"

"No, I just hate working on Saturday."

"And the dress code?"

"Ain't gonna happen. As long as we work, I should be able to wear a bra and panties…which gives me an idea for next week."

"Please, no more practical jokes?"

"Fine. Over until April, first. Can't ignore April Fool's day. Deal?"

"Deal."

They shook hands. Casper was about to leave and then stopped. He decided to offer a gesture of good will. "Uh…Sue. Me and my friends are meeting at The Pepper Grind. If you want, you can hang out with us?" He regretted asking her the minute he said anything.

"No thanks, I'd rather have a pit bull pull my eyelids back over my head than hang out with you."

"Al-righty then." He exited breathing a sigh of relief. "Later Fat Butt."

"And no more FAT BUTT!"

Casper stepped out into the night air and started his skateboard ride home. He briefly looked up at where the ring was. The military on the outside had placed a couple of spot lights on different sections of the ring, illuminating a couple of areas and giving them a general idea of the borders of the force field. The towns people still had no idea there was a force field around the town, they accepted the military and the governments quarantine story. As of yet, no one had dared to try to leave the town for fear of affecting the rest of the world with whatever was wrong with them. Casper, like most of the people in town had no belief that the rings effects on them was a bad thing. The only language he had come close to learning was Spanish and for those living in California, Spanish is used so much you actually learn words without picking up a text book. He tried to get Ami to teach him Japanese but the many rules of Japanese proved too fatal for him: formal Japanese versus informal, and women and men having different words for "you" was enough for him.

He was actually getting used to seeing the ring. It was like moving next to the Eiffel Tower. After a while you get used to it and start focusing on trying to live in Paris. You have a feeling of joy and excitement that you are near something so life-changing, but if the object remains the same for a week, you learn to stop running into telephone poles from starring at it while walking. The hours working at Big Red Groceries were a nice distraction. He wished his astronomy classes would start again. The absence of Professor Pascal along with many other teachers and students at the college proved fatal to the University. Restarting classes in any form was not an option. Casper felt that with the landing of a UFO, this was the equivalent of a work study program. Surely a ship that travels 600 light years has the answers to any question he would have about space in a classroom environment.

There was one individual in the town who had not benefited from the physical upgrades caused by the ring. Hiding in the shadows of a fast food restaurant, Yolanda Iesha Washington watched Casper skateboard past. The night was her time. She spent the day sleeping and the night hunting for food. Her mind was still a mixture of personalities and voices directing her into illogical behavior. She was no longer acting like a 'gangsta' rapper from the 80's but had now transformed into an antisocial hermit, prone to quoting poet Emily Dickerson and convinced that the ring was bringing nothing but doom and gloom to the Earth. Covering her identity with a long grey parka, she hurried across the street like a rat and started searching through a garbage can. She found some old hamburger buns and devoured them as if it were her last meal. Mid bite, she stopped and looked up at the ring. As if she were hearing it speak to her, she spoke back to it: "Yes…I know…My wheel…My wheel…My wheel is in the dark! I cannot see a spoke, yet know it's dripping feet go round and round." She grabbed a bag of garbage, hissed at a nearby cat and backed away into the darkness.

In a café, miles away from the town, Professor Pascal and Aarti were eating a dinner, barely above the level they could have made themselves. Pascal took a bite of the well done steak which he had ordered rare. Aarti ignored her Caesar salad; she was more interested in the data on her laptop computer. "The more I find out. The less I know," she mumbled. The laptop was showing the footage captured by some flying drones which had been deployed around the force field. The small, model helicopter-like devices were doing measurements on the field, looking for any weak spots —so far, they'd found none. "Well, that's the last of the survey."

"And?" Pascal asked.

"According to Dr. Roselli, there are no weak spots, no holes. The field is shaped like a cylinder. It not only covers the entire area of the ring, but it covers the top of the ring and comes within a meter of the ring itself, so there's no way you can blow up the ring. The Army Corps of Engineers tried tunneling underneath the field, but no matter how low they dig, the ring expands and covers the hole like an invisible dam. They captured a bird that flew out of the ring and dissected it; it was no different than any other bird, meaning, if there is a change to the townspeople, it's only when they're inside the field. According to Dr. Wright, the blood tests show no differences in the 1000 plus samples they examined, except an elevation of red blood cells which can also be found in people when they're in high altitudes or receive more oxygen. No explanation of the scar or tattoo removal but we did discover a lost of allergies and, in one case, a disappearance of an unnamed STD. And yet there have been no changes in genetic traits like myopia or ADHD. A couple of soldiers that suffered from Gulf War syndrome before the ring showed up, still suffer from it, and a soldier that was afraid of dogs, still freaks out at Fido."

"Same, but healthy."

"Pardon?"

"They're keeping all of our personality traits, but upgrading the physical."

"Like giving farm animals antibiotics?"

"Perhaps. Maybe they plan on eating us?"

"Louis!"

"No, I'm serious. Maybe they want to come to our planet and eat us. Maybe the ring is a farm pen. They're fattening us up for the slaughter. Cosmic Farmville."

"600 light years, just to eat us?"

"Intergalactic rest stop?"

"Whatever you do, don't tell the President that." Aarti opened her internet browser and started looking up cannibal recipes.

Pascal moved his head until he could see her computer screen. "You do realize I'm joking, right?"

"Nothing is off the table."

Speaking of tables, Don was sitting at a table at The Pepper Grind bar. Do you see what I did there? The table segue? Anyway, Don was sitting at a table at The Pepper Grind bar. The Bar was crowded. Not with the usual local, drunken sports fans, but a mixture of locals, army grunts and FEMA workers. They were taking advantage of the off-hour scene to drink, laugh and make fun of each others (you know, like guys act in bars). The army guys called the FEMA workers "fe-males" and the FEMA workers called the army guys "ground pounders" after the marching they did.

Casper came in, ending his skateboard ride from work. "Donny Boy," he said before realizing how much he hated using the words "Donny Boy" and vowing to never use them again.

"Captain," Don said before realizing how much he hated using that nickname for Casper and also vowing not to use it again.

"Wow, haven't seen this place this packed since we found out the world was going to end."

"Yeah, now it's crowded because an alien ship is hovering overhead."

"It's been an interesting month."

"Too interesting. Let's erase it with a couple of beers."

"Agreed." Casper raised his hand. "Hey! Baboosh. Two beers, please."

From behind the counter, Baboosh looked up after serving a pink cocktail. "$50!" he yelled.

"Wha-wha-what?" Casper yelled. "How much?"

"$50!" Baboosh yelled back.

"Are you kidding?"

"No kidding, all beers $25."

"$25 for one beer? Why?"

"Have to ration all booze. I don't know how long we have to be in town. So I ration until I run out…And make money."

"Fine! We'll take one beer and two cups."

"Cups, $10!"

"Forget the cups!"Casper turned to Don. "I can't believe that pirate!"

"He's not the only one that has to ration. They told me not to sell more than one cup of coffee per customer, per day. Have you ever seen people when they instantly have to go from three cups per day to one?"

"Not pretty?"

"There's only so many times I can hear the 'F' word thrown at me."

"What about the chain coffee place across the street from you?"

"They all actually made it out of town. Good news is, they left all of their supplies, so I get to take those for Don's Café"

"Don's Café? Is that what you're going to call it?"

"Soon as I paint over the old sign."

Coming in the entrance, across the room, Don saw Ami. Don smiled. He saw Private Finn come in behind her, Don stopped smiling. "Oh for crap sake," Don said shaking his head.

"What?"

"Ami bought Beetle Bailey with her?"

Casper looked at the two. Finn was helping Ami with her coat. "What? Finn? What's wrong with that?"

"I just wanted it to be us three. What do we need him here for?"

"He's all right. Not the brightest firefly in the yard, but he's okay. I mean, it's not like they're dating or anything."

"Dating? She better not date him."

"Why not? What's your problem with him? Is it because he's military? I thought you liked the military? Your family is all military."

"No, it's not that. I just think she can do better."

"Like who? Me? You? Ha! That would be funny! You and Ami together, can you imagine?" Casper started to laugh. He looked at Don. Don was not laughing and seemed to be deep in thought. Eventually, Don gave the third worst fake laugh in history.

In the field of Quantum Psychology, there is a method of thinking called English Prime. Part of using English Prime involves the method of not using the word "is" as in: "Don is in love with Ami." Casper applied English Prime to his thoughts and proposed: "It appears from my observation of Don's current statements and behavior since the appearance of Private Finn, his feelings for Ami have evolved from friendship to affection." Thanks to Quantum Psychology, Casper was also able to use GIGO also known as Garbage in Garbage Out part of his brain. It's the part that processed and dispersed such brief thoughts as: I should take this candy bar and not pay for it; wouldn't it be funny to trip that nun walking next to me; if I put this gin in my mouth and light it, my friends will think it's cool, and I wonder what Aunt Fay looks like naked. So, Casper tried not to think about Don being in love with Ami–garbage out.

Ami and Finn came over and sat down."Hey guys," Ami said. "How was work?"

"We super glued Sue's office supplies to the ceiling," Casper said.

Ami laughed. It had been a while since Casper heard her laugh. "Don?"Ami asked.

"It's fine," he said in a huffy voice.

"What about you, Dr. Ami?" Casper asked

"It's good, they're training all of the medical students to be field medics."

"What does that mean?"

"It means if something comes out of the alien ship and starts turning people into burnt skeletons, we can treat them…Well, treat the people that get injured before they're turned into burnt skeletons."

Baboosh came to the table carrying the one beer Casper had ordered. "Here you go, $50."

"$50!" Casper yelled. "You said $25!"

"Sharing fee!" Baboosh answered.

"$50 for a beer?" Ami asked. "What is this, price gouging?"

"Exactly what it is!" Casper said. "He's taking advantage of the rationing!"

"The American dream," Baboosh said shrugging his shoulders in apathy.

Casper started digging through his wallet to see if he had $50, he did not. "You guys have any money for our ONE beer?"

"You know, Baboosh…" Don said. "Casper works at Big Red Groceries, I work in the only coffee shop in town and Ami is working at the medical center. "

"So?" Baboosh answered.

"So, if you ever need…say, food and you go to the grocery store and you buy something, how much are you gonna charge, Casper?"

"$300 per ounce," Casper answered.

"And Ami, if Baboosh gets sick and needs some antibiotics, how much are those?"

"$795 per pill."

"And as for me, need a coffee fix? I'll let you smell the old empty cups for $99, provided you sing a song and dance around a little first."

The three of them stared at Baboosh to let him know that they were quite serious. Slowly Baboosh smiled and pointed at them. "Ooooh, I give special discount to my friends, $25 per beer."

"We also have a pharmacy at Big Red," Casper added. "Condoms are $2000 each and hemorrhoid cream is $1357 and your car."

"Okay, okay! Regular price beer for you." Baboosh grabbed a few bucks from Casper and huffed away from the table.

"Three more beers, please!" Casper yelled.

They laughed in victory.

"I feel like a Yakuza!" Ami said.

"That's weird: 'Yakuza' didn't translate into an English equivalent," Don said.

"It does seem inconsistent," Casper said. Like I can say 'nǐ hǎo' but when I watch TV, if a Chinese person says it, it comes out as 'hello.'"

"Speaking of inconsistent broadcast transmissions..." Don said breaking his segue license. "...When is the military going to restore our phone and internet connections?" he asked Finn.

"What make you think it's the military?" Finn asked, insulted.

"Of course it's you guys," Don said. "Who else would cut off all communication out of town?"

"Maybe it's that big UFO over the town?" Finn said pointing up.

"I wish people would stop calling it a UFO." Casper complained. "I mean, seriously, it's not unidentified. They should fall it an F-O."

Ignoring Casper's rant, Don continued. "Why would Aliens cut the power to the internet and phone service, and leave the one for cable TV?" Don pointed at the bar's television, showing a soccer match from Brazil.

"I don't know," Ami said. "Maybe they like soccer."

Don and Finn almost started to raise their voices in an argument until Casper interrupted them. "Oh look, my friend Darla is here!" Darla came in and shoved her way through the crowd, towards the group.

"Hey! You made it!"Casper said, hugging her.

Darla said hi to everyone and introduced herself to Finn. "Did I miss the band?" she asked, taking off her leather jacket.

"What band?" Casper asked her. Darla pointed to a little stage near the corner of the bar. From what they could see, a drum set and a microphone stand was being set up.

"No," Casper answered. "I had no idea, Baboosh was gonna have a band. Think I'll hit the little boy's room before they start." Casper excused himself and went to the mens room.

He stood at the stall and thought about Don's attitude. "Is he in love with Ami?" He tried to erase the thought. He instead thought about his feelings about a situation like that. Ami and Don were his two favorite people in the world. They were his world. If they got together and heaven, forbid, broke up, it would ruin the good thing they all had going. He didn't know if he could take some kind of back and fourth he said she said fighting situation. As he buried himself in thoughts, Finn came in and broke many of the rules of manliness. *The Alphabet of Manliness*, established by an internet personality, known simply as Maddox, list in the "U" section for "urination," that when there are three urinals, the first man in should use the one on the far left or right. The second man in should take the urinal on the far opposite side of man #1 and the third man, if the other two urinals are busy, only then does he take the one in the middle, therefore bringing him shoulder to shoulder with another man and in glance sight of another man's private parts. Finn came in and stood in the middle, right next to Casper. He also broke another rule; talking while urinating. After all, talking to another man while holding your private parts is rather awkward.

"How's it going, Mr. Cornbregger?" he asked, cheerfully.

"Uhh, it's okay. And you can call me Casper."

"Okay, Mr. Casper." After a sigh, there was a few seconds of silence, broken by the sounds of liquid hitting ceramic. "Mr. Casper, can I ask you a personal question?"

"It's Just Cas…Whatever, ask away." Casper hoped Finn wasn't looking in his direction when he talked, another rule: eyes front!

"You and Miss Nakajima. Have you guys ever…you know?"

"Practiced witchcraft?"

"No…you know…" Finn rotated his right hand.

Casper hoped that his other hand had taken care of aiming, otherwise things were going to get messy. "Have we ever, ran an underground hamster fight club?"

"No, no! You know…together, you and her…"

"Make-a the sexy?"

"No! I mean dated."

"Uhh, you do know that sex does happen when you're dating?"

"Not with me."

"For reals, you've never had sex while dating?"

"Course not, that's for marriage!"

"Wow…Really?" Casper zipped, flushed and went to the sink to wash his hands. Finn followed seconds later but didn't wash his own hands.

"So, did you?"

"Sex? No. Dated, sorta."

"Sorta?"

"Yeah. Ami was in my computer class along with her ex boyfriend. We became friends and after she broke up with her boyfriend, tried to see if you know, we could start something. But it was too late."

"Too late? For what?"

"Friend zoned. You see, when I meet a girl, the only way I see them as a romantic interest is if they aren't dating, married or are just so different that a relationship would be impossible. Ami was dating so I had already pegged her in the off limits section. Turns out that she had also put me in the friend zone so it worked out well, no feelings were hurt and we were able to become even better friends. Little later, I moved in with her and Don and the rest is hysterectomy."

"Hyster–what?"

"I mean't history…It was an attempt at a joke."

"I don't get it."

"That's okay, most people don't get me."

"So you never slept together?"

"Oh no, we did it like oyster eating rabbits in Vegas. She's a sexy beast!" Finn had a look of shock on his face. "I'm joking, again! No, we never did it. I don't have sex with friends, not even Don."

Finn breathed a sigh of relief and laughed. "I'm gonna have to watch out for you," he said shaking his unwashed finger at Casper.

Casper checked his hair in the mirror to make sure it was still messy. "So, Finn. I assume by your inquiry into my sexual history and that you probably aren't gay because I don't know any gay virgins—otherwise, what's the point, right? That you're sweet on Miss Ami."

"Can't pull anything over on you, Mr. Casper. Yeah, I think she's great. She's so sweet and smart. I wanna ask her out but I haven't found the courage. Any advice you can give me?"

"Advice? From me? Uhh…just remember to always be yourself…unless you're an ass, then it's okay to be someone else. But, I thought you had a girlfriend?"

"Who me? No."

"Then what was that picture of a blonde girl you were crying over, right before we were gonna get smashed by the comet?"

"Blonde girl? What? Oh, wait."Finn laughed and pulled out the photo from his wallet. Upon closer inspection, it was revealed the photo to actually be a picture of a long haired dog. "No, that's Queen Elizabeth II. She's a prize winning Afghan hound. My family breeds show dogs. She's my best friend."

"Wait, didn't you say you were going to get married to her?"

Finn left the bathroom without answering the question.

Casper finished his business in the restroom and returned to the table. He was just in time for the start of the show. Soldiers and FEMA workers hollered and hooted with delight when Baboosh took control of the microphone on stage. (as in he grabbed it. It's not like the microphone was alive and wiggling around like a snake).

"Good evening, ladies and gentlemen of Pepper Mill," Baboosh said. There was lots of cheering from everyone. "Tonight we have a special treat to celebrate the reopening of my bar and grill in this time of crisis and quarantine. This band is newly formed and will play their first live gig here, tonight."

More hooting and hollering. "Ladies and gentlemen, I give you: The Alien Ring!"

The band took to the stage, consisting of three guys and a female. The female was of interests to most of the men in the audience. Her short black hair and face gave her the appearance of 1920s movie starlet Louise Brooks, wearing a pair of blinking, bobbing antenna on her head band. Her curvaceous figure was accentuated by a long, sparkly vintage, green dress. The men in the band took their places behind various musical instruments; drum, guitar, synthesizer. She took hers behind the microphone. When the cheering died down, she turned to the synthesizer player and nodded. He started to play. It was a rather jazzy cover version of David Bowie's, *Life on Mars*. She sang it to match the tone. The room grew quiet, transfixed, as if they were all transported to a 1920s Café in Paris. The singers eyes were closed as she swayed not only her body, but the room itself.

Casper, like most of the men couldn't take his eyes off of her. "Who is that?" he wondered. Usually, he was pretty aware of all of the local music talent, being such a small town. Perhaps she had come in with the emergency crews or maybe she was here all along and volunteered to fill in for the lack of entertainment. There was something familiar about her. Casper nudged Don. "Nice, huh?"

"Yeah," Don said. He was busy looking at Ami and Finn. Finn had managed to put his hand on top of Ami's. Don had a look of distress. Ami moved her hand out from underneath Finn's. Don smiled.

Casper whispered to Darla: "She seems familiar. Have you ever seen this band?"

"I've seen the three guys, they used to be in a band called 'Chakra Zulu'. But the girl? I've never seen her before. Maybe she's an alien from the ship?" Darla elbowed Casper.

If she was an alien, Casper was quite ready to submit to the alien overlords. There was something about her face—he's spoken to her before, but from where?

The Alien Ring finished their song to lots of applause and whistling. When the lead singer said thank you, that's when Casper figured out who she was. The group started another song. This time, it was *Planet Claire* by The B52s. This song had a really long musical lead-up until actual lyrics would started.

During this part, Casper leaned over to Don and whispered his observational result: "It's Lori!" he said.

"What?" Don asked.

"It's Lori. The lead singer, It's her!"

"Wait, THE Lori?"

"Yep."

"But…I thought you told me she was a blond hippy looking girl?"

"She was…She must have cut and dyed her hair, but that's definitely her!"

"Wow! She's download, internet porn hot."

"Yeah. Too bad she's a dope smoking airhead."

"Sorry, Cap." Don patted Caper's shoulder.

"What's too bad?" Ami asked.

Don relayed the information about Lori to Ami.

"Really?" Ami asked. "Not what I expected her to look like."

"Who's doesn't look like you expected?" Finn asked Ami.

Ami told him about the lead singer. Finn's eyes lit up like a caffeinated deer in the head lights of a freight train. "Lori?" he asked. "Did you say her name is Lori? Is it Lori Katz?"

"No idea," Ami said. She leaned over to Casper." Is her last name, Cat?"

"Not Cat, Katz," Casper answered.

"Holy Mother of Elvis!" Finn said loud enough to be shushed. "It's her!"

"It's who?" Ami asked.

"General Katz' daughter! We got orders to look for her, and if we find her, to bring her to the general, immediately!"

"Wait," Casper said. "She's is the model daughter of a modern major general?"

"Oh, right. She's the one the general told me about," Ami said.

"I gotta go get her!" Finn stood up. Ami grabbed his shoulder and pulled him down.

"Whoa, whoa, whoa, cowboy!" she advised. "Don't do it now, she's in the middle of a set!" Some people shushed them.

Finn was patient enough to let The Alien Ring finish their song. As the applause continued, he stood up and rushed the stage. As anyone would respond, Lori, backed away from him, he grabbed her arm. "Miss Katz. I have orders to bring you in, please come with me."

"What the f–" Whatever F word Lori was going to say (Faboosh? FIFA? French fry?) was blocked by annoying microphone feed back. "...are you talking about? My name's not Lori!" There was a brief struggle. Lots of boos and yelling from the audience. FEMA and soldiers alike started to approach the stage.

A musician grabbed Finn. He wiggled free. "We have orders to bring her in!" he repeated.

"Your boyfriend has lost his mind." Casper told Ami.

Even though Ami said "my" and Don said "her", they both yelled: "He's not__boyfriend!" at the same time and then looked at each other. Finn tried to pull Lori off of the stage. She ended this idea by promptly kneeing him in the groin. As he hunched over, looking for the things that felt like they had just rolled down his pants leg onto the stage, some soldiers approached Lori again.

"Hey! You can't do that to one of our guys!" One of them yelled. Lori did the same thing to him causing his voice to be three octaves higher. The other soldier tried to grab her shoulders. It was uncertain how she did it but there were two more knees to two more groins. "Let's get her!" yelled some soldiers in the audience. Before they could rush the stage, some FEMA workers stepped in their path.

"Pipe down you ground pounders, she's only a lady," one of them yelled.

"Out of the way, FE-MALES!" a soldier yelled back. As soon as they got within striking distance of each other, a fist connected on a FEMA worker's face, sending him backwards against his friends. This was followed by a fist on a soldier's jaw, sending him against the bar. The synthesizer player in the band touched a few buttons on his keyboard and changed the keyboards so that it sounded like an old fashioned, out of tune piano. He then started to play *Camptown Ladies* while more fists hit more jaws. During the melee, Casper was trying to get Ami and Darla out of the bar to safety. It wasn't as if he had a chance to stop anyone from hurting them but he would rather it be him that ate a knuckle sandwich with pickle punches than them. An army grunt picked up a FEMA worker by the back of their shirt and pants and rushed him through the door, in an attempt to throw him out. At that exact moment, two guys were walking pass the door carrying the front window of a 1929 Stutz M-22. The FEMA worker went flying through the windshield and it disintegrated into useless micro shards.

On the stage, Lori was still doing relatively well in keeping the attackers at bay. She must have realized the situation was getting out of control and turned around to make a run for it. At that moment, Finn tried to grab her shoulders. When her heel met his crotch, he collapsed onto the ground, but not before grabbing the back of her hair. It easily slid off of her head and unsheathed the blond hair underneath a wig.

"Ah ha!" Casper thought.

Ami went away from him and made her way over to Finn.

"Ami!" Casper yelled.

"Finn is hurt!" she yelled avoiding an empty beer bottle smashing against a nearby wall. Don ran over to her and shielded her from any more assaults. They reached Finn. Ami made sure he was still conscious.

"Lets go!" Don yelled.

"Don! He's hurt!"

Don thought for a second. "Fine." He picked Finn up as best he could and drunk-walked him to the exit.

Casper looked around for Darla, She reappeared from behind the bar, carrying a mini keg of beer. "Let's go," she said.

"Wow! You're like the direct opposite of morals," he said running behind her.

"Thanks!" she said.

They made it to the safety and more quiet of the outside. A few seconds later, Ami, Don and Finn appeared. Finn had a stressed look on his face and kept saying "ow".

"There you go, Finn. You'll be okay, just walk it off," Don said.

"I should take him to his tent," Ami said.

"What are you talking about? He's fine," Don complained.

"No he's not, he may need medical attention."

"From what?" Don started to yell. "A knee to the groin? What the heck is the treatment for that?"

"I'm sure it involves lots of ice," Casper said.

Ami looked at Don with a bit of anger. "What? Don, you want me to dump him on the sidewalk and leave him here? Is that it?"

Don threw his hands up briefly. "I don't know, but you don't have to go to his tent with him!"

"Why not?"

"Because he's a man! You don't go to tents with men!"

"He got kicked in the groin, What's he gonna do?" Ami complained

Finn lifted his head. "Can you two please stop talking about my groin?"

"It's okay, Finn," Ami comforted him. "I'm gonna take you back to your tent, you're gonna be alright."

"Thanks Miss Ami, you're an angel."

Ami and Finn walked towards the army camp. Finn looked back at Casper, smiled and did a thumbs up as if to say: 'I got a date with her and she's taking me back to my tent!'

Casper gave a thumbs up back and silently said: "Good luck scoring tonight with that groin injury."

Don looked furious: "Can you believe that? He's fine. It's all a trick to get her in the sack."

"Who-whoa-whoa." Darla said. "Sounds like someone's got a case of the green eyed monster."

"What are you talking about?" Don asked.

"You." Casper answered. "She's saying you're jealous."

"What?" Don said taken aback. "Me? Jealous?" He crossed his arms. "Of who? Ami? Why would I be jealous of her? What do I care? She can do what she wants with her: raven black hair, and her cute little butt. I couldn't care less—stupid Ami and her hands as soft as Easter lily petals–can't stand her! Makes me so mad I could kiss her—Kick her! What did I say?"

Casper and Darla stared at Don in shocked silence.

"I'm out of here!" Don turned around and hurried away towards their apartment.

Darla looked at Casper. "He's got it so bad."

"I've never seen him like this," Casper said. "Kinda cute and scary at the same time."

The fight in the bar had attracted the attention of some military security officers, and the local Pepper Mill police force, which consisted of Earl and Clem. They approached the bar with their sirens blaring for the whole two blocks they had to drive to get there. Casper and Darla snuck away from the crowd forming outside before any questions were asked about the mini keg she was holding.

They found themselves on the bleachers of the nearby high school football stadium. Taking turns, they each took sips of the beer which turned out to be a low quality, American style lager, but it gave the necessary buzz. Casper looked up at the spot-lighted part of the ring he could see. He followed an imaginary line down to the ground and realized the field where Ami, Don, Finn and he almost died was actually the dead center of the ring's circumference. "This is weird," he said.

"What's that?" Darla said wiping her mouth.

"All my life, I dreamt of a UFO coming down and taking me away, and there it is, right above us, hovering like a halo. And instead of an alien coming out of it, all we get is some virus that let's us speak French. No enlightenment, no information about how we can save our planet from destruction, just French lessons."

"Yeah." Darla looked up. "Kinda sucks. I spent $1000 on my tattoos and they all faded away."

"Tabula rasa."

"What?"

"Tabula rasa. It means blank slate. It's like you lost your tattoos but now you can get new ones."

"Hmm. Never thought of that…" Darla took a swig of beer and set the keg down. "…Sorta like you."

"What? What about me?"

"Your Ta-blah ross-whatever"

"Tabula rasa."

"Whatever. Your blank slate is that UFO." She pointed at the ring.

"How so?"

"Not what you expected. Not the one you love but the one you're with."

"I guess so. Like what Ty what's-his-name said when he told everybody to remain calm. We're safe, we're protected and we're together."

"Those Grunts and FEMA guys didn't seem like they were together."

"They're just blowing off steam–I can't believe that was Lori."

"That some girl you were interested in?"

"WAS is right. She turned out to be a callous pot head."

"Throws a mean knee to the groin, though."

They laughed.

"What about you?" Casper asked Darla. "What are you gonna do? No Gregory; must suck for you."

"It does, but it wasn't like we were gonna get married some day; he's too immature."

Casper raised an eyebrow, thinking of Darla stealing beer kegs and super-gluing office supplies to the ceiling. Darla turned sideways on the bench and laid her head on Casper's lap. "I think the ring is great. It's like a big fat reset button on our lives."

Casper looked down at Darla's face. In spite of the heavy eye shadow and black lip stick, there was a bit of softness to her face— a vulnerability. He wondered what would happen if he leaned down and kissed her. He thought about his rule. She had a boyfriend–he put her in the friend zone. The boyfriend was out of the picture which mean't she was on the market. He started leaning down as a test to see what she would do. She didn't flinch or have a disgusting look on her face. He pulled back. "Should I?" he thought. "It would be weird. Dating someone you work with. And what if we break up? She would super-glue my genitals to the ceiling."

Sensing his apprehension, Darla lifted herself up so that she and Casper were face to face. She stared at him and breathed a deep, soulful breath. She had a look that said : "Your move."

Casper moved his head. With every heart beat, he moved half an inch closer to kissing her. She closed her eyes, he was about to close his, but then, he noticed something. The part of the ring he could see over her shoulder, had stopped. He pulled back to give his eyes a better view. It was true, the ring had stopped rotating. "What…the?" he said.

"I wasn't going to do anything!" Darla yelled really fast. "I was going to trick you, when you got really close I was going to do something really weird and funny to you!" She was rambling. "That's me, Darla, the funny girl! I swear, nothing was going to…"

"Darla! The ring!" Casper interrupted. "The ring!" He stood up, causing her to also stand up or fall off his lap. "It stopped."

"Stopped you from doing what?" Darla rambled some more. "Because nothing was going to happened!"

"The ring has stopped rotating!"

Professor Pascal knocked hard and fast on the door of the motel room occupied by Dr. Aarti Panjwani. Aarti answered the door at fire-in-the-hallway speed. Her hair was wrapped in a towel, matching her white bathrobe and slippers. Her face was covered with some type of green goop used to remove wrinkles and prevent sexual encounters. Professor Pascal gave a brief scream at the sight.

"Lewis? What is it!" she yelled.

"The ring! Aarti, the ring!"

That was all he had to say, Aarti ran inside her room, grabbed her laptop computer and without changing her appearance, rushed past him. "Let's go!"

A few miles away, in town, General Katz stepped outside and looked up. He radioed for his men to clear the streets of all civilians or unauthorized personnel. He got a call from Professor Pascal.

"General! Is the force field still up?" Pascal asked.

The general looked at one of the captains. "Tell someone on the bridge to throw something at the force field!"

On the bridge, everyone looked around for something to throw at the bridge which wouldn't come back and hurt them. A soldier had the common sense to walk up to the field and just push on it. "It's still up," he said.

The information was passed on to Professor Pascal who was driving as fast as his Audi 5000 would go. He conveyed the

164

information to Aarti. She was busy on her laptop, looking at the live video footage being broadcast from one of the flying helicopter drones. "It's glowing!" she yelled. The pattern around the ring was glowing first red then orange, yellow, green, blue, violet and finally settling on white.

Casper looked up at the ring, now resembling a halo more than ever. "Wow!" he mouthed.

"Should we get out of here?" Darla asked.

"No way. I'm not gonna miss this."

Army vehicles rushed around the streets. An alarm of some sort was going off. A megaphone announced for all civilians to shelter in place. Casper ignored it all and walked down the bleachers to the middle of the field. Darla remained in her seat.

"Uh, Casper, I'm gonna do what the announcement says and head back to my place."

"Oh, okay."

"You wanna come?"

"Pardon?"

"Back to my place…to escape the danger?"

"No, I'm gonna watch this."

"Oh…okay." Darla walked away. She paused for a moment, wondering if she should stay with him. It was also a pause to wonder what would have happened if they had kissed.

The near kissing incident meant nothing to Casper; seeing the ring glow was his world at that moment. He could see something happening to the inside edge of the ring. To him, it looked like the inside edge was producing a ring of bubbles, moving towards the center.

The drone camera being watched by Aarti produced a much more detailed account of what was going on. "It's like there are these tiny droplets of water coming out of the ring and flowing towards the middle," she told Dr. Julius Xiang, "The water drops are gathering together and flowing inward towards the center; it's like it's forming a film inside the ring!"

"Do you think it's water?" Pascal asked Xiang.

"More like the air itself?"

"Pardon?"

"It's not water—the droplets are a refraction of the air itself, like how a mirage creates the illusion of water by making the air jellied. But this is tiny pieces of bent light bubbles, coming together to form one big refraction of light. It's incredible! It's like a tiny version of gravitational lensing!"

Once the center of the ring was filled, it resembled a bubble wand which was just dipped in soapy water. The inside sheen was swirling with refracted color. Then there was a deep groaning sound, just like the whale sound the ring made when it first arrived. It was deep enough to be felt in the chest. From the outside of the ring towards the center, ripples appeared in the film, like the circular waves you see after putting your finger into a puddle but in a reverse direction. More and more ripples moved towards the center. They went faster and faster, until there was another whale groan, much higher in octave than the other sound. At this point, it resembled a bubble wand even more, as if a giant was slowly blowing on the top of the ring, the film slowly stretched downwards towards the center of the high school baseball field. Casper, like anyone else watching this event, got down lower, expecting something horrible to happen. At the last moment, just when you would expect a large bubble to be formed, the film quickly retracted back up and burst in tiny refraction droplets. In the center of the ring, a reflective sphere had formed, about the size of an elephant. It slowly floated to the ground. Casper couldn't see it land; he was too far away. Before he could start running towards the bubble's landing site, a soldier grabbed his arm. "On the truck, now!" The soldier yelled. Casper saw the gun the soldier had strapped to his back. Rather than risk being shot, Casper complied.

On his walk to the truck, from what he could tell, the ring had returned to normal. There were no more lights and the rotation had resumed.

General Katz had managed to maneuver a large group of troops within 200 feet around the center of where the bubble was floating. Weapons of all sort tracked the object as it slowed down more and more, the closer it got to the ground. He held his walkie-talkie up to his mouth and was ready to give the order to fire. He ignored the chatter from Pascal and the other scientist asking him to send them footage.

The silver sphere came to a dead halt by the time it touched ground. Everyone held their mental breaths. The sphere stood still for what seemed like days. There were few sounds heard, everywhere at that moment. General Katz exhaled, just when the sphere changed. There was a sound, similar to the fizz you hear from a carbonated drink. As this was heard, the bubble dissipated into tiny sparks. The sparks flew upwards and virtually disappeared. There was an unveiling of an object inside the sphere; an oval, greenish-gray object. Covering the object were squares of various size and thickness and in the center a blinking red light, about the size of a tennis ball. All around, there were the sounds of cocking guns. "Hold your fire!" Katz yelled. There was a standoff; the egg shaped object and the soldiers maintained their positions for at least 15 minutes. General Katz wanted to walk over to the object, but, after being in Iraq, he knew better than to approach a strange object. This gave him an idea. "Kowalski!" he said into the mike.

"Yes, sir!" Kowalski answered.

"Get one of the bomb disposal robots over here, STAT!"

"Sir! Yes, sir!" Kowalski answered.

In no time at all, a truck pulled up. The back ramp was lowered and a tank-treaded robot made its way to the ground. It was a very basic model, large enough to fit into the trunk of a car. It had one arm on it and three cameras. Kowalski controlled everything from a remote location. The general gave the order to slowly approach the object, but back away at the first sign of trouble. The robot camera was patched to the scientists' monitors.

"What is that, an egg?" Aarti asked. "And what's that red light, blinking?"

"We're going to find out," Katz said. He gave the robot driver orders to approach the object at three feet intervals and wait a few seconds between movements. This made the approach very slow but eventually they made it within five feet of the object. The robot camera's zoomed in on the egg's surface.

"Looks like a metal object about six feet high," Pascal said. "Zoom in on that blinking light."

"Standard electronic set up," Kowalski said.

There was a sound heard from the egg. "Wait, what's that sound?" Dr. Xiang asked.

"I can't hear anything," General Katz said.

"Is there a microphone on the robot?" Dr. Xiang asked.

"Sure," General Katz said. "Kowalski, turn up the volume for the mike."

When the volume increased, so did the realization that the egg was making a sound.

"What the? I can't believe it!" General Katz said.

"What is it, General?" Aarti asked.

"It's a message."

"Message?" Pascal asked. "All I hear is a bunch of gibberish, like a squeaky wheel underwater."

"Me too," Dr. Xiang agreed.

"I as well," said Aarti.

"I can understand it perfectly," Katz said.

"Oh! Wait! I get it." Pascal said. "He's inside the field! You can understand every language! Tell us please, what is it saying?"

"Sounds like instructions…" Katz said. "Keeps repeating the words: Please, press the red button…Please, press the red button."

Chapter 6

Sesos

Casper unlocked the door to the porta-potty and stepped outside. Before him, he saw a sphere sitting on what looked like a metal flower petal, unfolded and lying flat on the grass. "What the?" he said, drying his hands on a paper napkin. The sphere was about the size of a large fitness ball. It was off-white; more towards the blue end of the spectrum. Looking around the grassy, green field, he noticed everyone else in the park. They surrounded the grassy field in a circle at least 45 meters away from him and the sphere; it was like he and the sphere were radioactive and everyone else were trying to escape from them. "What in the world is going on?" he said aloud. There was some waving at him from the crowd–it was Ami, dressed in a French maid's outfit. "Ooo-kay," Casper said. Someone next to her was pointing at the sphere. It was Don, dressed like a butler. "Huh…" he said, "…that Baboosh Burger must have given me more than the runs—I'm hallucinating!" He tasted something tiny and metallic in his mouth and spat it out. "Yuck! So much for that." Casper pointed at the sphere, to see if it was what everyone was drawing his attention to. "This?" he asked. Many in the audience roared in approval, at least, that's what it sounded like. It could also have been a warning. "Maybe I should get out of here," he thought. An army soldier was gesturing "come here." The way the soldier was waving, it could also be interpreted as "give me the ball." Casper thought back to his days in as a young child, walking from the library while reading a copy of *A Wrinkle in Time* by Madeleine L'Engle. A group of kids were playing some type of game that involved a ball–perhaps soccer? It's irrelevant information. Anyway, the ball they were using ended up getting kicked over the fence and onto the street. Casper was so engulfed in the novel, he didn't even noticed until they ran up to the fence and yelled at him to retrieve their ball. Being told never to play in the street, he ignored them and kept on walking. A second later, the ball was squished by a pickup truck. The boys from that date, made it a point to make Casper's life difficult whenever they spotted him walking pass that spot. Eventually, he just changed his trajectory home, costing him 10 more minutes of travel time and missing the beginning of the Pokemon cartoons. "Not this time," he said, "this time I will pass the ball to them." He walked over to the ball, it looked very smooth and flawless. There appeared to be no place to blow it up or even a seam to indicate how it was put together. "Maybe it's not made of rubber" he thought. "Perhaps it's made of concrete or something and if I pick it up, I'll strain my back out; lift with the legs," he concluded. Casper bent down onto his haunches and grabbed the ball. It was not concrete, "Rubber–swede?" he wondered. But softer and warm. warm like a giant soft puppy. "Whoa!" was all he could say to describe it. He, let go for a second and grabbed it again and squeezed. It didn't feel hollow like a fitness ball. It was full of something–not liquid but not heavy like a liquid, a gas perhaps, a gas that was heaver than helium. He lifted it up with no effort at all. It might not have been a helium filled balloon, but it was no heavier than one. The weight confused him so much, he let the ball drop to see how high it would bounce, When he let it go, it stayed in the same position, meaning it levitated in the air in the exact spot he had released it, Casper smiled and laughed. "Awesome! What is this? Is this a joke?" He looked at the crowd again. A FEMA worker did the "come here!" or "pass the ball!" gesture. "All right," Casper said. He moved the ball until it was back on the petal. He took a couple of steps back, paused for a second and in spite of the uproar from the crowd which was definitely in the "don't do it!" range started running to give the ball a really big kick...

Let us pause here. Imagine this scene is completely frozen in time. Casper with his foot back, ready to send the white ball flying in the air at the FEMA worker. The FEMA worker with the look on his face that says: "OMFGWT(super)F!" Or Ami's expression that says "Oh great, Casper is about to end the world." Or, your expression that says "what's going on?" Let's address your concern, first: Where do we start? At the beginning would be the most logical place, but whose beginning?

In the beginning, God created the heavens and the Earth and then took a break on the 7th day for some strange reason. God gets tired? Have you ever worked on a dinner and got tired of cooking and decided: "good enough? That Baboosh burger may be squirting blood at me, but I'll eat it anyway?" Surely a planet creation requires more than seven days of labor? We put more effort into creating a bridge or even Casper's car, and we know how his car acts. Perhaps this is what's wrong with the Earth, we're a race of under-done hamburgers!...Where was I? ...Oh yes, Casper, being the main character would be the logical person to start on, but as you've seen, he really has no idea what's going on at this time and without knowing what else is going on, it won't be of much help. So of course, we'll start with…

Part 1

The Baboosh Burger

It looked like a storm had hit the one block radius of the downtown neighborhood of a small Toronto suburb called Hockey-eh. Police Officer Brian Clark stepped out of his squad car and walked over to the pickup truck, crashed into a telephone pole. The driver, Casey was dead. Slumped over the steering wheel. The victim of head and neck trauma. The head trauma, caused by the crash. The neck trauma, caused by an unknown source. Next to Casey, a farm-hand named Juan, also lay dead. No head trauma, but the farm hand's neck was bleeding.

Brian spotted Caleb, another officer. He ran towards Brian. His gun was drawn.

"Caleb, what's going on, eh?"

"It's a cow!" Caleb yelled, a little out of breath.

"What's are you talking a-boot?"

"There's a cow in the antique store across the street!"

"Like a cow statue?"

"No, a real cow! It's tearing the place to pieces!"

Brian started to run towards the antique shop. "How did a cow get in there?"

"Earlier, I saw the cow loaded on the back of the pickup truck. Before I could pull them over and ask them what the heck they were doing, the cow reached through the cab window, and starts biting them in the back of the neck. They crashed into the telephone pole, the cow jumps out of the cab and runs into the antique shop."

"You mean there's literally a bull in the china shop right now, for real?'

"No, a cow in an antique store."

"No, no. I mean like that saying: a bull in a china shop."

"Brian, it's a cow."

"Caleb, it's a saying."

"A cow is a saying?"

171

Brian pulled out his pistol to shoot Caleb. Before he could take aim, there was a crashing sound from the shop. A moment later, the cow jumped through the front window of the antique store and started running towards them. Tied to his body was the corpse of the shop's owner, Mr. Ahab, the victim of a failed attempt to lasso and constrain the beast.

"Holy hockey mother pucker!" Brian yelled. Caleb unholstered his gun and together, the officers fired a total of 27 rounds of ammo into the beast before it stopped charging, staggered into an alley and fell sideways, instantly killing a resting homeless man, who had just discovered his lottery ticket was a million dollar winner. His last words where: "Good one, God."

The officers walked over to the steaming dead beast. Caleb was about to nudge the cows head to make sure it was dead. Before he could get within one inch of the snout, the cow, using the last spark of it's nervous system, lunged it's mouth at Caleb's leg and tried to bite him. Brian fired another round at the cows head, sending what the Mexican culinary recipe calls "sesos" onto the wall.

"What are we gonna do with the carcass?" Caleb asked.

"We'll call the slaughter house and have them take care of it."

"We can't do that! This cow was obviously mad, and besides, the meat is full of bullets."

"We can tell them not to sell it. I just figure the slaughter house has some sort of way of disposing of bad meat like a furnace or something."

A call was made to Slaughterhouse #5. With strange promptness, a black van with tinted windows showed up, driven by two men who looked more suited to covering up mob mistakes than dead cow disposal.

"Lookie, lookie, lookie what we got here," said a short man wearing a black suit and tie. "This the body you want to get rid of?"

"Uhh, yeah, it's a cow carcass." Caleb answered.

"Never dealt with live stock before."

"Why are you wearing a suit?"

"Gotta look professional. See, I'm The Cleaner."

"I'm not sure what you're used to, 'Mr. Cleaner,' but all we want is for you to take this to the furnace at the slaughter house and throw this thing into the incinerator."

"Now that part I'm used to. What'd he do?"

"Who?"

"The stiff? What'd he do, squeal to the cops?"

"We ARE the cops."

"Suuuuure you are." The Cleaner snorted, laughed and nudged one of the officers.

"Just get the carcass off the streets and take it away!" Brian commanded. "And while you're at it, take those other bodies to the morgue."

"Sure, sure." The Cleaner said. "I don't see nothing." The Cleaner and his assistant known as Ten Fingers Eddie (because he had 10 fingers?) loaded the cow carcass into a large body bag and placed it into the van, next to the bags containing Mr. Ahab, Casey, Juan and a homeless man clutching a lottery ticket.

Now I must point out, under most normal circumstances, an animal suspected with any type of disease would be taken to some place where they would do an autopsy to discover what its problem was, this would lead to really large reports in 5" binders, media coverage, quarantines, accusations, all of that stuff–but, the Canadian Prime Minster had recently declared, if he hears of one more case of mad cow disease, he would personally pass a law that bands all meat including Canadian bacon. Besides the fact he couldn't do this, what he mean't was he wanted the meat standards to be so high, that you never have to worry about it, NOT please take all cases of bad meat and hide them, which is what's happening here.

The van sped around the curvy road which lead to the slaughter house. Ten Fingers Eddie, despite having 10 fingers, forgot to use all of them to secure the back of the van. Around one particularly sharp curve, the back doors swung open and both the bags containing the mad cow and the homeless person flew out and tumbled down a hill into an algae filled pond. The Cleaner slammed on the breaks. He and Ten Fingers got out of the van and made their way down the hill. Both the cow and the homeless man's bag were still floating in the pond. The Cleaner grabbed a really large stick and managed to pull the cow's body bag to shore. Before they could get to the homeless man's, it sprung a leak and like a gurgling hobo Titanic, sunk to the bottom.

"Should we go in after it?" Eddie asked.

"Naw, that's God's problem."

They slowly dragged the other bag up the hill. When they were just to the top, the bag broke and the cow carcass slid back down the hill into the pond.

"Son of a something-or-another!" The Cleaner yelled. They ran down the hill. Lucky for them, a leg was still sticking out of the murky goop. They grabbed on and pulled with all of their might. The carcass had picked up a hitchhiker—a dead, maggot infested raccoon had become attached to the cow's belly.

"What-the?" The Cleaner yelled. He kicked the Raccoon off the cow, sending it flying into the pond. "Disgusting!"

The two pulled the carcass up to the top, yet again.

"Hey, its head is missing." Eddie pointed out.

Upon closer inspection, it was realized that the cow's head had come off and slid down the hill, back into the pond.

"Should we get it?" Eddie asked.

"Naw, that's God's problem."

The journey was continued.

They made it to the slaughter house without any more incidents. The slaughter house was a dark industrial complex. Lots of trucks delivered animals to be transformed from living to liver in just a short time. Plumes of smelly smoke rose from two smoke stacks which coated the air with a haze of animal souls. Checking in at the front gate, the travelers asked the guard where they should go to get rid of bad meat.

"Just take it to the back area and put it in the chute that says: 'Bad Meat, Here.' Just make sure you don't put it in the chute that says: 'Bad Meat, NOT Here'. That one leads to the good meat to be processed and sold in the super markets in the United States."

The two drove the van to the back of the factory. The extremely smelly carcass was pulled out—or in the Canadians' case, "oot" the back and placed on the ground. Ten Fingers started smelling something. "Phew, what's that smell?"

"It's the cow."

"No the other smell."

They smelled around the area. The Cleaner lifted up the cow carcass. "Eww, there's a dead raccoon underneath the cow!" They quickly dragged the cow away from the dead raccoon. "What the heck is wrong with this town? Everything is accessorized with dead raccoons!"

With great difficulty, what was left of the cow was dragged over to the two deposit chutes. There were signs over each door in French:

Viande Gâtée, Ici

and…

Viande Gâtée, Pas Ici.

"For the love of Gretzky." The Cleaner complained. "Why is it in French? I failed French."

"I understand a little." Ten Fingers studied the letters. I know that 'pas' means not or don't so maybe that's the one that says not here. Maybe that's the one we should avoid."

"That doesn't make any sense. If it says not, then that means this is the chute NOT for bad meat. So let's stick it in there."

"Ouais, c'est ça. Works for me."

After lots of heaving and hoeing and an occasional cow part falling off, they were able to shove the carcass into the chute.

"There," The Cleaner said. "Glad that's over with. I tell you, all this stuff almost makes me want to become a vegetarian."

"Not me."

"I said almost."

They departed to go drop off the other bodies at the city morgue (or the highest bidder for organ donations).

Part 2

The Honorable, Mayor, Renée Sandra Duncan

"No more lock downs!" Someone yelled. Everyone cheered.

"Yes," the mayor said. "I will be discussing the possibility of no more lockdowns. Until then, go about your business."

"When are we going to get some answers!" Another person yelled.

"I'll let you know by 4."

"Why is there rations on food? How come the army can't just parachute more food in?" Yet another person yelled.

175

"Meet me back here. I promise, I'll get you some answers." The city hall meeting ended with a combination of cheers and mumbles.

Renée took a second to breathe; her doctor told her to do that. It was a silly thing to be reminded her of, to breathe. People do it all the time, but apparently people don't always do it at the right times. "What am I supposed to do?" she thought. "If I go to General Katz and he gives me the usual military run-around, and I come back and tell the towns people that I have nothing new, they're going to tar and feather me with super glue and poison oak." She began to walk back to her office. Within five minutes she had received three greetings and three inquires about what was that thing that came out of the UFO last week. She wished she could have told them that it was an egg shaped object, with a blinking red button, saying; "press the red button" over and over. This would probably cause panic and more questions and eventually a riot. Renée felt just as guilty as the military for withholding information from the public. She knew the reason for withholding information but sometimes you have to decide your emotional reason for it. Is it safety or your reputation?

"Mama!" A little girl called out from across the street.

Renée looked and saw her wife, Lilith and their five year old daughter, Abigail. Lilith, an African American woman with long dreadlocks, was the same age as Renée. Renée made her way over across the street, met them and hugged her daughter. "What are you guys doing here?" she asked, "Shouldn't you be in school?"

"The other two children in town were sick..." Lilith answered. "...So I figured I'd call it a teacher's work day."

"That's weird."

"What's weird? That woman that I just saw take a rat out of the garbage can and throw it into Don's café?"

"No...Well yes." The mayor looked across the street at the supposedly homeless woman scurry away. "...No, I have a feeling, those other two kids were either playing hooky or something has changed."

"What are you talking about?"

The mayor paused. She knew she shouldn't talk to Lilith about anything that was discussed between her and the officials in charge. She sighed. "Well, I guess I shouldn't talk about it."

"Is this related to that egg that came through the ring you told me about?"

"Uhhh, no."

"The force field around the edge of town you told me about?"

"N-no."

Abigail started dancing around and singing a song about a force field around town.

"The way we can understand different languages, thanks to the ring, you told me about?" Lilith asked.

Abigail started dancing around and singing a song about everyone being able to speak different languages.

"No—geez!" The mayor complained. "I've told you everything, haven't I? I have a big mouth, surprised the army hasn't shot me with a fire ant bazooka."

"You can't keep those things in, Renée, it'll eat you up."

"I know. And now they don't want me to tell everyone about the fact that the ring has healed people with chronic illness and as far as they are concerned, we're like vaccinated from everything–crap! There I go again! My big fat mouth!"

"I like your big fat mouth." Lilith leaned over and kissed the mayor. She pulled away and pulled something tiny and silver colored out of her own mouth. "That's weird...Anyway, instead of spilling your guts to me all the time, you should level with the citizens."

"I know, sweetie. I swear, if the military forces one more lockdown, people are going to riot. And God knows what the military response will be to that."

"Do you remember when we protested the war?"

"Which time?"

"The first one."

"Yeah."

"Remember what I said to you when you were so afraid that it was useless to protest against it because we were going to have no effect on anybody."

"Yeah, and I was right, the president started bombing even before the paint dried on our signs."

"True. But what did I say."

"You said; We may not be able to stop this war, but history will remember that we tried."

"Exactly. And even after that cop tazed me while I was standing in a puddle of water and spent a week in the hospital, I never regret the stand we took, because we were in the right.

"So what do you want me to do, Lil? Tell everybody everything and risk their safety?"

"Sweetie, there's an alien object over town affecting everyone in town and we're all trapped here. What could be more threatening to our safety than that?"

The mayor looked at her partner and then her daughter. Abigail was hitting the side of an army vehicle with a skinny stick. "They've been so brave" she thought. "Why am I the one afraid?"

She remembered back to the time when she came out to her parents. She and Lilith had already been living together for a year in a small apartment in San Francisco. Her parents were visiting from San Diego and had taken her and Lilith to a fancy restaurant downtown in the tourist area. In between conversations, a cable car on Powell Street would go roaring by and interrupt everything including the part where Renée said the words: '...am gay.'

"What?" Her father asked. "You're in a play? You're back in theater? That's a waste of a perfectly good English major education. Surprised you aren't looking for a job as a mime."

Instead of correcting him, Renée looked down and continued to eat her steak.

"We're gay!" Lilith said.

Everyone stopped eating and looked at Lilith. Renée's heart sank into her feet (Not literally, that's a different story). She looked at Lilith with shock and anger.

"Of course you are." Renée's father said. "Pass the salt."

Renée felt stupid. Something she had been afraid of saying for years was already known. Of course they knew, they were her parents. Even ones in denial know everything about their kids. Lilith had spoiled Renée's moment of becoming an adult.

The mayor sighed. A part of her had never forgiven Lilith for that moment, but mostly, she had never forgiven herself for not coming out herself. What was she going to do this time, let Lilith take the lead, again?

"What are you thinking?" Lilith asked her.

"I'm thinking we should get some coffee. Then I'm going to see the general."

"And then?"

"Then...And then. I'm going home."

The mayor could tell Lilith's sigh was not just from frustration but also pity for her spineless response. They continued their journey to Don's café.

Part 3

Donald Thelonius Byrd, Jr.

"Please, just one more cup, Don," said the woman in the low cut red dress. Usually, this trick would have worked on Don and he would allow this woman to buy an extra cup of coffee, breaking the food rationing law, but not today. No amount of heaving bodices would make Don dip into his valuable supply of coffee beans. He knew once he ran out, he would be as important as a the crazy hooded figure he had just spotted looking through garbage cans. The figure pulled what seemed to be a giant, dead rat out of the garbage can and threw it through the open door of the coffee shop, in his direction. Don avoided the rat. Unfortunately the rat hit a soldier in the back of the head, he turned around angrily and glared at Don. "Hey! What's the purpose of throwing a dead rat at my head!" he yelled.

"And why in the world would I throw a rat at your head?" Don asked the angry gentlemen.

"I don't know. Maybe it's some sort of editorial comment about me or something!"

"Pertaining to what, exactly?"

"I don't know, it could be about the novel I'm writing!"

"And how would I know about this novel? Apparently a novel so bad that your reading public would pick up a dead rat with their bare hands and hurl it at you. Is it a controversial novel on the same level as *Satanic Verses*, *The Catcher in the Rye* or *A Clockwork Orange*?

"That's a movie!"

"What is?"

"A Clockwork Orange. That's not a book!"

"Written by Anthony Burgess, before it was a movie."

"Shows what you know—idiot! Thinks Clockwork Orange is a book!" The guy left the coffee bar, laughing at how stupid he thought Don was.

Don sighed and started cleaning up the dead rodent off the ground. "That's great," he thought. "If this were regular business times, I would have to close down and sterilize the whole place; but not now. People are so desperate for coffee, I could dunk this rat into the pot and yell 'what do ya think of this Rat roast, coffee zombies?' and people would still drink it." Don looked outside. He saw Baboosh carrying a sack of groceries. Something dropped out of the bag which looked like a package of meat. Baboosh lunged and accidentally stepped on it. A stray dog came out of nowhere and tried to pick it up. The dog sunk its teeth into it before Baboosh had a chance to whack the dog on the top of his head, sending it yelping off into the bushes. Baboosh picked up the meat, set it back in his bag and continued on this way. "Eww!" Don said, "I hope nobody eats that!"

The mayor entered the establishment with her family. Her daughter, Abigail saw Don and smiled. "Don-don!" she yelled."

"Hey Abby-wabby!" Don yelled back. They had been doing this name game since Abigail was able to speak. Don didn't need their drink orders, he knew they would order the same thing: Coffee, black for Lilith, latté for the mayor, made with soy creamer and a cocoa for Abigail, extra whipped cream. Supplies were running low for special orders like this one but Don liked them so much he would make their orders the way they wanted until he heard the death rattle of the whipped cream canister, sputter its last hiss. The family sat at the bar. "What's new, your honor?" Don asked the mayor.

"Same old, same old, Don."

"Hey Don-don!" Abigail said. "Guess what?"

"What's that Abby?"

"This morning, we were passing by an apartment, and we saw someone throw a magazine out the window, and it landed in the street, and this army guy said "Whoa!' and he tried to pick it up and he got hit by a jeep!"

"Oh my God, was he all right?"

"He was fine." Lilith said. "He just picked the magazine up, said 'sorry God,' put it in the garbage and limped on."

"Jesus! Exciting morning for you," Don said.

"Another average day in Pepper Mill." The mayor said before sipping her latté. "So, Don?" she asked him. "How long do you think your coffee supplies are going to last?"

"Don't worry Mayor, I'm sure we have enough to last the quarantine."

"Yeah…quarantine," she said sadly.

"What's that about?" Don thought. "Does she know something I don't know? No wait, of course she knows everything I don't know; she's in the loop. I wish I was in the loop. From the looks of it, it sounds like Ami is now in the loop; and she calls herself a conspiracy theorist! Lousy in-the-loop conspiracy theorist!" Thinking about Ami made Don mad. Why was he so mad at her? She hadn't really done anything mean to him. "Sure she was hanging around Finn a lot but so what. Finn may not be the most well read book on the shelf, but he's not malicious and definitely a better person than Mark could ever be." Don thought about how things were when Mark and Ami were dating. Don was quite miserable during that period, watching Ami suffer at the hands of Mark's cheating and disrespect. When Mark was finally out of the picture, he felt sorry that Ami had to go through the breakup, but he was secretly glad: Schadenfreude, as the Germans say.

"Yes, Ami is my friend," he thought ringing someones order up on the register. "Of course I'm interested in her happiest. That's all, right? But am I okay with her dating Finn? She could do so much better. She should date someone that's smarter and knows her, and someone that's been there for her—Casper? No, they've already tried that and it failed. Me? Should we date? Won't things get messy if we break up? Does she even feel that way about me? What was that she said at the end of the world? I…L? I lied? I can't imagine she would even say I love you. Isn't that a super major thing for Japanese people? It's not like they throw out I love you, like Americans do. We say I love you to our dogs and football. If she loved me, that would be like challenging the entire Japanese culture…and a Black man? Surely her parents would have a problem with that. They were nice enough to me when I took that trip to Japan with her, but maybe they were just being nice. Like, We'll treat you with respect to your face but if you cross the line, We'll slice you open like a giant tuna." Don continued about his work day and tried to concentrate on his job.

At the end of his business day, which was only four hours long, Don closed up the shop. Because of the food rationing, he was not allowed to be open for a full eight hour day. Any day now, he was quite confident the quarantine would end and everything would go back to normal. The question was, what would happen to his business? The army had given him full control and ownership of the company, but of course the old owners would return and try to reclaim it. What where his rights? Would his new ownership hold up in court? This could all be a temporary capitalist dream. Don did want to own his own business one day but that one was going to be I.T. based. He would make $100 per hour fixing computers or perhaps he would work some more on a program he called Piggy Back, a program which takes a locked wi-fi signal's log in page, uses the signal that the page is using to broadcast to you, turns that around and uses it to create a separate signal which you can be used to surf the web. He was pretty sure this program was illegal and the feds would come after him for it. He should have accepted the job offer from Mark he didn't tell Ami about. Mark offered him a partnership right when his start-up was taking off. Had Don taken Mark up on his offer, they both would be knee deep in money, Mountain Dew™ and Doritos™. 'Why did I say no? Sure Mark was a scum bag for what he did to Ami, but the fact that I kicked had him out and yet, he wanted to stay in touch with me obviously mean't that he valued our friendship more than I did.'

Don finished putting all the chairs on the tables and cleaned the floors. He looked out the front window at his homemade sign that read: 'Don's Coffee.' "Face it Don…" he said, "…You're in love with Ami." A feeling of relief and a loss of guilt came over him. "I'm in love with Ami," he said. "I-Love-Ami-Nakajima." Don was happy. He wanted to tell her. He wanted to hold her. His belly became warm and his heart beat increased. "Yep, it's love." He wanted to do something for her—anything. Something to impress her before he told her how he felt. "Dinner out?" He remembered Baboosh stepping on the piece of meat. "Perhaps dinner somewhere, but not there. Where did rich people used to eat, that's still open?" No other restaurants were open. All of the rich people were gone and took the good restaurants with them. Don thought about the rich people and he remembered he was going to go look at the abandoned houses on the edge of town. "A new house! How about that as a gift to Ami?" Don smiled at this prospect. "I bet nobody has ever given her a house before." Don locked up the coffee shop and started walking towards the edge of town.

The updated edge of town was only a year old at the most. This part of town did not exist when Don first moved to Pepper Mill. This used to be all farm land. Back then, there wasn't even a proper road, just dirt trails, perfect for mountain biking. Today, the biking trails were paved over to make it easier for golf carts to get back and fourth between the course and the gated community. The gate proved to be a temporary problem. Don wasn't a professional climber, but being motivated by love, he was able to scale the iron gate in no time at all. When he finally reached the ground, exhausted and tired, the wind blew the gate open and told him that perhaps he should have tried to open it first and not assume that it was locked.

The neighborhood was a ghost town, Don expected to see a tumbleweed blowing across the street or perhaps the sound of a coyote howling in the distance. He was amazing people would live in such large grandiose houses—almost perverse that people would need such large, opulent structures with much more room than one could possibly use. Don wondered if it was possible that some of the people had actually stayed behind, after all, why would anyone work so hard to build these giant dream houses and abandon them, just because the apocalypse was happening? He took a chance and walked over to one of the large structures and peered through the window. It was apparent that most the good things were already taken out. He saw some furniture but he couldn't see things like: televisions sets, video games–even exercise equipment seem to have been loaded onto giant trucks and taken away. Don didn't know what to expect, of course people would take all of their prized possessions. He figured this would make things easier. It was one thing to move into somebody else's house but it was a lot easier to move into an empty house. No matter who the owners used to be, it felt more honest. Don never thought about what exactly his criteria was going to be for looking for a new place to live. Looking around he had so many choices; an entire neighborhood full of ripe fruit, ready to be picked. The houses were in different shapes, different sizes and different architectural styles. 'What would Ami like?' Of course she'll want something that's pretty he assumed, but he knew she wouldn't go for something that was too frilly 'Maybe I'll find something that looks like a Japanese house around here, something with those fancy gardens in the back, sliding doors and some kind of dojo thing where Japanese people pick up sticks and get out their aggression.' In spite of his many years of living with Ami, the Japanese culture was still a complete puzzle to Don. Even traveling to Japan and spending time with Ami's family proved to be a lesson in futility.

Don remembered the many times he sat at their dinner table and although Ami's mother was quite polite, bowed, smiled and seemed to honestly like Don, the father never said a word. Was it the Black thing or the fact he didn't know any English? Ami assured him, that to her family, Don was about as different as any White person—all foreigners are the same to them—if you're not family or friend, you're a gaijin. Back in the olden days, when foreigners were trying to get a trade foothold into Japan, the only way they could be accepted was if they did things like denounce their god and act like idiots, or in other words; "how low can you go?" Of course most foreigners with their pride would never act like idiots and especially denounce their God in the time of a flat earth and witch burnings. Perhaps Ami's mom liked Don because he was cracking jokes all the time—a way of dealing with nervous situations.

'How did Ami feel when she meet my family? Was it the same way?' Don's mom would accept anyone as long as Don liked them. But, his conservative father, who actually had Asian people shoot at him during the war, didn't seem too keen of their visit to Seattle. Don had to get away from them. If he stayed, he would have turned into his church going, anti-gay, 'White people are all evil' older brother. When Don's brother asked him 'why couldn't he date a 'sister', instead of some Chinese girl?' Don's response was to say that Ami was Japanese and they were not dating. This never sat well with him, he never rebuked the racist statement, and what business was it to his brother or his family, who he dated? This was Don's life, and if he had to move hundreds of miles away to live it, this is what he was going to do–and he did. Ami and Casper were his freedom and now he was addicted to that freedom—he wanted more of it. He wanted Ami. "I-Love-Ami-Nakajima," he said out loud and smiled.

Every house Don looked at, boldly displayed the warning that they were protected by a very loud alarm system, or a dog, which was either taken with the family or was now a new, skeleton statute in the master bedroom. This never occurred to Don, why abandon your house in an apocalypse and set the alarm? Only the Newbies would want to protect their worldly possessions, even to the very end. One house got his attention. It was the same as any other mini-mansion model. Situated on the very edge of town. In the back it had an infinity style swimming pool, overlooking the river. It was still filled and apparently still being cleaned by some type of wandering, white robot pump on wheels, rolling around the bottom, with a tube running from its back to the shore. The peculiar thing about the robot, it wouldn't clean the last five feet of the pool. It rolled along normally until it hit that area and then it switched directions and rolled in the opposite direction. "Weird" Don thought. "Must be defective from having to clean all this time."

Besides the pool and the robot pool boy, the thing that mostly caught his attention was the note, tacked onto the side door; it was in Russian. Don knew this only because part of the note mentioned that it was being written in Russian. To him, and any other towns people that saw that note, now had the ability to read it:

Hello, Natasha:

For privacy reasons, this note is in Russian because I'm sure my stupid American neighbors can't read it.

By the time you read this, I will be taking your place on the International Space Station with your lover, Marvin Lecehavitz. That's right, you cheating harlot, I know all about your affair. But how can I take your place, you ask? All it will take is a blonde wig and some make-up to trick that near-sighted fool. But don't worry, in your final hours of life, I will give you what you've always wanted, everything! You can have: the house, the car, the swimming pool, the dog skeleton in the master bedroom —everything! So enjoy your last hours of life as you look up to the heavens and I look down and watch you have an affair with Armageddon!

Love, Boris Tudef

P.S. The key is under the mat, the Alarm code is Vodka. Happy dying!

Don rolled his eyes at the terrible closing sentence. He checked underneath the door mat. Sure enough, underneath were a group of keys, one of which had a Porsche logo on it. "Sweeeeeeet!" Don said. He unlocked the front door. There was a constant beeping sound. Don knew he only had a certain amount of time before the alarm would sound and then the local police department, or worst, the army would show up to investigate. He desperately looked around for something that looked like a key pad to press in the deactivation code. There was nothing near the door, 'Where could it be?' he wondered. "It has to be somewhere away from the front door, but close enough to walk to before the alarm goes off." He thought about the password 'vodka.' He looked for something that held alcohol. Off to the side was an empty liquor cabinet. On its side was the key pad. Don ran over to the device, punched in the code. With a little beep, the alarm system went off. Don felt like he was an astronaut who had just safely landed on an alien planet.

Looking around, he noticed this house was a lot more furnished than the other houses. The liquor cabinet was empty but the fridge was full. The contents in the freezer could be saved, but not the yellowish eggs or the old, green yogurt with vines growing out of it, which made a lunge for him. On the walls, some paintings were taken, perhaps for sentimental reasons, well, not taken as in taking a picture but taken down (this is why English is one of the most ridiculous languages). The bedroom closets still had clothes for a woman, but all of the male clothes were gone except one suit which looked like it belonged to a butler. He then found an outfit for a maid. "Either these clothes were for the servants or this couple were into some kind of kinky dress up." Over all, this place was ready to be moved into.

Don remembered the Porsche. He found his way to the garage. Now, to the male brain, even if he is: heterosexual, homosexual, heteronormative, queer, transexual, transgender, tranerasure, pansexual, bisexual, bicurious, polyamorous, polysexual, gynosexual, monosexual, androsexual, allosexual, questioning, or varioriented, there are three things which will get the testosterone levels raising and the heart pumping: running from a tiger, oral sex and spotting a fancy sports car. The black, 2013 Porsche 911 Carrera 4 Cabriolet convertible was sorta like all of those things at once. Don was pretty sure that when the Russian bought it, he also received a tiger steak sandwich and oral sex, right there in the office while he was signing the papers. I won't go into too much detail because I'm sure you can just Google what this car looks like, but to put it simply, it looked like a Hot Wheels for James Bond, dipped in sex. There was only one problem with the car: written at least ten times in red Spray paint on the car was the word "suka" (pronounced soo-kah). To put it simply, this is the Russian word for female dog. If it were still in Russian, it wouldn't be as bad because perhaps people wouldn't know what it mean't and perhaps thought you were bragging like: "So long suckers, look at my Porsche Carrera!" Alas, being automatically translated as the 'B' word, made Boris' last gift to Natasha, bitter sweet.

Don wondered if it were worth it to drive a really cool car, if it has the 'B' word plastered all over it. "What about my reputation?" he wondered. "I might end up being the guy driving around town in the "suka" mobile. He looked at the inside of the car and discovered the $5000 stereo system. Two minutes later, Don was headed into town at 130 miles per hour. He adjusted the pair of golden sunglasses he had found in a drawer. They were a little feminine and perhaps lady's sun glasses, but it didn't matter. Neither did it matter that it was very hard for him to see without his regular glasses, evidence by the stop sign he ran or the one way street he drove up in the opposite direction, because for the moment, he was the coolest heterosexual in town, which he yelled at two women walking down Main Street (at least he thought the two blurs were women).

Squinting hard, he saw Ami and Finn leaving The Pepper Grind. "Perfect timing!" he said. He tried to make a U-turn. Traveling at such a high speed, he ended up making the car do a screeching, 180° spin and ended up parallel parked on the opposite side of the street, right in front of Ami and Finn. Finn grabbed Ami to prevent her from being hit. She slapped his hands away as if he were putting the moves on her, She turned her attention to Don in the sports car. "Don! What in Buddha's name? Why are you wearing woman's sun glasses?"

Un-phased, Don, tapped the side of the car and cleared his throat. "Ah-hem!"

"And why are you driving around in a car with the 'B' word all over it?"

"Thought you'd never ask. Like my new ride?"

"Why would you buy a car that has the 'B' word all over it?"

"Ignore the 'B' word! This is a Porsche!"

"Is that how they're painting Porsches these days? Rich people are weird."

"Ignore the paint job, Ami! Check out the fact that I'm driving a cool sports car!"

"And wearing girly sun glasses."

Don took the glasses off and threw them at the ground; they went into the sewer.

"Don!" Ami complained. "Don't throw stuff in the drains, they end up in the ocean!"

"No, it won't," Finn said. "The force field keeps everything from going to the ocean…" When he realized what he was saying, he put his hands on his mouth and excused himself. "Uh, excuse me, Miss Ami, I gotta go back to guarding The Egg…I mean I gotta go to work–excuse me!" Finn hurried off, leaving Ami and Don in confused silence.

"Ooooo-kay" Don said. "Anyway, what do you think of my new set of wheels?"

"Very nice Don, how much did you pay for it?"

"Zero down, zero interest, zero payments due by zero days."

"What? Someone gave this to you?"

"Sorta."

"Don? Did you steal this?"

"No, someone gave it to me…Or her. Whichever. It was left behind. Just like our sweet new petite maison!"

"Donald Thelonius Byrd, what are you talking about? Please tell me you've become a drug dealer and haven't started a rapping career, because I really hate rap music."

"Wow. I hate every part of your sentence—No to all of those. No, you are looking at the proud new owner of all of the prized processions of a Russian guy's mistress."

"And first of all, how do you know this person?"

"I don't"

"Second of all, did you kill someone and take their stuff? Because I'm okay with that over you starting a rapping career."

"For snakes sake, Ami. I'm not a rapper! I didn't steal or kill someone for it! This stuff was all abandoned on the edge of town."

"And you just took it?"

"I moved into an abandoned house, yes."

"With an abandoned sports car?"

"That's right."

"And what are you going to do when the real owner shows up?"

"No one is showing up, the owners are gone. One is apparently living on the International Space Station…Name's Boris something."

"And the mistress?"

"She must have beat it out of town."

"How do you know?"

"Boris left a note for her, she never took it off the door. Anyway, we have a new place to live and a new car."

"Don, the owner of that house is going to come back once the quarantine is broken."

"So."

"So, you'll have to get out. That could be a month from now or next week."

"Fine and when that happens, we'll leave—In the meanwhile, let's live a little–la vida loca! Odd, that and petite maison didn't translate…. The place even has a swimming pool! Do you know how many years I've always wanted to swim in a pool that someone didn't pee in?"

"Here we go again. You and your pool pee phobia."

"Hey! I can't believe 100 kids in a public swimming pool, can swim two hours straight without once, getting out to go to the bathroom! Anyway, until Boris comes back to claim his house, it's mine…It's ours." Don decided to be bold. Perhaps it was the testosterone injection from the sports car, but he took a chance and reached out and grabbed her hand.

Ami smiled, her face blushed and she held his hand for a brief moment. Her smile faded and she removed his hand from hers. "Don, when you make it big, I want it to be because of your hard work. Not because you took advantage of someone's situation and took their stuff."

"But they left this stuff. You gotta jump on opportunity sometimes."

Ami smiled. "Don, I have every confidence that you're going to make it one day. And when you do, it's going to be big…And real. That house and car are only pretend. I want something real…I want…Don, I…"

Ami's words were cut short by Finn. "Mr. Don? Why are you driving a sports car around with the 'B' word on it?"

Don rolled his eyes. "Hold on Finn, Ami was about to tell me something. You what?" he asked her.

Ami looked embarrassed. "What? Who me? I wasn't going to say anything."

Finn put his hand on Ami's shoulder. "We should get back to the base, Miss Ami."

"What? Oh, sure," she nervously said. "Don, I'll see you later at dinner time," Ami said. She and Finn began to walk back to the high school.

Don's heart sank. He felt like he and Ami were going to have a revealing moment. When she smiled and blushed, his heart skipped a beat and he came very close to saying: "I love you." When Finn showed up, it was like he had thrown cold water on him. When Ami was leaving, he felt he had to say something. Something to start the fire in his heart again. "Ami!" he yelled. She turned around. "I'll be at 55 Cerada Street."

"Don, I told you we shouldn't…"

"Ami-chan, just take a look. If you don't want to stay there, I'll go back with you to home…Our home."

Ami smiled. The warmth in Don's belly was ignited. He slammed on the gas of the car and it screeched away, much faster than he thought it would. His head was thrown back, He felt something tiny and metallic in his mouth, he spat it off to the side. The car swerved out of control until he regained mastery of the steering wheel and put it in the right lane.

"Watch where you going, Mr. 'B' Word!" someone yelled.

Part 4

Nakajima Ami, MLT, EMT, CPT

It's been a week since the ring started turning and something came out of it and landed somewhere near the park. Ami was scared, more scared than when the comet was about to land. She hadn't heard from her friends in days; she didn't know if they were safe—she didn't know if she was safe. She was surrounded by military personnel. They had their guns, tanks and bazookas but would that be enough to defend against the thing she saw floating down to the ground?

'Where is Finn?' she asked herself. It would be nice to see a familiar face; anyone she knew. A female private, first class, entered the tent where she and a couple of other females were being housed. She didn't know the names of the others. Ami was not good at becoming friends with women. She had no girlfriends, Only Don and Casper…if they wore dresses. She missed Don–a lot. The private told them they were all going to pack up and move into the nearby high school. There was no information about why they were not allowed to go home. There was no information about what the ring did and what that bubble was that floated out of it. The new camp wasn't that far from where the bubble would have landed. It was logical for them to move further away from it. It was illogical that the high school was only a four block difference.

Private Finn came into the tent. Ami felt a little better seeing a familiar face. He spat something out of his mouth into is hands. There were a couple of pewter looking pieces. He looked puzzled, put the objects into the garbage and turned his attention to Ami. "Hello, Ms Ami," he said.

Ami hated it when he called her that. She had grown tired of trying to correct him. "Hello, Finn. How are things, you all right?"

"Yeah, I don't know what that was in my mouth—anyway, we're moving everyone out to the high school. That way we don't have to be sleeping in tents. Guess they figured it made no sense having a high school and all of the teenagers were evacuated. You guys are going to get your own classrooms to stay in."

"Us guys?"

"The medical students."

"What about you?"

"Me?" Finn's eyes lit up, as if Ami's concern for his welfare was more than just interest. "I'm going to be guarding The Egg—oops, I guess I'm not supposed to talk about it with non military folk."

"What egg?"

"That's what they're calling the thing that came out of the— Darn it! There I go again!"

"It's an egg? What's inside it?"

"I don't know? Giant space chicken?" Finn laughed at his joke. "Don't you worry Miss Ami. If it's dangerous, I'll protect you with my life."

"Thanks, Finn." She thought he was sweet for offering to protect her but it also made her sad and a little creeped out because she was not on a "risk your life" level with him or even a stand between him and another person throwing a Q-tip at his head, level. Ami packed up the little possessions she had, all of which were supplied by the American military. The only items she had bought with her, besides the clothes on her back was a necklace Don had given her for her birthday. Even tough it was gold colored, she knew it wasn't made of gold. On the end, was an oval shaped piece of jade. "Jade is good luck in Japan, right?" Don said when he gave it to her. She didn't want to point out that that was more of a Chinese thing. She picked it up off her sleeping cot, looked around to make sure no one could see her and then kissed it before putting it around her neck.

The short ride with Finn to the high school could have been walked. She accepted a ride because she knew Finn would volunteer to walk with her and that would extend their time together. "What am I going to do with him?" she thought. "It's not like he's a bad guy". She felt nothing but friendship towards him. There was no 'tingle' if you understand my drift. If you don't, I suggest you study female anatomy and especially female sexuality. Don't worry, I'll wait right here until you're done.....................
....Okay, done? So basically Finn didn't do it for her.

At the high school, the army was busy moving things in and out, taking what they could use and throwing the rest into a pile in the back–mostly students desk, not the best seating in the world. The computer room was kept mostly in tact as was the biology class with it's scientific equipment. On one of the boards in the classes, someone had written: 'Hello students, my name is General Cats'. Underneath it, a cartoon picture of a cat. She assumed the general didn't do that. The subject of said cartoon drawing was in another classroom down the hall. From what Ami could see, he and some other high-ranking officials were having some kind of video conference with the President of the United States. A captain saw Ami and ordered someone to close the door. It was done unapologetically, cutting off her view. "They were having a video conference" she thought. "They have communication?" She tried her best not to get angry about this and instead tried to think of a way to get access to the system. How could she get access to that video conference system in order to tell her mother that she was still alive and quarantined in the town? Why were they denying civilians the right to communicate?

Ami's classroom was moved into. Her classmates were two female students (not of the high school but from her medical school. I'm sure you knew that, but sometimes I have to make sure you understand, you'd be surprised how people take everything so literal) one was a medical student, studying to be an EMT, the other was trying to take a bunch of prerequisites like Ami in order to transfer to a larger medical college. Ami was cordial to them, but once again, she didn't want to bond with other females–a pity because the one with the glasses has a secret, lesbian crush on the one that looks like actress Heather Graham. This is of course not a reason to friend someone, but without access to a television to entertain you, real life can substitute quite well. They all finished putting their things away, just when a female lieutenant entered the room. "Do any of you guys know how to run a X ray machine?" This was a strange question to ask. Of course it was logical for you to ask a group of medical students that question, but surely the army would have had an X-ray technician stashed away among the hundreds of human, killing machines. Then again, if your job as army doctor was to end people's pain (or to end them, completely), looking at the bone of the broken arm that you were going to saw-off no matter what the patient yelled, was a waste of time on a battlefield. Sort of the equivalent of a Medieval doctor having access to a speculum and a bottle of Vicodin (sounds like a party).

Ami had no idea why she raised her hand. She had zero experience working an X-ray machine. It was an automatic reaction to the other girls NOT raising their hands. Her father once told her:

'教師がクラスに質問をするとき、手を上げ、最もよい推測を与えることはよいより手で置かれ、愚か者であるために'

Or rather: "When the teacher ask the class a question, it is better to raise your hand and give your best guess, than to sit on your hands and be a moron."

"Okay, you!" The lieutenant said pointing at Ami. "Come with me!"

Ami did a little stagger dance, unsure about what she had just done, and how much trouble she was going to be in once they discovered she was a fraud. As she followed the soldier down the hall, her mind was trying to come up with a back-up plan to keep from being shot for lying. She convinced herself the American military never shot anyone for lying, they only shoot those that lie and get caught. Passing by one of the classrooms, Ami saw that the room had been converted into a makeshift library; not just a library, a medical library. She recognized one of the books on the desk as a ICMD guide book which is used to code various medical conditions. "Hold on," she told the lieutenant.

"What's the problem?"

"Are these books from my school library?"

"I don't know, maybe–why?"

"Can I stop and get a book?"

"What for?"

"I need it to…I need it to calibrate the X-ray machine."

"Oh, okay, sure."

The minute the soldier agreed to let Ami into the library, she did a mental high-five with Godzilla. Knowing that she didn't have too much time, she rushed into the room and prayed (or rather meditated, in her case) that the books would be in alphabetical order. Her prayer was answered thanks to a very anal retentive sergeant who ordered all books to be put in the exact order that they were in the campus library. She found what she was looking for: The Official Operating Manual of the Skeletor Mobile 300 milliampere X-ray machine. She picked it up and from the time she walked from the classroom to the principal's office, she was at least able to read the section called:

How Not to kill Yourself and Others Around You with Large Doses of Radiation, OR Transforming You into a Giant Laser Spewing Monster Lizard (Part 1A).

It might have seemed rude to the Military Doctor, in his office, explaining to Ami what she was going to be doing, but Ami kept reading while he talked. She acknowledged his existence with agreement sounds and head nods. This was apparently good enough for him and he never called her on her rudeness. She was escorted to the outside to get into a Jeep, still reading and processing what she had heard in the office. From what she could tell, she was supposed to X-ray something and it was very important she didn't discuss the job with anyone else. This lead her to the conclusion it was probably some high ranking officer who swallowed something embarrassing or worse, had something embarrassing go in the other direction and didn't want to labeled with a new nickname involving small animals or vegetables. "Whatever" she thought. 'What people do in their off hours is their own business.'

The Jeep took her, the doctor and an armed guard away from the school through town and eventually to the baseball field, It clicked in Ami's brain that they were going to the place where the bubble had floated down. She craned her neck around looking for whatever had landed. All she saw were a couple of guards in the outfield and where the pitchers mound would be, a very large white tent with tubes coming out of it attached to some kind of air compressor. Like an all-white inflatable jumpy house for a kids birthday party. Ami put the book down. This was far more interesting than the chapter labeled:

There is No Reason EVER, To X-Ray Your Own Genitalia!

"Wha-What is that?" she asked.

"You'll find out in a minute," the sergeant said. "But first, I have to make sure you understand, that anything you see is top secret. If you reveal this to anyone you know, who is not part of your team, this will be considered treason and you can be jailed, or under worst circumstances, shot by a firing squad."

"What? Seriously, firing squad?"

"Well, probably not that. But you will be thrown off the team and sent back to your home. And believe me, you don't want to do that after you see this."

'Wow!' Ami thought. "How fascinating can an object inserted into an orifice be, for this kind of secrecy?"

"Do you agree? Or do we have to send you back home?"

"Yes of course."

"Of course you agree to secrecy or yes you agree to be sent home?"

"The first one."

"I forgot, which was that one? Secrecy or going home?"

"Secrecy."

"I didn't offer a third option did I? Like going home in secrecy?"

"No, you didn't."

"Are you sure?"

"Tell me more about that firing squad option."

Without any answer to her question, the Jeep pulled up next to the white tent. Ami was taken to an area off to the side and fitted with a red, hazardous materials (or hazmat) suit. Her name was written (albeit, misspelled) 'Amy Yamaneko' on a piece of duct tape and placed across her chest. She ignored the fact the soldier that did it, had to touch her left boob for a second. After-all, unless he's some kind of super-freak into girls in hazmat suits, this won't do much to stimulate him. Before she entered the tent, someone sprayed her with what can only be described as a fire extinguisher full of disinfectant. The thought: "what have I got myself into" came to mind. Inside the tent, there were a few others in hazmat suits, (can we stop using the word hazmat, because I'm pretty sure it's obvious that everyone in the tent is wearing one) writing things down and typing on computers which were covered in a plastic film. Before Ami saw the object or person which had caused so much commotion, stationed in the middle of the room, she saw an individual in a green camouflaged pattern hazmat suit–(for christ sake), holding an automatic rifle. Although his voice announced his familiarity to Ami, his piece of duct tape (taped upside down on his suit), gave his name away.

"Hey! Miss Ami!" said Finn.

"Finn?" What are you doing here?

"I'm here to guard The Egg, remember"

"Oh, right…Where is it?"

Finn pointed to The Egg. It was an oval, greenish-gray object. About the size of a small, upright car, covered with squares of various size and thickness and in the center, a blinking red light, about the size of a tennis ball. It still spoke the words' "please press the red button" over and over.

"What is that thing?"

"That's The Egg."

Ami had a strong desire to touch it. She held back, remembering they were all wearing protective gear for some reason. "This came from the ring?"

"Remember that bubble thingy that floated down the other day? Well, this thing was inside it."

"It's a UFO, or is it an alien?"

"That's a good question." The sergeant interrupted. "That's where you come in. Now that we have an expert X-ray technician, we can look inside of this thing and see if it's organic or machine."

"Expert what?" Ami had forgotten why they had picked her to come along. "…I mean, yes—expert! That's me!"

The Skeletor Mobile 300 was loaded off the back of a pick-up truck. It was, as it said, a mobile version of an x-ray machine. It was a white, box shaped, wheeled device, about the size of a washing machine in a French apartment, with a crane like arm containing a square, camera-like device on the end, not unlike the set-up you see for a swing-arm lamp. The men who had unloaded the device, wheeled it over to Ami and stepped back as if the machine would explode if they attempted to do anything else to it. They all looked at Ami. She got the clue that she was the one to set it up, after all, she was the "expert" with her few minutes of instruction manual reading.

"What in the freaking world have I got myself into?" she mumbled and panicked. "Once they find out that I don't know what I'm doing, they're going to shoot me, or worst…Which I guess would be super-shoot me. Oh merciful Buddha, I don't want to be super-shot! Please get me out of this predicament!"

I will not pretend to be an expert in Buddhism (at least not in this chapter), but I'm pretty sure, Buddha is not some type of spiritual ATM you can withdraw favors from just by prayer or meditation. That would be closer to those that pray for winning lottery tickets, their favorite team to win a football game or smite the liberal political candidates. Perhaps God can do both, multitask smiting. Rival football team throws a bad pass into the stands, where the candidate is sitting, and the ball knocks his head off; happens all the time; that's how Wilson got nominated–but, this time, Ami's prayer will be answered, not by Buddha but by the X-Raymond company who were smart enough to print the entire step by step instructions of how to set up and operate the Skeletor Mobile 300, on its side panel.

'Didn't anybody look on this thing?' Ami asked herself. She looked around as if she had found a $100 bill on the ground, covered in chocolate, her P.B.T.

She followed the instructions line by line and only paused when she came to the part about protecting yourself or the patient from radiation. "Uh," she said "Do you guys have a 'mobile barrier' she read in the instructions.

"A what?" Finn asked, even though the question was not directed at him.

"A wall or something that keeps radiation from zapping the person working the machine."

"Don't worry," answered the sergeant. The suit you have on is lined with lead to protect you from radiation…Provided it's a model 345 and not a model 344"

"How can I tell?"

"You have to look at the tag in the inside."

"So I have to take the suit off and expose myself to possible 'god-knows-what' from that egg thing, to read the label?"

"...Pretty much. But if you think about it, if you have the wrong suit on, you're already exposed to whatever, already."

"So I'm dead either way."

"Unless The Egg is not an alien weapon."

Ami rolled her eyes and continued setting up the X-ray machine to take pictures of The Egg. The blinking red light and the voice saying: "press the red button." were very distracting. "Why won't they press the button?" She remembered the Americans obsessions with alien invasion movies, involving ne'er-do-well aliens and their nefarious plans to enslave the planet. American paranoia was the only reason not to trust the message of the object. She would press the button herself, if it wasn't for her fear of being super-shot, or worst, super-shot with a fire-ant bazooka–she was fairly certain the military had one of those.

Ami figured out the timer on the X-ray machine. Her plan would be to set the timer and run out of the tent when the machine was operating, in order to avoid cancer. She placed the camera against The Egg, pressed the timer and started running as she planned. She didn't get far because her path was blocked by Finn.

"Ms Ami? Why are you running? Is The Egg doing something?" he said moving to whichever side she moved to, like a dance, more annoying than the quick-step. After the 4th switch in her position and him getting in her way again, she shoved Finn to the side, sending him into a tent pole. "Move it! Idiot!" she yelled. She made it outside the tent right when the beep from the X-ray machine sounded.

Ami walked back in. She felt a little bad about knocking Finn to the side (a little). "Finn? Are you all right?"

Finn picked his dropped rifle off the ground and gave a fake laugh. "Of course—I'm in the army. I get pushed around more than that in the mess hall."

"Sorry to hear that. I was just trying to avoid radiation exposure."

Ami checked a monitor to see exactly what she had taken a picture of. The Egg may have looked like a machine from the outside, but the inside was more like a black and white photo of organic digestive system. Round globular structures, tubes and other shapes filled the image. The armature of The Egg looked more like a skeletal structure than a metal frame. This startled Ami so much that she backed away from the monitor and looked at The

Egg. "Is that thing alive?" she thought. "Maybe it IS an alien." She slowly walked back over to it. It continued saying: "press the red button." She put her head closer to it. "Maybe it's an alien trying to communicate with us," she thought. "Has anyone even tried to talk to it?" She leaned down to the area where the blinking red light was. "Hello?" she said to it. "Can you hear me?"

Ami's concentration and her nerves were broken when Finn came close to her ears and yelled: "WHAT ARE YOU UP TO, MISS AMI?"

After she had regained her composure and resisted the urge to gut Finn like sushi-grade tuna, she ignored him and went back to the camera to take more photos.

"Can't communicate with it, Miss Ami," Finn said. "Some people were trying all kinds of things before you got here, including: sign language, pictures and music—nothing worked. I think that's why they called you in, to look inside."

Ami wondered why Finn was always in her face. 'Does he not have anybody else he can talk to?' she wondered. 'Crap, is he in love with me? Ugh!' She shivered. 'How can I avoid hurting his feelings?' She looked over at him. He had realized his duct tape name tag was upside down. Attempting to remove it with a quick yank, caused him to tear a small hole in his suit. In a panic, he peeled the tape off completely and used it to path up the hole. 'Buddha's beads…What am I going to do with him?' She went back to the task at hand and snapped more x-ray photos. Each one revealed a mystery on top of a question. The area where the sound was coming from didn't have a speaker but long, flat objects. Where the blinking red light was, tubes ran into it from two different directions, each connected to something that looked like a balloon full of liquid. "It's like it's alive, but it isn't alive," she said. Looking at the monitor, connected to the X-ray machine, the sergeant and a couple of army engineers discussed the findings and oohed and awed at anything they didn't understand.

Finn (once again) interrupted Ami's train of thought. "Miss Ami, you're pretty good at taking those pictures, do all medical students have to know how to do that?"

Ami had had enough of Finn's interruptions. She decided to put an end to it. "Finn? Is there anything you want to talk to me about? I can't be interrupted like this when I'm working."

Finn was visibly shaken. "Oh my, no! I'm sorry Miss Ami, I didn't mean to get in your way. I'll let you get to work and I won't bother you anymore!" He returned to his side of the room.

Ami went back to setting up a downwards shot of The Egg. Her mission was of course, interrupted again.

"Miss Ami?"

Ami came very close to using a harsh Japanese curse word– "zackanayo" on Finn. She remembered at the last moment that it would be translated into English. "Yes…Finn ? Is there something you want because I have to admit I'm getting angrier than a pit bull with a mullet hair cut." This was a strange thing to say, but the reason she was saying it was because she actually saw one earlier in the army K-9 unit.

"I'm so sorry Miss Ami, it's just…I was thinking…If you and I, if you can find…You know if you are free…kind of like…"

"Finn! Are you trying to ask me out on a date?"

"Ye-yes. That's it one of those. A date, thing."

Ami mentally rolled her eyes and tried to think of a way to let him down easily but harsh enough so that he will understand the finality of her words. The truth was her best answer. "Finn…It's very sweet of you to ask…"

"Uh-oh," he said

"What do you mean 'uh-oh'?"

"Whenever a girl uses the word sweet it means she's about to stick you in the 'friend zone.'"

"Friend zone? Where did you hear that?"

"One of your roommates."

"Really? It's funny you should mention that because, I'm actually—I can't believe I'm telling you this…I actually want to move beyond friends with one of them."

"Oh, yeah, I know, I already talked to him about it."

"What? Really…and what did he say?"

"He said that he had already put you in the friend zone and there's no way your relationship was going to go beyond that."

"He…He said that?"

"Yep, during that concert that broke out in a fight. We talked in the bathroom."

"Are you sure?" Ami's heart sank. She had no idea Don felt that way. It was like they had been flirting with each other for over a year. Perhaps it was just that, flirting. She remembered the time she hugged him for her birthday present. How it felt so real and appropriate. How she wished they had turned their heads slightly and been able to kiss. She remembered him taking care of her when she was sick. How she overslept and was going to miss her plane to Japan. He drove her to the airport and ended up getting fired from his job at Big Red Groceries. She felt foolish as if all this time she was experiencing a school girl crush on a teacher who only looked at her as a child. She took the final photo of The Egg and started packing up the equipment as best she could.

"So…" Finn said. "Now that you know how he feels, do you want to join me in the mess hall, or I can splurge and take you to the Pepper Grind bar?"

"Mess hall," she thought. "how appropriate." She touched her jade necklace and said: "Sure, why not."

"All right!" Finn yelled.

It was getting dark. The sergeant and the rest of the staff left to go have dinner, leaving Finn and Ami alone with The Egg. According to Finn, his replacement was late. Ami was almost finished packing away the machine, when she heard a voice say: "Look at what I found!" and then "cool! Toss it to me!" A moment later, she saw a baseball roll into the tent. Finn walked over, picked it up and went outside.

"Little help, Finn!" an army guy's voice said. A moment later, Finn walked back into the tent, without the ball. He was about to interrupt Ami's task—again when the ball bounced back into the tent. Outside, some men could be heard laughing. "Little help!" One of them said.

Finn picked up The ball and walked outside. "You guys, you have to throw that in a different direction," he pleaded.

"SOR-REE! Army Guy # 2 said.

"Okay, just don't do it again," Finn said almost joking. He barely finished his sentence, when the ball rolled inside, this time, under The Egg. Finn hurried over like a dog playing fetch and reached under The Egg; his other hand dangerously close to the blinking red button.

"FINN!" Ami yelled. "Your hand!"

Finn looked at his hand and realized what a mistake It was to rest it there. "Holy cow granola!" He moved it away and stood up."

"Whew! That was a close one!" He picked up the ball and took it out side.

"Please tell me he's not going to return it," Ami thought. "C'mon Finn, grow a pair!"

"Here you go, guys. Maybe you should throw it in that direction," He was heard saying.

"Thanks Finn," Annoying Army Guy # 3 said. Before Finn could come back inside, the ball flew into the tent and hit The Egg itself, three inches away from the button. The laughter outside infuriated Ami. She stomped over to the tent exit to translate: 'zackanayo." Finn blocked her from the tent's exit. "Don't worry, Miss Ami, I got this. They're just fooling around."

"Fool is the correct word! Those idiots are going to press the button!"

"I'd like to press HER buttons." Annoying Army Guy # 4 said. Ami tried to leave but was blocked by Finn, again.

"It's okay. Miss Ami, they're good guys, they're just having some fun."

"Yeah MISS AMI, better listen to your BOYFRIEND." Annoying Army Guy # 2 said.

The word: 'boyfriend' was the last straw. Ami tried to leave again, but was held back by Finn

"Finn! Move!" she yelled.

"Whooa! Check it out! Finn finally got to second base!" Annoying Army Guy # 3 yelled. Ami didn't know what they were talking about. She knew they were on a baseball field but they were more near the pitchers mound. Finn looked at her and then looked down to where his hands were. Both of them lay firmly on her chest, cupping both of her radiation proof suit covered breast. For a split second, Finn produced a look of panic and joy at the same time. This sent Ami into what Don Called 'War Goddess" mode. She was not only furious for him touching her lady parts but also he was touching them before she would let Don touch them.

It's true that not all Japanese people know karate, but that didn't mean she had never taken a summer Judo class at the YMCA. On automatic, Ami grabbed Finns arms and with a rolling motion to the ground, sent him flying over her, causing him to land near The Egg on his back. This was accompanied by much laughter from the outside. Ami realized what she had done and felt remorseful for doing it to Finn in front of his associates. She ran over to him. "Oh Finn! I'm so sorry! I don't know what..." she didn't finish her sentence. In his haste to get up and perhaps regain his man hood, Finn had once again used The Egg as something to lean on. His hand was one inch away from the red button. "Finn! Move your hand!"

"Move my hand? Okay," he said moving his hand directly onto the red button.

"THANK YOU!" The Egg yelled. As if a computer was starting up, The Egg hummed, whirled and groaned into activity. It started to vibrate. White smoke started to pour from the bottom.

"Let's get out of here!" Finn yelled. Ami wanted to run but she also wanted to see what was going to happen next. Finn picked her up in a fireman's carry, over his shoulder and started to run away. Around them, numerous others beat a hasty retreat away from the area near the white tent. The tent was now shaking with activity and glowing as if there was a yellow strobe light inside A weird roaring sound came from the tent like a jet engine starting up in reverse. Ami diverted her attention to the sky and the ring in particular. It had stopped spinning and was doing it's light show and rippling sky routine again. Once they were a few blocks away from the tent, Ami wiggled off of Finns shoulders. "We have to keep going!" he yelled.

"Why?" she yelled back. "So far, what ever has happened, hasn't killed us, yet." The ripples in the sky stopped. Burning it's way through the tent, The Egg rose, propelled by a streaming ball of fire and leaving behind an orange plum of smoke. Ami was afraid and fascinated—like she was watching a roller coaster on fire.

The Egg headed to the center of the ring. When it reached the middle, it disappeared. The area where it had vanished resembled a water drop in a pool of mercury. A sound followed shortly. A quick whale moan. The ring glowed for five seconds and then returned to normal.

"Well…that was different," Finn said.

Part 5

General Flint Francis Katz,

Leader of NORAD and Pepper Mill Task Force Operations

General Katz started to look at some paperwork on his desk; his office used to be the principal's office in the old high school. Now it housed him as well as the special forces sent to Pepper Mill to originally evacuate the citizens. Now, they were assigned to protect them from whatever that thing is floating over the town, keeping them captive. One of the papers was a report on Private First class Anthony Finn. There was nothing particularly remarkable about Finn. He got high marks for discipline but low marks on leadership skills and competence. "Why would Captain Kowalski assign him to watch after The Egg?" The general used the high school's intercom system and announced: "Will Captain Kowalski please report to the principal's office." Moments later, Captain Kowalski entered the office. He was a tall, thin man with thin lips and a beak-like nose. If he were at Hogwarts, he would probably be picked for Slytherin. "Yes, General?" he said nervously.

"This Private Finn, the one who caused us a world of trouble, he was assigned to The Egg under your orders, right?"

"Yes, sir, a grievous order on my part. I take full responsibility."

"Yes, you will, but we'll get to that later. Why would you assign a chuggernut such an important assignment? And why was he left alone with it?"

"Sorry, sir, I thought it would help improve his performance. Finn is a good soldier. He's hardworking and does what you tell him to…albeit wrong some times. I thought giving him something high priority would help him to step up. Sorry that it ended in disaster."

"Me too: Second question, what was the punishment?"

"Three months of latrine duty."

"Not good enough."

"Sir?"

"From what I can tell from the report on what happened, there were other's involved. One was late for his shift guarding The Egg."

"Yes, sir three or four others, I believe. I already disciplined the one who was late, myself."

"And what happened to the others, that caused the disaster?"

"…Unfortunately, Private Finn refused to name names. That's why I extended his latrine duty."

"Not good enough."

"Sir."

"Captain. We have a code of conduct problem, here. In spite of being in a high school, we aren't dealing with a bunch of high school students gossiping about shoes, dating and all of that other crap, teenagers do. The army is life or OUR death. We can't have some incompetent duffer running around here making our lives miserable. This isn't some sit-com where we let the whacky neighbor barge in here without knocking, turn everything in our life SNAFU and then return next week to cause chaos. If that were real life, you'd shoot that S.O.B. the minute he walks in without being invited."

At that instant, a soldier came into the office wearing a pair of sunglasses. "Heeeeey Genre-roni! What's up?" The general and the captain stared at the man without speaking for what seemed like an eternity. The man's smile faded and he backed out of the office, waved and slinked away down the hall.

"Should I increase Finn's punishment, sir?"

"You should have gave him six, six and a kick."

"Imprisonment, loss of pay and discharged, sir?"

"Of course. We don't need Finns running around here. He's put our lives in danger. It's the last time he'll do that."

"Yes, sir, I'll let him finish the day and do it."

"You do that. AND, I want you to find the other members of the incident. If Finn cooperates, he looses the two sixes and just gets kicked out."

"Yes, sir." Captain Kowalski left the office.

"Oh great, now what?" Flint thought as he saw the mayor coming towards his office. It wasn't that he disliked the mayor, it was a complaint that he wasn't doing anything to help the people he was sworn to protect. He sometimes looked forward to seeing her. She was easy on the eyes and had a nice petit figure. He sometimes wondered if she had ever had a relationship with a man and if so, what would that man think of her sexual choice, now. Would he think: "so that's why we broke up" or would he think: "I was such an awful boyfriend, I ruined men for her." Then again, maybe they broke up for obvious reasons: personality differences, he cheated, he got hooked on pixie sticks and Red Bull™.

"Morning, General," she said.

"Madam Mayor. What can I do for you, this morning?" He looked at her red hair. It looked like it had recently been re-colored. He liked the color. It made her look like an Irish school girl. "Reminds me of that cute girl from the Bangles," he thought. "What was that song they sang? Our lips are sealed?" As the mayor talked about how the citizens were complaining about the constant lock-downs. The general was busy looking at her neck. "I wonder what her neck feels like? I bet it's really soft. I wonder what she would do if I asked right now, can I feel your neck? She'd probably take it as a threat—who wouldn't—Jesus Flint! What's wrong with you? Why are you fantasizing about a lesbian, 15 years younger than you? It's been too long—how long has it been, 21 years? I should seriously start dating again! I think 21 years is long enough to start dating. Boy, Lori would kill me—if she'd ever talked to me again, she'd kill me for trying to create a mother for her."

As the mayor went into passionate detail about the rights of citizens or some other American myth, the general was thinking back to a fatal day, 21 years ago.

He was in one of those countries with a 'stan' on the end of it. They had finally pinned down the leader of a terrorist cell. In the morning, they were going to make their move on his hideout. A radio call came through. It was a medical doctor taking care of the general's wife back in Washington, D.C. He informed the general that a decision had to be made as his wife's health was deteriorating. If they operate now, they could get rid of the baby or deliver the baby and she wouldn't live through it. The general had to make the worst decision of his life. He remembered what his wife had told him before she had become sick: "If the chemo doesn't work and you ever have to choose between me and the baby…" She never finished that sentence because he told her not to say such things and it wouldn't come to that. But it did come to that and he knew what she was going to say. Perhaps he subconsciously blamed Lori for killing his wife years ago and didn't bond with her for that reason. But that was in the past—he has to move on. He has to find his daughter and tell her everything.

"…People eating each other like cannibals!" The mayor said breaking the general out of his deep thought.

"What? Huh?"

"I knew it, you weren't listening!"

"I was, I was."

"Then what was I talking about?"

"Your townspeople are P-Oed because of all of the lock-downs."

"Lucky guess."

"Yes. And you want me to do…Do what exactly?"

"Put an end to them?"

"How?"

"The next strange event, no body get's shut in. So far, no harm has come to anyone from the aliens, therefore it begs to reason that they mean us no harm."

"Yet, we still don't know what we're dealing with and I'm not going to risk every ones lives on a hunch."

"Fine then. Prepare for an uprising!"

"What are you talking about?"

"You don't get it, the people have had it! If there's another emergency, they are going to dress up as apes and start throwing feces!"

"Come again?"

"Go crazy! They are really at the end of the rope of tolerance! They're going to hang me and then try to come after you guys! I feel like I'm the only thing stopping them from marching in here and holding an Occupy movement!"

"Wait, that's it!"

"What's it?"

"A protest. They need to protest, blow off some steam."

"Wait, you WANT them to march in here?"

"Not here, but somewhere. The park near here where that thing was."

"What was that, by the way?"

"You don't want to know."

"I do."

"No, you have to be in the dark. You have to be on the side of your Peppermillians...Peppercornys—whatever you people call yourselves. You have to be the mayor that's on the side of her people, fighting against the oppressive military ne'er do wells."

"Are you on pixie sticks? You <u>want</u> us to protest against you?"

"That's exactly what I want. The people will blow off steam and direct all of their anger at us. You'll be with them and therefore they won't...What did you say, throw poop at chimps?"

"Something like that. You want to stage a fake protest?"

"Oh, I'm sure it won't be fake. I'm sure the anger is real, but I'm also sure people's rage get's less and less, the more they protest and realize it doesn't do any good unless you form an actual movement or political party to back it up. Otherwise, it just fades away until it's made up of a couple of smelly hippies or some crazy gun totting shut-ins."

"Did anyone ever tell you, for a person sworn to uphold the Constitution, you have a real cynical view of democracy?"

"But, I'm right and you know it."

"When I was out protesting against the war..."

"Which one?"

"Doesn't matter. The one with all of the killing in it—anyway, It wasn't to blow off steam, it was to stop the war!"

"And did you break stuff or hurl your poop at the mayor?"

"As tempting as that was, no."

"People need an outlet for their anger. That's why terrorist cells always pop up in the crappiest countries. No economy, no future, no outlet, pow—monkey poop!"

"Okay, enough with the monkey poop. You actually sorta made sense there. So what do you want me to do?"

"Go back to your people. Tell them I told you to grease your opinion and where to put it. They'll turn their anger on me, lead a protest to the middle of town, they'll get over it and go home."

"Or, they'll get madder and break stuff."

"And if that happens, we step in and shut it down cause then we have a legitimate excuse for why there should be lock-downs."

The mayor held the sides of her head. "My head hurts."

"Go home, paint some signs, rally the protesters. Be the good guy...Er, ah, gal. I'll be along later and let them throw eggs at me."

"Eggs, if you're lucky."

"I'm made of tough stuff, I won't break."

The mayor left the room. The general caught himself looking at her rear end. He shook his head. "I seriously need to start dating."

Part 6

Private First Class (or rather) Private Travis Anthony Finn

"I have a date! I have a date! I have a date! I have a date!" Finn said in his brain. It was true, Nakajima Ami had agreed to meet with him at the Pepper Grind bar for dinner. "I wonder what I should wear?" he thought, forgetting the fact he only had two outfits, both of which were covered in camouflage colors. "Should I take her a gift?" He looked around in his corner, located in a classroom. There was nothing on his weapons locker but a photo of his parents, a photo of his family prize winning dog; Queen Elizabeth II and an empty frame with a really terrible (borderline racist), crude drawing of a Japanese girl and the words 'Miss Amy' (yes, misspelled) written on the bottom. "Maybe I should give her my drawing of her? Then again, If I do that, she'd have it and I won't have a picture of her." Finn took his hand gun and put it away. "Probably won't need that...unless it turns out she's a spy and I'll have to shoot her—naaw, what are the chances of that? She is pretty tough, she could be a spy trying to trick me into betraying America. She-yeah, right, Finn. No way she can talk me into that... Unless she gave me a kiss. Then I might betray America a little. Not all of it, just a little. Maybe the recipe for Grand Mammy's apple pie or the best place to catch cat fish, which strangely enough are in my Grand Mammy's apple pie recipe. Now that I think about it, Grand Mammy's pies are pretty awful. I need something better to keep a secret from a Japanese spy."

A Hispanic male soldier entered the class room. "Private Finn, my man, what are you doing in here? Isn't it your turn to guard The Egg?" he laughed.

"Hi Diego. That's a good one, I guess you found out what happened. I was just taking a break, thinking about something to take on my date."

"You have a date! YOU?"

"Yes. Something wrong with that?" Finn said angrily.

"No, no. With who?"

"Miss Ami."

"That Japanese girl?"

"That's the one."

"Finally going to bag her eh?"

"No, I'm not going to put her in a bag. That's wrong and probably illegal...except in Oklahoma where it's part of courtship."

Diego paused to think about what Finn had said. "Anyway, you asked out your dream girl? You want me to tell the guys to hang out someplace else so you can bring her back here and...You know." He elbowed Finn.

"Do the chicken dance?"

"Is that a metaphor for sex?"

"Sex? No, that won't be necessary, I don't believe in pre-marital sex."

"But what if you don't want to ever get married?"

"Sex without marriage? That's ridiculous. That's like milking a cow with a blind fold. You don't know what you're getting.

"I'm confused. Are you wearing the blind fold or is the cow?"

"YOU, silly. Cow wearing a blindfold. That doesn't make any sense."

"But milking one while wearing a blindfold does?"

"Because you're milking blind. Like what if you were milking a mad cow or something?"

"I guess that make sense. My second cousin, Juan lived up in Canada—got killed by a mad cow."

"That's awful. Sorry to hear that. Now I feel terrible about my cow reference."

"Yeah I know, thanks a lot, Finn." Diego lowered his head in depression and shuffled out the door.

"Don't go Diego, don't go!"

Diego left the room.

"Fine! Go Diego, go!"

Finn had to leave, also. He was on latrine duty for the whole month. It wasn't as high priority as guarding an extra terrestrial object from far away, but it wasn't as boring. For all of the days Finn had been guarding The Egg, there had been zero changes in The Egg's appearance, sound and size. Guarding The Egg was his one opportunity to be promoted, to go beyond private first class and he blew it–big time.

Just once, he wanted to be successful in something. So far careers seemed to slip through his fingers just like romance. He wasn't going to fail with Ami. He's never had very good luck in romantic matters. His only relationship started two years ago and ended one year and 11 months ago. Amanda Picklechest, his high school sweetheart, was relentlessly teased for her name. Finn thought it was because the name: "Amanda" had the word "man" in it. When he learned it was Picklechest, he thought she was made fun of as someone having a wooden container full of pickles. When she broke up with Finn for not being 'smart enough' in her words, Finn was quite confused at how she could make fun of him for not being smart enough when she had a name that sounds like a container for pickles. Finn threw himself into his career, being a dog show trainer. Unfortunately after the tragic accident with the family show dog, Queen Elizabeth I, involving an electric razor and a puddle of water, the family decided Finn should perhaps pursue another career. Therefore he decided to become a pilot. He joined the army because he didn't realize the army were not the ones with the airplanes, but it was too late. Finn was shipped off to Fort Bragg and then, during the crisis, Pepper Mill. He wasn't so upset at the fact he didn't get to see the world as his recruiter said he would, nor did he get to fly airplanes which made the recruiter have a really confused look on his face when Finn mentioned it. He just wished the recruiter along with other people could have been honest with him. He's always had a problem with people not being honest with him. Perhaps this is why he liked Miss Ami so much. There was something about her, maybe it was her delightful attitude or her pleasant demeanor. He didn't know if she is in love with him as much as he was in love with her, but he knew when the time comes, no matter what she will tell him, the truth was much more important than people pretending to be his friend.

After cleaning toilets sinks and floors, he hurried to the high school to pick up Ami. When he arrived, she had packed up all of her clothes and limited supplies.

"What are you doing?" he asked

"I'm packing up the rest of my stuff to go home."

"Go home? I thought you were staying here?"

"I live downtown in an actual apartment, with Don and Casper I was only here because of the lock down. And now that the lock down is over, I can go home."

Finn's heart sank. It was his fault that the lock-down was over. Without the lock down, she was going to go home and not be as available as she was the past week. "Are we still on for our date?"

"Date?" She paused, and fumbled the toothbrush in her hand, almost dropping it.

"Did I say date? I mean't lunch?" Finn apologized. He didn't understand why he had to explain himself. Was it or was't it a date? "So, are you ready to go?"

"I guess." She packed the last of her items and they started walking to the Pepper Grind for their non-date.

At the Pepper Grind, they took seats near the window. Ami sipped some tea and Finn had a Baboosh burger and a chocolate milkshake. His nose had some whipped cream on it. "So…" he said. "Quite a week, huh?"

Ami didn't hear him and seemed to be deep in thought. She looked at two guys carrying picket signs down the street.

"What's on your mind, Miss Ami?"

"Nothing Finn…well…are you sure when you talked to my roommate, he said we could only be friends?"

"Yep. Sure did. He said he doesn't date his friends." Ami looked sad. Finn was at a loss for what to do. This is not the attitude he wanted from someone who was on a date with him. "So…Miss Ami. You like noodling?"

This question broke her out of her somber mood and moved her into confusion and a little anger. "What? What is that some sex thing?"

Finn laughed. "No, no! It's like fishing for cat fish with your bare hands! You put your hand in the catfish hole and wiggle your finger around and when the catfish goes after it, you grab him and pull him out of the water—It's tons of fun. Me and my cousin, Skid Mark used to do it all the time."

Ami looked at him as if he had just explained noodling with his cousin, Skid Mark to her. "No…Can't say that they have that in Japan."

"Really? What do they do for fun in Japan?"

"Same stuff as you do here…except more efficient…and without sticking your hand down a cat fish's throat.

"But what did YOU do for fun when you lived there?"

"Same as here, Finn. Go to the movies, go to restaurants in Shinsekai, go shopping. You know, expect for a couple of shrines and the Japanese writing, Osaka could be New York or Los Angeles."

"Then why did you come here?"

"Pardon?"

"If it's all the same as here, why did you move here instead of staying there?"

"It's a long story, Finn, but I can tell you how it ends. I'm here now; that's all that matters, right?"

"Right." Finn felt this was a hint of affection. He reached out to try to hold her hand. She pulled her arms up and crossed them. "Why does she alway resist me when I try to touch her? Am I going too fast? I already touched her boobs, that's like 2nd base, right?"

After lunch, they left the restaurant and were heading back towards the base. They heard a screeching sound. A black sports car zoomed towards them. Painted all over it was the 'B' word. The driver slammed on the breaks, making the car do a screeching, 180° turn. It ended up parallel parked, right in front of Finn and Ami, Finn grabbed Ami to prevent her from being hit. She slapped Finn's hands away. "Again with the not touching." Finn complained in his head. She turned her attention to the driver. It was her roommate, Don. "Don! What in Buddha's name? Why are you wearing woman's sun glasses?" she yelled. It was true, he was wearing golden, ladies sun glasses. As Don and Ami seemed to argue, Finn took the opportunity to look at the car. It was some type of foreign sports car. He didn't know much about European cars but from what he could tell, this one was expensive. "How in the world can he afford that?" Finn wondered.

Don was angry at something Ami said. He took his glasses off and threw them into the sewer drain..

"Don!" Ami complained. "Don't throw stuff in the drains, they end up in the ocean!"

"No it won't," Finn said. "The force field keeps everything from going to the ocean..." When he realized what he was saying, he put his hands on his mouth and excused himself. "Uh, excuse me, Miss Ami, I gotta go back to guarding The Egg..." He remembered what happened to The Egg last night. "I mean I gotta go to work–excuse me!" Finn hurried off to the side leaving Ami and Don to talk among themselves. He looked back at Don and Ami. They smiled at each other. "Wouldn't it be weird to see them together?" he thought. He wasn't sure if his opinion was based on their racial differences or the fact they were usually arguing with each other. Ami looked sad. Finn didn't want her to be sad. He walked back over to the two and put his hand on Ami's shoulder. "We should get back to the base, Miss Ami."

"What, oh, sure," she nervously said. "Don, I'll see you later at dinner time," Ami said. She and Finn began to walk back to the high school. "Ami!" Don yelled. She turned around. "I'll be at 55 Cerada Street."

"Don, I told you we shouldn't..."

"Ami-chan, just take a look. If you don't want to stay there, I'll go back with you. To home...Our home."

Ami smiled. Don slammed on the gas of the car and it screeched away. He spat out the window. The car swerved briefly out of control and almost ran over Baboosh. "Watch where you going, Mr. 'B' Word!" he yelled.

"You okay?" Finn asked Ami.

"I'm fine, Finn."

"So I was thinking, on our next date..." Finn wondered if he should have been so bold and said: 'date.'

Ami cut him off. "Finn"

"Yes?"

"I...I think I'm going to go check out this house Don found on Cerada Street."

"He found a house?"

"Yeah, it's abandoned."

"So he bought it?"

"Not exactly. It's abandoned."

"So he's squatting?"

"I guess."

"Isn't that illegal?"

"Probably. But the owners evacuated out."

"But won't they come back?"

"Finn, I've had this talk with him."

"And you're okay with it?"

"Finn, again—I already had this talk with him."

"But you're going to check it out?"

"Yes…It has a pool."

"So you're okay with taking someone's house if there's a pool?"

"Finn. I said I'll check it out, I didn't say I was moving in… Yet."

"Miss Ami, I think it's wrong to take someones house without their permission."

"Finn, it's really none of your business."

"The army is responsible for security in this town. If you're doing something illegal, I have to report you or stop you."

Ami stopped walking and held up her hand. "I'm going to cut off our little 'Date'(air quotes), I don't like people automatically judging me and making assumptions about me or my friends. Yes, it's wrong to take peoples abandoned houses, but Finn, we're stuck in this town, there's a freaking UFO over our heads and a talking egg just came to visit, so I think a little leeway on what's right and wrong can be accepted."

"But just a little leeway can lead to bigger and worst things."

"Finn, I said I'd look at the house. I didn't say I was going to murder someone and wear their skin." Finn looked scared. "Okay, slight exaggeration. All that I'm saying is, the law is here to protect us, not constrain us. You want to know why I left Japan? Freedom, Finn! That big American trade mark that you people yell to everyone in the world, unless they don't agree with EVERY-single thing you say, then you cut off our communication with each other or blow cities up! I follow three principles, Finn. One of them is morality, but morality can be broken down into so many parts— like a morality fractal: Yes it's wrong to steal, but is it wrong to steal a loaf of bread to feed a starving child? Just like killing is wrong, but I kill mosquitos like they ALL carry malaria! And you guys kills TONS of people everyday because your crazy leader doesn't like another crazy leader! Don't tell me what's right or wrong Finn, until YOU can figure out what's right or wrong.! Ami stomped away from him.

Finn stood on the sidewalk, he was confused. It was like his entire world had been dropped like a plate of dishes. He had no idea what to do. Sure he liked Miss Ami but he had a duty to stop her and Don if they were doing something illegal—and, how dare she insult the United States of America! Its the best country on earth and no foreigner is going to tell him otherwise, no matter how cute she is! "I've got to stop them," he said.

Finn returned to the base and flagged down some Military Police (MP) in a jeep. He told them that some civilians were going to move into an abandoned house without the owners permission. The first MP said: "So what, it's abandoned." and the second one said: "Aren't you the idiot that was guarding The Egg?" Unfazed by their lack of concern, Finn took it upon himself to stop them himself. He went back to his room and retrieved some supplies. He didn't want to take his gun because he assumed they would come along peacefully, plus, in his child-like mind, it might ruin a chance for a second date if he pulled a gun out on Don and Ami. Instead, he took a baton and a flash grenade because we all know, nothing gets you a second date like throwing a flash grenade at them and a good beating (perhaps I should leave my personal life out of this).

Unable to find anyone who wanted anything to do with his mission or give him a ride, Finn walked to the edge of town where Cerada street was. It was a gated community filled with lots of mini-mansions. He scaled the front gate and tore his pant leg on the little spiky things on top. The wind blew the gate open right when his feet landed on the other side. All of the houses appeared to be abandoned. Finding which house Don and Ami were in was going to be a chore. "Miss Ami!" Finn yelled, while walking down the street. After 20 minutes of this he knocked on door after door. Again, with no success. He remembered Don saying 55 Cerada Street. "Oh yeah, that must have been the address! Oh Finn, sometimes you're a genius!" he said. He ran six blocks back to 55 Cerada Street. In the front were tire marks as if the sports car had done a doughnut in the street. "That's illegal, too!" he thought. He went up to the front door and prepared to confront the two. He hoped he didn't have to get violent, not for fear of hurting them but because he knew Miss Ami could toss him like a rag doll. "Hmm. Maybe I'll just toss the flash grenade into the room first; soften things up a bit." The front door was unlocked. He slowly turned the knob and opened it. There were voices in the living room. Finn knew, once they spotted him, there would be no element of surprise. He pulled the pin on the Grenade and tossed it in. It exploded and produced a flash of light and a lot of smoke. Finn rushed in with his baton. There was a silhouette of a person in front of him holding a gun, staggering around from the flash and smoke. "Oh sweet lord Jesus Christ crisscrossed on the crooked cross!" he thought. "They're armed! I knew just one little act leads to bigger and worst things! Sorry Miss Ami, I hate to do this, but…" Finn bought his baton down on the silhouetted person's head.

Part 7

Dr. Lewis Pascal, Ph.D

When the President called him "Professor Pac-Man" Lewis tried not to roll his eyes or sigh. This was becoming a habit whenever there was a meeting with this president. Being that the meetings were being done via video conference call, it was a lot easier for Pascal to keep from strangling the commander in chief. As usual, the meeting started with a debriefing about what each person knew about the current activities of the ring. In this case, it was more about the object which had appeared out of the ring, floated to the ground and then started broadcasting the message: 'Press the red button' over and over. The President gave strict orders that no one was supposed to touch the red button for fear it was a bomb, this, over the reservations from Pascal. Because, why would they send an object millions of miles away, just to blow up anything it made contact with? The point of not pressing the red button was moot, someone had pressed the button. It apparently made a weird sound and then shot up into the sky and disappeared through the ring which activated for only a split second and then returned to it's normal state. This made Pascal very happy. He couldn't imagine living the rest of his life wondering what would have happened if no one had ever pressed that button. When the President used the word "lie-berry" instead of library, Pascal couldn't hold his comment in. He was bursting at the seams and it was almost a civic duty to correct the commander in chief. It is possible the President was just saying it that way as a joke, part of his usual method of operations, but, Pascal's mouth outran his thoughts and made him blurt out the correction.

"Pardon?" the President said.

"It's library." Pascal said before stopping himself from speaking any more.

"Oh, I'm sorry," the President said sarcastically (which was strange because sarcasm is usually reserved for people being smarter than the recipient). "I didn't mean to pass vocal gas like that, professor. Sorry if I offended you."

"No it's fine." Pascal said nervously.

"Oh, no no. I'm sure my misuse of George Washington's English offends you more than Al Qaeda is offended by Jewish pornography.

"Mr. President, it's really no big de…"

"No, no." the President interrupted. "I'm sure with all of your fancy schmancy college degrees in what is it, English? No, Astronomy, you know more about things than I do. Especially when it comes to this mission where an alien space craft has landed here on Earth and we are trying to figure out what they want and how to deal with them…Oh wait. I just got a thought. Your job as astronomer is to look up at the sky and tell us about them purr-dee stars and me-tee-your-rights flying around and—hold on! We aren't dealing with purr-dee stars and me-tee-your-rights. We're dealing with something on this earth that has NOTHING to do with looking through a telescope. Now, I know that your girl wonder, Ms. Pack-man has a secondary degree in astrophysics so I'm sure she can help us figure out how that ring is floating around without piano wire, but YOU, you Dr. Grammar, You are about as useful as an all-you-can-eat buffet at a vegan restaurant."

"Mr. President, I can assure you I have many things I can offer an understanding of the nature of our alien…"

"Sorry son, but I don't think you have anything to offer at this time."

"Mr President, I…"

"Tell you what, Dr. P., If we see something else approaching the planet, we'll make sure to give you a call. But for now, this meeting is closed to non essential personnel."

Before Pascal could protest again, the President gave someone off-screen a head nod and Pascal's video monitor went blue and a message read: "404 ERROR. YOU CAN NOT ACCESS THIS NETWORK.'

Whenever he was stressed out, especially after dealing with the President of the United States, Professor Pascal liked to do some Tai Chi. He was happy to have found a space to do this in private. This secluded area on the river bank was over grown with wild flowers and blackberry bush brambles. Pascal had found a small, unobstructed path to navigate to his private spot. He only knew 17 movements but that was enough. He "parted the wild horse's mane, spread the white crane's wing and brushed his knee and side stepped. It wasn't until "kick with right heel" did he realize he was not alone. Across the river, two figures were siting on the opposite bank. It was a girl and a male, in their early 20's.

He waved to them. The male looked at him and then stood up.

"Hey!" The male yelled.

Professor Pascal recognized him. It was one of his former students, but what was he doing in the town? Surely all of his former classmates had escaped and were already enrolled in other colleges by now. Apparently not this poor soul. "Mr. Cornbregger?" Pascal yelled.'

"Professor Pascal?" Casper yelled back.

"Oh god, no!" Pascal thought. He felt responsible that one of his students was trapped inside the force field, unable to leave and must endure whatever shenanigans the ring throws at them. "Are you alright?" he yelled.

Casper said something to the female and then turned his attention back to Pascal. "Yeah, why wouldn't we be?"

"The ring?" Pascal pointed upwards to the ring."

"Yeah, it's giving us super powers and stuff but nothing bad."

"Super powers?" Pascal was about to state how the two can't leave the town because of the force field. He stopped himself." "Do they even know about the forcefield?" he thought. It was located about five feet away from them. If Casper or the female were to jump off the bank, they would either bounce back or hit the wall and slide down to the sandy area down below. Is it possible that the army inside the town were that good at keeping the force field a secret? "Is there any thing you want me to do for you?" he asked.

Pascals student paused for a bit. "Can you tell my mom that I'm all right?"

The request saddened and shocked the professor. The reality of the townspeople being stranded in town with their only means of communication cut off was something he didn't think much about. He was too focused on the scientific elements of the mission. If he honored Casper's request, he would be thrown off the mission, permanently. It would be breaking national security, but what had he signed up for? Was it right for a government to isolate it's own citizens under the false pretense of a virus? He was torn and deep in thought.

"Professor?" Casper yelled.

This woke Pascal out of his trance. Was he really needed at this point in the mission? He was an astronomer, dealing with things far away. Objects closer to home were more of a puzzle, especially people. If he got kicked off the mission, he would go back to studying objects far away. He would have a new understanding that the things he saw had life revolving around them. He would get his old life back without government censors and leaders more interested in monopolizing alien technology. "Do I have her contact information?" he yelled.

"Yes," Casper yelled. "It's in my list of emergency contacts."

"I'll do whatever I can. Meet me here next Friday at this time. I wish to know what it's like on the inside."

"No problem. Thanks!"

"No…Thank you. The professor picked up a pine cone. "Mr. Cornbregger!" he yelled.

"Casper and the girl looked puzzled. "Yes?"

Pascal threw the pine cone at them. It bounced off the forcefield and returned back to the professor's hand. Pascal took a second to look at the shocked expressions on Casper and the young lady's face and then he turned around and walked back towards his car.

Part 8

The P.O.T.U.S.

It didn't matter what the liberal senator from California said, President Jarrod was going to disagree with it. It would be easy to say that it wasn't personal, but in this case, it was personal. The

President and the liberal senator went way back. All the way to their college days. The President was barley 18, fresh out of Cactus Texas. Ready to take on the world and get away from his starchy conservative, evangelical upbringing. The campus in Austin was just what he was looking for. A place where youth rejected their parents, Texas and all inhibitions. It's hard to imagine the President with long hair, but there he was, with shoulder length hair, blowing in the breeze, trying his best to get the attention of the numerous girls in shorts and tank tops. Unfortunately, the girls were already paying attention to Chaz Dodge. Chaz, a classmate of Jimmy was a Sophomore. Chaz also had long hair, a guitar and could get ahold of marijuana, faster than you could find a cigarette. Chaz was very popular, and because Jimmy wanted to also be popular, he took everything about Chaz (minus the easy access to pot) and copied it onto his own self; it didn't work. One of the reasons, although Jimmy had a guitar, he could only play fast and slow versions of 'Michael Row Your Boat Ashore'. The other reason, Chaz was very well read. He could quote from Ulysses, The Unbearable Likeness of Being and the Karma Sutra. Jimmy could quote from Garfield comics and The Big Dirty Joke book. None of this mattered, Jimmy had a bro-mance crush on Chaz. He had no desire to have sex with a man or even any physical contact, but he wanted to be close to Chaz, so close that some of Chaz will metaphorically rub off on him and he would become Chaz: a handsome, musical, well-read god.

Chaz was sitting underneath a large fig tree and ironically, singing a song about a fig tree. Four girls sat near him, listening as if he where   a young Charlie Manson and with one word, they would hop up, grab a knife and turn your brain into sesos. When Chaz saw Jimmy, he asked him if he knew how to play guitar.

"Sure." Jimmy said.

"All right, maybe we should jam sometime."

"Jimmy couldn't have been happier. After that, he would stop by the tree with Chaz and play their guitars. After learning how limited Jimmy's guitar skills were, Chaz took it upon himself to tutor the young padewan. In no time at all, Jimmy had graduated from "Michael Row Your Boat" to "Smoke on the Water." Jimmy was also being schooled in the way of liberal politics: Human rights, environmental rights, the right not to wear deodorant, etc. This was a revolutionary time. Not just for the country but Jimmy's personal life as well. He had grown up underneath the ultra conservative shadow of his father, Representative Abraham Jarrod. Congressman Jarrod was an unapologetic, evangelical dictator in the public realm and an unapologetic, evangelical dictator having a bad day, in his home life. For Jimmy and his siblings, they couldn't wait until they got out of their Texas home. One child had already moved to California and was living the life of a bohemian, rent hating artist while the other had become a lesbian missionary (not a missionary for lesbians or a lesbian in the missionary position but a girl missionary that liked girls) in an African country famous for photos of small, dusty children eating, while covered in flies (seriously, how hard would it be for the photographer to shoo the flies off their subjects before snapping a photograph?) Jimmy's lifestyle did not please Congressman Jarrod, whose only comment was: "You'll never be anything but a loser." Jimmy has been hearing this comment his whole life: When Jimmy didn't make the little league team, when he got fired from his job at the fast food tripe restaurant, when he failed to get into Yale and instead ended up in Texas A and M University. Even when he got all As on his report cards, his dad would say: "What, an A+ too hard for you?" So when he became friends with Chaz, It was like being adopted by a new dad; an improved dad.

In their senior year, Chaz decided to run for student council President. Jimmy jokingly said: "Hey, maybe I should run too, that way, we have a better chance of someone decent or cool getting in." this was one of those "pick up the penny" moments for Jimmy. If Chaz had said "sure" or even laughed and said: "right," life would have turned out different for Jimmy. Instead, Chaz said: "Who would vote for you?" To which Jimmy responded: "What's that supposed to mean?" And Chaz said, really digging the quantum penny into the pavement: "Dude, nobody likes you. The only reason anybody puts up with you is because you hang out with me. You're like Robin to Bat Man, 'cept you can't fight. Now, take some of these flyers and hand them out." With this, Chaz tried to hand him a stack of "Vote for Chaz" flyers. Jimmy looked at the stack and then at Chaz. He didn't see a friend of four years, he saw his dad, in secret form: 'You'll never be anything but a loser.' The next thing that happened, Jimmy had knocked the stack to the ground and stormed off.

He ran across the campus and ended up sitting under a statute of Ronald Reagan, holding up a baby by it's legs, about to smack its bottom. Jimmy's few minutes of sobbing and anger was interrupted by a voice—a female one.

"Look at you," she said.

"What?" he asked looking at her. It was one of the cheerleaders, Betty McLincoln. Betty was ultra-popular, fetching, blonde from a rich family which owned a chain of fast food tripe restaurants. She was leaning against a lamp post, smoking a cigar.

"I said, look at you—pathetic!"

"What? That's rude—and why are you smoking a cigar? That's bad for you!"

"Know what else is bad for you? Crying!"

"No, it's not! It relieves stress and expresses sadness and joy."

Betty leaned over. "Excuse me for a second..." she pretended to vomit. "...I'm sorry. So much liberal pixie dust was coming out of your mouth that I think I may have choked on a fairy."

"You're rude."

"And you're a weak minded, lily-livered coward."

"I don't have to take this."

"Yes, you do and yes you will." Betty extinguished the cigar in her left palm. "I've been watching you, J.J., always acting like the Hagi to that guitar playing Johnny Quest hippy, and do you know what I see?"

"What?"

"Nothing! That's what I see. I see a person that could be so much better than that smug, righteous, prig. Running around like he's in touch with the world more than we are. Thinking just because he recycles and eats rice cakes, that gives him the right to go to school on a trust fund while you had to earn a scholarship to get here or work at some crappy fast food tripe restaurant..." She looked up "...Sorry daddy. You earned everything you got and yet he makes you feel inferior? Like you did something wrong?" She walked over to Jimmy and ran her finger from his stomach to the top of his head. "Don't you know what this country is about?"

"S-sure, freedom, truth justice..."

She interrupted him with more fake gagging. "No! You wuss!" She grabbed his shirt. "It's about power! Real power! If you want to change the world, you think wearing Birkenstocks and eating tofu is going to change anything?"

"Every change helps."

"Bull——" The second part of this word was obscured by Betty producing a really loud horn sound on her megaphone (A megaphone I forgot to mention because I really didn't think she'd use it). "Do you know the best way to change the world, J.J?"

"He was about to say something but was interrupted."

"POOOOOOOOOOWEEEEEEEEEEER!" she said through the megaphone. "If you want to change the world, you can't be in the caboose, you gotta be up front, knocking cows off the tracks. If you want people to eat tofu, you can't ASK them, you gotta shove that horrible white paste down their throats! And if you want to get R-E-S-P-E-C-T," she sang. "You gotta prove to Chaz that you're not a follower, but a leader!"

"How?"

"How? How he ask? Tell you what, there's a guy you need to see, hangs out on the cross roads of Mississippi Way and Mississippi Avenue. Names Carl Something. You meet him on the Mississippi crossroads, make a deal with him, he'll give you whatever you want!"

"And then what?"

"Then what? After that, you'll be like a samurai that just lost his entire family to bandits. You won't spill anymore tears—only blood!" Betty turned on her heels and headed in the opposite direction which happened to be a small, wooden lamp post. She ran into it, stumbled back a little, growled and hit it really hard. It bucked and fell to the ground. She stepped over it and continued walking. "Power!" she said through the megaphone.

Carl Something (which really was his last name) turned out to be a political consultant. He was a short, bald, 68 year old guy, wearing an ugly peach colored suit and yellow tie. Like a desperate student, Jimmy waited outside the closed office door on the corner of Mississippi way and Mississippi Avenue for two days as a sign of discipline, until Carl Something took him in and taught him about power. Unfortunately, Jimmy realized on the second day, that the reason Carl wasn't letting him in the building was because the entrance was actually on the other side of the building.

It was a very modest, cluttered little office with lots of pictures of famous people, all autographed: Ronald Reagan, Bill Clinton, Saddam Hussein, Darth Vader and Barney the Dinosaur, among the many.

"Come in, come in!" Carl said. He cleared some paperwork off of a seat and made a place to sit for Jimmy. "Do you want something to drink: water, tea, whisky?"

"Whisky?"

"One whisky, coming up."

"No, that was ...Never mind."

Carl pulled a bottle of whisky out of a waste basket and poured J.J. a shot. "So, J.J....What brings you here?"

"It's Jimmy...Jimmy Jarrod."

"Jimmy, what's your story?"

"This girl I know sent me here, said you could give me power."

"Give you power?" Carl laughed a raspy boisterous laugh. "I can't give you power. Power is something you're born with, like sex organs. Everybody's got a tally whacker and a hoo-ha. No, I think what you mean is you want to learn how to use it, am I right?"

"I guess...Well no, I already know how to use my sex organs."

"Of course you do. This girl. She your girlfriend? Sent you here to man up"?

"Betty? No—"

"Betty McLincoln?"

"Y...Yeah, how'd you know?"

"She was one of my best students."

"She's been here?"

"Among the many, yes. Should have seen her; pudgy little thing, came here because her boyfriend dumped her. Saying he was going to date someone better. Could have knocked her over with one insult. By the time she left here, she could rip a horse in half... which I never recommend anyone witness more than once. So, good Ol' Betty sent you here. I guess she must like you."

"What? Me, no. She's a rich socialite cheer leader and I'm..."

"You're what? Nothing? Don't you think you're good enough for her?"

"No, we're just in two different worlds."

"Same sky outside as the one she looks at."

"You know what I mean."

"But you don't know what I mean."

"Actually I don't—actually I don't even know why I'm here. How are you supposed to teach me about power? You work in this crappy little office in a crappy part of town. If you had power, you'd be in a high rise building...And not wearing...that!" Jimmy gestured to Carl's suit. Jimmy stood up and started heading out. "This was a waste of time. I can't believe I skipped classes for this."

"Wait, wait. Before you go, I want you to answer one question."

Jimmy paused at the back door entrance. "What?"

"What does Jesus, Martin Luther King Jr., and Gandhi have in common?"

"Huh? That's easy, all religious men who taught peace and non-violent actions for change."

"Besides that?"

"They're all men?"

"Besides that?"

"I don't have time for guessing games. Just tell me."

"Money."

"What are you talking about? None of them had much if any money."

"I didn't say their money. I mean't other peoples. The Philistines, The British, the U.S. military industrial complex."

"Not following."

"Why were those people killed?"

"They were killed because of those that hate peace."

"Enough with the liberal close-and-play version of history. Think logically and without emotion. Jesus was in his 30's before they killed him. Plenty of opportunities to kill a younger Jesus, preaching the same stuff. Pretty sure claiming you were the son of God is enough to get a stone to the noggin. Gandhi taught peace and all that stuff, why kill someone for that? Peace would be perfect for the British overlords. Martin Luther King had a million opportunities to get killed until something happened. What do you think changed for these men?"

Jimmy shrugged that he didn't know.

"Jesus messes up the Philistine's farmer's market in the temple, Gandhi was killed by Nathuram Godse, a guy who used to support Gandhi until Gandhi fasted to get the Indian government to transfer a bunch of money to Pakistan as part of an agreement, Godse didn't like that. Martin Luther King Jr., soul brother number one, around for years, suddenly gets killed at the same time he was talking about uniting the poor against the rich and how bad the war in Vietnam was. I'm sure the people that make money off of wars didn't like that. You see where I'm going with this?"

"They all involve money?"

"Not just money—Power! They got powerful. So powerful that suddenly they were changing the world of those that control the planet; those with the money! Money has been around since the Ancient Sumerians and has been plucking the strings of our mortal coils for thousands of years. Some idiots think America was founded by a bunch of people yearning for religious freedom. Pilgrims weren't a bunch of naked hippies running around, they were just as conservative as any body else in England. No, The pilgrims went to Holland for 12 YEARS and had their religious freedom. But they didn't have any MONEY and were working their blunderbuss off, so they left and went to America for all that free stuff! Caesar couldn't care less about Jesus until those whiney Philistines started complaining about him and his supermarket wrecking ways. Jesus was getting too close to the sun, you see? All of those men got killed for being too close to the powers that be: The banks, the politicians, the corporations."

"So, what does this have to do with me."

"If you want power, Jimmy, REAL power, you have to have money. But when you have money. You have to make a choice between fear and respect."

"How is that related?"

"Those people I mentioned were all respected and will live on in history for that. But, there were others that took a much easier path to attaining the same level of power, and they lived a lot longer than those other guys and for only two reasons. They worked the system and they use fear! Adolf Hitler, Caesar, Couple of U.S. presidents—you never saw any of them walking around healing the sick or getting hosed by redneck police officers. They worked the system and played it like a triple necked electric guitar. Fear of the Jews, fear of the Greeks, fear of Mexicans, fear of Muslims. Fear is the quickest route to the top. But, it usually leads to a bullet in the head or in Caesar and presidents case—betrayal by senators."

"So you're saying I have to make people afraid of me?"

"I'm saying you will NEVER be a Gandhi or John Lennon but you can be a Genghis Khan or a Ilyich Lenin. You will never be respected. I'm sorry Jimmy. I don't see it, you don't have the spark. I can see you becoming powerful. Maybe even great, but it won't be real. It'll be based on fear."

Jimmy slumped down into an office chair. "Well that sucks. Might as well kill myself now. I don't want people to be afraid of me."

"I'm sorry Jimmy. I've helped hundreds of people become powerful. They all had to choose; getting power by respect or fear."

"Can't I have both?"

"Many have tried and failed. People can see through a fake, every time. Remember when Michael Dukakis was riding around in that tank?"

"Maybe I can be the first."

"Are you saying you want to take the easy way to power?"

"I'm saying I want to change the world for the better."

"There are two worlds Jimmy. Which one are you referring to, your world or the outside?"

"Both, I guess."

"Fear is going to be your only path to attaining great power."

"I refuse to spend my life deceiving people, though. That's probably how my father got to congress."

"Your dad? You're Abraham Jarrod's boy?"

"Yep."

Carl had a look on his face as if a pile of gold had been place before him. "Oh...Oh my! Now it makes sense!"

"What makes sense?"

"This isn't about a girl. Oh no, no-no-no!" Carl walked over to a dusty bookshelf and started looking for a book. "What we got here...is a classic Greek tragedy." Carl found a book of Greek mythology and turned the pages until he found a wood engraving of a winged man falling. "You're Icarus, my good man and your father is Daedalus. He escaped form Crete. Your wings melted and you fell in the ocean."

"Believe me, in my father's eyes, I've never gotten anywhere close to the sun."

"Neither did he."

"He's a congressman, that's a lot higher than most people."

"Does he treat you like dog garbage?"

"Pardon?"

"Has he always been treating you bad, all your life, even if you make good grades and have never done anything wrong?"

"Pretty much."

"He's Daedalus all right but this time he doesn't want you to fly so close to the sun. Not because he's afraid for your safety..." Carl walked over and patted Jimmy's head. "He doesn't want you to do it because he can't...And he knows that you can."

"What? You're saying he's jealous?"

"He's afraid. He's afraid that you'll be a better man than he is one day."

Jimmy laughed. MY father, jealous of me? I doubt it."

"And it's that doubt that's kept you right under the level of his belly buckle. Right where he wants you." Carl walked over to the back door and opened it. "Jimmy. You have two choices right now. You can leave, have a nice quiet life and be just like everyone else in the world. Or you can drop out of school and study under me. By the time I'm done with you, you'll be on a path to becoming a greater man than your father could possibly imagine."

"Drop out of school? Why?"

"College isn't for everybody Jim. For you, it's just a hiding place from your father. Doesn't matter if you get straight As or shotgun beer cans in the best fraternity, you'll still end up living a mediocre life. No, your school is everywhere else, outside the college walls. If you want to be great, you gotta leave the palace and come sit under my Bodhi tree. Choice is yours."

There was a long pause. Jimmy looked at Carl and the exit and Carl again. "But, what about that path to power, with all of the fear? That doesn't sit too well with me."

"Tell you what. I'll make a deal with you. Once you get to the top. You can do a switch-a-roo. Be as honest as Abe Lincoln hooked up to a lie detector, high on truth serum. But, like I said. No one has ever successfully done it."

"Well, I'm going to be the first."

Prove me wrong, Jimmy...Prove HIM wrong."

There was another long pause. "Close the door." Jimmy said.

...Anyway, as I was saying many pages ago, The President and the liberal senator went way back.

After the session with Congress was over, it was obvious Senator Chaz Dodge and his constituents didn't have enough votes to pass the bill. The President and his loyal congressional pit bulls had the veto power. It didn't matter how important or right the bill was that Chaz was presenting, Jimmy would vote against it. It didn't matter if it was a bill to provide free oxygen to babies (which it was), Jimmy was against it, if it had Chaz's name on it. After the President closed the video screens of the other congressmen, the one for Senator Dodge came back on.

"Chaz-O what can I do you for?" the President asked him.

"I can't believe you would veto that bill."

"Course I would. It has bureaucratic, tax dollar, spending waste all over it."

"Free oxygen tanks for low income asthmatic kids?"

"Yeah, sounds like Socialism."

"You're a moron."

"Nice talking with you Chaz, way to respect the office of the President, sorry again about whooping you in the election." The President cut the conversation short and disconnected Senator Dodge.

The President sat back in his leather recliner and thought for a few seconds. He pressed a button on his computer and connected himself with a congressman from Oklahoma. "Marty, how are they hanging?"

"Mr. President, how can I help you."

"Mart man. I was thinking about the asthma bill for poor kids."

"You think we should have voted yes on it?"

"Oh my, no! There's no way I'll let anything that smells like Chaz see the light of day. No, what I was thinking was, we create a bill of our own that basically does the exact same thing, but maybe we'll add some tax break, cake sprinkles on it for the health care companies."

"But why would we help a bunch of kids with asthma?"

"Because it's the right thing to do." There was a long, silent pause. The lack of a followup comment let the Oklahoma Senator know that the President was quite serious.

"Won't Senator Dodge just complain that we took his law and called it our own?"

"Not when I tell him that if he brings that up or bashes us in the media, we'll take it off the table and it'll be a loss for him and those poor wheezy kids. See, if he really cares about those kids, he'll keep his big, capped teeth mouth shut."

"I hope you're right."

"Hope is the religion of fools, gotta have faith, Wal-Marty. Anyway, write up the new bill and give it a fancy name, maybe something like "Americans for Air Freedom Act." Have it ready to go by noon." The conversation over, the President leaned back in his chair again.

Barry came into the room. "Mr. President?"

"What do you want Barry, I was in the middle of some really important–insert anything else more fun than talking to you, stuff."

"Mr. President, I just want to remind you that in a few minutes you have a conference call with the scientist and General Katz about the object that came out of the ring."

"Okay, fine. Time to talk to the Justice League again."

"Oh, and sir, the hospital called and said your dad is in serious but stable condition. Do you want to set up a video call with him, too?"

"Nope, anything else?"

"Sir he's your fa—" The look the President gave Barry was worst than "I'll kill you!", but more like: "I'll super kill you if you bring this up again!" "Very well, Mr. President. That's all for now."

"Okay Barry, out you go, faster than you came in."

Barry left the room. The President walked over to the window and looked out over the barren Arctic landscape. "I'm going to prove Carl wrong," he said.

"But why did you have to make the dark side so tasty?" he asked no one in particular.

Part 9

Yolanda Iesha Washington, Head of FEMA

Yolanda finished looking through the garbage can. The only thing she could find was a dead rat. She picked it up and looked for a good place to un-throw it away. Her mind told her: *'rats do not belong in the garbage, let them run free like the gazelles.'* She threw it in the direction of a café and it hit a soldier. *'Eat what you kill'* her mind said. The soldier turned and yelled at a Black man. The Black man was late actor Robert Guillaume in the role of his famous character: 'Benson DuBois'. From the show 'Benson' which ran between the years 1980-1986.

"Benson! Benson is there. Must find out where he's hiding Kraus!" It took a long time for Benson to leave the coffee house. Yolanda stayed out of site and followed him. He walked for a long time and ended up on the outskirts of town. He studied a gate outside an apartment complex. "The walls of Jericho will not fall without lettuce, lots and lots of lettuce!" Benson climbed over the fence and then turned around and opened the gate in the regular way. "Benson wants me to follow him." Yolanda kept to the shadows and followed Benson from house to house. He looked in the windows of each one and checked the doors. "Bricks and Stones do not make a home!" Finally he came to a house with a note on it. Benson read the note, bent down, picked up a key and used it to gain entry into the house. When she was sure he wouldn't spot her, Yolanda darted across the street and ran around to the back of the house. There was a full swimming pool. Crawling along the bottom of the pool, a large white rat, the size of a car. "The rats of the rich breathe under water and are too big to throw." She watched the rat for a while until she heard Benson's footsteps approaching. He came outside and was completely unfazed by the giant white rat. He walked around the pool and headed towards the garage. Yolanda looked through a tiny window at him. He was looking at a sports car. The sports car had writing all over it that told her it was a dog, and a female. "Dog spelled backwards." After admiring the car, Benson got into it. The car roared like a lion and then left the garage at a very fast speed. Yolanda tried to run after them but it was too fast. "Benson! Come back! Governor Gatling needs you!" She entered the house and examined each room. There was nothing she was interested in. Even the food in the kitchen was spoiled. "Benson has an iron stomach!" In the living room, there was an old coo-coo clock. She turned the hands to 12— nothing happened. She hit the clock with her fist and still nothing came out of the little door over the Roman numerals. She became bored with trying to get it to work and went up stairs to the master bedroom, Over a dresser was a huge mirror. She looked into it at her own reflection; a stranger was there. "Who are you? Yolanda? Yolanda is that you? Come back, come back to the land of the living! No! Not yet. They have to be stopped. It's coming, it's coming. I'm not going until I stop them!" She turned away from the mirror and looked around the room. In the closet was a suit and a maid's outfit. "Benson's and Kraus!" On the closet shelves, was a wooden shoebox she took it down and looked in. Inside was a snub nosed 38 hand gun. She felt something loose in her mouth. She spat and little pieces of silver came out of her mouth. A wave of panic came over her. She picked up the gun and pointed it at the mirror. "This will stop the wheel from turning. This will stop them!" She fired a single shot at the mirror and sent millions of reflections of herself scattering around the room.

For about 40 minutes, she sat in a chair, waiting for Benson to come back. The hum of a sports car announced his presence. Yolanda jumped up and ran to the side entrance door. Benson came inside, he was happy and whistling a tune. He didn't see Yolanda off to the side. He went to the refrigerator.

"Now, what can I fix for her in here that's not old and moldy?" he asked.

"Her?" Yolanda wondered. "Who is she?" She thought about the female cast members of the show. It would have to be Gretchen Wilomena Kraus. The starchy uptight German maid who usually exchanged barbs with Benson. "Why does he want to fix her food? He wants to be nice to Kraus? He wants to apologize for being so mean to her. A date? Benson loves Kraus?" That last part of her thoughts was actually said out loud. Benson reacted how you would act if you heard a stranger's voice yell something weird, as you were looking in the refrigerator and had no idea that someone was in your house. If it were possible for him to jump out of his skin, he probably would have. The sounds of his scream told of a desire to do just that. He turned around and looked at her. In his right hand he was holding an old salami, if he could, in his other hand, he probably would have been holding his heart. "Who are you! What are you doing here?" He threw the salami at her, she dunked and then pointing the gun at his head Benson raised both hands. "Okay, okay, everything is cool! I don't have anything! This isn't my house! I'm just visiting! I don't have any money! Take everything you want–burn it down I don't care, it's not my house!"

Yolanda had no idea why he was raising her hand or had a look of fear on his face. She ordered him to shut up and sit down. He looked around for a chair but there were none nearby. He pointed to a wooden one far off to the side. "That one over there?"

She didn't understand why he was pointing at a chair she knew what a chair was. Perhaps he didn't know. She nodded her head 'yes'.

Benson walked over to the chair. He turned it around and sat down. His hands were still raised up over his head.

"Stop praising Jesus!" she yelled.

Benson had a confused look on his face. He lowered his hands. "You mean my hands? Sure, I'll put them down. They were getting tired anyway. So…What do you want? Do you want money? You want food? Please, oh please don't be sex. Who are you, am I under arrest? Are you a cop? You don't look like a cop I'm sorry I'm rambling. I'm nervous and people keep pointing guns at me. Starting to develop a phobia. Is there a phobia named from people who fear having someone point a gun at you? Probably pretty common in some hoods, right?"

Yolanda didn't understand why he was complaining. She was there to help him. Perhaps he was upset with the gun she was pointing at him. "I'm here to protect you, Benson!" she yelled.

"Benson? My names not Benson."

She pointed the gun at him again. "Not Benson? You die now!" She cocked the trigger on the gun.

"Oh! Benson—Yes! I'm Benson, whoever that is—he and I are the same! Me! Benson that's me…Yep! I'll be anything you want me to be! And who are you?"

"I'm nobody! Who are you? Are you nobody too? Then there's a pair of us–don't tell! They'd banish us; you know!"

Benson looked around the room as if he were being filmed. "Uh…come again?"

"What does he mean?" Yolanda wondered. "Where does he want me to go?" "You're asking so many questions, Why? You're just a butler!"

"Butler? I'm not…" Yolanda pointed the gun at him. "Sure, butler, why not! You must be the boss then…The boss…wait! This is your house? OMG! You're that Russian guy's mistress! It all make sense now! You're mad because I broke into your house! Oh my crap! I'm so sorry, I didn't think anyone was living here! There was a note from your boyfriend on the front door saying take every thing and stuff! I had no idea that you would come back—I mean, everyone left town and hand't come back—actually, how did you get back, did they lift the quarantine?"

Yolanda was ignoring his words and concentrating on what he was wearing; a T-shirt with the words "Drink more Ale!" on it and a pair of blue jeans. "Your uniform, where is your uniform!"

"My butler clothes? I don't have anything to wear? Unless… You seriously want me to wear those clothes you had up stairs."

'I Don't like the way he talks! He's constantly questioning your every word!' The voice said. If she wasn't already crazy, this would have driven her over the wall. The only solution her mind told her was to agree to whatever he said. Perhaps then, he would just do what she said without challenging her every word. "Yes—do that!" she yelled. Benson stood up and slowly walked up the stairs. She followed close behind, aiming the gun at him. He went into the upstairs bedroom closet and pulled out the butler's outfit. "Uh, could I have some privacy in here? He suggested."

"The Horror not to be surveyed, but skirted in the dark, with consciousness suspended and being under lock!" she yelled. She didn't know were the words had come from.

Benson had a look that one would give another person if that person were covered in red and yellow paint and had a sign next to them that said: "hot dog." "Almighty then," he said with fear. "I don't know what that means but I'm going to assume it means you'll kill me if I close this door. So, enjoy the show." Benson changed into the butler outfit.

There was a knock on the front door. "Go down!" she yelled. Benson led the way downstairs to the living room. Yolanda peaked through the peep hole on the door. There was a woman standing there. It was Gretchen Wilomena Kraus, the maid from the TV show. "Kaus!" Yolanda yelled. She yanked the door open, fast. Gretchen screamed in surprised. When Yolanda pointed the gun at her, Kraus screamed even louder. *Why is she screaming?* Benson jumped between Kraus and Yolanda:

"Whoa-whoa! Whoa!" Benson yelled. "No need for that! Let her go!"

"Who is that?" Kraus yelled grabbing onto Benson's back. "Way is she pointing a gun at us?"

"I think this is the Russian guys mistress," he answered. "I think she's mad because I was in her house," Benson answered.

Kraus hit Benson on the side of the head. "You idiot! I told you this was a bad idea!"

"Ow! How I'd know she'd come back!"

"Years I had been from home and now, before the door I dared not open, lest a face I never saw before!" Yolanda yelled.

"What-the-crap is she talking about?" Kraus asked.

"No idea," Benson answered. "I think she's a week off her meds."

"Stop talking! Inside!" Yolanda waved them into the house with the gun. They slowly walked inside while raising their hands up. Once inside, she slammed the door closed. Kraus continued to hide behind Benson. *Why is she hiding behind him? Is it because she's naked?'* "Your maid clothes! Where are your maid clothes!"

"What is she talking about, now?" Kraus asked.

"Well, she wanted me to dress up like a butler I guess she wants you to dress up like a maid. I saw some costumes upstairs, I guess the people who used to live here were into some kind of kinky costume play or something so she made me put on this thing, I guess you're next."

"Wait, what?" Kraus asked. "She wants me to cos-play in a sexy maid costume, or are <u>you</u> trying to get me to dress up as a sexy maid and you're using this crazy lady as an excuse to live out your hentai, maid café fantasy?"

"Believe me, my fantasy of having you dress up as a hentai maid does not involve a third party pointing a gun at us…Hey! 'hentai' didn't translate."

"I'm not putting on a kinky costume for anybody—and stop telling me when things don't translate, I know that already!"

"If you don't put on the costume, I'm pretty sure she'll shoot you and put the costume on your corpse."

"Sooo…Where is this costume?"

A short while later, Yolanda sat in the living room with Kraus and Benson. Each wearing their respective costumes. Yolanda dressed in an ill-fitting mens suit and assumed that she must be the character: Clayton Runnymede Edict III, a sort of stuffy antagonist to Benson. She held the gun on them because the voice told her to do so. It also told her to tie them up or they'll fly away. She looked at Kraus. She was both nervous and angry. It was unsure why she was angry but occasionally, she would look at Benson and yell: "Would you stop looking at my boobs!" to which he yelled: "I'm not looking at your boobs!" It must have been hard NOT to look, because the sexy hentai maid café outfit did provide some lift, push and shove in the bust area that would even make a fat man's boobs look sexy. *This is not right! They are laughing at you!* said a new voice in her head. *Kraus has Blonde hair and round eyes, Benson is older. Clayton is a man! This is wrong, this is all wrong!* She tried to silence the voice. "Shut up!" she yelled.

"Who? Me, or her?" Benson asked.

Yolanda ignored him. *This is wrong! Come back Yolanda! Come back…Jolantha! You are Jolantha not Yolanda. Yolanda is a Black woman from Compton, you are a 42 year old White woman from Connecticut! Come back! Let them—*' "Shut up!" she yelled again.

"Don, I'm scared!" Kraus said.

"Don?" Yolanda asked. "Not…Benson?"

"I'll be anything you want, just set the gun down!" Benson said.

Yolanda looked at Kraus. "Your hair…it's black!"

"Don?"

"It's okay, Ami," he said.

"Ami? Don?" Yolanda said feeling dizzy. "Not Benson or Kraus? *It's them! They are trying to trick you. It's the work of the wheel! Kill them now before the wheel consumes you!*"

"So proud she was to die, It made us all ashamed," she said

"What?" Benson asked. "I know that poem...From high school English class...that's Emily Dickinson. I think she's quoting Emily Dickerson," he said to Kraus.

"NOT EMILY! YOLANDA!" She pointed the gun at Kraus and cocked the trigger. "SO SATISFIED TO GO WHERE NONE OF US SHOULD BE!" There was a sound of an explosion and a bright flash. Someone said: "Sorry Miss Ami, I hate to do this, but..." and then there was a sharp pain on the side of her head. All went black.

Sleep...Sleep now.......Sleep Jolantha..................

The coo cook clock on the wall was heard.

In the distance, an alarm screamed. Yolanda awakened, she was flying. No, not flying. She was in the back of the sports car, the convertible roof was down. Her hands and feet were bound by cable. Benson was driving and Kraus was siting next to him.

Kraus was staring up at something. "You okay, Finn?" Kraus asked.

"I feel like a ferret and a mongoose are having a knife fight in my stomach. "G.I. Joe answered. He was sitting next to her, hunched over in pain.

The Wheel was turning, turning around and around. "Because I could not stop for Death, he kindly stopped for me." Yolanda said.

"The carriage held but just ourselves and immortality." Benson added.

Part 10

Dr. Aarti Panjwani, Ph.D.

Aarti laid on the grass and looked up at the ring. "Oh Lewis, why can't you keep your big mouth shut?" she wondered. She put her hands over her eyes, removed them and looked at the ring again. "Still there; still hovering and spinning. No idea how, but it's still doing it. I guess it could be some type of positivity buoyant force at work. But even if it's floating as if it were in water, air has all of those currents so when the wind blows, that thing should be moving around—yet, there it stays. It hasn't moved one centimeter away from it's original position—Agrrgh!" she moaned. "I hate you, space ring! What do you want, and what was The Egg for; was it a beacon of some sort?" She held up her tablet computer and looked at some x-ray photos of The Egg. "It's more like an animal than a machine; maybe that was one of the aliens? An alien that can fly apparently; it's possible. How would an amoeba look at us?"

Her cell phone rang. The caller I.D. told Aarti that it was her mother. She let the voicemail get it. When she was sure the message had been saved, she retrieved it.

"Hello? Aarti?" Her mother's voice said. "Are you there? Aarti? This is your mother calling. Pick up the phone, long distance is expensive. Do you not care about how much money we are spending on you and you aren't answering? Fine, don't answer, I will leave a message. I need for you to give me an answer about your engagement to Aneck. I know you told us a long time ago that you weren't going to follow tradition and live in America but you aren't getting any younger. Aneck is a good man and he owns his own chain of motels in Cleveland. I'm sure with your high-paying professor job, money is not a problem, unlike us–did I tell you we had to sell your pet goat Punjab to pay for this call? Anyway…I know you'd say you will help us but we are the parents, you are the child. We help you and I want to help you get you married. Do that, I can die a happy woman with lots of grand kids…Unless you are already acting like an American veshya and are doing the sex with lots of men and have kids already, then don't call me back— ever! Anyway. I'm sending you a picture of Aneck by e-mail. Your cousin, Ravi works at the call center at the American flag factory in Bombay. He can do all of that computer internet stuff for me. Be sure to call me back and I can start the wedding planning."

The message was ended. Aarti sighed. There was a message from her cousin in Bombay; it told of how her mother wanted him to send her a photo of Aneck. She looked at the attached picture on her smart phone's screen. The photo was of a very attractive Indian male. He looked like a Indian cinema star. "Whoa! Aarti said. "Maybe I should reconsider arranged marriages." She read the text from her cousin Ravi that said: "JK!" Under that, the real picture of Aneck. Instead of a Bollywood star, he was closer to Ganesha the elephant god, not that there's anything ugly about Ganesha but you wouldn't take someone that looked like a blue elephant to the prom.

Her cell phone rang again. It was Professor Pascal.

"Lewis?" she asked.

"Hello Aarti," he said cheerfully.

"Lewis what the devils? What did you do?"

"I got fired, Aarti."

"I know that, I mean why couldn't you hold your tongue?"

"I don't know, Aarti. I guess I just got so sick of them treating this as an opportunity to advance their technology, instead of thinking of it as our first encounter with our brother and sisters from space."

"Lewis, you don't have to over romanticize everything."

"Sorry, I'm a little drunk right now."

"Lewis! Where are you?"

"I'm on a plane."

"To where?"

"Can't tell you."

"Why not?"

"Because I'm pretty sure this conversation is being recorded, right now."

"Don't be so paranoid. Why would anyone record you?"

"I'm quite certain they don't want a person who knows what I know wandering around freely"

"Lewis, if they wanted to record you, why would—"

Aarti's speech was interrupted by a strange sound coming from the phone and a thumping noise followed by a little bit of feedback. "What is…"

A voice interrupted Aarti, again. It wasn't Professor Pascal.

"…Like this?" a man's voice asked.

"I guess," said another voice.

"I can't hear them."

"Did you plug the red cord into the blue input?"

"Oh? I put the red into the red input."

"Oh! No-no-no! If you do that, it reverses the audio and it makes it so that they can hear us instead of us hearing them!"

"Who is this!" Aarti yelled.

"Oh Crap snacks! She can hear us?" yelled the second voice.

"Unplug, unplug!" yelled the first voice. A second later, there was a quick feedback sound and then silence.

"Anyway…" said Professor Pascal. "…They may be recording this conversation."

"I'll take your word for it. But Lewis, are you alright?"

"I feel… feel. I feel lighter."

"Lighter?"

"Yes. That's how I feel. Like I can go and do anything, now."

"But you aren't going to do anything stupid, right?"

"I'm happy, Aarti. I'm not going to do anything to take that away. Don't worry about me."

"But, Lewis. I AM worried about you."

"I know. And I'm sorry. I'm sorry for everything."

"Sorry? What are you sorry for?"

"I'm sorry that I never told you…"

There was a bunch of static on the phone.

"Lewis? Lewis are you still there."

"Is that right?" asked mysterious voice #1.

"No! They can hear you now, unplug!" Yelled voice #2

There was a static feedback sound and then Professor Pascal's voice. "…Never told you that."

"What? Lewis, I didn't hear you, those C.I.A. Guys interrupted."

"You didn't hear me?"

"No, what did you say?"

"Oh…Nothing much, never mind. I'll keep in touch. I gotta go…I think my wing is on fire."

"Lewis, don't wiggle your way out of this one. What did you say?"

"No, seriously. The wing of my plane is on fire."

"Oh, my God! Lewis?"

"Don't worry about me. Just keep working on the project. No matter what happens. Stay in the loop!"

"Lewis, what in God's name is happening?"

"Gotta go."

There was a crackling sound and then silence as the signal went dead.

"Lewis?Lewis!LEWIS!" Aarti dropped to her knees. She felt like she might be going into shock. "Please…Please be all right," she begged.

An alarm went off. It took her a second to acknowledged the sound. She looked around. Soldiers and scientist alike scrambled around the camp site, grabbing equipment and cameras. She remembered what the alarm was. If for some reason, the ring stopped rotating, the sensors would sound the alarms. Whenever it stopped rotating, something always came through it. She looked up at the ring. It was still and the light bending waves had started in the center. She was awakened out of her despair about her friend's possible death and stood up. The same light show took place as when The Egg appeared a week ago. At the end of the cycle when the jellied air stretched through the ring to appear like someone blowing through a bubble wand, it produced yet another bubble which floated from the ring down to the center of town. Even with her binoculars, she couldn't see where it had landed exactly. She grabbed the nearest scientist sitting in the outside office, looking at a computer monitor. "What was it? Where did it go?" she asked him.

"It was another bubble, just like before. It landed in the middle of the city park." On his screen, someone was broadcasting a live video feed of the events in the middle of town. Apparently at this time, there were lots of towns people holding picket signs, some read :NO MORE LOCK DOWNS! They were being held back from the object landing in the background, by armed soldiers.

"Are they there to protest the aliens? How did they know they were coming?" she asked.

The floating bubble landed in the park and like the container for The Egg, dissipated in a shimmer of light. The ring made a moaning sound and then stopped spinning. Sitting still, in the middle of the park was a silvery blue, oval sapped object with a texture like a pine cone. There was a humming sound. The angry crowd of protesters had gone silent. Starting from the top, the object's walls peeled away until they lay flat on the ground, giving the appearance of an unfolded flower. In the middle was a large white sphere, about the size of an exercise ball. A long period of quietness followed. No one made a sound or a move. Off in the distance, there was a clicking sound. On the field, behind the sphere, an outhouse opened and a young man stepped out of it.

"Oh no!" Aarti said. "He's right next to that thing. He could get hurt!" The man looked around and then pointed to the sphere. People started to yell for him to get out of there. He seemed to not be able to understand them. "We got to get him out of there!" She looked over at a tent where some army colonels and captains were watching their own video feed of the events. She ran over to them. "You need to tell General Katz to get that young man out of there, he may be exposed to high doses of radiation or some type of contagion!"

"Don't worry, Professor..."one of the colonels said. "The general has some snipers on the roof ready to take out him OR that balloon thing, if necessary."

"You're going to kill him?"

"If necessary. He makes one wrong move and we'll turn him into a drop and drag."

The young man did a spitting gesture to the side and then, pointed at the sphere. Everyone in the crowd yelled for him to get out of the way. He ignored them and walked over to the sphere. He bent down onto his haunches and grabbed the sphere. Everyone, including Aarti and the soldiers gasped. The young man lifted the sphere up and then let go of it. The sphere didn't fall to the ground and levitated.

"It's floating! It's floating!" Aarti yelled

The young man smiled and laughed. He looked at the crowd again. They all yelled for him to get away from the object. He grabbed the sphere and moved it back onto the center of the . He took a couple of steps back, paused for a second and started running towards it

"Is he going to kick it?" Aarti wondered.

"Drop and drag it is," The captain said.

Part 11

Plürreannedunadugavas

Although the spectrum reading said the atmosphere outside of the ring's boundaries was made up of 78% nitrogen and 21% oxygen, from her view, even without scientific equipment, she could tell years of industrial progression had added high degrees of carbon monoxide and other chemicals to the air. From the transparent wall, she had a nice 360° view of everything. She could see the manicured plant life, indicating an agrarian society, straight paths, and buildings, indicating a structured intelligence. This was what she had wanted. Of the 99 other purges she had gone on, she had never seen a level three society. The timing could not have been more perfect. Her 100th purge on the 100 cycle of her birth; a great way to celebrate. She remembered what her mothers had said. They of course mentioned how proud they were of her but First Mother told her to remember, when she made contact with her first life form under level 5, not to be judgmental. To remember: all life forms are constantly evolving while struggling with a constant feeling of wanting to return back to their evolutionary beginning, before they could float, roll or walk. This land sprawled out before her was major proof of an insecurity in advancement; what society would poison their atmosphere on purpose?

"Bosq?" she asked.

"Yes?" Bosq answered.

She couldn't see Bosq. At this time, no one could see him. She knew he was somewhere in the transport with her, but she was feeling insecure. It was strange for her to feel this way. She has purged to places where the ring's inhabitants were large carnivores or the landscape was a volcano. This landscape was different, it contained aware lifeforms who thought and schemed. This visit could go in any direction at any time. She looked up at the ring. It had stopped it's spinning and glowing. She couldn't see it, but she knew, outside, the ring had cast a bubble around them. She knew, whichever intelligent lifeforms existed on this planet were probably looking up at her and wondering what this silver bubble was which just came out of the ring. "Fear" Her Second Mother said, is one of the 88 emotions that all creatures discovered so far, share.

"Remember: No sudden moves, put the lifeforms at ease and remember who you are and where you came from," she thought.

To ease her nerves, she quietly did some meditative chanting. "Until I reach enlightenment, I take refuge in the spirit. Through the actions of my merits; giving, meditation, patience, effort, concentration and wisdom, may I achieve enlightenment so that I may help all who suffer." She repeated this three times until the lander was 300 feet from the ground. "Definitely level 3," she thought. The little structures–probably buildings, the manicured vegetation around them, the systems of black paths–and, what's this? Little box-like objects traveled along the paths. "Are those the dominant life forms?" she asked Bosq. She could feel Bosq move next to her in order to see what she was looking at.

"Hmmm, unknown…It looks like another creature just came out of it." Bosq and Plür looked at a man exit his Prius. "I guess the creature could be excreting,"

"Walking excrement?"

"It's possible, remember that 3rd place we went to."

"Could be a parasite."

"Possible. There seems to be a lot of them inside the larger creatures."

"A transport vehicle? See, look, those green ones just unloaded a group of the smaller creatures onto that green field."

"I think we're going to land on that green field. The smaller creatures are gathering around our landing site."

"Curiosity! That is one of the 88 emotions!" she said excitedly.

"So the excrement is the intelligent life on this planet?"

"Please do not call them that to their faces."

They slowly came to a rest on the big green field, surrounded by large plants. The creatures which may or may not be excrement, kept their distance. Some of them had matching green skin and held black sticks in their claws. The others were multi-colored except their heads and appendages seemed to come in many shades of orange. The creatures were bipeds. This was another sign of level three intelligence; so many creatures were also bipeds. Plür wished, just once to run into another race that floated besides her and the Aœqé. The bubble around the lander burst and it softly settled onto the green field. The small creatures withdrew briefly. "Fear?" she thought. A good sign but also a bad one if their fear translates into violence. She waited for Bosq's to say all was safe. She heard him walk from one end of their vehicle the other, looking at the lifeforms, checking for small insects on the ground or anything flying in the air. She hoped the intelligent life form were not small insects or bacteria, being destroyed underneath them—You only make that mistake once.

"Look!" Bosq said pointing.

"I can not see you, look where?"

"In the sky."

Plür looked up and saw something flying. It perched onto the large plants. She recognized it. "Is that a bird?"

"I think so, it has feathers."

"It is so…Small."

"I know. How did they evolve so small?"

"Maybe these creatures killed all of the big ones?"

"Aggression? Genocide? Carnivores? Perhaps we should leave?"

"No! We do not know for certain. We will not know until we make contact."

"Are you sure? I don't know if I can protect you if all of those green ones started beating you with those black sticks."

"I trust you...I trust them. Go ahead, unravel the doors."

"Plür, are you sure? I know you're kind of impatient because this is your first level 3, but theres nothing wrong with coming back with a heavier security contingent."

"It is not necessary. If we return with others, it may trigger an attack, then all diplomatic missions would be a disaster. No, go ahead, open the doors." Plür floated to the floor. She was told floating sometimes put biped creatures on edge when they saw her.

Bosq triggered the lander's doors. Starting from the top, the doors peeled away like a large blue-grey banana. The doors kept peeling until they lay flat on the ground, giving the appearance of an unfolded flower. Plür remained still. She knew the creatures could see her now. They talked among themselves and pointed their arms and claws at her. She felt Bosq walking around her and hear the hum of his weapon, ready to force anything that came near, back. "Please do not use it." Plür whispered. "No matter what,"

"Are you sure?" he whispered back.

"Yes...No matter what."

The humming stopped; Bosq turned the weapon off. Moments went by. She stayed still as did the creatures. A bird flew nearby and landed on the field. Plür resisted the urge to say anything about how cute this planet's birds were. There was a clicking sound. She turned around, On the field, behind them, was a large green box. The box opened and out stepped one of the creatures. "Do they live in small structures like that one? A smell floated from the box to her. It was terrible, like sulfur. "Excrement?" she thought. "Is Bosq right about them?" The creature turned, what Plür guessed was its tiny head. "Confusion?" she thought. The other creatures around the field started making noises and gesturing at the smelly one. She couldn't hear what they were saying but, she could pick out a few words like "get" and 'Casper'. This proved they were the dominate intelligent life-forms on the planet; the ring only translated the words of the dominant life forms. She felt a little disappointed. She wished it were the small birds.

"Ooo-kay." The smelly one said. "Okay…That Baboosh burger must have given me more than the runs—I'm hallucinating!" It did a spitting gesture to the side. "Yuck! So much for that." It pointed at Plür, "This?" he asked the yelling crowd.

"What is bur-gur?" Plür thought.

Smelly one walked over to her. She got a better look at it. His flesh was in the light orange-pink tone. The paws were split into five small tentacles. She concluded they were phalanges. It had thick fur on its head, meaning it was some kind of mammal.

It's pink parts disappeared into colored fur. "It is wearing clothes," she figured. "But why; shame, religion?" she wondered. Smelly One bent down onto it's haunches and grabbed her. She heard Bosq step into action and then back away.

"Whoa!" The creature said. The way it said: "whoa" was not in the tone of something that was attacking you, but of curiosity. It felt warm: "Defiantly a mammal" she thought. It let go of her for a second and grabbed her again and squeezed. "It's just curious about me. It's amazing, I've never seen a creature so fearless before," she thought. "It is so unafraid of me, unlike the rest of them. Maybe it is their leader. Maybe that green box was the leader's throne room or something." He lifted her up and then let go of her. She decided to levitate to prevent herself from hitting the ground. If it was as brave as she thought, then her natural form shouldn't scare it.

Smelly one smiled and laughed. "Awesome! What is this? Is this a joke?" It looked at the crowd again. "All right" it said. He grabbed her and moved her back onto the floor of the lander. It took a couple of steps back, paused for a second and started running towards her. In spite of her wishes, she heard Bosq's weapon start up. "Is he going to kick me?" she wondered.

Part 12

Casper Simon Cornbregger

"I am the very model of the major-modern general—" Don sang

"No-no-no!" Casper complained. "I am the very model of a modern major-general, I've information vegetable, animal, and mineral!" he corrected.

Don adjusted his Major-General Stanley hat, made out of newspaper. "Don't be such a perfectionist."

"Hey, if you're gong to do Pirates of Penzance, you have to do it right. Mr. Snedleman, how's the dress coming for Mabel?"

Mr. Snedleman came into the living room. He was one of the remaining neighbors Casper and Don had left in the apartment building who did not escape a while ago. He was a man in his late 60s and could be considered good looking, in that silver-haired fox kind of way. He was carrying a red frilly dress which used to belong to his long deceased husband, a former actor in off-off-off Broadway plays. "Does this work?" he asked Casper.

"I'm not sure, does it fit?"

"What, me? You want me to play Mabel?"

"Of course, I'm playing the Pirate King and Sergeant of the Police, Don is Frederic and Ruth. We can't sing all of the parts."

Casper and his companions were all dressed in makeshift costumes for their upcoming roof-top production of the Pirates of Penzance. Their downstairs neighbor, Howard something-or-another (Casper never could remember his last name) a gaunt, red headed White man in his 30s (By White I mean caucasian, not white as a ghost), was busy creating a backdrop and lighting using cardboard and house lamps. After a week of being cooped up, Casper and the other residents needed something to stimulate and pre-occupy their minds at the same time. There was only so much TV, music, porn, FPS video games or checkers you can take, in 80 or so hours of lockdown.

Across the street, another lock-down victim; Mr. Cane, a 42 year-old African American gentleman wearing a wife-beater shirt, yelled to the group: "Hey! What time is the show?"

"In a minute, Mr. Cane!" Don yelled. We need to figure out who's going to play Kate!"

"I could do it!"

"But you're across the street!"

"I could yell my songs: TAKE ANY HEART BUT MINE! TAKE ANY HEART BUT MINE!" he sang, or rather, bellowed.

"Okay, Mr. Canes, you're hired!"

"Let me go put on a dress!"

"Don't you go touching my dresses!" His wife Laverne could be heard yelling.

The production was right on schedule; it was almost curtain time, but the show they were going to be putting on was delayed by a strange rumbling sound. It was a deep, choppy and thunderous like the air was being cut.

"What the French is that?" Casper asked. "The army copters coming to tell us to get off the roof, again?"

"Look, over there!" Don yelled pointing in the direction of the baseball field in the park.

Over the trees and eventually over the buildings, rose an orange plum of smoke and a streaming ball of fire.

"What's that, a missile?" Casper asked.

A flaming projectile rose and headed to the center of the ring. When it reached the middle, where so many helicopters have tried to escape and were bounced back like toys, it disappeared. The area where it had vanished resembled a pebble drop in a pool of mercury. A quick whale moan sound followed shortly. The ring glowed for five seconds and then returned to normal.

"Well…that was different," Casper said.

From across the street, the song: *Poor Wand'ring* was being sung.

In the early hours, after the blue light of morning had filled the streets. Casper was awakened by a megaphone announcement being broadcast out of the window of an FEMA SUV: "Attention citizens of Pepper Mill, shelter-in-place is officially over. You may return to your lives and jobs. All food service employees please report to work for food distribution. All those without lives and jobs, please be more productive."

Casper woke Don up with the words "We're free!" They got dressed as fast as they could. They were sick of being in this apartment building, they had explored very part of it including the apartments which were vacant. Not many interesting things were found, except in apartment 2A; the chalk outline on the floor of where a body used to be and a spray painted swastika on the living room wall along with the words 'We'll be back!'

When Casper was tying his shoes, the front door was unlocked and Ami walked inside. It was a joyous and loud reunion. The last time they had seen her was when she was escorting Finn back to his base. They had no idea where she was or even if she was safe. She and Casper hugged but didn't break the five second rule. What's the five second rule, you ask? Or maybe you don't care to know. Maybe you like to blindly meander along through life not learning anything, considering education a distraction from your religion or a liberal plot to allow gays to marry farm animals…The five second rule, being applied in this situation, unlike the one where you drop food on the floor and think it's still safe as long as you pick it up before five seconds, which is odd by the way because I have yet to see a germ, wearing a watch, shooing away other germs from the food saying: "Not yet guys, it hasn't been five seconds yet!" No, this is the five-second "hug" rule. It states if you hug someone and it's been over five seconds, you are now expected to kiss them on the cheek, even if it's between two straight guys. This is why straight guys show affection by punching each other instead of hugging. It's a warning, like saying: 'If our sports team scores a basket-touch-field-down-goal-murder thingy and we hug for more than five seconds, I'll have to kiss you and then possibly hit you to regain my standing as the Alpha.' So, as I was saying, Casper gave Ami a 4.35 second hug. But Don, gave her one for 7.48 seconds. There was no indication that she had a problem with this and when they pulled away from each other, there was this awkward moment when they looked at each other. It was like there was a question of 'Are you going to kiss me or not?' No kisses were exchanged but Don did give her a quick double back pat, like two guys would do and Ami leaned on his shoulder for one second, venturing into another rule's territory: the one-second plutonic cuddle.

"Where have you been?" Casper asked her.

"At a camp site and then the high school."

"You were staying at the high school?"

"Yeah, the army moved in there and converted it into a base. They put cots and stuff in the class rooms and they already had: a cafeteria, the showers, and all the other things already there-so it was easy to convert."

"But why were you there? Why didn't Finn take you home?"

"It was all shelter-in -place stuff. They wouldn't let us leave the grounds—by us, I mean the civilians who also got trapped there."

"You spent the entire week inside a tent?"

"I got to go out…But I can't talk about it."

"What? You saw something weird, didn't you? Did they tell you about that big bubble light show that I saw before they told everybody to go home?"

"I…I'm not allowed to talk about it."

"Ami-chan? What do you know?"

"Casper, seriously, If I talk about it, it could get me kicked off the medical team, and maybe jail time. I'm not sure."

"Hmmm, how interesting that the Queen of Conspiracy Theories is now part of one. I don't know what you guys are covering up, but I'm going to find out. I saw something that looked like a silver bubble come out of that ring and land somewhere in the park; was it an alien spaceship?"

Ami remained silent and looked around the messy living room. Pizza boxes, clothes and remnants of their production of the Pirates of Penzance littered the floor. "Holy crap pile, look at this place! You guys made such a mess when I was gone!" She picked up a pool cue and used it to lift up a pair of underwear. "You guys are like raccoons–in pants!"

"Don't try to change the subject!"

"Seriously, this place looks like the cover of Hoarder magazine."

"Hey, we were trapped all week in here, we got cabin fever," Casper complained.

"Cabin ebola," Don corrected.

Ami reached down and picked up a magazine. On the cover was a half-dressed Japanese girl, straddling a giant stuffed panda, underneath the words: Nippon Nerd Gals "What the? And hentai magazines?"

Don grabbed the magazine and threw it out the front window. "How'd did that get in here? Hey, Nippon and hentai, didn't translate!"

"Now who is changing the subject?" Ami complained "I swear, I can't leave you for…"

Ami's complaint was interrupted by the sound of a car outside screeching and then a thump. "What was that?"

Casper looked out of the open window. "All I see is Finn limping across the street, go figure."

"What's he doing here, is he stalking you?" Don complained

"He was giving me a ride from the base," Ami said rolling her eyes in the literal sense, otherwise what a Japanese horror movie that would be if she really rolled them towards Don.

"Does that mean you spent the entire week with Finn?"

"He was around a lot but we weren't in the same class."

"You can say that again!"

"Oooh, social snap!" Casper said

"You know, if I didn't know better, I'd swear you were jealous," Ami said poking Don.

"And why would I be jealous?"

"I don't know, you tell me!"

A thought went through Casper's head: "Tell her, you idiot!"

Don didn't say anything. Instead he grabbed his jacket and started to head out. "The only thing I'm jealous of, is that you and Army Boy doing the in-and-out all week."

"Huh?" Ami said.

Don got the sexual double entendre and corrected himself:

"You guys got to leave your building and go anywhere you want while us regular folks got stuck in here putting on roof-top productions of the Pirates of Penzance."

"Oh my God!" Ami said. "I love the Pirates of Penzance! I wish you would do Mikado so I can be Yum-Yum."

"Well, the next time we're trapped inside, we'll keep that in mind–anyway, it sucks being trapped like a convict all week! I'm so sick of this apartment! If I spend one more day in here, I'm going to pop!"

"Are you saying you're going to move out on us?" Ami looked like she was about to burst into tears.

"I'm saying I'm sick of living inside this apartment, if you want to help me find a new place to live then you are welcomed to join me. If you want to stay here, then you're on your own!"

"And where are you planning to live?" Casper asked.

"I don't know, I'm sure there are plenty of vacancies; half the people beat it out of town, I'm sure I'll find something."

"That's actually not a bad idea," Casper said.

"What are you talking about?" Ami protested. "Even if you find a place, where are you going to find the landlord? Ours is in jail, who knows where the rest are."

"Rent?" Don laughed. "Who says we have to rent another apartment. There are plenty of abandoned houses in town."

"What are you going to do? Break into someones house and take it? Isn't that like stealing?"

"Not if they abandoned it," Casper said.

"What? Casper? You too?" Ami complained.

"I'm with him," he said. "I can't spend another week in this 1000 foot box. I am seriously considering sleeping outside, tonight."

"That's two for new place—Ami?" Don gestured at Ami.

"I don't know, Don," she said sullenly. "It doesn't seem right to take someone's house without their permission."

"Is this some kind of Japanese thing?"

"Why does it always have to be a Japanese thing when it goes against your beliefs? Are American values all about dirty, girly magazines, pirate operas and pillaging?"

"Yeah, pretty much, nailed it," Casper said.

"No" Don said, "but it'll be nice if you considered MY feelings for once and stopped assuming I'm always wrong!" Don stormed out of the apartment and headed downstairs.

Ami plopped down on the couch and sulked. "lately I can't talk to him any more without getting into an argument."

"I wonder why that is?" Casper said sarcastically. He rolled his eyes and spotted a pizza crust which had been thrown onto the ceiling.

"Huh-what? What did I say?"

"It's what you two aren't saying," he thought. Casper patted her on the head and headed out the door. "I'm going to go to work for a few hours." He looked back at Ami. "We really missed you Ami-chan…Both of us." He left and quietly closed the front door.

Stepping outside was like breathing fresh air which had been infused with peppermint. Sure, he and Don were able to go onto the roof whenever they were sure the military wouldn't force them back inside, but this was a truer freedom. The streets were packed full of citizens coming and going. When he walked by the park, he saw the mayor standing on some milk crates and giving a question and answer session in front of a crowd of 48 people and the statue of Sacajawea.

"…I'm going to ask the head of the military about that later," the mayor answered. "I have no interest in being locked up for another week." Some people in the crowd grumbled their approval of frustration.

"Why are we still here?" A guy wearing a baseball cap asked. "And what the heck was that thing that shot up into the ring last night?"

The mayor paused. "I…I'm not allowed to talk about that." This time the grumbles were of disapproval. The mayor held up her hands. "I'm meeting with the general this afternoon and I'll discuss the lockdown situation."

"No more lock downs!" Someone yelled. Everyone cheered.

"Yes," the mayor said. "I will be discussing the possibility of no more lockdowns. Until then, go about your business."

"When are we going to get some answers?"another person yelled.

"I'll let you know by 4:00. Meet me back here. I promise, I'll get you some answers." The meeting ended with a combination of cheers and mumbles.

Casper had no faith the mayor would return with any answers. He saw the thing that came out of the ring last week and he saw the thing that went back through it. Why would the people in charge tell them anything? He looked up at the ring. It spun in its usual spot, as if nothing unusual had happened. In spite of his scientific curiosity, Casper was starting to resent the ring. Not for landing over their town and changing the citizens, but for the way the humans were processing all of the ring's actions with lock downs and cover-ups. If indeed the military was blocking their internet and telephone service, it was unfair of the people in charge to be hoarding so much information which affects them all.

He started to skateboard to his job. "What were things like for the Native Americans when Columbus first arrived?" he thought. "Probably the first thing that happened was them saying, 'Hey, idiot, we're not Indians and this ain't India.' But Columbus didn't secretly communicate with the natives and then sneak off. It wouldn't make sense to travel 500 light years on Alien tax dollars and then sneak quietly into a small country town and talk to a small handful of people. If I went through so much trouble to get to another planet, I want a welcome committee waiting for me with bouquets of space flowers and a group of space cheerleaders with the word 'welcome' painted on their bellies."

The field, where he guessed the bubble had landed and later, the missile had taken off was stripped of any evidence that something had happened there. There was one army soldier, carrying some tent poles away. On the field, two civilians had already started playing a game of catch with a baseball. "I'm glad they can enjoy themselves," Casper said. "While the rest of us have no idea what's going on." He took out his cell phone and checked to see if he had a signal; it didn't. He wondered what his mom was doing right now. Did the government tell them they were okay? Would his mom push for more information or be satisfied with not hearing from her kid for week? He held his phone up higher and wondered if he could get a better signal if he went to the edge of town. He made a mental note to do this later.

As he had expected, there was a huge crowd outside the grocery store. A week without shopping presented many shortages in many refrigerators and pantries. People bought large bags and boxes to fill up. Casper knew this was a mistake for them. If they sold these people gallons of this and cases of that, what would the rest of the town have? All items were being regulated. It didn't matter how rich you were, or in one person's case: "Can I have more than one box of cereal if I sleep with you?" Being a man, which are genetically, 18-50% pig, Casper considered it for a second. He dismissed the bribe of the attractive woman in a low-cut red dress, as a Freudian joke. In case you didn't know what that was, a Freudian Joke is a serious statement said and then explained that the speaker was only joking and wasn't serious. For example: "Sure, you can borrow my Lamborghini, but if you get a scratch on it, I'll erase you like a cartoon doodle of genitalia on the Declaration of Independence." If you think this threat was a joke, then you're sadly mistaken. If you were to damage that car, the next words out of the owner's mouth will be: "You don't even know you're already dead." So yes, In exchange for a box of sugary carbohydrates, Casper had a shot with this woman, but since she had given him this proposition in front of Darla and Sue, Casper decided to maintain his reputation as a "good" pig.

It was good to see Darla again. During the break, she had been locked up in her apartment by herself. "How did you keep yourself from going bonkers, day after day?" Casper asked.

"Remember that expensive tequila I bought?" she asked Casper. He nodded yes. "Whelp, it takes a week to finish it."

"You were drunk the whole week?"

"I'm still drunk. I wasn't sure if we were going to go back on lock-down. It's amazing how time flies when you have no idea what time actually is."

"Wow…" Casper thought. "…she a professional." A part of him felt sorry for her. Having her loved one abandon her in town and then forced to spend the whole week alone in her apartment. His thoughts drifted back to their near kiss. She had joked it off once the ring started acting up; Freudian joke?

He continued to ring up peoples purchases. The internet and telephones were down but the credit card machines were working. Casper sighed at this frustrating support of commerce and lack of support for the freedom of information. A light bulb appeared over his head, well, not a real light bulb but the metaphor for when someone gets an idea: "What if you could somehow communicate with the outside world using the same lines of communication that the ATMs and credit card machines were using?" He had zero computer skills to do this but he wondered if Don could do it. He added another mental note to try this later. As Casper and Sue frantically rang up hundreds of people, Sue was keeping tabs on how much each of the customers were buying, using a lap top with the names and addresses of every remaining citizen in town. On the sides of Sue, keeping the peace, were two armed soldiers. Casper had yet to know their names. They always appeared bored. Obviously, watching people shop was far less invigorating than shooting radical Islamist at Disney Land, Iraq. Whenever anyone would question the rationing system or say anything remotely troublesome, the men would spring into action with a "move along" or a "is there a problem over here?" Casper looked at Sue. Sue seemed to love it. It was like Big Red was being run the way a grocery store was supposed to be run: a monopoly on products, low overhead and armed guards to keep out the riff raft. Speaking of riff raft, Baboosh was next in Casper's line.

"I felt like I've just been insulted from someone," he said.

He was buying some steaks. A strange smell caught Casper's nose and he realized it was coming from one of the packages of meat. "Eww-hey, Baboosh, I think one of your steaks has gone bad. You may want to replace it with a new one."

"Really?" Baboosh said, sniffing the cuts of dead cow's belly. "Can I get a discount, then?"

"What? You're still going to eat that?"

"Of course, if I get a discount."

Only your life span will be discounted."

"Cornbregger! What's the hold up?" Sue yelled.

"Baboosh wants to get a discount on this bad steak."

"What-ever, give it to him! We gotta keep the line moving! We got at least 80 more people in line, here!"

Casper shrugged his shoulders and rang up Baboosh's purchase. The ringing and crowds continued to be exhaustive. When he looked at the clock he realized he had not only skipped his morning break but he had overshot his lunch break by two hours. He bought this fact up with Sue. "Hey, Sue, I think I'm going to take a lunch break."

"Later," Sue said. "We have to get this crowd down!"

It was then that Casper realized the crowd was never going to go down. There was always at least 100 people in line. "The crowd hasn't gone down in hours, it's never going to go down."

"Sure it will, by the end of the day, it should be less people."

"You mean when it's time to go home?"

"What do you want me to do, Cornbregger? If you go on break, it's just going to be me and Darla. Do you want that?"

"No, but I'm not going to work eight hours straight without taking a break."

"You can break when the crowd goes down."

"I see that we've returned to that circular fallacy. Sue, it's not going to go down. We need to take breaks, it's in the Constitution, I think."

"Just man up and grow a pair, Cornbregger! We don't have the work force to be taking breaks!"

"Here's an idea: We close the store down for 45 minutes, then we can all take a break."

"No way! We can't force people to wait outside while we go out for lunch!"

"Well, I can." Casper cut off the register light. "Sorry folks, this lane is closed." There was a huge groan of anger from the 40 people in his line. Someone yelled "come on!" another yelled mother-something or another.

Sue had a look on her face as if someone had taken all of her shoes and filled them with spaghetti. "What? Where are you going?"

"To lunch," he answered, heading for the front door. There was a gnawing guilt in his gut. It was a mean thing to do, leaving all of those customers to suffer in line but he knew that if he didn't take a stand, now, then when would he? Sue was in Big Red customer service mode but this was a different era. He wasn't working because he was afraid of being fired, he was working because the head of FEMA said it would be a good idea to help out at the store, while they waited to be released from the quarantine. "Casper!" Sue yelled.

"Back in 45 minutes!" he yelled and went outside. He made it to the middle of the parking lot. There were more citizens queuing up to buy supplies. The feeling of guilt made him stop and think about going back, for any other reason, to help his friend Darla. He began to turn his body back towards the store.

"Casper!" Darla yelled from the front entrance.

"Oh great..." he thought, "...she's coming to make me feel like Captain Crap for abandoning her." "Okay-okay!" he yelled. "I'm coming back, I won't take a break! I'll work until I spit blood and pass out. Just throw some dirt on my corpse at the end of my shift and say a quick eulogy!"

"Dude, what are you talking about?"

"Aren't you here to drag me back?"

Darla looked confused. "Uh-no. I'm gonna go to lunch, too."

"Oh," Casper said confused. "What about Sue?"

"She's fine. She's trying to drag the army guys onto the registers."

"I see. We've been replaced—that was easy."

"I think one of them was a cashier before he was sent to Afghanistan."

"Probably a prerequisite."

"So, where are you headed?"

"Me? Are you coming with me?"

"Yes, I told you I was coming with you."

"Oh, I thought you mean't lunch at the same time."

"No, together."

"Like a date?"

"NO!" Darla yelled "I mean—no! It's not a date. Just us having lunch together!" Darla started to ramble. "What's the big deal! It's just us having lunch together, it's not like we're about to get married or something—"

"Okay, okay!" Casper interrupted. "It's just lunch, Darla." He raised an eyebrow and thought about the near kissing incident on the night the ring was active. "Why can't I ever date a normal girl?" he thought.

Le restaurant du choix for eating downtown was The Pepper Grind which was now featuring something called a Baboosh burger. It was advertised as a burger with plenty of character, aged just like a fine wine to bring out all of it's true potential. Casper expressed reservation about eating any steak from Baboosh after witnessing the buying of bad steak earlier. Darla used some illogic to convince Casper that they were eating a ground-up hamburger, not a whole steak and therefore, instead of eating 100% of bad steak, they were eating 1% of bad steak, ground up with 99% other cows. While she was explaining this, Casper had discovered that she was wearing a low-cut shirt and he could see the mole on top of her left heaving bosom. Nonetheless, he was hypnotized by radiating cleavage protons. At that time, he could be tricked into eating a dead mouse, still in a mouse trap, between two pieces of moldy bread and not notice—speaking of which, that's exactly what that hamburger tasted like, except inject the word "maggots" into the sentence.

"Alcohol will make it better," he thought. "Alcohol-make-anything-better." He sucked down a $25 bottle of beer (sold to him for $5). He made the mistake of taking a second bite of the burger. Beer had not made it better. If possible, he felt like his teeth were trying to eject the burger and spare the tongue any harm. Casper bit on something hard and pulled it out of his mouth, Upon closer examination he discovered it was a bullet. "What the? Why is there a bullet in my burger?" he complained.

"Gotta kill it some how." Darla answered

"Baboosh!" Casper yelled. Why is there a bullet in my hamburger?"

"Oooh. Mr. Casper. You er-ah got the "special" burger. In Yakistan, we hide a bullet in our meals and whomever gets it, get's a prize."

"What? Really? What do I get?"

"You…You get to keep the bullet."

Casper shrugged his shoulders and put the bullet into his shirt pocket. "How about you, Darla, how's your salad?"

"It's a little burned."

"Burned? A salad? Is that even possible?"

"I know, right? Baboosh is like the Escoffier of Bizzaro world!" Darla had a look of distress on her face.

"What is it?"

"I think my food had a bullet in it too…" She put her finger in her mouth, pulled something out and showed Casper some tiny pieces of metal.

"That's not the same color. That's more silver."

Darla Looked at it. "O-M-G. I think I must have broken a filling on his food! She rubbed her finger in her mouth. "Can't feel where it is. Can you see it? Probably one of the bottom wisdom teeth." She opened her mouth, wide.

Casper looked in. He didn't see a hole or any other place where a crown would have been. "You don't have any fillings back there."

"What are to talking about, Cornbregger? I've had like a billion dollars of dental work back there."

Casper looked in her mouth again. "Well, they did a good job because I can't tell where any work was done. You have perfect teeth back there."

Darla picked up a large spoon and used it as a mirror to look in her own mouth. She moved her finger around her back teeth. "Goly gfhit! Guy hucking geeth grew gack!"

"What? Take your finger out of your mouth and say that again."

"I said my wisdom teeth grew back. I had my cavities drilled and filled and now it's just regular teeth."

Casper checked his wisdom teeth. He had gotten similar dental work done on his own. There was no change. "Mine are the same, for now. Guess it's like the scars and tattoo thing—new, repaired teeth. Maybe the aliens are tattoo hating dentist."

"Just in time to protect us from Baboosh and his bullet burgers." Darla admired her regenerated molars by holding up two spoons,

"And we have to live with his cooking for as long as we're stuck here."

"How long do you think it'll be before they let us out?"

"No idea. I don't see anybody dying of an alien disease, yet"

"I guess we can just sneak out."

"Maybe. I personally am in no hurry to leave."

"Are you kidding? Don't you want to see what's going on in the outside?"

"I'm pretty sure everyone on the outside is talking about how much they wish they could be here, with front row seats to a UFO."

Darla looked through the window as if she could see the ring from her seat inside the restaurant; she could not. "What do you think they want?"

"No idea, same as what you would want if you traveled 45 thousand light years just to come here: A chance to say howdy, start trading beads for land?"

"Or eat our brains."

"Everyone's so obsessed about the 'evil' alien invaders that they can never imagine an actual positive scenario. If it wasn't for all of that stupid, commie paranoia in the 1950's, who knows what people could have accomplished. Even today, every time there's a sci-fi movie, you got to stick an ugly evil villain in it. It's just fueling people's xenophobia of anyone that's different from them."

"Okay, Michael Moore. you've made your point. But isn't there anything you miss doing, before that thing showed up?"

Casper thought for a second. "You know, it's funny, but all of the things I can think of that I missed doing were all indoor activities: The internet, cable TV–that kind of stuff. And now that we don't have those things, I started reading more, getting out of the house—at least when we're not on lock down. It's like I'm more active in this tiny little world than I was in the big one.

Darla put her head into her hands: "I'm just sick of seeing this town. I'm used to touring with my band–who I'll never see again. I want to go to the mall, in a big city–and I hate malls. I miss my alcoholic dad and my credit card identity theft, mom. I miss taking long walks in the woods, looking at nature and setting things on fire—don't you?"

"You had me until the fire part."

"But don't you miss walking in the woods?"

"Sure, but we have some woods here."

"Woods we can't get to."

"Well, from what I can tell, the army won't let us go outside the ring, That thing stretches from the lake shore to the edge of Nowhere mountain–plenty of hiking places."

"Where did you like to go?"

"Me? I like to walk along the river's edge where my dad and I used to hunt for crayfish."

"There are crayfish, in California?"

"There were when I was a kid. Not so much now, but you never know."

"Let's see if we can find one!" Darla said, excitedly.

"What? When?"

"Right now."

"Darla, we have to be back at work in five minutes."

"Oh BFD!"

"Berkeley Fire Department?"

"No! I mean who cares, Sue and the grunts can ring people up for a few extra minutes."

"I guess…Okay, let's do it," Casper said, exhilarated.

After a 20 minute walk, the two ended up not only by the path along the river's edge, but also the edge of where the ring hovered overhead. They made it a point not to go beyond the ring for respect of the military orders, about them being infected with something, and the fact that they didn't want to be shot with a fire ant bazooka. Looking at all of the wild flowers, picking a couple of blackberries and listening to the sounds of the water flowing by, created a mini vacation for Casper. He didn't know why he hadn't done this earlier. They walked along, looking for a good place to go down to the river's shoreline. Every area they saw was a little too treacherous. One area was just plain gross and even contained an old rotted cow skull. Casper insisted they continue walking until they could find an area less dangerous and disgusting. He looked over at Darla. She slowly crushed a California Poppy in her hand (which may be illegal) and looked down. She smiled slightly and seemed to be thinking of something. "What is it?" he asked her.

"Oh, nothing," she answered. "I'm just thinking, it's funny how things work out."

"What things?"

"How we both get quarantined in this town, together."

"Yeah. It does make it easier that your friends are with you."

"Yeah, friends…Right," she said a little sad.

"What does she mean?" Casper thought. "Is she saying we're more than friends, did I just miss a romantic chance?" He reached down and picked up a pine cone. He threw it at the river and looked away. The pine cone bounced off the force field and hit him on his neck. "What the!" he complained. He looked back in the direction of the river. A squirrel was sitting on a branch in that same direction, eating an acorn. "That squirrel just threw a pine cone at me!"

"Don't worry, I got it." Darla said picking up another pine cone. She threw it at the squirrel, it hit him and sent it flying off the cliff with a squealing complaint. "Yeah, that's right!" she yelled "Tell your friends!"

"Wow," Casper said. "Er-Thanks?"

"No problem; freak'n <u>hate</u> nature!"

"Wait, what? You don't like being out here with me?"

"Uh, no, this is fine. I like being here with you. I just prefer the city life, you know?"

"Right, you said you missed that kind of stuff."

"Yeah." Darla looked away from Casper.

Casper wondered why she had become silent. "Feel bad about hitting the squirrel?"

"Huh, no! I was just thinking of something."

"Things that you missed."

"Something like that."

Casper sat on a large rock. Darla sat down next to him. He looked at the ring above, silently rotating. Would it really be so bad if they just left the town for a little bit. Sure they may be carrying an alien diseases but so far, it didn't seem harmful in the least. Perhaps it would be a good thing for everyone in the world to be infected with a virus that get's rid of ugly tattoos, let's you watch Spanish television and repairs old dental work. He looked over at Darla. She appeared very sad. She was definitely having a bad time with the quarantine. He wished there was some way he could make her feel better. He walked over and grabbed her hand. "Hey," he said. She turned and looked at him. "Buck up little cowgirl, it ain't that bad."

"What?"

"Being trapped in this town, it ain't so bad, still got your friends."

"Friends. Right, just friends."

"What, we aren't friends any more?"

Darla sighed. "Maybe I want more."

"More of what?"

"Everything." She squeezed his hand and looked at him in the eyes.

"Is she talking about a relationship?" Casper wondered. "Should I try to kiss her again?" He grabbed her other hand and decided to play it safe in case he was reading her incorrectly "Don't worry, we'll get out of here. Then you can have all the things you want again."

"Not everything I want is out there."

"That's true. Won't find hamburgers with bullets in them at McDonalds."

Darla laughed and nudged closer to Casper. He put his hands on her shoulder. "But seriously, I am not the most optimistic person in the world. But I know nothing last forever. Good or bad. Look at the universe. Far as we know, this could be it's millionth time around, maybe it's been expanding and contracting forever. A new you and me created over and over."

"What are you talking about?"

"Some people think the universe is static—you know, standing still. Others that it's expanding because the light from the stars look like they're getting further away. But some think that if you were getting sucked towards the center of something, the only reason stuff looks like it's getting further away is because you're being sucked in and everything that hasn't gotten affected is actually just waiting in line."

"I wish I understood what you're talking about, some times."

"I basically like the idea that the entire universe feels the way we do."

"How's that?"

"The way we—humans want to be together, always pretending like we're drifting further and further apart." He clasped his hands together. "But actually we're all being drawn together until one day BOOM!" He moved his hands apart. "Another big bang."

"Then we'll be drifting apart from each other again."

"Then we wait billions of years until we come together again, again and again." He bought his hands back together.

Darla gave him a look, the same one she had when they were on the bleachers about to kiss. Casper took the opportunity to move in for a kiss. She looked at him and closed her eyes. He was about to close his until he saw something.

Someone familiar was waving at them from across the river. "I think I know that guy." Casper turned his head away from Darla.

"What, seriously, now?" Darla said before she opened her eyes. She angrily looked across the river at the man waving his arms.

Casper stood up and yelled "Hey!" back at the man. "Is that Professor Pascal?" he wondered. "What would he be doing here? Oh crap! I think I just ruined the kissing scene with Darla." He looked down at the angry Darla which coincidentally, was the name of her first rock band.

"Mr. Cornbregger!" The man yelled.

"Professor Pascal?" Casper yelled back.

"Are you all right?"

Casper was unsure how to answer that question. They were alive, so he guessed that was a good enough answer. He looked at Darla. "It's my own Astronomy professor." He looked back at the professor. He looked a little sad as if Casper and Darla were supposed to be dead. "...Sure, why wouldn't we be?" Casper yelled.

"The ring?" Pascal pointed upwards to the ring.

"Yeah, it's giving us super powers and stuff but nothing bad."

"Super powers?" Professor Pascal paused for a second. "Is there any thing you want me to do for you?"

This was a good opportunity to communicate with the outside world. Casper wondered how much everyone knew about what was going on. He wanted to put his mother at ease. "Can you tell my mom that I'm all right?"

The professor looked down at the river without speaking.

Casper and Darla looked at each other as if asking: "What's wrong with Professor Pascal?"

"Professor?" Casper yelled.

"Do I have her contact information?" he yelled.

"Yes," Casper yelled. "It's in my list of emergency contacts."

"I'll do whatever I can. Meet me here next Friday at this time. I wish to know what it's like on the inside."

"No problem. Thanks!"

"No...Thank you. The professor picked up a pine cone. "Mr. Cornbregger!" he yelled.

Casper and Darla looked puzzled. "Yes?" Casper prepared to catch the pine cone if it was thrown at him.

Pascal threw the pine cone. It bounced off the forcefield and returned back to the professor's hand.

"Wait, what?" Casper was shocked.

Professor Pascal walked away.

"Did that pine cone just bounce off of something?" Darla asked.

Casper picked up a rock. He tossed it at the force field. It returned and hit him on the leg. "Ow! No freak'n way!" He picked up a stick, another rock and a tin can. Every time he threw them, each returned and hit him. He thought back to the incident with his bike and his landlord. "There was no trip wire! He ran his bike into an invisible wall!"

Darla stared at the invisible wall (which is illogical). She took a step back and sprinted towards the field. When she hit it, instead of bouncing, she came to a halt and slowly slid down into the river below. She came to a rest, knee deep in water "Ow!" she said rubbing her nose. She walked back to shore. Casper reached down his hands and pulled her back up.

"Are you alright?"

"Yeah, I thought I would bounce back and it would be fun like jumping in a bouncy house. Instead it was like hitting the <u>wall</u> of an inflatable bouncy house."

Caper looked up. "That's why they won't let us leave, it's because we can't! My landlord hit this wall on the way out of town, when he stole my bike!"

"Are you saying we're trapped?"

"That's exactly what I'm saying."

"That's just great! This is wonderful! I was looking forward to when the quarantine broke, but there is NO quarantine! This is a prison! I'm stuck in this stupid little town!" Darla picked up a bunch of leaves and sticks and threw them at the field, it all bounced back and sprayed her in the face. "Son of a–why does crap fly back at us and I didn't!" She was visually upset.

Casper wanted to comfort her but he was upset as well. Who was going to comfort him? No wonder the professor looked so distressed. No wonder the military was keeping them from the border, no wonder their internet and phones don't work. "No wonder, no wonder!" he thought. He was angry. It was one thing to want to be in the same town with a UFO, but it was another to be forced to. Suddenly, the ring didn't seem so innocent. Now, it was aggressive. "What are we going to do?" he asked.

"What do you mean what are we going to do?" Darla yelled. "You're the scientist? You tell me? There's a force field around the town, how do we get through?"

"I'm sure the government and military have been working on this since they discovered it."

"Seriously? You trust the military and the government to get us out of here?" Darla yelled again.

Casper was a little scared. Not from being trapped in the town, but by Darla's panic attack. He walked over and grabbed her. "Don't worry, Darla. We'll find a way out of this. Nothing last forever, remember."

"How can you be so calm? There's an alien ship holding us hostage! God knows why? Food? Our brains? Our women? Maybe they want to impregnate all the women in town with chest busting aliens!"

"Darla! No one travels a trillion miles just to eat everything in site and then go home…Except people from Minnesota…and barbecue."

"Tell that to those sailors that ate up all of the Dodo birds! Face it Cornbregger, we're toast! English style toast with some disgusting human meat on it and a side of peas! Do you want to know what the peas represent, Casper, DO YOU?"

Casper hugged her. "Calm down, Darla, you're scaring me waay more than the aliens. We have to figure out what to do."

"We can't do any thing!"

"Not without help, we have to tell everybody."

"What good would that do, everyone will just freak out like us!"

"Like you…Yes. But the more people that know about a problem, the more answers you get for solving it."

"But you said every brainiac in the world has been working on this thing."

"Those people are working on the outside. Maybe the forcefield is weaker on the inside, we don't know until we try to get everyone together in here, trying to break through from this side."

His words seem to calm Darla down a little. "Who do we tell?"

"Everyone, but we'll have to start at the top. The mayor, that General Cat guy, Earl and Clem? Anyone who'll listen. The mayor said she was going to have a town meeting by 4, that'll be a great place to start, right?"

"I guess."

"Good enough. Let's go find the mayor!"

"What about work? We were supposed to be back like 30 minutes ago?"

"Darla I don–"

Before he could finish, Darla broke into laughter. "Got ya!"

"Good one, Darla…jokes. Jokes are good in a stressful situation."

Caspar and Darla ran to the center of town. The closer they got, the more people they noticed holding picket signs. Words like: NO MORE LOCKDOWNS and LET US LEAVE TOWN! Were among the messages.

"What is this some sort of protest?" Darla asked.

"Looks like it—over there, look!" Casper pointed to the city park. A crowd of protesters had gathered around the mayor. She was literally standing on a soap box, giving a speech. "There's the mayor, lets go talk to her!" Casper and Darla squeezed between the audience, trying to get to the mayor. Mixed in with the crowd were some FEMA workers and army personnel, holding rifles. Casper didn't know what was going on, but he did know that protesters plus guys with guns never ends in a make-out love session.

"...And I believe that the army owes you and me an explanation for why they keep locking us inside our houses!" the mayor said to clapping and cheering in the crowd. "And they need to tell us why they won't let us leave town!" More cheering.

"I know!" Darla yelled raising her hand. Some people looked back at her.

"Shh!" Casper said to her. "We should only talk to the higher ups, first. We don't want these people rioting and getting shot right now."

"I also know why..." The mayor continued. "They want to keep us in the dark about what the ring is about and those things we saw floating out of it. Well, I'm not going to be satisfied until they tell us the truth about whats really going on!" yelled the mayor. Everyone applauded. The mayor stepped off of her soap box and a minute later General Katz took the podium. Many boos were heard. "Now, now, give him a chance to speak," the mayor pleaded.

"Thank you." General Katz said. "Towns people. Unlike you, we have experience in dealing with things which can be friendly as a butterfly or hostile like a honey badger getting neutered. So unless you have honey badger neutering experience, I suggest you do what you're told and stay out of our way. Thank you." The booing in the crowd was louder than the booing at a pro wrestling match. The general stepped down and made his way to a jeep.

"Worst–speech–ever!" Casper yelled over the booing. "Quick, lets go grab the mayor." Casper and Darla tried to get close to the mayor, but others blocked their way with concerns of their own.

"This is bogus!" Darla said. "We'll never get close to her!"

"We'll have to wait."

"Hey Mayor! There's a force field around town!" Darla yelled.

Everybody stopped. The general stopped walking to his jeep, the mayor stopped talking to a citizen and looked at Darla and Casper felt like his heart had stopped. "Wow!" he thought. "Darla really needs to get tested for ADHD!"

This time, the mayor started to squeeze her way over to Darla, as did some armed soldiers.

"Crap. Darla! I told you to..."

If you were to take a toilet, fill it full of Pop Rocks™ candy, Vegemite ™ paste, some needles and a box of lit matches and then flushed it, that would be a good representation of how Casper's bowels felt at that moment. The awful gurgling sound was so loud that even Darla forgot about the trouble she might be in and noticed him, "Casper? What end of you did that sound come out of?"

Casper held his belly. Above his short pants (or shants as some call them) "Oh boy, I really gotta go, really bad!"

"Now?"

"Right now or else I'm going to pit my shants!" Darla looked around. "Over there! In the middle of the field, there's a porta-potty." She pointed to the green out house.

Casper shoved some people out of his way, while saying: "excuse me'. The mayor made it to Darla, as did General Katz. They both seemed to want to drag her away from the crowd. Casper wished he could help her but the words 'bowel movement" were more like a bowel warp drive. He ran to the out house, opened it, stepped inside and proceeded to do that disgusting thing you do on a toilet when your stomach feels like jello made with lard and little marshmellows.

After he was almost done, he heard a rumbling sound outside. An alarm sounded in the distance. Some voices from the crowd screamed. "Oh great, Darla, what did you do now? Geez, what am I going to do with her. She's like pure id. What am I thinking of dating someone like that–been there, done that." There was a whale moan sound. "Is that the ring? Now what? I gotta get out of here and see what's going on." In spite of trying to hurry up, Caper let nature take its horrible course and finally was rid of all of the stomach sensations.

Casper unlocked the door to the porta-potty and stepped outside. Before him, he saw a sphere sitting on what looked like a metal flower petal, unfolded and lying flat on the grass…

Okay, we've repeated this scene like a Brazilian times this chapter. I'm getting deja vu–DEJA VU! DEJA VU! That's the word I was trying to remember in chapter 2! Thank goodness, I've been racking my brain about that one forever! Anyway, where was I? We know what's going on, so let's skip to the part you haven't read yet…

...He took a couple of steps back, paused for a second and in spite of the uproar from the crowd which was definitely in the "don't do it!" range started running to give the ball a really big kick. Suddenly, something hit him, hard. It was like getting side swiped by an NFL line backer. Casper fell sideways and landed on the grass. Dirt and grass mixed in his hair and mouth. Something heavy laid on him then got off and ran towards the porta potty. It was Finn. "Sorry Mr. Casper, I really gotta go!" he yelled opening the door and hurrying inside. A shot rang out from a nearby building. A bullet hit the porta potty. "Hey, occupied!" Finn yelled.

Casper was about to get up but something else knocked him down, again. He looked back. It was Don. Don had run across the field and tackled him.

"Don? What the French? Why is everyone tackling me? Is it Tackle Casper day? Because I'm pretty sure that's in December... And why are you dressed like a butler?"

"Cap!" Don said panting, trying to catch his breath from running across the field. "...That...thing! It...just came out of... the ring!"

Casper looked at the white sphere. It rose up and floated over to them. Casper wiggled from under Don and fast crab crawled away from the approaching sphere. Don saw the sphere and rolled sideways away from it as fast as he could. Some soldiers were running over to Casper. Casper hoped it was to get him out of there and protect him for what ever the sphere was. Casper's escape was blocked when he backed into the porta-potty's door. The sphere came closer and cornered him.

It floated closer and closer until it was five inches away from his face. Casper could feel the warmth of it. The soldiers, picked Don up and pulled him away. Some others were cautiously tiptoeing over to Casper. Casper knew they were going to drag him away as well. He also knew that this might be his last chance for a real life close encounter with an alien life form. He lifted his hand, touched the sphere and rubbed its surface, like petting a cat. He felt a strange sense of calm. It was like a wave of peace came over him. The sphere lifted up and floated back to the middle of the metal flower petal. Some soldiers arms grabbed Casper and dragged him to the side where the crowds had gathered.

"Casper! Are you all right?" Ami asked.

He took a quick look at her French maid costume. "Ami...it's alive!"

Don joined them. "You alright, man?"

"It's them you guys...It's them!"

Chapter 7
Baka!

In the kitchen of a condo in Florida, an older woman sat at her kitchen bar, smoking a cigarette and drinking a vodka martini. Physically, she resembles author, Fran Leibowitz: Frizzy graying hair, high forehead and stern eyes which can see the truth through a dark lake of lies. Mounted underneath her kitchen cabinet, she has a small television set playing the local news. She knows she shouldn't be smoking but it is one of the few things capable of calming her nerves.

It's tough when a parent looses a child and it's almost worst when a parent has no idea if their child is alive or not. The news focused on any negative stories they could find: Person A shoots person B. Politician C hates politician D and terrorist E wants to F ABC and D. The male newscaster didn't surprise her with no news on the town of Pepper Mill California. After all, people are more interested in the latest celebrity baby. There was a short piece on someone connected to the town. When she heard the town name, she turned up the volume.

"...Authorities have given up any hope of recovering the body of Professor Lewis Pascal, the famed scientist accredited with the discovery of Pascal's Comet which crashed harmlessly into the Baltic sea." There was a birds-eye view of the pacific ocean and some Coast Guard boats. "Professor Pascals plane went down earlier this week and crashed into the ocean 70 miles off the coast of Monterey California. He is believed to have died on impact, or drowned in the freezing cold waters. A memorial service will be held by his former colleagues and students in Monterey, later this week. Authorities aren't commenting on his last communication where was believed to be intoxicated and stated that his wing was on fire. We'll keep you posted as this story develops. In other news; does your baby formula contain asbestos? Find out after these commercial messages..." The woman cut the TV off.

"Always with the bad news," she said. "Didn't anything good happen in the world?" She took a drag on her cigarette, sipped her martini and then stared at the telephone, laying on the counter. "Should I try it?" she wondered. She picked it up and dialed a long number. She knew this number by heart; she had called it so many times. A recorded voice message answered; "Hello. You have reached the Federal Emergency Management Agency information center for the town of: *Pepper Mill California*. As of this date, *April 28th*, there are no new developments or changes. Please call back later. Our thoughts and prayers are with you. Thank you, goodbye."

"Bupkes!" she said hanging up the phone. "I don't want your thoughts and prayers. I want my son!" She checked her text messages on her extremely outdated Razor flip phone. There was only one, dated from a couple of months ago. It read:

SRY I WONT B HOM 4 HANUKAH. LUV U 4 EVR.

She felt like crying. A part of her held the tears back and fought back the pain and sadness. "No! I will not cry! He's still alive! I can feel it! A mother knows!" Her door buzzer went off. "Who in the world would be visiting at this hour?" she said walking over to the intercom. "Hello?" she asked pressing the talk button.

"Uh, this is Pizza Face Pizza, We have a delivery for Hazel Cornbregger," said a teenager with a cracking puberty filled voice.

"Pizza? I didn't order a pizza! Why would I order a pizza? Do I look like a dope smoking college student? Take it away, you have the wrong Hazel Cornbregger."

"But, it says Hazel Cornbregger, Number 39A, North Miami. Is that you?"

"Yes, it is. But, I didn't order a pizza. You've been had. I don't eat Pizza—with my cholesterol? Are you trying to kill me, is that it? You kill them with Pizza and rob them?"

"Ma'am, I'm just the delivery guy, I don't know who ordered this pizza but it has your address on it. If you don't sign for it, they take it out of my paycheck, or make us clean out the deep fat fryer —please don't make me clean out the deep fat fryer! Last time I found half a rat in there—half a rat! What happened to the rest?"

"Sorry to hear that. But I'm not paying for a pizza I didn't order!"

"It's already paid for, you just have to sign for it."

"Already paid for? Well, Bring it on up!"

A few minutes later. The pizza delivery man had made his way up the stairs and was knocking on her front door. Hazel cracked the door open and kept the two chains engaged to prevent him from coming inside. "Don't try anything, I have a pit bull behind the door, I own a gun and have a flesh eating STD if you are thinking of getting frisky with me!"

271

"Great Caesar's ghost, lady, I just want you to sign this so I can get out of here!" He slipped the receipt pad through the door crack with a pen. Hazel checked it over to make sure it were real. She confirmed its legitimacy, signed it and handed it back to him.

"Just leave it in the hallway."

"Believe me, I'm a step ahead of you." He put the pizza down and swiftly walked away.

To make sure it wasn't a trick, Hazel looked through her front window and watched the pizza delivery car leave. "Now then, let's check out this so called 'free' pizza," she said bringing the pizza inside. There was a look of disgust on her face. It wasn't that the pizza was disgusting. It was actually quite tasty looking with its fresh baked bread crust and it's glistering cheese topping. What she didn't like was the flavor. "Is that pork? What type of sadist sends a pork pizza to a Jewish person?" She took the box to the compost bin and tossed the pizza in. In the box, where the pizza used to rest there was a white envelope taped to the inside. "What's this, a love letter?" She untaped it and ripped it open. It read:

Dear Mrs Cornbregger:

My name is Lewis Pascal. I was your child Casper's astronomy professor at the University of California, Pepper Mill. Although I'm sure you are a fetching woman, this is not a love letter. Let me say first, that I am sorry for the stress the recent events have caused you. The feeling of uncertainty you must feel about your son's fate must be heart wrenching. But, there is no need to feel despair. Your son is alive and well Mrs Cornbregger. He is alive and well and told me to pass on that message to you. I'm sorry for sending it to you in secret like this, but I'm afraid my life is in danger I can't tell you anymore than that, for it would jeopardize your life as well.

Signed, Lewis Pascal, Ph.D.

She sat down in a chair, laid the letter on her lap and put her head back on a cushion.

In a small Pizza parlor, Tim the pizza delivery boy was occupying his time, waiting for an order to come in by hitting on the boss's daughter, Sandy who worked as a cashier.

"Man, you better lay off of her, else Mr. Forman will come after you," his friend Carlton advised."

"Pfft!" he said (a sound used to represent discontent). "I'm not afraid of that guy. What's he gonna do, fire me?" At the completion of his sentence, three masked men, dressed in black and holding machine guns, burst into the restaurant. Tim, Carlton and Sandy screamed, raised their hands and prepared to be robbed. The men, ignored the other employees and went straight for Tim. Within seconds, he was put in a large black bag, zipped up and carried out the door leaving a stunned Carlton and Sandy with their hands still in the air. "Man." Carlton said. "Yo' daddy really wants you to stay a virgin."

A short car ride later, a hood was removed from Tim's head. He discovered he was in a dark room, in a chair at a wooden desk. Two mysterious black suited men wearing white shirts, skinny, black ties and sunglasses, stood sightly off to the sides, in the shadows.

One of the men sat down in front of Tim and introduced himself. "Mr. Ficus...I'm Mr...A. This is Mr...B. He gestured over to the other man in the room. Tim noticed a third man, far off in the darkness of the room that was never introduced. "You're Timothy A. Ficus, delivery boy for a respectable pizza company....you have a social security number, you pay your taxes, and you...help your landlady...kill rats in the alley. The other life is lived on the 'internets', where your social media title is: 'T Fi', and are guilty of virtually every spelling error we have a grammatical law for. One of these lives has a future....the other does not.

"Recently you sent a pizza to a Mrs...Hazel...Cornbregger, One Southwest Ave, Pembroke Pines, Florida 33027...Is that not correct?"

"Y-Yes—who are you people? The cops?"

"Sure, let's go with that...Anyway, Mr. Ficus. Mrs Cornbregger contacted the authorities and told them that someone played a very, very cruel joke on her, using a note inside the pizza box...you delivered."

"Hey man! I don't know anything about that note. It wasn't me. I swear."

"Did you not deliver the pizza containing the note...Mr. Ficus?"

"I delivered the pizza, but I had no idea what the note said. It was slipped in by this guy when he placed the order. Said it was a birthday wish or something."

"A guy? To whom are you referring...Mr. Ficus?"

"I didn't know him."

"You let a complete stranger slip something into your pizza box?" asked Mr B. "Not very sanitary."

"Hey, for a $100 tip. They can put a finger in the box."

Mr. A. raised an eyebrow. "Okay...Suppose you can tell us what this mysterious man looked like."

"Sure. He..." Mr A. stopped him with a raised finger. "Get a sketch artist in here." 15 minutes later, a man dressed in plain clothes, carrying a sketchbook and a pencil entered the room and sat across from Tim. He seemed uncomfortable. "Okay Mr Ficus...continue,"

"Okay, he was about five or six feet tall. Wore a grey tench coat. Had a grey fedora on."

"His face Mr. Ficus. We don't care how he's dressed."

"He had these thick, round, black framed glasses on. A long and wide nose. A really big bushy mustache and his eye brows were really prominent, like, as bushy as his mustache. Oh, and he was smoking a cigar. I remember that too."

For a few seconds the sketch artist worked on the drawing. At the end, a look of confusion came over his face and then he rolled his eyes and handed the sketch book to Mr. A. Mr. A looked at the sketch and even though his face remained emotionless, you could tell he was a little angry at the results. "Mr. Ficus...Do you seriously want us to put an APB out on..." He showed the drawing to Tim. "...Groucho Marx?"

Over 2000 miles away in a jail cell in Pepper Mill, Casper was wearing an orange track suit and playing a harmonica with handcuffed hands. Actually it wasn't a harmonica, it was a makeshift kazoo; a piece of wax paper wrapped around a small black comb. In between hums, he sang the words to *Amazing Grace*. His face had a five-o'clock shadow and there was a band aid on his head. Sitting across from him in the cell was Don, dressed the same and trying to see how to turn a toothbrush and a razor into a weapon or "shank" as they call it. A guard came to the cell door and opened it up. "Okay Cornbregger, time to go," he said . Casper handed his harmonica-kazoo to Don. "Looks like my time is up. Time to walk the green mile. Take this to remember me by."

"I'll always remember you, Cap." Don said.

Casper got up and started walking down the hall. "Dead man walking." Don yelled. Casper and the guard slowly made their way down what is actually the hallway of the high school, now being used as an army base. The cell is just a classroom with some cots. While walking down the hall, Casper noticed through the glass window of one of the classes, Finn was also a prisoner.

"Finn?"

"Hi, Mr. Casper." Finn happily waved.

"What are you in for, kid?"

"Sorry, I can't say."

"Okay then, take care." Casper waved goodbye.

Casper and the guard kept walking. They reached a class near a stairwell "Okay Cornbregger" the guard said, "go on in and sit in the chair."

"The chair, eh. I knew I'd get the chair one day."

"Okay, okay, inside!" the guard said, getting impatient.

The room had a couple of hospital beds, medical equipment and his friend Ami, dressed in pink, Hello Kitty™ hospital scrubs under a white lab coat. She was at a school desk getting some equipment ready. When she saw him she rolled her eyes. "Casper? Why are you wearing that orange jumpsuit?"

"Oh, my clothes got dirty when Finn and Don threw me on the grass. They let me borrow this from the track team supplies while my clothes are drying."

"And what's that on your face. It can't be a beard. You've only been here for two days!"

"We had chocolate pancakes for breakfast...me and Don were playing with the chocolate."

"The hand cuffs?"

"Oh, these?" Casper raised his hands. "One of the guards does magic tricks, he was showing me how to escape from handcuffs— Huzzah!" he said. A moment later, the handcuffs fell to the ground.

Ami put her hand to her eyes as though she had a head ache. "...And the band aid on your head?"

"Some guys tried to get fresh with me in the shower."

Ami looked up with a serious face. "Oh my God! And you got hurt fighting them off?"

"No, I bumped my head on the sink when they were having sex with me." Realizing he had taken the joke too far, by the look on her face, Casper let her off the hook. "Just kidding! I bumped my head on the ground when I got tackled." Ami picked up a clipboard, walked over to him and hit the back of his head with it.

"Ow! Sorry, I'm bored. When are they gonna let us go? I can't believe they locked us down—again!"

"Not everyone, just you guys." Ami wet a paper towel in a little sink off to the side and handed to him. "Wipe your face, please." She then washed her hands

"What? No lock down this time?" He cleaned his face.

"Yeah, there's no lock down, the whole town is running like normal, 'cept they walled off the area with a tarp where that alien thing showed up."

"What was that thing?"

"You know as much as I do. I'm just here to poke you."

"Oh, oh. Really?"

"Yep. Sorry, we need to check your blood. Probably want to make sure you're not carrying an alien virus after you touched that thing." Ami put on a pair of latex gloves.

"It was incredible, Ami. It was like touching something that… Like we're so far apart in the universe, and suddenly we have an opportunity to connect like that. I'll never forget it."

"It's pretty exciting. A real extraterrestrial in our back yard. And you touched it. And now, I'm going to touch you. Lay your arm on the table palm side up and make a fist." Casper did as she said. She wrapped a latex tourniquet on his upper arm and poked around for a good vein to draw blood from.When she had found one, she swabbed the area with alcohol, and after she had arranged her test tubes with different colored tops in a certain order, she inserted the needle with virtually no pain to him and started transferring his blood into the collection tubes. "You can unclench your fist," she said switching from one tube to another.

"You gonna do Don next?"

"What do you mean DO him?"

"As in, shot? What did you think I mean't?"

"Shot, of course! He's next."

Casper looked at multiple medical color posters on the wall. One was of a heart. "So, what do you think of Don?"

"What do you mean?"

"I mean as more than a friend?"

"I don't think Don would ever want to be more than friends."

He found it interesting that she actually avoided the question. "Really? Where'd you hear that?"

"Finn told me."

"Finn? FINN, Finn? What is he some type of love guru? How would he know what Don thinks?"

"Don told him."

"Really. Don said he only wanted to be friends? Why would he tell Finn that?"

"Why are we talking about this? Did Don say something to you?"

"I think maybe you and Don should have a talk, I'm just saying...." Ami appeared to be spacing out. "...That and I'm pretty sure that tube has enough blood in it."

Amy looked at the tube and grimaced. It was quite full. "Oops, sorry! She pulled out the needle and had him hold a cotton swap over the draw area while she taped it on. "All done."

As Ami cleaned up her work station a woman entered the room. Her combat booted height put her at six feet. She was wearing army fatigues with a lab coat over it. Her very short bond hair and model-like features gave the appearance of a Russian gymnast or a character in the Street Fighter™ video games. As a gymnast, she would have trouble doing any flips with her very prominent breast (I will be proven wrong, later). Casper's eyes widened. "Hello Mr. Cornbregger. I'm Major Chambers. I'm the head medic," she said.

"For reals?" Casper said. "Please tell me you're here for my physical." Ami hit the back of his head with a clipboard. "Ow!"

"Excuse him Doctor, he's an idiot." Ami complained.

While the major looked over some paperwork on her own clipboard, Casper leaned closer to Ami and whispered: "Aaaa-Me! Why didn't you tell me your boss was like, jpeg download hot?"

"Because you're a pervert," she whispered back. "And she's out of your league."

"She's not out of my league...What do you know about my league? How do you know she's out of it?"

"Look at her! She's like a super model injected with unicorn blood! Even I'd do her; you have no chance!"

"I'll show you!" Casper turned his attention to the major. "Soo, Doc, what are you doing after..."

"I'm out of your league," she said abruptly. "Now then, Mr. Cornbregger, I'm going to ask you some questions, try to answer them as truthfully as possible."

"Is one of them: 'is your ego crushed?'"

"No. Unless it's relevant to your experience with the life form the other day." The major listed off a bunch of different symptoms such as: "Have you experienced any headaches? Have you had trouble sleeping? Any blurry vision?" When she got to "any sexual disfunction?" Casper looked at Ami who raised up her clipboard and prepared to hit him again.

"I'm gonna have to say no," he said, holding his joke in.

"Okay, then. We'll run your blood work and see if there is anything new in there."

General Katz entered the room. "Hello Mr. Cornbregger, I'm General Katz," he said.

"Not THE General Katz?" Casper said.

"You heard of me?"

"No." Ami hit him with the clipboard. "Ow! I mean yes, you're like the head of the army."

"Correct. I need to talk to you about what you and Miss Marbles saw."

"I think the whole town saw that ship land and that white ball thing."

"No, not that. I mean't the force field."

"Technically, it was invisible, so I didn't SEE it." Casper covered his head and looked at Ami, preparing for a head whack.

She didn't do anything. "That's actually a good point."

"Sure. Anyway…"the general continued. "You and your friend went into an off-limits area and discovered the force field."

"Yes. So we're all trapped here, right?"

"For now, yes."

"I was wondering why you guys just didn't air-drop supplies into town, and made us start rationing. Is the top covered too?"

"Top and bottom. Like a cylinder."

"Is it ionized air or an electromagnetic field?"

"Huh…Oh, I don't know, you'd have to ask the scientist."

"There was this plastic factory in South Carolina in the 90s that had this area where the static charge was so high, people couldn't walk through it, but it only worked on low humidity days."

"Okay…Again. I'm leaving all of the speculation up to the scientists. Anyway, I want to talk to you about the social implications of the force field, Mr. Cornbregger."

"Casper. Mr. Cornbregger was my father's name."

"Sorry, Casper. Casper, what you and Miss Marbles–Darla know–I assume just you two, did you tell anyone else?"

"Nope, not even my roommate. I wanted to talk to you guys first."

"Good, because it can have dire consequences if you left here and started talking about it to everyone. Panic would set in, maybe out-of-control mobs, all kinds of civil disobedience. Do you see what I'm getting at? We can't play protectors while wasting our time on policing the same people"

"You're going to keep me locked up, until the forcefield goes away?"

"No, we can't do that. You see, we don't know how long we're going to be here so all of our supplies can't be wasted on housing too many prisoners that don't do anything but eat, drink and poop and aren't contributing to the community as a whole."

"Holy crap!" Casper said in a panicky voice. You're going to kill me? Or worst, recycle me into solent green?"

"What? No! We can't kill you. Our job is to keep all of the citizens alive. But like I said, if we can't have you running around talking about the force field, there is another solution besides murdering you."

"I'm at a loss for a solution the army uses over murdering."

Ami hit him with the clipboard. "He means for you to keep your big mouth shut, idiot!"

"Oh, right, that. Yeah I can do that. Not so sure about Darla. Controlling her is like trying to control a fire while wearing piñata pants thats been doused in fingernail polish remover."

"…Huh?…So, you're saying she's not much of a team player?"

"Definitely not. But, she does respond easily to bribes. I once got her to cover three shifts at Big Red Groceries–Wow! I just realized I haven't been to work in days without a notice, good thing I can't get fired–anyway, I gave her a couple of six packs and that's all it took."

"So maybe we'll offer her some bottles of our weaponized vodka."

"Totally, but then what about me? I don't get a bribe?"

"What do you want?"

"How about…"

"Ain't gonna happen." Major Chambers interrupted.

Wow, she's like a sexy psychic! Okay, besides a date with her. How about you let me in?"

"In what?" The general asked.

"In the inner circle. I want to be an insider. I want to know what's going on, see the aliens, get all the dirt that you guys get instead of always being in the dark and getting shut in a classrooms or my house."

"I'm sorry, but what do you have to offer us?"

"Well, I'm studying to be an astronomer and I'm also interested in physics. My friends Don is an ace programer and Darla is also taking biology. I'm sure our knowledge can come in handy?"

"Possibly but we just got rid of a top astronomer. Not much use for someone that looks at stars when the inhabitants are sitting in the middle of the park. God, I can't believe I agree with the President."

"Top astronomer, who?"

"Lewis Pascal."

"Oh? But he's the guy that was tracking this thing since the very beginning."

"Doesn't really matter much now, he recently died in a plane crash."

A wave of shock came over Casper. Besides his dad, he has't had many people die that he's had long conversations with.

The general sensed his sadness. "I'm sorry, where you one of his students?"

"Yes." He remembered their short conversation a few days ago and how they were going to meet up at the river bank. "He was kind of a friend, too."

"I'm sorry, I truly am. I've lost more friends than enemies."

Ami walked over and put her hand on Casper's shoulder. "I'm so sorry, Casper."

He patted her hand and gave a slight smile. "That's okay, thanks. Well, if you guys don't need someone with his resumé, I guess I'm pretty useless."

"Every single citizen in this town is useful," the general said. "Just go back to your normal life and do what you usually do. That's the best thing you can do for our mission right now."

"Fine. What about Don and Finn? You gonna free them too?"

"Finn?" Ami asked.

"Don, is he the Black guy that works at that café downtown?" asked the general.

"Yeah," Casper answered. "He's also my roommate."

"He's free to go too, if his medical exam clears, you two can be out of here within the hour." The general turned and left the room. Ami followed him into the hallway.

"General!" she yelled.

He turned around. "Yes, Miss Nakajima?"

"Private Finn, why is he locked up?"

"Finn? He's the one that caused The Egg to be sent back up the ring."

"But, that's not a reason to lock someone up. We all make mistakes."

"Is he your boyfriend or something?"

She tightened her hands on the clipboard and resisted the urge to hit the general with it. "No, sir, just a friend."

"He didn't get locked up just for that. He refused to tell us who the other participants were that caused the probe to launch. Add that to his constant knuckle-headed theatrics, we can't have him in the army, operating weapons."

"Couldn't you just kick him out of the army? Like you said, isn't he wasting resources by being in there?"

"So he can do what? What can he do? He'd starve to death. It's more humane to have him locked up like a zoo animal. Least here he gets three hots and a cot."

"Please, sir. For my sake."

"Sorry Miss Nakajima but…"

Before he could finish, Ami got down on her knees and bowed her head to the floor on top of her hands in a Japanese apology bow. "I'm sorry. I'm afraid I was one of the people involved in Private Finn pressing the button on The Egg."

The general was very shaken by her display. He quickly walked over and picked her up. "What? Whoa! No need for that. What are you talking about?"

"Private Finn was probably keeping me from getting in trouble. I had no idea he would be locked up for that. He was protecting my honor from some ruffians when I accidentally threw him onto the ground and he pressed the button trying to get back up. So, it's not all his fault, I deserve to be kicked off the team and locked up as well."

The general sighed. "True, but you aren't in the army and took an oath like he did. You're part of the medical team and what Major Chambers tells me, hard working and a very fast learner. We really do need you here. Tell you what. I'll let him out and by out I mean he's out of the army. Your punishment, you can help find him a place to live out there and a job that's productive. But, if he starves to death, it's your fault."

"Thank you very much, sir."

The general started to leave and then stopped. "You threw a U.S. soldier on the ground?"

"Yes, sir. I took a Judo class."

He chuckled and continued walking.

Plür was alone for a long time but not bored. Her view of the town and it's inhabitants was being blocked at this moment by a large green, plastic wall, but she had plenty of things to observe and keep her busy. The green grass was an interesting color. She had seen it mostly in blue, yellow and red but not this particular shade of green. On closer inspection, she had discovered tiny insects and some kind of tree pulp based leaf with the words 'McDonalds' written on it. "Why would they put words on their leaves?" she wondered. Bosq had been gone for three of her hours. She knew that with just a sign from her communicator, he would come running back and defend her from any hostile movements by this planet's inhabitants. Luckily, she has only had to call on his help once, and that was on a planet without a dominate life form. The plastic wall moved. She knew it was Bosq slipping in between an opening in it. She waited until she was sure he had walked over to her before speaking. If she yelled, it might alert the natives and cause trouble.

"Plür, I'm back," he said.

"Safe journey?"

"Yes, thank you. I've discovered many, many things."

"Please, enlighten me."

"First of all, that wall they put around us is very weak. As you can tell I was able to slip in and out and wander around the town without any obstacles."

"Are their defenses that weak?"

"I thought that at first but then I noticed there was a large structure full of the natives that like to wear the green clothes and sometimes had black sticks. They are surrounding our enclosure and seem to wander around the town with impunity. The natives that aren't wearing green, always get out of their way or do whatever they tell them to do."

"A cast system or army?"

"Possibly both. The green ones are definitely the Alpha creatures here, as are the ones with the words FEMA written on their clothes."

"What level of technology are they?"

"They aren't as advanced as my people but they are a lot more advanced than yours. Their vehicles all seem to run on flammable liquids. I saw some vehicles fly over the ring using propellers on top and far away, some type of rocket engine craft, spitting smoke out the back. A couple of aircraft with propellers were parked in the Alpha's compound. I guess they are the only ones allowed to use them."

"What about the non Alphas? What did you learn of them?"

"Anatomy wise, bipedal motion, their legs bend the wrong way, only two arms. All of these creatures are basically the same with slight differences: some are tall, short, rounder and come in different colors. The pink ones seem to be the most prominent color but I really didn't see any problems with the darker skin ones or those with different eye shape and hair interacting with them."

"That's promising. Perhaps their races have learned to coexist peacefully."

"I wouldn't assume that. Even your people have some discrimination."

"I am not going to debate that right now. Please continue."

"They are definitely mammals with sporadic hair. The males sometimes had hair on their faces, the women usually have longer hair and only two breast. I assume there are teats for feeding for the young."

"Only two breast? How can they feed more than two babies?"

"No idea. I did see three baby creatures but they looked so different from each other, I doubt they were from the same litter and were with a female even more different than them. It's possible they have a system where females take turns taking care of the youth. Either way, I never saw any large litters.

"What about sex?"

"No idea. I followed a male, female pair for hours but they never engaged in it. Although at one point, the male tried his best to get the female to come home with him but she refused and said she had to get up early tomorrow."

"Maybe that is when they can only have sex. Early in the morning."

"I wan't going to wait around until morning to find out."

"So their society is heterosexual based?"

"I did see at least one female, female couple and among the green Alphas, two male, male couples. But the male, male couples were very secretive in their interactions."

"What about the planet itself?"

"Great potential for farming. Theres a large water source not far from here and the ring has already conditioned the soil. I don't think the natives have realized it yet because I didn't see evidence of organized crops."

"No crops? Where are they getting their food?"

"Storage buildings. They go in, get what they want and leave."

"But, where did that food come from?"

"Perhaps it was here before the ring landed. Another thing, in the food storage area, they had frozen animal carcasses."

"They eat, meat?"

"It looked that way to me."

"Is the meat lower life forms or are they cannibals?"

"I didn't see any evidence of cannibalism, but we both know that's what happens when meat eating inhabitants run out of lower life forms and vegetation to eat."

"They need to start crops before they run out of food. They are going to need our guidance."

"Definitely, I mean, things look peaceful now, but they don't seem to be working together to make their imprisonment functional. I didn't see any water conservation. They take their transport vehicles to travel the most mundane distances, there's no sign of waste recycling. It's like they're acting like nothing significant has happened to change their lifestyle. Maybe they're not very smart?"

"Bosq! lack of panic could also be a sign of bravery or they are at peace with their situation."

"Perhaps, it's hard to gauge them, at least without actually interacting with them."

"I guess that's what we…I will have to do. Thank you, Bosq."

"It wasn't a problem, Plür. Do you want to slip through the plastic wall?"

"No, if it is so easy to get through it, I can only assume they put it up to either block our view of what they are doing, or block the non Alphas view of us. No, I shall wait until they approach us."

As far as approaching the aliens, The person who will be making first contact with them, albeit video feed, will be the American President, Jimmy Jarrod. President Jarrod was dressed for the part, wearing a nice black suit, red tie and the obligatory American flag on his lapel. But he was not dressed for bowling, which is what he is doing in the two lane alley, located in the secret Antarctica base. He held the ball up to his chest, took a few steps and threw a perfect gutter ball. Before he could finish his expletive, the First Lady entered the room. "J.J.? What are you doing in here?"

"Let's see, in a bowling alley, holding a bowling ball, Hmmm. Can I phone a friend, Regis?"

"I know what you're doing, I'm saying why are you here instead of in that room with all of your people, running the free world or something?"

"They sent you in here to get me?"

"They know better than to disturb you when you're bowling."

The President concentrated, rolled the ball down the lane, and scored a zero. "For The love of ... They're right. Gotta lot on my mind, sugar lumps."

"I can tell. Last time you went bowling while wearing a suit, we went to war with some country with the word 'stan' in it. Is this something you can talk about or is it so secret even the vice president doesn't know about it?"

"Oh-my-lord! I forgot all about the vice president! Last time I saw him, we were boarding Air Force One and he said I have to go to the bathroom and I said go on the plane and he said I hate going to the bathroom on a plane and I said if you don't come now, we'll leave you here to deal with the comet and he said if you leave me, I'll just wait right here until you come back because you can't run the country without me. That's the last I heard of him. Don't suppose he's still waiting at the airport, do you?"

"I don't know J.J. Who'd be stupid enough to wait months at an airport just to prove how stubborn they are?"

....
....Oh, I'm sorry. I guess you were expecting a cut scene of the vice President of the United States, still at the airport, dressed in an old tattered suit, perhaps begging for spare change. Move along, nothing to see here!

"Betty, I can't tell you what's going on, but I can say: soon I'm going to have to introduce myself to someone and make a good first impression. And if I screw up, we could be going to war with someone bigger than another 'stan' country."

"Oh J.J. Don't you worry..." She walked over to lane #2 and picked up a bowling ball. "...But sometimes the occasion rises..." She rolled the ball down the lane and got a strike."...And sometimes you rise to the occasion. You don't need to worry J.J. This is what you signed up for. Just be yourself."

"But sometimes I can be kind of an ass."

"Then be someone else." She bowled another strike.

"For the love of–you bowl better than I do and you're smarter." The President walked over and kissed her. As he left, she slapped him on the butt.

"Go get-em tiger!"

The President entered a room which was set up like a small movie studio. There was a podium with an American and United Nations flag behind it. They called this the 'Thoughts and Prayers' room because this is were the president gives the speech to the American people, right before the giant tsunami hits the East cost, the Mayan calendar earthquake slides California into the ocean, or they use all of the countries resources to create a giant robot to destroy the giant fire breathing lizard. Today would be a more positive use as the President will be the first human to greet visitors from another world. Many suited gentlemen approached the President and handed him paperwork full of speeches and directions on what he should say and do. He looked them over and nodded. On monitors behind the camera, he could see many world leaders listening in and being informed about this historic moment.

"Make sure you tell them that you are only a representative of the many races and cultures on Earth." The German chancellor said.

"And that you stand for peace," said the Dali Lama.

"And don't tell them you're an American," said the Prime Minister of Canada. "Because let's face it. I'm an American, as well as people down in Argentina and there's no way I want them to lump us into one big country."

Many other words of advice and suggestions were being said until it all melded into a people talking-over-each-other garbled noise.

The President held up his hands to quiet them. "Listen up!" he yelled. "the alien ship landed on our property and I think they did it for a good reason."

"Because you fired missiles at it?" said the French President.

"Be that as it may, it's on our property and I'm the land lord. As the land lord, I'm going to be the one to decide what to say."

"Mr. President, can you at least give us a preview of your speech." Asked the President of Mexico. "After all, one wrong word and they could turn our planet into burned palomitas."

"We don't know that," the President answered. "As far as I can tell, if they wanted to do that, they would have done it already. After all, on D day, we didn't storm the beach, set up a nice spot with towels and umbrellas and hung out, we kept on invading!"

"How can you say that, when they have one of your cities hostage?" asked the President of the People's Republic of China.

"Oh, believe me, I'm going to address that. First part of my speech is going to be a treat" There was a collective gasp in the room. "First I'm going to tell them to release the force field around the town of Pepper Mill or else there will be dire consequences."

"But, won't that just provoke them?" said the President of South Africa. "You need to establish a dialogue of mutual respect and friendship. You said so yourself that you don't think this is an invasion."

"It may not be. OR they're trying to catch us with our underwear down, bent down looking for our glasses. When Columbus showed up and looked all nicey nice. Next thing you know, Wham! Indians reduced to casinos and football mascots. If I establish us as tough sons of guns, then they're gonna go whoa! These guys mean business, lets build our alien casinos elsewhere!"

"Mr. President…" the Italian prime minister was about to argue against his point. His point of view was interrupted by seven other world leaders raising their concerns and their voices. This created a symphony of muttering and confusion and was rapidly slipping into chaos. The President took out a gun and fired it into the air. This of course bought the room and the meeting to a shocking quiet. No one expected this to happen. Most wondered where he got a gun.

"Gentlemen!" He gave the gun to a Secret Service agent. "Here Carl, don't leave your gun in the men's room next time." Another person was about to speak. The President quickly cut him off. "Let me tell you gentlemen a little story. Back when I was a fledgeling musician and played guitar, I wanted to be a drummer, but not just any drummer, I wanted to have a band made up of nothing but rock AND or roll drummers. I met up with three other drummers and we formed an all drum band. Another name for the drums is the skins, so since there were four of us, we called ourselves the four skins. Now, can anyone tell me why we failed?"

"Because of your horrific name?"Asked the President of Iceland.

"What? No, what's wrong with the name? Anyway, we failed because there were too many drums. Too many people trying to set the beat. That's what we got here. You all want to be the Four Skins and nobody wants to be the head of…"

"Oh for the love of god, please stop your story!" the President of France pleaded.

"What? You all want to be the lead singer is my point. So for now, we do this my way! Next time an alien ship lands in your country, you can be in control. My country, my town, my alien visitor—my speech!"

"And if they respond negatively?" asked the President of Walmart, a large campaign contributor.

"We have nuclear bombs in all shapes and colors Tom, I'm sure we can find one that can crack open that hard nut."

Listening in on the meeting, via video conferencing, General Katz was right outside the tarp wall enclosing the two alien visitors. "Oh my god," he muttered. "He's gonna kill us all."

A monitor device was being set up which would allow the President of United States to be seen by the aliens. The monitor was wheeled inside the enclosed tarp area in full view of Plür and Bosq.

"What do you suppose it is?" Plür asked.

"It could be a weapon of some sort, except I don't see any exit chambers or indication of a ballistic weapon. Also, the absents of protective armor around the green suited ones pushing it, shows a lack of concern for danger."

"I assume that means, whatever it is, it is not dangerous or an act of aggression."

"I'm going to get ready for an attack, just in case."

"I fail to understand, how the more advanced a society is, like yours and theirs, the more paranoid and weaponized. It is like you spend half of your lives attaining technology and the second half defending it."

"I can't help but feel a hint of smugness in your words."

"I am sorry. That was not my intent. I do have a request and that is, if you do feel they are showing aggression, we leave without any confrontation."

"If I hear one threat, I'll evacuate us immediately."

"Thank you for your support, Bosq. Since you feel they are probably not setting up a weapon system, I have one surveying mission for you."

"Yes, by all means."

"You mentioned how you witnessed them storing and distributing food in a structure."

"Yes. Lots of containers and some frozen carcasses."

"Yes. I'm very concerned about the carcasses. I need to know if they are eating higher or lower life forms.I think this could play a role in deciding if we can deal with them on equal grounds."

"I shall examine the area again and return shortly."

"Thank you, Bosq. Safe journey."

"Thank you."

Plür could hear his foot steps as he trotted away, towards the direction of Big Red Groceries.

In 1997, Theoretical physicist Juan Maldacena proposed a model, that the universe you are seeing around you right now, is nothing but a hologram of the real universe. That's right, everything you see and feel are projections of a 2D object, projecting itself into a 3D universe. As fantastical and unbelievable as this theory is, it's much more believable than Casper's faith in the U.S. Army, the government and the idea that the alien ring meant them no harm. The ring was no longer whimsical. It was a danger; a trap and had nefarious intentions. It was one thing to build a wall between you and your neighbor than it was for your neighbor to build a wall between themselves and you. While he skateboarded to the store, for once, he was looking forward to getting to work. He needed a distraction. A distraction was soon presented to him. Before he could reach the parking lot, a figure ran across his path. He came to a halt as best he could but still collided clumsily with the other person and he almost fell down. "Opps, I'm sorry!" He grabbed their arm and realized the stranger was Lori. "Move, micro brain!" she yelled pushing him away. She started running away. A few seconds later, two soldiers gave chase yelling "stop!" Casper watched until she disappeared over some nearby hedges. "Well… that was different," he said, picking up his board.

Things were as he had left them at Big Red Groceries. It was full of customers stocking up on what they didn't realize would soon be dwindling. Sue, the manager was running one of the registers as were the two soldiers, originally hired to keep the peace. When Sue saw Casper, her reaction can best be described as the expression you would give someone coming out of the bathroom as you're going in and they've just finished vacating a broccoli bean burrito and a large coffee milkshake. Casper smiled, it was genuine. He may not be able to use his science skills to help the town, but perhaps he could help them with their supplies. He could be part of the invisible support staff. Like pigeons in the city; everybody hates pigeons, but if they realized how much garbage the pigeons helped clear away, perhaps they would appreciate them more.

"Hey Sue, sorry I'm late."

Sue didn't respond to his joke.

He walked over to her, put his backpack down, the one I forgot to mention, because it wasn't really important, and prepared to work. "So, where do you want me?"

"In the back with Darla."

"What?"

"In the back."

"Why in the back? I'm a cashier."

"As you can see, I already have cashiers."

"Those guys aren't cashiers."

"They are now, and they're a lot more reliable than you and the Queen of the Goths."

"Hey, I have a good excuse for being gone all this time."

"Okay, I'm listening."

Casper thought about his vow of silence. "And...I can't talk about it."

"Fine. You can talk about it as you inventory every-single-item in the back room."

"Annnd what if I don't want to. It's not like you can FIRE me or anything."

"No, I can't but, I'm sure even the head of FEMA will have a problem with anyone that refuses to help out. Maybe even honor my request to make you the town janitor or better yet; the official crazy homeless person in town. Can you talk in gibberish while peeing your pants?"

Casper knew she had the upper hand on this one. Having no interest in being turned into the town janitor or crazy homeless person, He wandered to the back to join Darla. Strangely enough, she was doing her job in a calm and organized manner. There was no sign of goofing off or embezzling. Casper waved to her. "Hey, I see they let you out, too."

Darla didn't respond. She continued counting cans of black beans and writing down the numbers on a print-out sheet.

"Darla. You alright?"

"Not really." She put the paper down.

"Sucks, huh? Being back here."

"What?"

"Doing boring busy work—It sucks."

"What's wrong with you?"

"What do you mean?"

"We're stuck here, and you're acting like everything is okay!"

"No, I'm trying to distract myself from that."

"Good luck with that!" She picked up a can of what appeared to be Doc Brown's Lisbon soda. "You realize, this may be the last can of…" She read the can and scrawled. "…this stuff we'll ever see. Once this runs out–that's it! No more lesbian soda!"

"Unless the force field is dropped, then you can walk out of here and buy all the lesbian soda you want…By the way, you misread it. It's Lisbon, a city in Portugal"

"Whatever. My point is, we're screwed!"

"We're not screwed, were in a pickle."

"I don't get how you can be so optimistic, Casper! The Aliens put a forcefield around us that apparently the army can't break trough. Far as we know, we're running out of oxygen right now!"

"I thought about that and I'm not worried about it."

"Why not?"

"Wind."

"What?"

"When we were walking near the edge of town, I felt the wind blow on my face. Can't have that without oxygen getting through the force field."

"Fine. So why can't we just walk trough the force field? What's keeping us here?"

"Same thing that made the pine cones and the other stuff bounce off. It's no ordinary forcefield. It's obviously programed to keep only us inside"

"And THAT doesn't make you freak out?"

"I'm freaked out. But I also realize that this means the forcefield is being controlled by somebody or thing. Most likely, that thing that landed in the park I touched. If that thing is intelligent, then it can be..."

"You mean the one you were gong to kick?" she interrupted

"Yeah, I guess."

"You mean, the thing that controls the forcefield and is keeping us hostage was recently threatened by you?"

"Possibly."

Darla picked up the can of Lisbon Soda and threw it at his head. He ducked just in time, causing it to hit the wall and explode, sending red soda everywhere. "You moron! You've doomed us all!"

Casper made a hasty retreat away from her. "Whoa-Whoa-whoa! It's only a theory! Far as I know, that ball could also have been a probe or something unimportant!"

"I swear, Cornbregger, If I'm stuck in here because of your mistake, I'm going shove a bag of candy down your throat, tie you up and bust you open like a piñata!"

"Oookay. I'm going to work over here in the freezer until you cool down."

"Shove it!"

He backed away from her. His fear of being piñataed was quite real.

Caper started doing inventory on the fresh meat in the freezer.

Unbeknownst to him, Bosq had snuck into the back room and was already in the freezer looking at the meat. He was within three feet of Casper. Bosq looked at Casper's face. He found it interesting that Casper's nose holes were pointing downwards. "Perhaps it's to keep the rain out. Maybe they can't lower their heads and would drown, otherwise." He speculated. Although most of the humans looked alike, he remembered Casper from the earlier encounter with Plür.

Thinking that he was alone, Casper speculated out loud. He discovered it was a good way to problem solve. "Okay, force field around town. Must be a deflector shield. Deflector shield? What is this, Star Trek? How it works unknown. Ring is obviously causing it. Oxygen, wind and most likely water are getting through it, at least I assume water is getting through because our water is coming from the reservoir miles away and no one has told us to conserve water. What about natural gas pipes? Whatever. Two things came out of ring in a showy way, yet, ring appears to have no inside structure meaning it's contents are invisible or it's not even a ship. No idea what happened to the first thing that came out of the ring, but the second one had a big white ball in it that felt warm and floated. That could have been the inhabitant of the ring meaning Darla may kill me if I messed up our first encounter with an alien life form." He picked up some frozen steaks and noticed Bosq's suction cup claw prints on the ice crystals. "Weird…Anyway: Force field around town, wammy powers allowing us to speak Japanese and have good teeth–crap! This is looking more and more like setting us up to be hormone injected cattle! Any minute now the aliens are gonna start harvesting us! Well, if they eat me, I hope they choke on the years of mercury, genetically modified foods and non BPA plastics I've eaten."

Bosq found this creature fascinating. He liked the fact that he spoke to himself. Where he came from, those that spoke to themselves were considered crazy (we won't spoil it for him that the same rule applies here). Bosq sat down on a crate of frozen dinners.

"Who am I kidding! I'm only a student. I wish Professor Pascal was here–poor guy. I'm gonna miss him. So tired of men I look up to, dying. What would my dad do? He could care less what the army said. It's not up to them to save us all, it's up to me and everybody in this town to save ourselves. I gotta do something. I gotta help get us out of here or at least make things easier for us. What can I do? What do we need to do?"

The words "Make plants." Were heard in Casper's right ear. He jumped to the left and looked around for where the words came from. Bosq, realizing he probably shouldn't have spoken, quickly exited the freezer. "Who's there!" Casper yelled. A minute later, Darla looked into the open freezer door. "What?"

"Oh, ha–ha," he said sarcastically. "Very funny."

"What are you talking about?"

"Make plants? What does that even mean?"

Darla turned her head sideways. "Get out of the freezer. Your brain is starting to harden."

"Whatever. Your joke's not funny. Make plants. How's that gonna…"

"Seriously. Get out of the freezer." Darla left to go back to counting water bottles.

"I guess if we are stuck here, it wouldn't do any harm to prepare for the long haul. And if we run out of food in a couple of months, it would make sense to have some crops started." Casper left the back room and walked to the home and garden section. On a rack were many packages of seeds. He thought about what the easiest things to grow were. When he and his roommates tried to do a planter box garden on the roof, things like tomatoes did okay but the best were the things that grew like weeds in California, such as: arugula, fennel and mint. He took some packages of the seeds and saved them to be purchase later.

His thoughts focused on his grandfather on his dad's side. His grandfather was a large man, not only in body but also in spirit and energy. When Casper and his family visited him at his home in Sonoma, he liked to take Casper and his cousin Sonia out into the garden to put them to work, weeding and planting whatever was in season. Although nobody ever talked about it, his grandfather had a tattoo of six numbers on his arm. His grandfather went to the grave without discussing the numbers. "Are we in that kind of situation?" Casper wondered. "Who's to say that the aliens don't have a nefarious reason for locking us all in the force field? How did Grandpa survive? How did he stay positive in a situation like that?"

Darla came up from behind and startled Casper. "Relax," she said. "I'm not going to kill you...yet. What were you spacing out about?"

"Just thinking about my family and how they would handle being in this town."

"I know what mine would do and I'm sure it'd involve guns and crystal meth."

Casper wasn't sure if she was joking. He felt a little sad for her. "Sorry for maybe ruining our first encounter with an alien life force."

"It's not your fault. I'm just feeling stressed out. It's pretty heavy knowing that we can't leave."

"For now."

"Sure, for now."

He risked a violent reaction and gave her a shoulder hug. She leaned into him and put her head on his shoulder. "You asked me why I don't seem bothered about all this."

"Yeah. Why ain't this freaking you out?"

"It is. On a scale from one to ten on the freak-out scale, I'm on eleven. But I had relatives that went through a lot worse than even the comet that almost killed us all. Yet they survived and thrived. I'm trying to channel their super powers to keep me going." Darla gave him a hug. "I need something good to happen." With the proximity of her head to his head, and the feeling of her breath on his ear, he knew what could happen between them at this point. For the first time, ever, he was glad to see Sue.

"What are you two doing?" Sue asked.

They pulled away from each other and simultaneously yelled: 'Nothing!'

Plür was uncertain what the TV monitor on wheels was or why two men in white haz-mat (there's that word, again) suits were pushing it towards her. With just a thought, she could communicate an urgent message for help to Bosq and he would come running, or hopping in his case. She decided to take a chance and have faith that the orange hairless ape creatures meant her no harm. Unseen by her, the many snipers on the nearby roofs had orders to "pop the balloon" if she made any threatening movements towards the soldiers pushing the monitor towards her.

On the electronic end of the monitor, the President straightened his tie and prepared for his speech. "Should I start with a joke?" he said to the camera person. "How about: A priest, a rabbi, and an alien walked into a bar, bartender says, we don't serve your kind here and the alien says which kind: The first, the second, or the third kind?" The camera operator didn't laugh. This of course didn't affect the Presidents decision to use or not use the joke. He took a deep breath and tried to appear as if he wasn't nervous and knew everything that was needed to know about the world. He was it, he was the sole representative of the entire human race. Any mistakes he made would be recorded and remembered by the out-of-town visitors. As the camera on the monitor got closer and closer to Plür, his stress level climbed higher and higher. The problem was, whenever he was stressed out, he went into lizard-brain mode. Lizard -brain mode happened to all humans. It was that part of you that was leftover from our days of ape-like shenanigans. If there is no danger, we are in "rest and repair" mode. We are relaxed, our bladder is loose, we can have sex and our blood vessels are dilated. In "fight or flight" mode, or "lizard brain', we are being chased by a tiger; Our bladder shuts down, heart pumps more blood to get more oxygen to the muscles, our blood vessels constrict in order to minimize bleeding and the furthest thing we can think about is sex. When one is in this mode, the main thing they want to do is protect themselves. They are not thinking in any intellectual way about the fate of the Earth or what they should or shouldn't say. The only thing Jarod wanted to do was protect himself and his bladder from the alien. In other words, he was totally freaking out, dude!

The soldiers brought the video monitor within two meters of Plür. She levitated to get to an equal height with it. She hoped this wouldn't be taken as a sign of aggression. The soldiers pushing the monitor stopped and withdrew themselves from the scene in a calm fashion. A few seconds later the seal of the President of the United States appeared on the screen. Plür backed away briefly and then got closer to see what the pretty painting was. She could read the words. "President of the United States. I know what the words 'President of the' means, but 'United Predicaments' is confusing." The President faded into the scene with a star shaped video editing feature filter called 'star wipe.'

"Wait, what was that?" he said to the camera man.

"I thought it would be better for your intro if I faded in with a star effect."

"Listen, Spielberg, cut the fancy stuff and just fade in!" he said a little angry.

The screen faded back to the Presidential seal and then faded back to the President, this time using a circle opening type of fade in.

"What was that?" the President complained. "That was even worst! Looks like the intro to a Bugs Bunny cartoon!"

Again, the screen faded out and this time, the filter was a bunch of fake lightning bolts and the words: "Bob's Heavy Metal Vacation!" on the top of the screen.

"For the love of Texas! Someone get that idiot off the camera!" the President yelled.

The camera shook for a second, faded to black and then faded in with a normal fade in.

General Katz didn't see the last part because his hands were over his eyes in an attempt to alleviate his headache. "Someone please tell me when it's over and the aliens declare war on us," he mumbled.

"Hello?" said the President.

"Hello?" Plür responded.

The President was confused. Instead of "hello" the only thing he heard was a thump, similar to the sound one would hear, hitting a large inflated latex balloon with a drum stick. "My name is Jimmy Jarrod. I'm the President of the United States of America. The richest most powerful country on Earth...Which I guess makes me the most powerful man on Earth—sorta like Superman. You guys have Superman comics on your planet? Anyway, may I ask who or what you are?"

"Greetings Jimmy Jarrod, head of United Emotions of America, Similar to Superior Male. My mortal shell is called Plürreannedunadugavas. I am an ambassador from the Collection of Wanderers."

Again, Jimmy had no idea what she was saying, as did anyone receiving the video broadcast. "I'm sorry, we're not getting good audio on this end—keep hearing some weird thumping sounds. Is the mike okay on your end General C?"

"Kowalski!" the general called to the men in a broadcast van, one block away, designed in a similar way to a news van, complete with a large antenna on its top. "Are we broadcasting? They seem to be having trouble understanding what's going on."

"Everything's okay on our end." Kowalski responded.

"Then what's the prob..." The general remembered something. "Mr. President..."

"Yes, Tom Cat?"

(Pause for the general to take a meditative breath) "...Mr President, We can understand everything that she's saying. I think it's because, you're outside of the ring."

"Wait, it's a she?"

" Yes, sir, her name is Plür-re Anne something."

"How can you tell it's a girl? Looks like a beach ball to me... Unless it's a giant floating breast."

"I'm only going by the voice. I guess I should use the word 'they'."

"Could be like Richie Valens, Little Richard or Michael Jackson?"

"True, but for all intents and purposes, let's go with she for now, until they let us know otherwise."

"You can understand her and she can understand me?"

" Yes, sir. Because we can understand anyone as long as we're inside here."

"This is gonna make things more difficult."

"Not really sir, I'll translate whatever she says."

"Alright then, I guess I'll start with asking for their complete surrender or else we'll nuke…" The President's broadcast went blank.

"Kowalski! What just happened?"

"We lost the broadcast from Antarctica."

"Did the aliens do that? Get ready to–"

"It's not them sir, it's the broadcast van, the antenna just broke."

"What? How can that be? Fix it! Now!"

"Already on it, sir."

While they scrambled to unscramble the broadcast, Plür floated close to the monitor. "Hello? Jimmy Jarrod, head of United Emotions of America, Similar to Superior Male? I can not see your face. Are you sleeping?"

General Katz looked at Plür. "We gotta fix this train wreck or else this could ruin our chances for a dialog!"

"This is gonna take at least 15 minutes to fix, sir," Kowalski said.

"We don't have 15 minutes!"

"Go talk to her!"

"What?" The general was taken aback, as if Kowalski had given a command to him.

"Talk to her, sir. Before it's too late…like you said."

"Just do your job, and let me worry about the alien."

Plür continued to ask for the return of the President's face in the monitor. This made the general more and more anxious. He was afraid this scene could quickly escalate into her being angry and then what would she do? If they can create unbreakable force fields, what other weapons did they have at their disposal?

"Jimmy Jarrod, head of United Emotions of America, Similar to Superior Male?" Plür asked. "Is this a ritual greeting?"

"Enough of this!" the general said. He left his tent and walked to the tarp covered area. Like a child peeking in to look at Santa Claus, the general looked inside to see Plür talking to the dead TV monitor. "Hi," he said waving.

Plür floated around the monitor and came to a stop.

"Hello, can you hear me?"

She floated closer to him. "Hello."

"Greetings, I- I'm a- I'm General Flint Francis Katz, Leader of the North Atlantic Treaty Organization and the commanding officer of the Pepper Mill civilian protection division."

"Hello General Flint Francis Katz, Leader of the North Atlantic Treaty Organization and the commanding officer of the Pepper Mill civilian protection division. My name is Plürreannedunadugavas. I am an ambassador from the Collection of Wanderers and a member of the Ancient Orange Nimbus of the North Wind."

"Er-ah, Plür-era-re-anne…"

"Plürreannedunadugavas"

"Plür-ere-Plür-reanne…"

"Plürreannedunadugavas"

"Plür…Can I just call you Plür?"

"Oh…Oh my…Hmm,…well. Usually I am only called Plür by close friends and family. But if it is part of your custom, you may…It is considered a little rude where I came from but…"

"Oh! I'm sorry, I don't want to offend you. For my people, we shorten names also as a sign of friendship or family."

"No, it is all right. Please, whatever is easiest for you. I will consider it an act of friendship."

The general smiled. He was not used to being a diplomat. He'd assume stick a bayonet into a foreigner than negotiate with them. He looked behind at the base tent, for a sign that the President was ready to broadcast again.

Miles away, the President along with the rest of the world was in a panic, wondering what was going on inside the force fielded town.

"Don't blame us, the President explained to the world leaders. This is what happens when you get all your parts from China."

"Hi-yah!" yelled the Chinese President.

"Can anyone tell me whats going on at the scene?"

"Yes, sir" answered a technician. "We have a satellite feed from above." Everyone watched the satellite camera zoom in from miles in space to the tops of the general and Plür."

"Who is that?"

"Hard to tell sir. He's probably one of ours."

"I don't really care who he is, why is he talking to my alien?"

"We don't have audio sir, so it's impossible to know if he's having a conversation with it."

"Try and get my picture back. I'm not gonna let somebody steal my spot light!"

In Pepper Mill there was a silent lull in the conversation between the general and Plür.

He cleared his throat and looked back at the blank monitor and then back at Plür. She remain perfectly still. Hovering at his chest height. He wondered how in the world did she float and decided to pose this question, "Sorry about the wait. The guy whose supposed to do this is…Well, we're having communication problems."

"I see."

There were a few minutes of silence broken by the general. "So…What exactly are you?"

"Pardon?"

"Your species or race. We call ourselves humans. What are you?"

"I am an ambassador from the Collection of Wanderers and a member of the Ancient Orange Nimbus of the North Wind."

"That's where you're from? Or is that your race?"

"I do not understand the question."

"Okay, like if you look at me, I have arms and legs. And you're shaped like a sphere. So how do your people identify themselves compared to people that look like me?"

"I have to apologize. Some words you are saying don't always translate correctly. If I understand what you are saying, you mean what type of animal are you compared to me."

"Yes, that's it. What's your animal name?"

"I am an ambassador from the Collection of Wanderers and a member of the Ancient Orange Nimbus of North Wind."

The general resisted the urge to sigh. "Ok, fine. Can I call you a floater, or is that insulting?"

"Whatever is easiest for you. The ring doesn't translate everything correctly. There are some words that are so unique to different animals that they come off as…"

"Wait a minute." he interrupted. "You said the ring."

"Correct. The ring. Can you not see the ring in the sky?"

"Oh, yes. Very much so. Is that your space ship?"

"Space-Ship? I don't know that word. The ring is an artifact from the First Ordinal."

"First what?"

"The First Ordinal. They are the ones we credit with creating the rings and sending them to different parts of the Collection."

"You mean space?"

"Space?"

"You know, where you're from? Outer space."

"Space is an unoccupied area. I am not from an empty place."

"No, you see…" He was about to explain what "space" meant. He knew this would lead to other subjects not related to what he wanted to find out. "Okay. So these First Ordinals are not you?"

"No, I am a member of the Ancient Orange Nimbus of the North Wind."

"Oh, I get it. That's your planet or country name."

"Planet. That word translates as wanderer."

"Yes, it's what we're standing on…or at least I am. How are you floating like that?"

"I was told by another animal it has something to do with ourselves are made of that which is lighter than the things around us."

"You don't know?"

"We are not into technology like you and some others are."

"What about your space ship?"

"Space-ship? An unoccupied area that floats on water?"

"…I mean that thing you came in from the ring. Looked like an egg."

"We did not come from the ring. We came through the ring."

"Through? You mean like a door?" (Actually he means doorway because going through a door involves a kungfu soundtrack, crashing and lots of splinters).

"The ring is not a vehicle if that is what you mean. The ring is…It is a way…It is that which is uniting us…It is what lets you understand me…It is also what separated us form our people."

"Separates. You mean the force field?"

"Force?"

"The invisible wall that keeps us in here?"

"Yes. That is also the ring."

"And it has nothing to do with you?"

"It has everything to do with ALL of us."

"I mean your people didn't make it."

"No. We are not into technology. The ring was around millions, maybe billion of rotations ago. My people are only 20 thousand rotations."

"That sounds like a long time, Plür. Can you please explain why that thing is doing what it's doing? And how you know so much about it? And who are these First Ordinals? And if you're not into technology, what is that thing you came in?"

Bosq snuck up from behind Plür. "Plür!" he whispered a little loud. "Why are you talking to this creature? Why didn't you wait for me to make an evaluation before possible malign contact?"

"Sorry, Bosq. They approached me but he…I assume it is a male, he has not tried to harm me."

"Quick, before we scare him off, let us talk more in the transport."

"Who are you talking to?" The general asked.

"You'll have to excuse me, General Flint Francis Katz, Leader of the North Atlantic Treaty Organization and the commanding officer of the Pepper Mill civilian protection division." Plür apologized, backed away from him onto the metal flower petal. The petal folded up and formed an egg shape, enclosing her inside. A second later, communication with the President was reestablished and his face reappeared on the screen.

"…Throw you into a pit of snakes!" the President yelled before realizing he was on the air again. "What? Huh? What did I miss?"

"She's gone, sir. She went back inside the egg," The general answered.

"What? For the love of bacon! What did she say?"

"Lots sir, lots of things that I don't understand."

"That's why I have the scientist on the video chat. Gives us the 4-1-1. Is she a giant breast?"

While the general, now suffering from a headache, briefed the President and others about his conversation, miles away in Monterey, CA, Dr. Aarti Panjwani was in a bar, missing the most important meeting of two species since bacon met tomato. She was joined at her table by three others; two men and a woman, all with equal intelligence and academic achievements to hers. They were having a makeshift wake for the lost of their college and friend; Dr. Lewis Pascal. Aarti checked her video phone for any new feeds. So far, all she could see was the President explaining how to cup a gigantic breast. "Tuma êka bëvakūpha ho!" she said, basically stating: "he's an idiot."

"Why do you keep looking at your phone? Are we boring you" the White female scientist wearing glasses asked.

"I'm sorry, Linda. I'm on call tonight. It's rude, I should put it away, I'm sorry." Aarti put it in her purse and picked up her glass of water. "I should be here, for Lewis."

"Don't worry about it," guy scientist #1 said. "Life goes on. That's what he would have said."

"He would, wouldn't he? Except he would have added: Life goes on because of the Anthropic Principle." They all laughed at Aarti's joke. In case you are wondering what the Anthropic Principle is, It's basically the theory that the universe is compelled to create a life form to observe it, sorta like saying it can't exist without an audience. What a huge ego the universe must have. Perhaps this could be evidence for the theory of a higher being. "Hey everybody! Look at me!" yells God, four thousand years ago, on a flat earth, "Check out that garden I made! No wait, there is nobody here!' Zap! Man! "Hey look at my garden, man! Whoops, forgot the eyes." Zap! One eye. "Eew, cyclops!" Zap again: "Oooooh!' goes man. "Now, can you make something else for me to look at? perhaps with long hair and one gigantic breast?' "Two normal ones it is, ya freak!' God says. Anyway…They laughed at her joke, perhaps thinking about what I just said.

"So, Aarti, what are you working on, hows' your life?" Linda asked.

"We'll, I was working with Lewis until…"

"Right, right. But what were YOU up to?"

"I just told you. Lewis and I were on the comet thing and then some other stuff."

"Aarti, I know we came here to have a drink and toast Lewis, but I want to talk to you about something other than him."

"But why? That doesn't make sense."

"Just do it! Please!"

Aarti was quite confused. "Oh, okay. Well, I can't tell you about my job because it's top secret and I'll end up dead. Before the comet hit, I was taking a Zumba class but I quit because the only music they would play was Avro Pärt."

"Avro Pärt? In Zumba?"

"Avro Pärt. I bought a used car, a BMW which I think means 'Breaks Many Ways.' Before the comet thing, I was living in New York in an apartment that cost the same as the GDP of India. It had bad heat, a subway train that ran within 50 feet of my bedroom window and a view of a hairy guys bathroom, and he liked to shave his back every day. How's that?"

Linda raised her hands in the air and yelled: "Yes!"

"Whats your malfunction, Linda?"

"We passed the Bechdel test!"

Aarti looked at scientist guy #2. "What?"

"A movie or play must have more than one female character, and they have to talk about something other than a man," he answered.

"I'm totally applying that test to my life. I never talk to women unless we talk about something other than a man!" Linda grabbed a beer and took a big sip.

"So…Anyway, considering we're here for Lew—"

"Arrk!" Linda scoffed like an angry bird choking on a peanut shell.

"…Anyway. I think I'll talk to the guys instead. So, Lewis' body was never found?"

"No." answered scientist guy #2. "Don't get your hopes up. They found the wreckage in an area lousy with sharks and several witness saw it hit the water and sink. Unless he can survive shark attacks, a high impact into hypothermic, icy waters and a 10 mile swim to shore…He's gone, Aarti."

Aarti felt even sadder. She had not yet come to grips with her friend's death. She felt that any minute now, he would call her or show up and say: "just kidding" or something like that. The worst part, he was missing the reports of first alien contact.

"To Lewis!" Scientist guy #1 said, raising his glass. They all raised their glasses and clinked. "I don't know what happens to atheist when they die, but I'm sure it involves beer and a foosball table. Speaking of which, who wants to join me for a game?" Linda and scientist #2 joined him. Aarti said she would join them after checking her messages.

The video feed was now of the closed egg. It opened and Plür floated up and back over to the camera. The President's voice could be heard, apologizing for the technical difficulties. There was a thumping balloon sound. "What?" the President asked.

"She said don't worry about it." General Katz translated.

"Oh, okay. Now about your surrender and…." All communication was lost again.

Aarti put the phone away and went over to join her friends for a game of foosball.

Ami almost didn't recognize Finn. When she told him to meet her in the park across the street from the high school, she knew he wouldn't be wearing an army uniform, due to his discharge, but she didn't expect him to be dressed in rags and pushing a shopping cart, like a homeless person. "Finn?" she asked.

"Hello, Miss Ami."

"Finn? Why are you dressed like that and pushing a shopping cart?"

"I'm cutting out the middle man, Miss Ami. Without the army, I have nothing. I've failed at every single thing I've tried in my life. The army was my last chance to make something of myself. Now that I've failed that, The only thing I'm suited for is being a alcoholic bum, living on the streets. Least I can't fail at that."

Ami looked sadly at him and started to put her hand on his shoulder, she opted for giving him a light punch on the arm. "Oh, Finn, you're over exaggerating. You haven't failed at everything. My father always told me. "you haven't tried hard enough to fail." You're not going to turn into an alcoholic homeless person. For starters, you aren't drinking any alcohol."

Finn took out a brown bottle. "See!" He drank from it and winced in pain. "Ew-wee! That's strong beer, but I'll get used to it."

"Give me that!" Ami took the bottle away from him and read it. "It's not even beer, it's 'ginger beer'!" She threw it into a garbage can 15 feet away. "Ooh, nice!" she congratulated herself on her shot with an arm pump. "Get ahold of yourself, Finn! We're going to get you some new clothes, a job, a place to live and a new life as a productive member of society."

"You're gonna do all that for me?"

"Of course. You're my friend."

"Just your friend?"

"Yes? My friend…Also, I feel responsible for getting you kicked out of the army."

"Ah ha! So that's what this is about, you feel guilty! Well, don't you worry, you don't owe me anything! I don't need your help!"

"Finn, it's not about guilt, it's about my honor. If I can't help you, it would be dishonorable."

"This a Japanese thing?"

"Honor? Sure, why not."

"Well, I don't want you having to kill yourself with a samurai sword because of me." There was a clicking sound. "What was that?"

"I'm sorry. I rolled my eyes so hard they made a clicking sound —any way, let's head on over to Don's Café."

"Don's Café? I don't know anything about making coffee."

"I was thinking of getting a coffee, but that's not a bad idea. Maybe he can hire you to do stuff." They headed off towards the café.

Unfortunately, when they arrived at Don's café, they saw Don had placed a sign on the window that read: "Going swimming, be back at 4:00'. You see, after being held in detention for a couple of days and feeling cheated out of his dream house by the army when they told him he couldn't move into an abandoned mansion, Don decided to take it upon himself to at least take advantage of the swimming pool in its backyard. So, with towel in hand, and trunks underneath his clothes, he traveled back to the house of the Russian businessman to go for a quick dip. The pool cleaning robot was still operational as it rolled along on the bottom of the pool, keeping the water pure and scum less. Don pulled the robot out by it's vacuum tube, onto the shore so he wouldn't dive onto it. He looked around to make sure there were no army personnel to harass him as well or perverts who get their jollies by watching Black men change into swimsuits. (I think they sell that magazine at your best pornographic book stores). After a few stretches to prevent cramps, Don stepped back and plotted his trajectory. He calculated if he took a running jump, it would land him right in the middle of the pool where the water appeared to be at least six feet deep. Like a track runner, he hunched down and almost on the count of three, he took a few fast steps and launched himself in the air. His calculations were fairly accurate. His speed and height were going to cause him to hit the pool right in the dead center. At least it would have been that way if he suddenly didn't hit an invisible wall and his body went flat against it like a fly, hit by a gigantic swatter. There was a thump sound, mixed with a meat being hit with a cricket bat sound and then a squeaky glass sound as he slowly slid into the pool. For a moment, Don stayed under water. It wasn't because he was hurt or drowning, it was because he didn't know what to do. He slowly raised his head out of the water and stared at the invisible wall (which is hard to do because you can't see it). He lifted up a hesitant hand and moved it forwards until it hit the force field. The harder he pressed against the air, the harder it became. He made a fist and when he struck the wall, his arm was thrown back by equal force.

"What.......The........F—!"

The 'F' word was not heard because at that exact moment, a crow, which had seen Don hit the wall, did the crow version of laughing–or a squawk. The bird, satisfied with his afternoon entertainment, flapped it's wings and flew pass Don, right through an area to the right, where the wall would continue and flew out of site. Don treaded water to the area the crow had just flown through and reached out his hand. It hit resistance. He looked down at the water in the pool. There was no sign that the wall had any effect on the ripples of water that moved from one end of the pool to the other. "We're trapped!" he muttered.

The metal flower unfolded as it had before and Plür, once again, floated from it's center towards the general. Bosq whispered some final instructions to her, continuing their conversation from the inside of the transport: "Now remember, do not reveal anything which can jeopardize your security. We don't know what these creatures find moral or not. They have many things which I think are weapons of some sort. There is a lack of conservation which points towards decimation of their own kind which means a complete disregard of life and they eat meat, not just meat, I saw at least five different species in their food storage area. I'm sure they'd have no problem eating a large round morsel like you…"

"Bosq! That is enough." Plür said, rather cross. This was not like her. She was taught not to let anger even make an appearance in her personality. Many hours of meditation and studying usually kept it away like a cloud passing overhead, but this was her first meeting with a level three society. The level ones and twos were so much easier to establish contact with. They just wanted basic necessities: food, shelter, reproduction and a place to discard waste. These creatures were different with their leaders, weapons and organized roads with carbon monoxide spewing machines. The general waited for her to arrive. She wondered if he had been standing there the whole time, waiting for her to come back. "Patience" she thought. A good part of the 88 emotions.

"You're back," he said

"Yes. I am sorry for leaving, I...I had something I needed to do."

"That's fine. Everything all right?"

"Yes, thank you."

"So..." The general looked back at the video monitor. There was still no picture of the President. "I'm sorry that my leader isn't here to speak to you. There seems to be some sort of trouble."

"Oh, I thought the mechanical life form was your leader."

"Mechanical?" The monitor?" He pointed to the screen. "You think that's alive?"

"It is not?"

"Heavens no, that's just a picture of our leader. He's far away, outside the ring. We're using the monitor so you can talk to him."

"And what are you?"

"Me? I'm a man. A human to be exact."

"And this place is?

"This place is called Pepper Mill..." The general gestured to the ground and then waved his arms around. "...But this place is called Earth. Is that what you mean?"

"Oh! I understand, now. Many other creatures call their homes, 'Earth'. I think there are at least 500 by that name."

The general's legs became weak in the knees. "Five hundred? There are 500 Earths out there?"

"I am just estimating, perhaps more."

"Are there any creatures like us?"

"Similar, but never the same."

"I guess we're not alone in the Universe."

"We are all alone until we approach others with compassion. We are always together with all sentient beings."

"That's nice to know."

Plür paused for a moment. She knew what Bosq had lectured her about when it came to protocol and security, but she also knew what she had been taught. It is true, the human creature could be as dangerous as any race she had ever met, but she knew he was also a member of the Universal light as she was. Unless she made a connection with him, nothing would come of their meeting. They were two beings hiding their emotions and true selves from each other. They were both showing their outer shells. "General," she said very hesitant.

"Yes, Plür?"

"Will you show me your true self?"

"Pardon?"

"Your true self. I know that we are both behaving in a guarded state right now. I think for the sake of developing a rapport, we should shed our outer shells."

"That's true. But you have to understand. You people came to US and captured OUR town, changed us and we have no idea what you want."

"You mean the effects of the ring? The ring was created by the First Ordinal."

"You told me that. But as far as I'm concerned, you're that first Ordinal."

"I understand where your fear is coming from. What can I do to remove the barrier between us?"

"You can tell me how to remove the force field around the town."

"I can not."

"And why is that?"

"Because every planet, as you call them, in the Collection of Wanderers, have similar rings on them.

"And each one has a force field, surrounding a town?"

Bosq came up behind Plür again and whispered: "stop giving them too much information, their brains may not understand certain concepts. He may get frustrated and that can lead to anger and violence."

Plür paused again. "General. Put yourself in my place. I am scarred, very scarred."

"Plür!" Bosq whispered rather loudly.

"What was that?" The general asked looking around."

"Ignore that, please. Just know that I am going to ignore it as well." She couldn't see him, but she knew Bosq was angry. "I am here as a member of the Collection of Wanderers." It is my duty to connect to others joined by the rings."

"How many members are there?"

"8473 varieties of animals."

"Wow!"

"I do not understand, 'wow!'"

"It means I'm surprised and in shock."

"Now, I have given you information which we usually reserve for much later, after we have discovered that you mean us no harm. What are you willing to give me in exchange as a sign of trust?"

The general looked around at the large tarp surrounding them. This was not a very inviting scene. "Captain Kowalski!" he yelled at were the captain's tent would be located. "I want you to remove all of the tarps around here and have all soldiers pull back to the edge of the park."

Within a few minutes, one by one, the tarp walls came crashing down as soldiers dismantled them faster then they were raised. Armed soldiers walked out of the park to nearby streets. Like the sun had been let in, Plür found herself in the middle of the field, surrounded by trees, the town of Pepper Mill and a better grasp of the creatures level of technological advancement.

"Is that better?" he asked her.

"Thank you. It was not very inviting having a wall around you. And creatures holding weapons."

"Let's start over. Welcome to Earth, Plür. Our home is your home."

Watching the whole scene and listening in on their conversation by a one way radio, Captain Kowalski put his binoculars down and smiled. "Excellent." His cellphone rang. "Hello?" There was a pause as he listened to the voice on the other end. "Yes...Yes, sir...It worked. All is going according to plan." The captain hung up the phone and continued ease dropping on the general and Plür.

Don stood in front of Casper and Darla. He was wearing his swim trunks, a T-shirt and flip flops. In his right hand, he held a change or clothes. He could have changed into his clothes while he was still at the Russian's house but he wanted to get to Casper as fast as possible. Casper of course was surprised to see Don at his work as well as his attire. "Er-ah, Don? Is it casual Tuesday or are you in a Jimmy Buffet Margaritaville kind of mood?"

"I just came from that house that I found, the one with the pool."

"The one the army told you to stay away from?"

"They didn't say anything about the pool."

"And why are you here instead of your café?"

"The pool."

"Pool of what?"

"The swimming pool, Cap! I took a dive in it and I hit a wall!"

"Oh my god! Dude. Are you all right?" Casper walked over and put his hand on Don's head. There were no bumps bruises or blood.

"No, that wasn't it! I hit an INVISIBLE wall and I bounced off! I FELT an invisible wall! I ran my hand alongside it all the way through that neighborhood! As far as I'm concerned, it follows the edge of the ring! Probability goes around the whole town! That must have been what Mr. Campbell hit when he stole your bike!"

"Neither Casper nor Darla showed any concern for what Don had just said. If anything, Casper's expression was more like being caught in a lie. "Don't you get it, Cap? There's a force field around the town!"

Casper looked around to make sure none of the shoppers in the store had heard Don. He grabbed Don's arm and lead him to the stock room.

"Wait, don't you get it, man? We're trapped in this town! There is no quarantine! We're trapped...Wait, where are you taking me?" When they were out of earshot of customers, Casper stopped dragging Don.

"Alright. It's like this. Yes. There is a force field and yes we are trapped."

"Wait, did you know about this?"

"Me and Darla found out right before that white ball thing showed up."

"And you didn't tell me?"

"We can't."

"Can't tell your best friend something like that?"

"It's a secret."

"Secret? Casper, you told me once you have fear of pomegranates!"

"Argh! Don't mention the 'P' word!"

"Sorry, but there ain't nothing we don't share between us? Why would you keep something so important as our impending doom! From me?"

"Because of the way you're acting."

"And how is that?"

"Look at you, man. You're literally soaking wet and freaking out! The army told us to put a lid on it. Imagine if other people in town find out about that thing? It'll be a Busby Berkley bloodbath in here."

Don put his head on his hands and sat on a box of Lisbon soda. "I can't believe this, we're trapped! What are we gonna do? Can we fly out?"

"Nope, shaped like a cylinder with a lid."

"Under?"

"I assume the army tried that."

"How are we able to breathe? Should we be saving air?" Don's cheeks puffed out and he held his breath.

Casper walked over and poked Don's cheeks, causing him to exhale like a popped balloon. "Relax. Somehow, air and water are getting in here."

"How do you know?"

"Because our tap water, electricity and gas is still running. The reservoir and natural gas lines come from miles away. Has to go through the forcefield to get here."

"That's pretty logical."

"I have my moments. Just wish the army had a use for me."

"Wait-a-minute. If air, water and gas are getting through, electronic signals or satellite communications can get through."

"We already know that from the foreign television channels we can pick up."

"So the army really is making it look like the ring is blocking signals!"

"Yep. Probably to keep us from sharing info to the public about what's going on in here."

"Those sons of—stupid Finn, acting like it wasn't true! That's it! I'm gonna try to contact my family!"

"And how, may I ask?"

"Piggy Back?"

"I'm not carrying you anywhere—oh wait, that program you were working on?"

"Yep."

"But doesn't that just let you log on to locked wi-fi signals? You can't really use that if there are no wi-fi signals."

"You're right. It's useless." Don looked sad.

"Unless…"

"What?"

"ATMs and point of purchase machines."

"Come again?"

"People are using the ATM and the credit card machines at the registers. How are those things communicating with the outside world?"

"That's true! The ATM would be hard to crack into, but the cash register machines have been hacked a zillion times! If I can get ahold of one of the machines, I can check out it's program called Domain Center of Excellence which is Windows Embedded for point of service. I can duplicate it's protocols, and use Piggy Back to camouflage a signal coming from our lap tops or smart phones. Then boom! Ride the wave of the wi-fi!" Don had become very excited.

Casper felt like he was speaking backwards Swedish. "Sounds good…Whatever all that means."

"Basically I fool the signal jamming devices. There's only one problem."

"There's always is. What?"

"I need you to steal one of the credit card machines from one of the registers."

"Did someone say steal?" Darla asked, standing in the doorway.

"Darla," Casper said happily. "Just the amoral expert I was looking for." He walked over to her and put his hands on her upper arms. "Don may have a way for us to talk to people outside the Ring. But we need you to help us steal…borrow one of the cash register credit card machines."

"Does it have to be completely intact?" Casper looked at Don.

Don shook his head no. "I just need one chip inside it."

"I guess not, can you do it?" Casper asked looking her in the eyes.

"Sure, but on one condition."

"What…You're not going to make me kill someone are you?"

"No…no…maybe—I mean no! I want to go out on a date!"

This was not what Casper was expecting. "A date? As in drinking sodas together, parking the car at Inspiration Point, kind of a date?"

"What are you, in the 50s? Yeah, a date! One that doesn't involve alien rings, bar fights or anything else that can interrupt us."

"Okay. If that's what you want. After work you can go help me plant Arugula."

"Come again? That some Jewish saying for dating?"

"No, I'm going to go find a nice field somewhere and plant some crops. If we're stuck in this ring forever, then we'll be running out of food in a couple of months. Probably a good time to work on a backup food supply."

"Planting crops does not sound like a date. That sounds like Farmville, without the drinking."

"You drink while playing Farmville?"

"You mean you don't? Anyway, I want to go to a romantic spot."

"Oooookay." Casper was a little nervous about Darla's directness. She was obviously bothered by the numerous interruptions of their impending kiss. "Tell you what. This weekend, I'll take you to The Pepper Grind."

"Ugk!" Darla scoffed. "I'm tried of that place!"

"Well, there aren't many restaurants in town to eat at anymore." Don snapped his finger. "You guys could dine at my café!"

"Not exactly the French Laundry, Don. You don't serve food that does't rhyme with 'uffins.'"

"Fine then. Why don't you whip something up at home, grab a bottle of wine, and I'l let you guys have the place for the evening, after I close."

"That'll work." Darla said. "So, you guys need me to get one of those machines?"

"Yes, but how are you gonna do it? Sue kicks us out as soon as we're closed…"

Darla cut off Casper's question by leaving the back room and heading to the front. Casper and Don peeked out to see what she was doing. She walked pass the aisle containing toys and sports equipment and picked up a baseball bat.

"Oh, oh," Don said. "Is she going to kill your boss and take one?"

"I'll allow that, but I don't think so. Sue has two soldiers working the registers, I doubt they'll let that happen."

Without being seen by Sue and the two soldiers, who were quite busy ringing people up, Darla put the bat at one of the empty registers. She then walked up to Sue. "Hey, Sue, can I take a break?"

"What?" Sue complained. "You've only been here three hours, what do you think this is, France?"

"I'm pretty sure, you're supposed to get a break every two hours at least."

"Probably before I became boss of the store, and you two goof-offs skipped work for two or three days."

"Come on Sue. I need a break before I get goth rage."

"Goth what?"

"Goth rage. When a goth's blood sugar get's low, we either have to drink blood or eat something...preferably a baby or we go into a rage."

"Whatever. Get back to work and stop making up crap."

"But Sue."

"Now, Marbles! Back to the back with you!" Sue pointed to the back of the store.

"Oooooh nooooo!" Darla moaned. She held her head with her hands and moaned some more.

"For Elvis sake, Marbles, stop goofing around and go to the back!"

Darla moaned and swayed as if she were either sick or trying to keep her head from coming off, which would have been a brilliant trick; no one would see that one coming, not even me, and I'm the narrator...Alas she stumbled around until she made it back to the cash register with the bat under neath it. She picked up the bat and yelled: "GOTH RAGE!" and with two loud crashing swipes, she knocked the credit card machine off it's post and sent it flying into the aisle, towards Don and Casper.

"Whoa..." Don said. "That's your girl, Cap! Good luck with that!"

"I'm hoping she's soft on the inside...Like a marshmallow...in a hedge hog's mouth."

"WHAT THE FOX NEWS, MARBLES! Sue yelled. The soldiers stopped ringing people up and were about to leave the register to grab Darla. Darla raised her hands up and now pretend to be normal again. "It's okay, it's okay, sorry, sorry. Low blood sugar."she pleaded. This was enough to stop the soldiers approaching her and they went back to their registers.

"You're fired! Marbles."

"You can't fire me, remember."

"Then you're-you're-you're gonna clean up that mess and no 15 minute break until 15 minuted before you leave!"

"Woo-hoo! I get to leave early." Darla skipped down the aisle towards the mess. She picked it up and took the credit card machine to Don and Casper.

Plür had enjoyed talking to General Katz, but she was physically tired. It had been a long day and she needed to rest and meditate. She let him know about this fact after he had finished describing the different races on Earth.

"…And people use the words 'African Americans' even though I have a White friend that moved from South African and he's basically an African American. So you can see how it get's confusing."

"I can. General Katz, I would love to talk to you some more but I need to regenerate and meditate."

"I'm sorry if I kept you from resting."

"It is no problem. I will see you again when your sun has risen."

"Okay. Until then, Plür. Have a good rest." Once again, Plür floated to her metal pod, and as soon as it closed, once again, the President's monitor started working again. "The general walked over to the screen.

"Don't tell me. She's gone, ain't she?" the President sighed.

"Yep."

"Ya, know, General Whiskers. I'm starting to think it ain't no accident that whenever I try to talk to the out of town visitor. You guys C-block me."

"Believe me sir. I have no idea what's going on but I intend to get to the bottom of it."

"Whelp, while I got you here, I have my giant brain scientist friends on this call. Why don't you drop some knowledge on us, C-Dog."

"Well, a lot of what I'm saying is guess-work because what we say to her gets directly translated. Like if I said 'the Earth is round' she would ask around what?"

"So you should use the words the Earth is a sphere?" asked the voice of astrophysicist, Dr. Julius Xiang.

"That's right, professor. Many times I had to correct myself. Took a while to figure out how to tell her that the United States of America is a country on planet Earth, just like it took a while to figure out that her country is the Ancient Orange Nimbus of the North Wind—by the way, everybody seems to use the names: Earth and Sun."

"So what can you tell us about her space ship?" asked Theodore Larson from the Jet Propulsion Laboratory.

"First of all. The thing she came in is not a space ship. It's some kind of transport thing. She seemed confused when I talked about space travel, like her people had never been there.

"Then how did she travel so far to get to us?"

"The ring. It's like a door to thousands, maybe millions of planets. The egg things are how she travels between them. The rings all have area's locked inside, like Pepper Mill."

"Inside a force field? She gets in and out of the force field?"

"Only using her pod thing. And it can only go from planet to planet but can't leave the enclosed area, just like we can't leave Pepper Mill. Also, all of the planets, have an enclosed area full of what I'm guessing are other alien races, all trapped. With no where to go but from planet to planet."

"Are all of the alien races intelligent?" Aarti asked.

"No. Some are just simple animals, some are the same as us, but there are some that are far more advanced than us."

"The whole thing sounds like a giant hamster cage, where the only way to get from cage to cage is through plastic tubes," the President added.

"To put it bluntly, yes. This also means, if they don't know how to get out of the field, then we're trapped in here, forever."

"Not so sure about that," said Dr. Sal Roselli from M.I.T. She told you there are millions of planets, connected to the ring or rather, rings. If she has technology more advanced than us, someone else, yet to be contacted, can have technology to get in and out."

"She mentioned that. As part of her mission as ambassador is initiating contact for some type of alien alliance she calls the Collection of Wanderers. It took me a while to figure out the word wanderers was planets. But her job is to find an alien race that can get out of the force field.

"And how long has she been looking?"

"She said this is her 100th cycle on her 100th rotation of birth. No idea how long a cycle is but if she's 100 years old, we can say she's been looking for a while."

"Assuming there are millions of rings out there around millions of planets, how did she find us?"

"Remember that egg that was here before her? That was like a drone. It's job was to find planets with intelligent life on them. The message 'press the red button was an intelligence test. Soon as it's pressed, the egg sends a signal to her Collection friends so that they know there may be intellect life on a planet.

"How many of these drones are out there?" asked Dr. Xiang.

"She had no idea. She could be keeping it a secret for security reasons, just like she refused to tell me who made all of the spaceships and advanced stuff.

"Maybe the ones that created the ring, could also be responsible for all of the advanced technology."

"That's possible. Said Mr. Larson. They created the road and gave them the wheel. Did she mention what planet the ring came from or is there a particular planet that has all of the gadgets and things?"

"No. But that could be a security thing."

"What about weapons?" asked the President. How can a cute little beach ball like her go to all of these planets by herself? I'm sure not all planets have a welcome mat and a Waffle House."

"Not all races are paranoid and war-like." Aarti complained.

"Even the Dali Lama has to have someone to keep the crazy fans at bay, Doc." the President retorted.

"I can't really answer that," the general said. "It's possible, she's able to protect herself. But I also get a sense that she's not alone, I mean I haven't seen any trace of anyone with her, but It feels like she's not the only one listening."

"Getting back to me..." the President said. "Is she willing to share any piece of technology with us? Those flying eggs, a new type of computer, something that lets us float around like her? 'Cause that would be cool."

"We didn't talk about that. I'm just trying to find out if she's dangerous or not."

"And is she?"

"My gut says no. I like her. She's seems to be on the level."

"Then again, she is a diplomat and everything she's said to you could be a lie. Lord knows I can butter up a leader's bread while I toast his country."

"True. It's impossible to tell unless I get more info on her and those other Wanderers members."

Inside the pod, Plür was having a similar conversation with Bosq. "He seems to be an honest animal," she said.

"Because he's polite."

"No, because I feel it."

"You can not go on emotions alone. We can't make a judgment on them unless we have more information."

"I now have a good idea how their society works. It is very similar to your people. You two are very much alike."

"Don't compare me to those hairless mammals."

"It is not an insult, Bosq. All creatures are beautiful."

"But not all creatures are harmless."

"That is true, Many mistakes have been made by other members of the Collection, with detrimental effect. But, I like this…What did he say they are called? Humans. I think they can become members."

"Do not advance to conclusions. It can take many cycles of information gathering to make a decision like that."

"By that time, they could have starved to death or any contribution they can offer us could be decimated. Remember the Ya'toul. It took many cycles for them to become members, and in that time, they lost half of their population. Just because the Collection didn't understand that they greet each other by stabbing."

"I really don't like them."

"Understandable. But I would like to get them cleared as soon as possible."

"I think you are being impatient because this is your first, class three life form and you want to make a good impression."

"My ego is not that high, Bosq. I only want to help these animals."

"Then be patient. Perhaps some of them will die. It's much better than them causing harm to the Collection."

"All life is important to me, Bosq. I will not let harm come to anyone if I can prevent it."

"Patience. Plür."

Plür thought for a moment. "Unless…"

"No! I will not let that happen."

"Bosq, it is my decision."

"It's dangerous! Remember what happened that one time?"

"That was 18 cycles ago. I have had two successful ones since then."

"That's because the last two were simple life forms! These… Humans have complicated bodies and emotions. Also, who knows what they'll do with your body!"

"This is all part of my duty. Besides, if they are willing to do it, then it is a sign of trust on their side. We would both be dropping our guard and showing our true selves."

"As your protector, I must state that I am completely against this."

"Duly noted." Plür began to meditate on her decision.

With all of General Katz's information on Plür revealed, Aarti felt it was safe to bow out of the meeting when the President presented his theories on Plür being a possible space vampire. She put her secured video conference device on mute and stared out into the waters off the coast of Monterey. She had taken a short walk on the beach and sat down on the sand when communications with the general had been re-established.

Somewhere out in the Pacific, Lewis's flaming plane went down in shark infested waters. She found the timing disturbing. Soon as he is kicked off the comet task force team, his plane crashes. Would the same happen to her if she quits or is kicked off the team? She wished she could somehow channel his soul. To talk to him, to get his theories on Plür and her Collection of Wanderers. The waves off the shore crashed on and off as they have done for millions of years, turning shells and rocks into sand. Aarti put her chin on her knees. "Oh, Lewis," she whimpered. She knew the soul never died and Lewis had cast off his shell. She thought about a verse from the Bhagavad Gita: "The Soul never takes birth and never dies at any time, nor does it come into being again when the body is created. The Soul is birth-less, eternal, imperishable and timeless and is never destroyed when the body is destroyed." This gave her a bit of solace. But, there was still an empty part in her heart. "So many things I wanted to tell you, Lewis," she said. She picked up some sand and let if fall onto her toes.

Out in the water, she spotted something. Her eyes adjusted. It was a human figure—but why was it in these cold waters? There were no waves big enough for surfing and this area had nothing to offer to the scuba divers. the figure swam closer, she saw that it was a man. "Could it be?" she wondered. She stood up to get a better look. The figure swam even closer. He was Lewis' height and although covered in kelp, appeared to look like him. Aarti stood up and walked to the edge of the shore. The extremely cold waves washed over her feet but she didn't care. The figure fell down in the shallow part, preventing her from seeing his face. She risked getting her pants wet and met him half way. Reaching into the water, she pulled up the man. "Lewis?" she asked. The man was dressed in tattered clothing, perhaps evidence of a plane wreak, and a long swim to shore.

"No, Roscoe," he said standing up. He was now revealed to be a swimming homeless man. The look of disappointment on Aarti's face must have registered with him as an insult. "What?" he complained. "Homeless people can't go swimming? He took a live, flapping fish out of his pants, walked around her and headed towards a nearby pier.

Don had gotten dressed and returned to his work to open up shop. There were 20 people in line in front of his coffee house, waiting to get in. "About time," one of them said. Don understood their impatience. They had been waiting a couple of days for him to reopen so that they can get a better cup of coffee at three times the price than they could make at home, While he tried his best to keep up with the multiple orders and ignored the complaints, he occupied his mind with finding a way to hack into the POS device in his backpack, and convince the phone lines to allow him to send a message to his parents. Codes ran through his mind, over and over as he arranged the data and rearranged it as if he were programing in his head. A site broke him out of his binary day dream; Ami and Finn walked towards the coffee house. If they were holding hands, it wouldn't have surprised him. "Why is that dude always with her?" Don mumbled. They entered the coffee house.

"Hey Don," Ami said cheerfully.

"Ami…" Don looked at Finn. "…You."

"Afternoon, Mr. Don."

"What brings you two in here…Together; actually, why are you together?"

Ami was perplexed by Don's attitude. If she didn't know better, she could swear he was jealous. But why would he be jealous? Was he not the one who said, he doesn't date his friends? "Finn needs a job. I figure since you're the owner of the café, you can hire him as a barista or bus boy, or something."

"Bus boy? You want me to hire HIM as my bus boy?"

"Or, barista."

Don looked at Finn. "You got any experience making coffee?"

"Sure," Finn said happily. "I used to get up every morning and make a cup for Miss Chatterley."

"Miss Chatterly? She your neighbor or something?"

"No. She was our family cat."

"You gave coffee, to a cat?" Both Ami and Don had disapproving looks on their faces.

"Only up until she died."

"Let me guess, heart attack."

"No, she got ran over by a car."

"Sorry to hear that."

"Yeah. After coffee, she liked to run on the highway, REALLY fast!"

Don looked at Ami, trying to telepathically communicate: "Why did you bring him in here?"

"Any-way," Ami said apologetically. "No coffee making required for a bus boy, right?"

"Sorry, I don't need any help."

"You kidding? Don, look at this place, it's very busy."

"That's only because they've been waiting for days for me to open, I mean seriously, I think that White lady with the hat has been sleeping out front, like I'm selling concert tickets."

"Therefore, you need help with the big rush, right?"

"No thanks."

"Don!"

"Sorry Ami. Don't need him. Why don't you send him to the Pepper Grind bar?"

"Because you're my friend."

"Yeah, but he's not."

"Don!"

"We're not friends?" Finn asked sadly. He turned away.

"Don, that was mean!" Ami complained.

"What? Why is that mean? He's not. If anything, he's a bit of a hindrance!"

"Sorry to bother you," Finn said. He walked out the front door.

"I don't know what you have against him, but he could teach you a thing or two about manners!" Ami yelled.

"What? Like how a cat likes its coffee?"

"Baka!" Ami stormed out behind Finn.

Don ignored the people trying to place their drink orders and watched Ami join Finn. She patted him on the back and lead him away, towards The Pepper Grind bar. Don threw his tea towel on the ground in anger. "You're the one that's baka…Hey, that word didn't—What ever!"

Casper skate boarded towards the hardware store, with a back pack full of arugula, mint, and fennel seeds. He needed three things to accomplish his mission: garden supplies, land, and a watering source. His rooftop garden was a good spot for growing tomatoes and herbs, but he needed an area with a lot more space if he was going to be creating an alternative food supply. Rusty's Hardware store was chosen for tools, being the only hardware store left in town. The two, large chain stores had left town even before there were any evacuation orders. Casper was not very fond of coming here because Rusty himself must have been 1000 years old and was hard of hearing, as well as slow as universal change when he worked the register. Fused with the stool he always sat on, he was stationed behind the counter, with a corn cob pipe in his mouth. "Popeye" was always the first thing that came to Casper's mind. Casper nodded to him and started looking for digging instruments. He saw a display full of hammers labeled Micro Carbon fiber hammers, initialed as "M.C. Hammers." He wondered what they felt like and reached for one. "You Can't touch that!" Rusty yelled from across the room. Casper stopped what he was doing and walked to where the shovels were. He wanted to buy a garden hoe to break up any hard dirt he would come across. There was nothing in site but shovels and rakes. "Hmmm. Hey Rusty, where are the hoes?" Casper yelled to him. You need a what?" Rusty answered.
"A garden hoe."
"A hose?"
"No, hoe."
"Horse?"
"No, hoe. For digging."
"House for rigging?"
"No!" Casper said frustrated. "A Hoe! Hoe-hoe-hoe!"
At that moment, Rusty threw a bunch of white confetti into the air and yelled: "Merry Christmas!"
Casper looked for the rest of his supplies without asking for help."

Officer's Earl and Clem were taking a break near the exit of the store when Casper stepped outside. Earl questioned Casper about the tools he was carrying. "Hey son, where you going with that Corpse Digger 3000 shovel?"

"Hi, officer. I'm going to start a garden."

"Where?"

"I haven't decided yet. I need to find a large empty field somewhere."

"Can't just plant stuff anywhere, that's public property and belongs to everybody, not just you." Clem said.

"That's true," Earl agreed. "Like that time Hippy Joe tried to plant a community garden right in the middle of an abandoned parking lot."

"Hippy Joe?" Casper asked.

"Yeah. He was that crazy, long-haired fella that lived near the lake. Got busted 'cause he was growing pot up there; guy sure loved making trouble."

"So...his property is abandoned? Is it within the quarantine zone?"

"Yeah. The Feds bull dozed his house, his goats and his oats; ain't nothing up there but an empty field."

"Hmmm. Casper said, thinking of a large fertile field, away from everyone's view. A perfect spot for a secret vegetable garden. "And where exactly is this field?"

General Katz sat in the high school principle's office and finished looking through a bunch of documents. He picked up a walkie talkie and paged Captain Kowalski. Minutes later Kowalski entered the tent. "You sent for me, sir?"

"Yes. Please. Have a seat."

Kowalski sat on a metal fold-out chair.

The general shuffled some of the papers and selected a couple. "I want to talk to you about Private Finn."

"Private Finn, sir?"

"You remember him. That bumbling FUBAR that launched the probe."

"Sorry again sir for scheduling him for guard duty that day."

"That's just it. You scheduled him for guard duty that time AND you scheduled him for communications tower maintenance."

"That would explain the weird problem we were having with the President's communication."

"It would. But what I don't get is why you scheduled that idiot for such high profile jobs."

"Guess I had too much faith I him."

"You had a LOT of faith in him, because, since we got here, you seem to schedule him for LOTS of high profile jobs, and he always managed to screw them up. THEN when I ask you what happened, his name automatically pops up!"

"Like I said sir, I was just trying to give him a chance."

The general stared at Kowalski for 15 seconds and then sighed. "How soon until the communication problem is fixed?"

"Unknown, sir."

"So the next time I talk to the alien, there's no guarantee that the camera won't die again, just when the President starts talking about a giant breast or space vampires."

"Correct."

Five more seconds of silence passed. "Okay then. Dismissed."

"Yes, sir." Kowalski about faced and headed out of the office.

Once Kowalski was gone, General Katz leaned back in his chair. "Just who in the world are you, captain? And what's going on here?"

Casper stopped by Don's Café on the way to Hippy Joe's property. The crowds Don had to deal with earlier had decimated into a handful of caffeine addicts. Don was quite surprised to see Casper carrying a bunch of garden tools as well as a red plastic bucket and his clarinet case. "Ohh-kay, Cornbregger. Plan on starting a really interesting band?"

"No, I think I may have found a spot to plant my seeds near the lake."

"And your clarinet?"

"Something my family used to do when I was little. Whenever we started a garden, we'd play something. My Grandpa said it helped bless the garden so that things would grow."

"And did it?"

"I guess. I don't think we ever had one bad garden."

"That's cool."

"So how you doing, man? Has your newfound knowledge about our situation sunk in yet?"

"I guess. I don't know how you and Ami can act like everything's normal. "

"I don't know about Ami, but as for myself, I'm trying to stay busy." He wiggled the shovel handle. "It's a nice distraction."

"Maybe that's why she's hanging around Beetle Bailey so much, a distraction."

"You really hate that guy don't you?"

"Don't you? He's so freaking annoying." Don did his best impression of Finn: "Hello Mr. Casper'– Drives me nuts."

Casper chucked. "I don't think it has anything to do with Finn."

"What do you mean?"

"I mean, it's about your feelings for Ami."

"What feelings? My feelings haven't changed for Ami."

"C'mon Don, you…Whatever—Anyway, bottom line, Finn is not a threat."

"Okay, Finn's fan club."

"I'm not a…Let me put it this way. I love Ami. Do you?"

"WHAT, love?"

"I'm not talking about spit swapping, P into V type of love. I mean as a person. Do you love her?"

"Y-Yeah. Of course…I'd die for her."

"Depending on the situation, me too, unless of course she was a zombie, or a serial killer, or both. Although by definition, a zombie is a serial killer until his head is chopped off–my point being, I love Ami, you love Ami, and she likes Finn."

"Likes him how?"

"Does it matter? If she loves Finn, I still have to like him. You see what I mean? I trust her to like or love the right person. After all, she loves you, and you're a pretty cool guy."

"You think she loves me?"

"Are we talking in a spit swapping zombie serial killer way? Oops, I mixed up my metaphors—Bottom line, again, trust her. She's one of my top five favorite people, and yours, I'm assuming."

"The top…" Don looked forlorn. "…And I screwed things up by not helping her out, earlier."

"Well, that's the good thing about mistakes."

"What's that?"

"Science, my lad, is made of mistakes, but they are mistakes which it is useful to make, because they lead little by little to the truth."

"Who said that?"

"My professor…And Jules Verne. Any-who, I gotta get going before the sun goes down. I'll see you back at home." Casper picked up his gear and headed towards the lake.

It took a lot longer to walk to Hippy Joe's property than Casper had expected. He was careful to always see where the ring's boundaries were to make sure the army wouldn't harass him for getting too close to it. As luck would have it, the property was quite far away from it. He could tell that the force field cut the lake almost in half. As long as he didn't get into a boat and paddle out, he would be okay. As described from the officers, the land was abandoned. The only indication a house was once here, was a pile of wood and a toilet, tagged by graffiti by bored teenagers. The place where the marijuana crops had once been was overgrown with regular weeds but still more manageable than the surrounding land which contained thistle, blackberry brambles and a few boulders. Casper went right to work, chopping up the soil and trying to get as much air into the dirt as he could. Once satisfied with the fourth of an acre he had conditioned, he went about planting the multiple packages of seeds.

Again, he remembered planting a garden with his grandfather. How, one really hot day, his grandfather had rolled up his sleeve and exposed his tattoo of five numbers. Once Casper discovered the nazi atrocities on Jewish people in Europe, including the Korberger family (who eventually had their name changed to Cornbregger by a lazy immigration officer), he angrily questioned his parents about his grandfather and how he never talked about the horrors he had survived which had taken the lives of most of his family. How could he not be angry, all of the time? If it were Casper, he felt he would have spent the rest of his life, hunting and killing hiding-nazis. Their answer was his grandfather had seen horrible things done by horrible people. The most horrible things in America could never compare to the horrible things he had seen in Europe, just like the most wonderful things in America can never compare to the joy his marriage and his children bought to his life. His goal for the rest of his life was to never let the horrors in Europe and America overflow the joy, or else the demons win. They then showed Casper a photo of Dr. Martin Luther King Jr., speaking in Washington, D.C. on August, 28, 1963. Casper had seen many versions of the photo of the civil rights leader giving his famous" "I have a Dream" speech and didn't understand why her parents had it. His father took a red magic marker and circled an area near the Reflecting pond. "If what he told me is right." His father said. "That's where your Grandfather and my mother stood."

Casper studied the photo and couldn't see enough detail to spot either of their faces. "You see, your grandfather never gave up fighting the demons, even in America. Wherever he saw atrocities, he was there fighting for peoples rights. He hid the negative inside of him, like a lump of black ice, but he also hid his goodness inside, like a slow burning flame, always melting the ice."

Casper surveyed his farm. It was good and organized. He used rocks to remind him of what was planted where, so that in the weeks to come, he could distinguish the sprouts. He walked down to the lake, dipped his bucket in the water and made multiple trips, watering his seeds. On his final water dump, he discovered something on the ground. A small plastic baggie. Examining it, it appeared to be a package of seeds. Closer inspection and smelling them revealed the package to contain marijuana seeds. "Whoa! Hippy Joe lives." Casper wondered what to do with them. "I guess I can toss them or give them to Darla. Naw, she has enough inebriated behaviors." He dumped them out just when the wind blew. Some of them landed in his garden. "Oops. Oh well, if they grow, I can open up a hemp soap shop or whatever people do to pretend this stuff serves any other purpose." He put his tools down and took out his clarinet. It had been a while since he had played it. Not since his father had died. Casper racked his brain for any songs he still knew by heart. There were two. The first was *Hashivenu*. A very hauntingly beautiful and sorrowful Hebrew tune he had played with his school's band in middle school. In spite of being out of practice, he played quite well. There were lyrics to the song including the translated words: "Who will take us by the hand and lead us back?" Casper felt powerful. No matter what their situation was, he would try his best to melt the black ice. Once finished with the first song, he started on the second one he knew by heart. *Super Freak* by Rick James. Stopping periodically to sing the chorus.

Don was typing away on his computer when Casper entered his room. There where all kinds of electronic configurations all over the desk. Wires came and went into the P.O.S. Device that they had stolen from Big Red Groceries. Casper knew better than to ask Don what exactly he was doing because he was quite sure he wouldn't understand the answer. Instead, he focused on the result. "How's it going, Don Tron?"

"Great," he said. "This thing is <u>so</u> easy to break into. No wonder all those Russian hackers break into them."

"How soon until we can make a call?"

"Calling may be more difficult, but, I think we can at least send an email to somebody as soon as I crack this last protocol."

Casper patted Don on the back and went into the kitchen to get something to eat. Ami returned home. She walked by Don's room without saying hello. Don stopped what he was doing. "Ami!"he called out. She slowly came back and peered into his room. "Yes?"

"How did the job hunting go with Finn?"

"Not so good. He got the job at the Bar but Baboosh fired him for being too clean?"

"Too clean?"

"Yeah. Finn was in the army so he's used to things being sparking clean and organized. He applied that to Baboosh's kitchen and ended up throwing away a bunch of things that were covered in mold."

"As he should."

"I know, Right? But Baboosh never likes to throw things away if he can sell them. Moldy bread equals penicillin. Moldy steak equals steak marinated in vinegar and renamed aged."

"Wow."

"Yep."Ami turned and was about to leave.

"Ami!" She stopped. "I-I. Tell Finn to drop by the café tomorrow for work."

She smiled. "You're hiring him?"

"I guess. But if he screws up, I'm going to fire him faster than lightning in a super conducting super collider."

"No idea what that means but I take it to mean really fast. Thank you, Don! Don't worry. He won't screw up." Don went back to typing. Ami walked over to him and was about to give him a hug from behind. She hesitated and pulled away before Don could see her. Casper walked up behind her and pushed her into Don. She gave Don a clumsy staggering hug from behind. "Casper!" she complained.

"Sorry," Casper said. "You were in my way."

Don was confused by the whole scene. "You guys! You may have messed me up…No wait. That was it. You actually made me push the right code." A couple of beeps later and Don's Piggy

Back program popped up on the screen with a logo of a pig wearing sunglasses.

"I designed that." Casper bragged.

"Your art teacher must be very proud."Ami said. "What is this program?"

"This, my dear, is how we are going to communicate with the outside world." Don bragged.

"But you can't do that."

"Can and will." Don pressed a few keys. The words:
PLEASE LOG ON TO YOUR E-MAIL ACCOUNT
appeared on screen.

"But guys, you're gonna get in trouble!"

"No, we won't. If the aliens are blocking our signals, I'm sure everyone will be happy that they can now send emails to friends and relatives."

"But, they're..." Ami hesitated in her giving them any information which could get her in trouble.

Casper let her off the hook. "It's okay, Ami. Don already knows about the force field, you don't have to keep it a secret any more."

"You told him?"

"No." Don answered. "That house I want us to live in has an invisible wall right through the pool."

"I'm sorry I couldn't tell you about it." Ami apologized.

"Understandable. You have to work with the military...But I don't—Right, who do I email, first?"

"Your mom." Casper answered.

"Don typed a letter to his mom:

Mom:

It's me, Don.

In case you don't believe me, remember that time when I was 5, I really wanted a pet monkey? You got me a stuffed one and I was so mad I threw it out of the car window onto the highway?

I'm sending you this email to tell you that we're all alive and still in Pepper Mill. I don't know what the government are saying about us, but the ring over our town is not some kind of military experiment or whatever but an alien space ship. Not only that, but the spaceship has created an invisible barrier which has trapped everyone in town. The military have blocked all telephone and internet signals, preventing us from communicating with the outside world. I'm sending this to you using a program I created.

We are all well and healthy for now. The aliens have given us many abilities such as understanding all languages and near perfect health (In spite of me not getting better vision)…

Casper interrupted Don's typing. "Jesus, Don, wrap it up! Don't write a long winded e-mail when you know she may not even get it. Just send a simple note."

"You're right." Don saved the first draft and typed a simple message:

Mom. It's me. Don.

He pressed send. A minute passed as they all waited for an indication that the message was sent successfully. Finally a message popped up from his server:

This message was created automatically by mail delivery software.
A message that you sent could not be delivered to one or more of its recipients. This is a permanent error. The following address(es) failed: Hazelbyrd123@supernetmail.com SMTP error.

"Crap-Ola" Casper complained. "It didn't work."

"Not necessarily," Don said. "I got a message from the server which means I'm in. Let me try sending a message to myself." Don typed a email and addressed it to himself. When he sent it, it came back to him without a problem message. "See."

"Then why didn't the other one make it outside the ring? I guess they're blocking that too."

"Not true, Remember, the register signals are going out of town to somewhere outside the ring. I think I have to keep working on it."

"It's a good start." Casper returned to the kitchen.

"Ami was about to leave but stopped. "Be careful, Don. I don't want you to get into trouble."

He turned and looked at her. "I'm not going to do anything to take me away from you."

Ami smiled and looked down. Her skin got a little red.

"Are you blushing?"

"No, Baka!" She put her hands on her cheeks and hurried into the hallway.

"Again, that word.…" Don returned to his programing.

Casper was awakened by the sound of a cow mooing. He looked out of his window and sure enough, there was cow in the middle of the road. It looked like it was exploring. It slowly walked down the street, surveying the empty business. "He thought about the time he had heard a rooster crowing in the morning. "Where are these animals coming from?" He decided to get up and get out of the apartment. Perhaps he could go up to his farm and water the plants before he went to work. Don was slumped on his desk asleep. Lots of codes and numbers were on the screen. Evidence of an all night programing session. Casper didn't know if Don was successful, but he had faith in him that one day he will be able to get through to the outside world. He walked over, picked up a blanket from the bed and draped it over Don's shoulders. Don stirred and continued sleeping.

By the time Casper went outside, the cow was nowhere to be seen. The long skateboard ride was easier, thanks to the lack of traffic to deal with. When he arrived at his little farm, he wondered if he had come to the wrong location. Some shrub like trees and knee high plants were where he thought he had planted the seeds. He searched around the area but couldn't find any evidence of a cleared out area. He smelled something. It smelled like fennel and marijuana. "Hmm, did the cops forget to rip up one of Hippy Joe's trees?" Casper used his nose to try and locate the stray illegal plant. His nose lead him back to the area with the shrubs and knee high plants. The knee high plants were in rows and very organized for weeds. He reached down and picked up one of the leaves. He smelled it. It didn't appear to be a dandelion. He took a chance and took a bite. It tasted like arugula. He took another bite from another large plant. It was mint. "What the? Did someone already plant mint and arugula here?" Near the tall shrubs, he saw his watering bucket. He remembered leaving it right in the middle of his field. He looked up at the large shrub. It was a marijuana plant. "Wait a minute." He spun around and realized all of the plants he had sewed, had grown to full height over night. "Wow! Grandpa was right about the music!"

Chapter 8
Salt

According to Dr. Stuart Hameroff, Professor Emeritus at the Department of Anesthesiology and Psychology and the Director of the Centre of Consciousness Studies at the University of Arizona [his business card must be the size of a clipboard], and British physicist Sir Roger Penrose, the soul is basically a tiny piece of the universe contained inside of your brain cells in structures called microtubules, and may have existed since the beginning of time. However, the President of the United States believes that the soul was handed out to Christians (only) before birth and once they die, they are recalled by heaven. If you lived a good life the soul would be white as snow, but if you lived a sinful life, the soul would be dingy and dirty like a white rag on the floor of a cockfight's locker room. General Katz believed the soul was something you earned through good deeds, and until you die, you were nothing more than a soulless shell meandering through life. When these two gentlemen discussed the human soul they both had different religious, psychological, and philosophical reactions to the information that Plür wanted to switch souls with a human.

"Say wha-?" Because the President had taken the phone call while he was in the Antarctica base's steam room, he asked the general to repeat the question. "I'm sorry. Did I hear you right? She wants to switch souls?"

" Yes, sir."

"As in the floating white thing that goes to heaven or super heaven?"

"Yes, sir."

"How?"

"Plür's race, the Ancient Orange Nimbus of the North Wind, or 'Floaters' as I call them, have the ability to switch souls—her words, not mine—with other races. She uses this ability to instantly learn if another race is on the up and up and are worth joining the Collection of Wanders."

"But…is this possible? Switching souls?"

"Not sure, sir. I told you that the ring doesn't always translate things in a direct way. Plür believes that it doesn't translate what you say, it translate how you feel."

"And how exactly do they do this? And is it reversible?"

"She didn't give any details; she's waiting on our answer before she starts the process."

The President laid against the tiled steam room wall and took in a breath of hot mist. "What kind of religion are these Floaters? Do they believe in god, football and super-heaven?"

"She mentioned a spirit and us all being connected to it, so there is some kind of religious thing, but no specifics."

"So maybe soul's a completely different things to her. Like Democrats and Republicans look at the words 'French fries'."

"Hopefully not that different."

"What if we say no?"

"If we say no, we have to go through a lengthy evaluation process that could take weeks, months or years—I really don't know how she measures time, but it sounded like a long time before she could learn enough about us."

"And what would be wrong with that?"

"Sir, Plür's people have been trapped by the ring a lot longer than us. I can only assume we may be trapped in here for years. If that's true, we're going be running out of resources in few months. Without sharing resources with other races, it could have detrimental effects on our survival in here. I mean water supplies are good, but food is starting to look bad already. To put it simply, we need to establish contact with the other races ASAP."

"But we can't have her stealing our souls, not like we got spares—'less you're a cat, like you."

"She wouldn't steal it; she wants to trade the body it's in."

"So, one of us would go into her body?"

"I assume so."

"And while she learns everything about us, we'd learn everything about her people, including their technology."

"Maybe. I don't know how it'll work."

The President wiped some sweat off his brow and looked down at the tiled Presidential seal on the floor. "General, get the process started. Make sure our soul candidate is low on military secrets and such. The minute you even smell a trap, you eliminate that Pilate ball and take possession of her toys."

"Yes, sir."

When the conversation ended, the President pressed the off button on his phone and looked up. "God. You really are good with those curve balls, ain't ya?"

Casper knew Darla was a biology major and therefore had an interest in plants. But the intensity she put into studying the large cannabis plants was probably more related to recreation than science. She stroked the leaves as if it were a pet and smelled it as if it were a dozen roses.

"Uhh, Darla?" Casper said, trying to get her to pay attention to the other plants that had grown to full size in only one night. "There's also the mint, arugula and fennel, over here." He pointed to the rest of his little farm.

Don was already looking at the fennel. He had taken Casper's shovel and dug up one of the bulbs. It was the largest he had ever seen. Just moving the fronds around filled his nostrils with a licorice smell. "Wow. These plants are so healthy."

"I know, right?" Casper said. "And in only one night. So, considering you're our residential biology major, what's your theory, Dr. Marbles?" Darla was back to looking at the marijuana plants. "Darla!"

She shook out of her hypnotic state. "What, huh?"

"Focus, Darla. What's your theory?"

"Well…" She bent down, grabbed some dirt and smelled it. "The fastest growing plant on record is a type of bamboo at around 30 inches per day, once it's established." She plucked a mint leaf and smelled it. "As far as vegetables go, you can grow radishes, kale and lettuce in about a month."

"And overnight?"

"That would be alien Maui Wowie plant."

"Dude…" Don said. "Why did you plant pot? I thought you hated smoking pot?"

"I do. The smell reminds me of the teachers lounge in high school, but, I didn't plant it. I found a package of the seeds left by Hippy Joe and dumped it out. I never even buried it."

"Wow," Darla said. "That's some good soil. I should take this to the agriculture departments lab at the college and analyze all this stuff."

"College is closed, Darla…Oh, wait, you'll just break in." Casper answered his own question.

"…And of course, I should analyze the pot as well."

"I don't think so, Cheeky Chong. I'm going to get rid of those."

"What! Why?"

"We need to grow food, not something that makes you CRAVE food."

"But, what if this is part of the reason the plants grew overnight?"

"Nice try, Cannabis Lector, but we both know it's all about the soil; analyze that."

Don took a conservative bite of mint. "At my work we have some green coffee beans in a jar as decorations. I wonder what would happen if we planted them?"

"Probably pop up like everything else. Why?"

"If we're stuck here beyond a couple of months, we're probably gonna start running out of coffee, and when that happens…"

"Caffeine addicts will rip off your head and turn it into a French press?"

"Something like that. I think I should plant coffee beans."

"Problem is, it takes like two to four years for beans to even show up." Darla informed.

"Not with alien super dirt."

"Hey! How come he gets to plant coffee beans and I can't have cannabis?" Darla complained

"Because there's no way the army would let us! Still illegal in a LOT of places, you know!" Casper said.

"What about beer?"

"What about it?"

"We're going to run out of beer one day. I'm sure the soldiers wouldn't mind an endless supply of that."

"Probably not. But don't you need hops and barley to make beer?"

"You can make wine and beer from anything as long as it produces its own sugar. My grandmother used to make wine using dandelions. All we need to make beer is wheat, barley or even corn."

"And the hops?"

"Guess what plant is a cousin to hops?"

Casper looked at the cannabis plant. "These things? Then how come no one ever makes beer out of them?"

"They have, but it's obvious why no one does."

"How come you know so much about making booze?" Don asked.

"My ex boyfriend brewed his own…and I drink a lot."

Casper put his hand on Darla's shoulder. "Okay, brewmaster Darla. Our future inebriations are in your hands. Lets go to Big Red and corner the market on seeds."

"I'll check on those coffee seeds..." Don said. "...Provided Finn hasn't thrown them away."

"How's that working out for you?"

"Finn?" He's actually a good worker. Place is sparkling clean, good with customers. Real bummer 'cause I was really looking forward to firing him."

While they were walking back into town, Darla was looking at her soil sample in her hand. "What I don't get is, if it is the soil, then how come all of the other plants in town haven't turned into super plants? Like, shouldn't there be grass growing out of the sidewalk and weeds everywhere?"

"Maybe it's only the plants that grew after the ring landed or seeds that are planted from now on," said Casper

"But we should have still seen lots of new growth around town."

"It could have taken time to happen like the teeth thing," Don said. "Plus, have you even been paying attention to plant growth around town? We've been kinda distracted lately. I mean, who's to say that that tree over there wasn't here a month ago." He pointed to a young eucalyptus tree.

"Speaking of distracted," Darla said. "You owe me a date, Cornbread!"

"Sorry, I've been putting it off, I got distracted with the farm stuff." Casper was actually lying. Truth be known, he was a little afraid of going on a date with Darla. Her behavior was unstable and sometimes violent and criminal. He was physically attracted to her but he had been in a relationship with an attractive yet unstable girl and it had ended badly. If he could delay their date for as long as he could, perhaps she would lose interest in him and they could just be friends.

"Next Saturday. Be there or else!" Darla threatened.

"S-sure."

Ami Nakajima placed the test tube full of blood in the centrifuge. She was about to close the lid and press start when Dr. Chambers stopped her. "Ami?" She turned and looked at her boss. "Ami, make sure you balance out those tubes in there or else it could lead to breaking," Ami opened the lid and noticed the test tubes were crowded more on one side of the machine than the other. She quickly readjusted the arrangement. "Sorry, Doctor. I don't know what I was thinking."

"That's okay. You seem a little distracted. Is everything okay?"

"Sorry, Doctor."

"Stop apologizing."

"Sor..." Ami picked up her clipboard and checked for anything else she had to do for her morning shift.

Dr. Chambers walked over to Ami, bent down a little to Ami's level and looked her in the eyes. "Is it a boy?"

Ami dropped her clip board. "What? Huh? A boy, no!"

"Hmm." Dr. Chambers straightened up. "Let me try something. I grew up in a family full of men, so I'm not used to interactions with female friends when it comes to matters of the heart." She felt around in her lab coat and pulled out a red hair ribbon. She tied it over her short blond haired head in a bow. She then leaned forwards on a desk and widened her eyes to appear very enthusiastic and interested. "Oh-me-god! Girlfriend!" she said like a Valley girl, "So, like, what's his name?"

Ami of course was taken aback and a little scared. "Huh?"

"C'mon, girrrrl. Tell me his name, cause you're like TOTALLY buggin about something."

"OKAY! Okay! I'll talk! Just stop what you're doing!"

The doctor took the ribbon out and stood up straight.

Ami took a breath. "It's my roommate, Don. He told someone I know that he doesn't date his friends."

"But you obviously want to move beyond friendship."

"Yes, but it's stupid if it's just one-sided. I mean, I can't get over it. It's been building for so long but it's useless for me to be putting so much energy into it, right?"

"This friend, the one that informed you about Don. Is he a reliable source?"

"Finn? Well...not really."

"And would Finn have anything to gain by sharing this information with you?"

"Finn? Probably. He seems interested in being more than friends."

"Interesting: Unreliable source., romantic interest, competition. Shakespeare couldn't have said it better: 'Love looks not with the eyes, but with the heart." She went back to work on analyzing a urine sample in a jar.

Ami felt a little foolish for taking Finn for his word. "But what should I do? If I tell him I like him and he doesn't feel the same, I'll feel like a fool."

"Fear is a strange concept to me because I grew up on a gator ranch in Florida. Whenever I have to do anything that's difficult—in your case, confess your love to Don, as 236–excuse me 237—men have done to me—I think of it as lifting weights with my brain instead of my body. I believe the mind and body must match in order for a person to have perfect balance in their life. You're a smart person, Nakajima. But your heart is a bit of a knucklehead. Take it to the emotional gym and do 100 Kegels."

Ami picked up her clipboard and tried to get back to work. An announcement came over the PA system, interrupting her train of thought: "Attention! Will all unmarried civilian and military female personnel on the base, please report to the gym at fourteen hundred hours. That is all."

"What do you think that's about?" Ami asked.

The doctor had her eyes closed as if she were meditating. "Sorry, Kegels reminded me of something I forgot to do this morning."

Hazel Cornbregger was a latecomer to the internet, social media and online videos. When one of her friends told her that there was a social networking site for families whose children and relatives were in Pepper Mill, she made it a priority to learn everything she could about her lap-top's web browser and apps in order to find the site. Most of the web page contained lots of random conversations between strangers across the country who may or may not have relatives in Pepper Mill. Hazel scrolled through the hundreds of back-and-forth conversations, most of them discussing current events or insulting responses posted by racist, uneducated virgins who apparently had become bored with posting insulting racist, anti-gay responses on other video sites. Hazel sighed and felt her life being wasted with every scroll of her browser's side bar. Just before she was about to call it a day and go back to watching her court TV shows, a new post caught her interest. PeppermillFreedoom162@internet.com posted the words: "Have you seen this?" Ignoring the fact this could be a virus that plays a video of a monkey smelling his rear-end and falling out of a tree in an endless loop, Hazel clicked on the link provided. A dark figure in a dark room appeared in the video. His voice was digitally masked as was his face, resembling a pixelated eight bit homage to censored Japanese porno genitalia. "Greetings." the person said. "I am a member of the Pepper Mill Squad. I am going by the name 'Anonymous Ominous Unanimous.' What I am about to tell you comes with great peril to my life because the government–YOUR government doesn't want this information to get out. Thomas Jefferson once said, that..." His speech was interrupted when a light came on in the dark room, now revealed to be a basement. On the wall was a poster of a kitten wearing a Star Trek uniform, holding onto a clothesline. Although the guy's face remained digitized, his body revealed that of a overweight man wearing a Bullwinkle and Rocky t-shirt. "Ma!" he yelled. "Turn the light off!"

"What are you doing down here?" (Said a female voice, off camera.)

"I'm making a video!"

"I need to do the laundry!"

"Do it later!"

"You can do your little movie later!"

"MA! Just give me five freak'n minutes!"

"Fine, Ingmar Bergman! You can sit in the dark in your dirty underwear! What do I care? But the next time you want me to clean those awful stains out of your Spiderman briefs, don't you..." Whatever instructions the woman was going to give the guy were not heard after he stomped up a flight of stairs and slammed a door. He walked back down, sat for a second, stood up and walked offscreen. A second later the light was turned off and he returned to his seat.

"Anyway, as a member of the PMS, our goal is to expose the lies perpetuated by the government that the ring around that town of Pepper Mill, California is some sort alternative energy experiment and the citizens inside the town are quarantined because of a virus or, as some people think are all dead. As I speak, two of our agents are sneaking a third into the area around the ring who will report back to us with the true purpose of what we think is a military weapons complex and the truth about the citizens of Pepper Mill. Our agents, as well as I, are risking our lives to bring you the truth. As Thomas Jefferson said: "There is no truth existing–" the quote was never given. The picture went completely black. "What the?—Ma! What's going on?"

"You blew a circuit with all of your cameras and computers."

"For the love of…Fine! If you can still hear me, I'll report back later as we learn more about the ring. PMS out!"

Hazel pulled away from her computer. She stood up, walked over to her bookshelf and picked up the letter which was sent to her in secret from the late Professor Pascal.

'… Your son is alive and well Mrs Cornbregger. He is alive and well and told me to pass on that message to you.'

"What if?" she thought.

On Highway I-40, a white van made its way towards a small town bordering the off-limits area around Pepper Mill, California. Inside, two college students discussed a subject more important to them than the dangerous mission they have been sent to accomplish.

"Dude…" said the one with red curly hair. "…Every time you go to the bathroom, you need to wash your hands!"

"No, I don't…" said the one with glasses. "…When I go to the bathroom, I don't pee on my hands!"

"It doesn't matter. When you pee, ALL of the pee mist goes everywhere, including your hands!"

"I'm not going to worry about it."

"So, if you go to the bathroom, and then you start cooking, do you wash your hands then?"

"I don't know, probably not."

"OH-Em-Gee, I'm NEVER eating your cooking, EV-VUH!"

"Like I would even offer!"

"Whatever, Pee-Hands Herman!"

"Whatever, Perry Noid!"

The van rushed down the highway and eventually made it to The Dew Stay Inn. There was nothing spectacular about the 1980's style architecture of the motel that separated it from the storage facility across the street or the convenience store next door which had a sign that read: "Open 24 Hours, But Not in a Row." After parking around the back, the two gentlemen changed into brown jump suits. "Okay," said the one labeled Perry Noid. "You ready?"

"Yep", answered Pee Hands Herman. They got out, unloaded a large wooden box with the word "FARGILE" on its side (I'm sure they meant to write: 'Fragile') onto a hand cart and wheeled it into the motel lobby. Behind the counter, was a 53 year-old, East Indian clerk with more oil in his hair than the van driven by the two guys. The man raised a suspicious eyebrow at the large box making an appearance in his solitude. "May I help you?" He asked.

"Yeah, said Pee Hands. "We have a delivery for Aarti Panjwani, room 207."

"A delivery of what?"

"No idea. Is she here?"

"We're not allowed to discuss the whereabouts of our guests."

"Then can you sign for this thing?"

"Most certainly not! Is she expecting it?"

"Sure, why not?"

"Pardon?"

"I mean, yes! It's very important! Part of a religion thing."

"What religion thing?"

"I don't know, something important. DUDE! Why are you busting our chops about this? We're dressed like delivery guys and have a box with all kinds of official stamps on it. You either take the box or else we're gonna tell her that you didn't accept it and she's gonna go to the papers and say how racist you are against White people! Geez, I've dealt with sorority house moms that asked less questions than you...!" He looked at the Indian man's name tag. "...Aneck."

"How do I know you're not delivering something illegal or dangerous to my motel?"

"Jumping Jesus in high school, man! If we wanted to do that, we'd go through the back entrance, find a maid that was cleaning that lady's room, bribe the maid to let us put the box in it and skip talking to you, all togeth..." Pee Hands and Perry Noid looked at each other. "Excuse us." They lifted the box back onto the hand cart and wheeled it out the exit.

After paying the maid $50 and a box of chocolates, the delivery was completed.

The Pepper Mill high school gymnasium was filled with women of various races, ages and sizes, standing around, wondering why General Katz had summoned them there. He talked briefly with Dr. Chambers and the mayor and then turned his attention to the crowd. Raising his hand, he tried to quiet their chatter. "Ladies. May I have your attention?" They still talked among themselves. Dr. Chambers put thumb and index finger in her mouth and blew a really loud whistle. This made the general flinch, which was odd for someone used to the sound of explosions. The whistle silenced the room instantly. "Er-ah, thank you doctor. Now then, ladies, before I reveal the reason I've called you here, I must release some of you from the room for various reasons. First, any women who does not wish to take on a mission which may or may not be extremely dangerous, you may leave the room." Everyone looked around at each other but no one made a move for the door. "Oh, good. Next, all women who are pregnant or are going to be pregnant, you may go." Everyone looked around. A woman near the back walked through the crowd and exited to the right. "What? She was going to volunteer for a dangerous mission while pregnant?"

"Understandable," said Dr. Chambers. "My mother worked at the alligator ranch until month 8."

"Really?" said the mayor. "Thank god she stopped."

"She had to. She killed the alligator."

The general raised an eyebrow at Dr. Chambers. "Next, any woman in the infantry or involved with weapons of any kind or in the security area, you are dismissed." About half of the women left the gym. "All right, that should be it." The mayor leaned over and whispered something in his ear. "Oh, right. Will Tattle-Tale Tilly, leave the room."

"Aww, man!" said a woman in the back. She slowly walked out the door.

"Sorry Tilly…Love your newsletters, though. Now then, that should be it. Mayor Duncan and Dr. Chambers are also excused, but shall be involved in the mission as advisors and medical examiner." The general walked closer to the 22 women remaining and started pacing slowly. "We are not alone in the universe, nor are we alone in our situation. As most of you in this room know, we are trapped in this town. You also know that a U.F.O. landed a while ago carrying a large white floating ball. That ball is actually an alien who we have named Floaters. We've been communicating and establishing a diplomatic relationship with it in hope of finding a way out of our current situation." He paused and looked at a few faces in the crowd. "The Floaters have a unique ability to switch bodies with others.…" There was mumbling in the crowd. "…They use this ability to learn about others instantly; as you find out about them. It's a shortcut to trust and an easy way to get the diplomatic ball rolling. What we are looking for is a volunteer to undergo this process. Someone willing to do something which has never been done on Earth before. A volunteer willing to switch bodies—temporarily—with an alien." Lots of mumbling from the crowd were heard. "If you do not wish to do this, you may be excused." Eleven more woman headed out the door.

"I'm sorry" said one of the remaining women. "Did you say stay or go if you didn't want to switch bodies with an alien?"

"Go" the general answered.

"Gotcha." She ran out the side door, reducing the surviving numbers by one.

"Well, I'm glad we have some brave souls in here."

An African American soldier raised her hand.

"Yeah, Walden?"

"Sir. Why only women?"

"The alien said that it's easier with females because they adapt a lot faster than males. I think that's her way of saying men whine too much."

Ami raised her hand.

"Yes, Ami?"

"Sir. How does switching bodies let it trust us?"

"She's not only using your body, she's getting your memories, experiences, anything that makes you human. But, in exchange, you're getting the same. Everything that she's experienced and seen in hundreds of years on hundreds of planets, you get to experience. Imagine, knowing what it's like to travel throughout the galaxy, meeting different lifeforms, seeing incredible sites—instantly. If she allowed it, I'd volunteer myself in a heartbeat. But that's where we are. You ladies can be a new type of astronaut, of the mind—perceptio-naught, how's that sound?"

"Work on it," the mayor suggested.

"Anyway, you can see how this could be dangerous. She's done it dozens of times, so there's that. But she's never done it on us. We have no idea how she does this or how she reverses it; it's up to you to decide if you're willing to go through with it. But know this: If you succeed in gaining her trust, when we get out of this town one day, your name is going to be the first one with the label 'hero' attached to it."

The ladies talked among themselves. Five more left the gym. One of them said the word "crazy." The general went to congratulate the remaining five. "You five have my sincere admiration and gratitude."

"Six," said Ami."

The general looked at her. "Pardon?"

"Six, sir, including me."

"Are you sure, Ami?"

"Y-y-yes, sir," she said nervously.

Casper tried to think of the ingredients in chicken soup, latkes, spaghetti sauce and guacamole. In his mom's opinion, if you had the ingredients to make all of those in a heartbeat, then you have a well stocked kitchen. Carrots, celery, onions, potatoes, tomatoes and avocados would be easy to grow in the alien super-soil, but how would they get ahold of eggs, chicken meat or other proteins-like substances? True, he had heard a rooster roaming around, like the cow, but is it fair to kill the last rooster in town just for broth? All day he had been hoarding seeds and seeded fruits and vegetable from the dwindling produce section of the store. Some things were long shots, like the multi grain seeds in a loaf of bread. Chances of them growing after being baked were less than the pepper inside of a pepper grinder. It didn't matter, he was going to plant it all. Among the fruit he notices that there was only one moldy orange left. He hoped it wasn't one of those seedless oranges. It had an organic label on it it. "Yes!" he thought. "We can grow oranges and won't get scurvy." Before he could put it in a box and hide it in the back with the rest of his future crops, an elderly lady snatched it away from him.

"Oh goody, you still have oranges," she said.

"What?" he said shocked. "I'm–That's mine!"

"Yours?" She looked at his clothes and apron. "You work here!"

"Yeah, but I'm saving that!"

"Are you still on the clock?"

"Yes…"

"Then I'm a customer, and you're an employee!"

"But I'm saving that."

"Sorry kid, no saves!" She put the last orange in town in her hand basket and started to walk away.

"I can't let her get away!" he thought. "Should I tackle her and just take it? It is pretty important, but I can't beat up an old lady." He tried to think of a way to get the orange from her without violence. A nearby broom would make an easy weapon. "Ma'am!" he yelled She turned around. "If you want, we have a huge shipment of oranges coming in a few days."

She turned around. "Really? When?" She appeared skeptical.

"A day or two. So you don't have to buy that rotten old orange. I can give you first pick of a fresh crop, right off the truck."

"Really?"

"Yep. But you gotta hand over that orange…For health code reasons. It may have e-coli-botulism-salmonella germs. I was trying not to say anything because we don't want people to panic."

"How do I know that you're not just making stuff up just to get the last orange in town?"

"You don't. But I'm telling you the truth. I give you my word that within a couple of days, you'll see the oranges restocked. But you have to hand me the one you're holding." Casper extended his hand and had a very sorrowful look on his face. The old lady looked at him and then the orange. "Well…I don't think so, I'm keeping it!" Before she could put it back in her basket, Darla had snuck up from behind her and knocked it out of her hands, while yelling: "Give it up you old bat!" The orange hit the ground, Casper put it in his box. "I'm sorry ma'am, it really is important." The lady didn't hear him because she was yelling and screaming at Darla to have her fired. Darla yelled back something along the line of: "Take whatever you are saying, swallow it, and let it exit your body through your rear in a gaseous form."

"A few days!" Casper yelled "Just give me a few days."

"I'm going to have you both fired!" the old lady yelled. She turned on her heels and angrily marched away.

"Can't have us fired! Ol' bat!" Darla yelled.

Casper looked around the produce section for more essential plants.

"Can you believe that broad?" Darla complained.

"Yes, I can."

"What, you're defending her?"

"The way she acts? No But she's just crazy because she had the last orange in town. That's what things are going to be like. The less and less food there is the crazier, until it's going to look like Dystopia-opolis, Pepper Mill edition, in here."

"Hmm. Maybe we should raid the gun shop."

"No! No guns! That's what they always do in those sci-fi movies when there's the first hint of Zombie apocalypse,"

"Well, duh! Zombies? Hello!" Darla said sarcastically (as I'm sure you figured out because you're sooo smart).

"Perhaps if the heroes in those movies spent as much time in the lab as they did chopping off zombie heads, maybe they could cure the population by the end of the movie, instead of killing them until they inevitably get bit themselves."

"How boring of a movie is that?"

"You've never seen Andromeda Strain, have you?"

"Didn't they play at the Fillmore in San Francisco?"

"My point being, things are going to get worse. We can stop it in two ways. Chopping off of the heads, or actually solving the problem, in this case, starvation."

"We don't have to worry about starving. We got super soil, remember?"

"We is right. Us and our exclusive garden club."

"And the problem?"

"That old lady is a sign of things to come if we don't share the wealth."

"Share? With her?"

"With everybody."

"We can't just share with everybody. They'll take all of our crap and leave us with nothing."

"They aren't raiding this store. There's a nice organized line."

"That's because it's a store with armed guards."

"Then we'll use the store to share our crops."

"You're not making any sense."

"After we plant the new seeds and stuff pops up, we put it on the shelves in here and sell it."

"We can't do that. What about OUR share?"

"Of course we'll take some for us, but no more than we'd normally take for our weekly grocery run."

"You're so, so…nice." The expression on Darla's face told that she was not complimenting him.

"Yep. That's me. Mr Nice guy. But I'm not going to finish last." He packed up the secret seed supplies and took them to his locker.

The large white ball was in the middle of the classroom. All of the furniture had been removed except for one folding chair. Ami ignored the girl who was leaving the room as she was entering. If she had paid attention, she would have noticed how the girl seemed to be in a state of joy and at the same time shock. It was understandable. It wasn't every day you came face to face with someone who lived so far away from you, that the light from their sun had started traveling to your eyes, even before we were in the lizard phase of evolution. The ball was floating. Ami expected that, but the way it was standing perfectly still was not what you would be prepared for when it came to something floating in the middle of the room. Ami looked back at Dr. Chambers. She nodded to let Ami know that it was okay to walk on in. Ami entered and was about to sit down. She stopped and slowly bowed. "Hello. My name is Nakajima Ami. It is a pleasure to meet you."

"Hello, Nakajima Ami. My name is Plürreannedunadugavas. I am an ambassador from the Collection of Wanderers. It is my pleasure."

"It is an honor to meet you, Plürreannedunadugavas." Ami bowed again.

"Oh…" Plür said happily. "You are the first one to say my name correctly."

"I was practicing."

"Nakajima Ami, you may call me Plür. The General Katz said it is a sign of friendship to shorten your name, as do my species."

"Then you may call me, Ami."

"Ami. What does your name mean?"

"Where I come from, Beauty."

"As does my name. You are different looking than the pink and brown humans."

"Yes. I am a Nihonjin."

"There are so many versions of humans here."

"Are all of you the same?"

"There are only five different races on my cloud."

"Cloud?"

"Clouds are our territories. The Ancient Orange Nimbus of the North Wind, where I come from, there are no hard areas, or trees and grass, and things like you have here."

"This land must seem very strange for someone from a planet made of clouds."

"I've been traveling around for hundreds of cycles. I now find it strange when I go home."

"I know how you feel. I come from a faraway land and find it strange when I visit."

"And why are you here?"

"I was living in Nippon, but I was not happy. My parents were pushing me into a life I didn't want. So I came to this place. I made lots of friends and was able to be myself."

"And now you are happy?"

"Happiness is only temporary. My goal in life is joy and enlightenment."

"Then our goals are very similar."

Ami smiled.

Aarti was tired. She had been up all night going over the data gathered by drone satellites around the ring trying to find any weakness in it's force field. She had found none. Now it was almost lunchtime. To her it was going to be nap time. She has been at the Dew Drop Inn for months, commuting back and forth between the campsite around the Southside Bridge and the motel. She was sick of living in a motel. In spite of never having to clean her room or wonder where she could get a bucket of ice water, she missed her over-priced, loud apartment in New York. It wasn't paradise, but it was hers. She even missed using a key to enter her apartment instead of the motel's fancy credit card key. She went inside her room and closed the door. It struck her that her lights were on. "Did I leave my lights on?" she wondered. Figuring that she was tired, she continued on her quest to take an afternoon nap. The TV was also on. This she knew was out of place because the last time she watched TV, Happy Days was still on the air. Her heart raced. Her brain told her to get out of the room. By the time this message reached her legs and she was preparing to sprint out of the room, someone touched her back and said "Aarti." That was enough to go into self defense mode. There is a type of ancient martial arts in India called Kalaripayttu. Aarti's cousin, Deep was heavily invested (I guess you can say, deeply invested) in learning this form of self defense and at one point taught her how to take a victim, turn them around so that their back is against your back, grab them around the neck and flip them over you onto the ground in front of you. In this case, the victim, luckily for him, landed on the bed. Aarti was prepared to put fist to face, but paused for a second to see who her attacker was. It was Groucho Marx. She had never seen even one Marx Brothers movie, so to her he was just a creepy attacker with a bad mustache and eyebrows. What did stop her was the attacker saying: "Aarti, it's me!"

"Me who?" she said pausing mid strike. Groucho took off his fake mustache and glasses which were attached to the eyebrows.

"Lewis?" she said.

Lewis Pascal smiled through the pain in his back. "Hi." Aarti punched him in the chest, hard. "Ow! Aarti, it's me!"

She punched him again. "I know!"

"Then why are you punching me?"

"Zombie!"

He grabbed her hand. "I'm not a zombie! I'm alive, Aarti." She punched him again. "Why are you still punching me?"

"Because I'm freaking out! You're supposed to be dead!"

"Well, obviously I'm not."

"But–how, why, when? You were in a plane crash, in the middle of the ocean, among sharks and cold water!"

"Not really."

"What do you mean, not really."

"I faked my own death." She punched him again. "Ow!"

"Why would you do something so stupid? Why would you do something like that to your friends, and me?"

"Simple, to get off the government's radar."

"What are you talking about, Lewis?"

"When I was kicked off the project, I wanted to make sure that the government stopped keeping the information about the ring and the people in Pepper Mill a secret. I wanted to expose the cover-up and let people know that we have alien visitors and the government is trying to put a big copyright symbol on them and their technology. I couldn't do that if they were bugging my phone and following me around all the time."

"So you faked your own death?"

"I had to, Aarti, It was the only way to go underground."

"You're a fool, Lewis. When they find you…"

"They won't because they're not looking for me."

"How did you do it? I heard you in your plane."

"I took off from Santa Cruz, put it on auto-pilot and skydived over Monterey. I got picked up by a radical underground group who call themselves the Pepper Mill Squad, or PMS. They are dedicating themselves to finding out the truth about the ring."

"And now you're here. Near the ring and in the lion's mouth. When they find you…"

"They won't…unless you turn me in. You're not going to turn me in, are you?"

"I should. But I'm sure you know that I won't and that's why you're here."

"Bingo."

Aarti growled in frustration. "Why didn't you tell me you were going to do something like this?"

"Because I knew you would try to talk me out of it."

"Of course I would!" She punched him again.

"Ow. Can you please stop hitting me? I think I can taste blood."

Aarti got up to go get a wet towel from the bathroom. "Why are you here? What do you hope to accomplish?" She threw the towel at his face.

He put the towel on his chest. "Pictures, sounds...files from your computer."

"Ohhhh no," I'm not going to put up with you and your PMS."

"C'mon Aarti. Help a brother out."

"No, Lewis. What you are doing can get me in a heap of trouble. If they find you, you're gonna spend a million years in jail."

"I would spend a million years in jail, awakened, then spend one day in ignorant bliss."

"Who said that?"

"I did."

"I'm not going to jeopardize my career just so you can play revolutionary."

Professor Pascal looked very sad and disappointed. He sighed. "Fair enough." He picked up his Groucho disguise and put it on. "I'll let myself out. Don't worry. If they catch me, I'll deny ever seeing you..." He walked to the door and paused. "...I suggest you do the same." He left the hotel room.

Aarti sat on the bed. She thought about the time he hired her, how he put off buying equipment for the lab just to budget her in. "Masīhā khātira!" she said, which roughly translates into "for Christ's sake." She stood up, walked to the door and opened it. Professor Pascal was waiting in front of the door. Aarti made a squeak-like scream. "Lewis!"

"Hi. I forgot to get that box out of your room." He walked over and tried to pick up the large wooden box. "Wow...." he grunted..."this thing is heavy." He tried to drag it across the room while producing more grunts. "How did those...guys carry this and me in it? College boys are a lot... stronger nowadays than..."

"Lewis!" Aarti interrupted. He stopped. "You should stay here."

"Huh. Won't you get in trouble?"

"If I do, I'll say you threatened me with loss of tenure."

Don was quite happy when Casper came into the café. The lunch crowd had died down and he could actually relax and socialize. He held up a small plastic bag full of coffee seeds. "Check it out!" Casper took the bag and studied it.

"Awesome! After work I'm going to plant these and some other bad boys."

"I thought you were going to do your date thing in here after work?"

"Ugh!" His face formed into a scrawl.

"Ugh? That's not the right noise someone gives for a date."

Casper sat down and looked at the coffee seed carefully. "I know. I mean, Darla's kinda cute—she has a cute body from what I can tell under all of that black armor, but it's…it's I'm not feeling it."

"Of course you can't feel it if she's wearing armor."

"No, I mean relationship materials."

"Who says you have to have a relationship with her? It could just be for fun."

"Is that what you want with Ami?"

"Ami? No that's the real thing."

"AH-HAAAAAAA!" he yelled. "You finally admit you're in love with her!"

"Whatever, man, we're talking about you, not me!"

"Well maybe I'm looking for the real thing too; we both are. After 'The One Who Shall Remain Nameless' and that stint with Lori. I am so done with girls who are less stable than a roller skating goat on a half pipe."

"If you don't go on that date with her, she'll probably medieval you."

"True. Yuck, I'd rather work on the farm! I want to get the crops grown as soon as possible. Maybe I'll make her fall un-love with me. Give her the worst date ever."

"Easy. Just be yourself."

"Very funny, Don. But not Marx Brothers funny, more like that smells funny, funny."

"Tell you what, give me all of your seeds. You can have the keys to the café. You do your bad date thing, while I plant all of the seeds on your farm."

"I guess that's what I'll have to do." He sighed.

"Man, I've never seen anybody so sad to go out on a date with a cute girl before...except that time I set up a blind date for my gay cousin—Ami!"

"Holy crap! Your gay cousin is named Ami? Freaky!"

"No! I just spotted Ami heading this way." As Don had said, Ami was making her way towards the café. She entered and waved to Finn who was using the broom to clean another broom.

"Ami-chan! You off work already?" Casper asked.

"We're taking a lunch break. What are you doing here?"

"Same, 'cept I should have been back 15 minutes ago. Guess I'm cleaning the bathroom when I get back. Might as well take an extra 15."

Don had a spacey look on his face as he stared at Ami. "W-what can I get for you?"

"Have any muffins left?"

"For now. Soon, berries are going to be few and far between... Unless?" He looked at Casper.

"I got all berries and wheat covered. If we run out of sugar, I even got stevia seeds. If I can find eggs and milk, you got your muffins."

"What in the world are you two talking about?" Ami asked.

"Nothing, for now. It's kind of a secret."

"A secret? From me? Why?"

"No offense, Ami, but you might spill the beans to your military buddies."

"What! Who do you think I am? I can keep a secret, I'm insulted"

"Fine, I'll whisper it to you." Don walked over to her, put his cupped hand and his mouth really close to her ear and began telling her all about their secret farm. Ami's face turned red as she could feel his breath on her ear and neck. She reached down and loosened her shirt collar.

"Th-that's interesting. I want to make sure rice is in there somehow."

"If it grows, you got it," Casper said.

"After work, I'm going to go home and try to do some programing on Piggy Back, then I'm heading up there. You should join me," Don said.

"I might do that, If I'm not...never mind."

"Never mind what? What are you up to?"

"I can't talk about it."

"Wait, we talked about our secret project. How come you can't talk about yours?"

"Because mine is firing squad level."

"See. I told you you're part of the system!"

"What are you talking about?" she asked angrily, "I'm not part of a system! I'm trying to do something that could lead to us getting out of here!"

"But you're still a member of the ones locking us down, keeping secrets away from us, and treating the citizens like we should't be involved in rescuing ourselves."

"Every society needs order and leadership structure, otherwise It'll be anarchy in here!"

"This coming from a woman with a pink stripe in her hair?"

"What's that supposed to mean?"

"You've changed, Nakajima. You used to be a rebellious punk girl, and now you're working for the Man."

"Damare!" she yelled. "I'm still the same person. Maybe you're just jealous because the only way you can help is to caffeinate people, while I get to be part of the group that actually is helping the town!"

"Annnnnd, scene!" Casper yelled. "Ami, Don, you're both part of the Justice League. Ami has her army thing, who help protect us...sorta like Wonder Woman. Don runs the café...Sorta like... Alfred the Butler to Batman. Me, I'm Superman, because we're both awesome—everybody's important."

"Well, perhaps Don doesn't appreciate what I do, but I know Finn does—right Finn?" Ami gestured over to Finn who was now polishing the counter top so shinny, it looked like a mirror. "Who? What?" he asked.

"Never mind!" Ami yelled. "I'm going back to where I'm appreciated." She stormed off. If the pneumatic cylinder would have allowed it, she would have slammed the glass door. Instead it slowly closed with an angry hissing sound.

"Well. My date with Darla is definitely gonna be better than your date with her."

Don ignored Casper's comment and put his arms up and yelled "KHHHHHHAN!"

Professor Pascal scrolled the pages and pages of digital data on Aarti's laptop. Aarti had counted at least seven "fascinatings" and at least 12 "wows" uttered by him as he learned what he had missed during his faking death sabbatical. "This is astounding. The alien wants to switch bodies in order to learn more about us?"

"Yes." Aarti gave him a cup of coffee. "It makes you want to be inside there with them, doesn't it?"

"Definitely. But I'll accept just being near them for now."

"And what is your exit plan?"

"I sneak in the camp, gather footage and then sneak away."

"And you expect me to help you?"

"No. I expect you drive to the camp as you do every day as I hide in your trunk. And when you leave, I'll just happen to be in your trunk, again. This will all be without your knowledge...except what I just told you...Tell you what, If they catch you, you can say I threatened you with extreme violence."

Aarti laughed. "YOU, with extreme violence."

"My lack of aggressive nature aside, say whatever you have to. I'll take any punishment that comes my way."

"Lewis, Is it worth it? Why don't you just run away to Mexico? Find a hut in the Yucatan and live a peaceful life?"

"As nice as that sounds, I'd never live a peaceful life if I didn't try to do this."

Aarti sighed. "Lewis...just don't get killed."

"Can't kill me, I'm already dead, remember?"

When General Katz came into the café, Finn automatically stood at attention.

"At ease soldier, you're no longer in the army," the general said.

"Oh, right." Finn relaxed. "Can I call you Flint?"

"You do and I'll shove your eyes up your rear so you can see me kick the crap out of you."

"Yes, sir, General. What can I get you?"

"Just a coffee, black." Finn poured the general a cup and handed it to him.

"How much do I owe you?"

"Don't worry sir. It's on me. Think of it as a thank you for my time as a member of the armed forces."

The general sadly shook his head and sat down at a table near the window. After a couple of sips he called Finn over.

"Sir. Something wrong with the coffee?"

"No, It's good. I have something I want to talk to you about."

"Anything, sir."

"When you accidentally launched the egg into space…"

"I'm deeply sorry about that sir, it was my respond…"

The general stopped his apologizing. "Don't worry about that. We actually were supposed to press the button on it. I guess we can say thanks to you, we may find a way to get out of here. What I actually want to talk to you about is why you never gave the names of Ami Nakajima and the three other soldiers that were with you at the time."

Finn had a confused look on his face. "Sir?"

"Why didn't you name others involved with launching the egg?"

"But sir, I did."

"Huh?"

"Sir. I told Captain Kowalski that Miss Nakajima wasn't involved because it was those other guys and my fighting with them that launched it."

"You told him their names?"

"Not really sir, because I didn't know them."

"What do you mean you didn't know them?"

"Sir, I don't know people by names but I'm really good at faces. I know every face in our squadron and I never noticed those guys before, until right when we entered this town."

The general looked down. "You told Kowalski that."

"Yes, sir."

"Finn. Did you work in the telecommunications van at any point?"

"What's that?"

The general stood up. "Never mind. Thanks for the coffee." He exited the café.

Ami Nakajima, Private First Class Shante Walden, and Private Sarah Sachenbacher-Stehle were Plür's three choices for the people she could easily transfer bodies with. It was a perfect racial mix: Japanese, African-American and German Caucasian American. Ami felt as if she was the runner-up in a beauty contest. She was happy to be one step closer to going where no Earthling has ever gone before, but nervous she might not be able to come back. Once again, all three of them entered the gym. A presidential monitor was set up in front of the stage. It took Ami a second to recognize the live stream of the President because recognizing him would be like you recognizing the President of Japan, and also because he was wearing glasses, looking at each one of them and going over some paperwork that gave their various resumés. When everyone had assembled, including General Katz and Dr. Chambers, he started the briefing.

"Good evening ladies," the President said. "I'm your commander in chief, President Jimmy Jarrod. The good General Kitty has informed me that you three are the damsels de choice of our alien beach ball friend. First, I must congratulate you three on being the top sirloin cuts of humanity, so much so that you impressed an alien as the perfect specimens to swap noggins. Unfortunately, as you know there is only one winner in the Super Bowl and the rest of the teams that played through injures, rain and Gatorade being dumped down their backs are simply a whole lot of losers. The final decision comes down to me, because after all I'm sorta like the daddy of this Brady Bunch. So as daddy, I will announce my choice–drum roll…" There was a long pause. "…I said drum roll" Everyone looked around and at each other. "Fine, no drum roll. And the winner is…our fine candidate from Nebraska, Sock in Bock–Socker Gauche…"

"Sarah Sachenbacher-Stehle," the general corrected.

"Yes, her—congratulations, future pioneer. Your name shall go down in history, if not for the first human to switch souls, then the most difficult last name to pronounce. God speed."

The President was about to officially end the meeting, but was interrupted by Private First Class, Walden. "Mr. President, sir."

"Yes, Miss Nakajima."

"Walden, sir."

"Yes, Walden, what can I do you for?"

"Sir. If I may ask: Why did you pick her…" She gestured to Sarah Sachenbacher-Stehle "…over myself and her?" She gestured to Ami.

"That's confidential information, Walden," the general said.

"No…" said the President. "…it's okay. I'll tell you if you really want to know."

"I do, sir."

"Okay. Where did you grow up, Walden?"

"Chicago, sir."

"Grew up in a rough neighborhood, did ya not?"

"Y-yes, sir. But I made something of myself when I joined the army."

"I'm sure you have. But when you were in the hood, did you see things, say, like…drive-bys, drug use, police brutality, that sorta thing?"

"Sometimes."

"And when you switch bodies with our alien, and those memories transfer to hers, what do you think her impression of humanity will be?"

"Sir, I like to think that my hardships and my triumph over them are what makes me human. I already talked to Plür about some of it and she seemed quite interested to know more."

"All the good reason to take the angry horse out of the race."

"Sir, I'm not angry…"

"No, but as far as history goes, I have no interest in showing the alien 400 years of racism locked in your brain and then trying to convince her that humans are good, in spite of slavery, Jim Crow and Al Jolson."

"I think she'd understand."

"Not willing to take that chance, Walden. I mean, I think you're a fine America, but I can't risk gambling on you."

"Sir, I…"

"Dismissed, soldier."

Walden saluted the general and then wiped a tear off her face while walking out in a hurry.

The President turned his attention to Ami. "I guess you have the same question?"

"Yes, sir."

"Pardon?"

"I said yes, sir."

"General, can you explain to her, that from my end, all I hear is Japanese chop-chop coming out of her mouth."

"S-sorry, sir," Ami said struggling. "I—forgot…how to speak English…being able to speak freely inside the ring's borders."

"That's part of my following points: Ami Nakajima, age 22. Graduated near the top of your class, student of U.C. Pepper Mill. Four point oh my! Grade average. Studied: CPR, phlebotomy, EMT, Medical Lab Technology, Philosophy 101, Computer 1A and 1B, sociology, Drama 2B—or was it not 2B?—And Jazz dancing. Regular all-American girl–oh wait…not an all-American girl. Citizen of the Osaka prefecture, Kansai, Japan, here on a student visa."

"Sir, what does my nationality have to do with anything?"

"Let me put it to you this way. You like to watch Godzilla movies?"

"I fear where this is going, but yes, I used to."

"Okay. Godzilla is in the middle of the Pacific ocean, trying to decide if he wants to eat Japanese or California cuisine. He asks you: should I stomp on through Osaka and turn people into hot sushi or dance right on through California and eat a couple of surf board platters? Which one would you suggest to him?"

"Sir, that question is rhetorical, if not absurd."

"You know what's absurd? A real-live alien in our country that may or may not attack us. If your Japanese brain is in her head, there is a chance that your people will be spared her wrath instead of my people."

"That's selfish."

"Yes…yes it is and that's the way this world is. Your people attacked Pearl Harbor. We dropped a bomb on your people. Who's right? I don't know, but I'm glad we had the bomb first."

When Ami yelled "kutabare!" and then stormed off, the general and Dr. Chambers but not the President, understood her.

An hour later, preparations for the soul transfer had been made in the gymnasium. Plür finished her meditation and floated to the ground.

"Are you done?" Bosq asked.

"Yes, I am ready for the transfer."

"You seemed to meditate longer than you did for other animals."

"I want to get this right."

"It'll go fine, Plür."

"I want my mothers to be proud of me."

"They are. Did I ever tell you what your first mother said to me when I was assigned to you?"

"No, you did not. What was it?"

"I'll tell you later…your host are here."

General Katz, Mayor Duncan, Dr. Chambers, two armed soldiers and Sachenbacher-Stehle who was wearing an all white jumpsuit, filed into the gym. Bosq scampered off to a more strategic position on the stage. Everyone exchanged greetings. The general walked over to the Presidential monitor and cut it on. The image of the President appeared briefly then disappeared to a blank screen.

"Why am I not surprised," General Katz said.

"Are you ready?" Plür asked.

Sachenbacher-Stehle nodded yes.

"Do not be afraid. Fear will delay the transfer. Also do not touch me until I tell you to do so–no one else should touch me when I am preparing to transfer or else my body will try to bond with theirs instead of hers. Let the memories of your host flow into you. The first ones will be breathing, talking, moving, and later memories. Finally, remember not to touch other humans when you are in my form. The result could be…over-stimulating."

"Are you sure this is safe?" the mayor asked.

"As long as you follow the directions I just gave you, everything will go fine. Now, I ask you, Sarah, to walk close to me and when I say—now, you will touch me and the bond will start." Sarah walked over to Plür. The soldiers raised their guns. Plür started to produce a sound not unlike that of the word "ohm" and a didgeridoo but at one octave lower. Her surface seemed to vibrate and shake more and more until she was a vibrating blur. The didgeridoo sound stopped as did the vibrating. The room was quiet, so much so, that everyone could hear their own breathing. Suddenly, the silence was broken by screaming from outside.

All attention turned from Plür to Lori being dragged into the gymnasium by two soldiers. "Let me go!" she yelled.

The general angrily stomped over to the chaos. "JUST WHAT'S GOING ON HERE? Why did you bring her in here?"

"You gave us strict orders that when we caught her, we were to bring her directly to you," answered one of the soldiers.

"You MORON! This is the worst time to come in here! Take her somewhere else, anywhere!"

"What's that?" Lori asked.

"It's something you shouldn't be seeing."

"You bought me here just to show me something that I shouldn't see?"

"I didn't want you to be here. Take her to the cafeteria, I'll deal with her later!"

Before the soldiers could take Lori into another part of the school, she wiggled away from them.

"This is just like you!" she yelled. "You act like you want me but the minute I'm around, you want to ship me off to somewhere else!"

"Can we talk about this later?"

"No!" She quickly backed away from them. One of the soldiers tried to grab her. She applied knee to groin and he bent over and away in pain. Before the other soldier could try to capture her she ran away to the area where Plür and Sarah were.

"Stop!" the general yelled. "Get away from them, Lori!"

"No! If you have something to say to me, you say it here!"

"Lori. Please. Back away from the white ball." The general slowly walked towards her.

"Why? What is this thing?" She pointed to Plür.

"Lori, just back away. We can talk later."

She walked over and almost put her hand on Plür. "What's the big deal?"

Bosq slowly crawled off the stage and crept towards Lori. He wanted to make sure he could get her out of the area before she touched Plür.

"Should I grab her?" Sarah asked the general.

"No! Remain still. I don't want anything or anyone…" He gestured for the two armed soldiers approaching Lori to lower their weapons."…to mess up the transfer!"

"You didn't answer my question. What is this?" Again Lori almost touched Plür.

"Please, Lori, dear, don't touch that thing, it's dangerous!"

"You know, dad, the one thing I've learned from you is…"

"What's that sweetheart?"

Bosq was almost in range. He could almost grab her and drag her away.

"…I've learned that you're nothing but a big…fat…liar!"

"Now!" yelled Plür.

This startled Lori. So much so, that her pinky jerked and came into contact with Plür.

"Ooo. Soft," Lori said. A second later, Plür's body had liquified and spread from a ball shape onto Lori's entire body as if someone had poured white paint all over her. Lori, of course, struggled to remove the white stuff as anyone would, if a bunch of white stuff was suddenly coveting your body. Everyone else tired to rush to help her but Dr. Chambers kept them at bay. "Stop! You remember what Plür said—it can be dangerous to interfere right now." As everyone watched in anguish, Lori hit the floor and struggled, tying to wrestle the white goo off of her body. She stopped struggling and collapsed into an unconscious pile on the floor. A second later, the white goo left her body and collected into a white puddle, five feet away. Lori regained consciousness and lifted up on her hands and knees. She then proceeded to vomit up more white stuff which automatically moved and merged with the rest of the puddle. A small blue marble came out of her mouth and rolled across the floor.

"Lori! Are you all right." The general was speaking to the human form of Lori, but it was the wrong person. The human form, Plür, took a huge, labored breath as if she had almost been a victim of drowning. Within seconds, her hair, which had been blonde, turned as white as snow. She clumsily crawled over to the white puddle. "H-hello? Cc-can you hear me?" she said to the puddle, struggling to pronounce the words. The puddle bubbled and moved around. "Think–k-k-k-s-s-sp-sphere. Think about—s-s-sphere." The puddle bubbled again. A moment passed and the white goo started to move around. It gathered together more and more until it formed a large solid blob. This blob slowly took the shape of an abnormal sphere and eventually a perfect one. Plür grabbed the sphere and picked it up. "Think–lighter than air." She let go of the blob. It dunked down, bumped the ground hard and then started hovering in the air. "Wh-what's going on where am I?" Lori's labored voice came from the sphere. General Katz ran over to it. He almost touched it but stopped. "Lori! Are you all right? It's me, daddy."

"Daddy?" it said. "What's going on? What happened to me?"

Dr. Chambers walked over to Plür. "Can I touch either one of you?"

"You can touch me," said the human form of Plür. "If you touch her it could be too much for her." Dr. Chambers started checking Plür's vital signs.

"What about my daughter?" General Katz asked.

"I'm at a loss as how to examine her; Plür?" the doctor asked.

Plür got close to Lori. "C-can you s-see?"

"Yes, but it's a lot of information!" Lori said very fast. "It's like I can see every single color in the world all at once and everybody keeps changing color depending on what they're saying! It's like my sinuses have been clogged for 22 years and now, they're clear! The colors, dude! The colors! This is like the ultimate high!"

"This…is bad," Plür said, struggling to move her hands and legs.

"What's wrong?" the mayor asked."

"Her mind. It is unfocused…un…disciplined. Why I chose other three girls. They had good…focus."

"You need to switch back, now!" the general commanded.

"If we do…this moment, it…destroy her mind. We wait for… half a sun's rotation…she is not stable enough…I not stable enough to…soul transfer."

"But can't we…"

Plür interrupted him. "Sorry. I can not do now. I am trying– adjust. Everything…so…heavy. The world…feels so heavy for you humans. I…aware…my own mortality. Give me moment to adjust…your world…so heavy…so heavy. Like universe holding me down." Plür picked up the small blue marble and put it in her ear. It disappeared inside her head.

"What was that?"

"I can not talk about it."

"Plür! I thought we had a deal. You said if we do this, there'd be no secrets between us!"

"All will be…revealed. For now…adjust to bodies.

At Don's Café, Darla arrived for her date with Casper. She had picked out her best loli-goth outfit resembling a black wedding dress, accented by her dark makeup. She was happy, which seemed counter-productive for a goth. Inside the café, Finn was cleaning up. She waved hi and had a seat.

"I'm sorry, ma'am but we're closed," he said.

"I know, I'm here for my date with Casper. Don said he was going to let us use the place."

"Oh right. He did say something about that. Hey, I've seen you before. At that night of the bar fight, right?"

"Yep, that's me."

"Boy, that was a wild night."

"The wildest."

"A date with Casper? huh. I guess this will make things much easier for Miss Ami."

"What are you talking about?"

"She said she was in love with one of her roommates. So if he's going out with you, she can get over him easier."

"Dude."

"What?"

"She has two roommates."

"Yeah, so?"

"Dude. She's in love with Don, not Casper."

Imagine a deer in the headlights of an oncoming truck. Now imagine instead of a truck, it's a 747. That's the look on Finn's face.

"Noooo…No way."

"Why not?"

"They're always arguing."

"Of course they argue, it's all foreplay."

"No idea what that is, but I understand the word play." Finn sat down and looked depressed. "Ahh man."

"I guess you had your heart set on Ami, huh?"

"I even had our kids names picked out: Ikea, Rambo and Vader for the boys and Assia, Shady and Damiracle for the girls."

Finn didn't see Darla do a gagging motion. "Well, now you can save those names for someone who'll actually let you impregnate them."

Plür got up from the cross-legged lotus position on the floor and stood up. She clumsily walked around while looking at her toes. On the other side of the room, Lori was still having a hard time adjusting. She slowly floated up and down like a yo-yo, as too many thoughts flashed into her undisciplined mind.

"Why did your hair turn white?" the mayor asked Plür.

"It is a sign of an imperfect transfer. I am supposed to take on a pure appearance of the host.

Plür did a ballet pirouette. "What is that? She asked everyone.

"It's called a pirouette." Dr. Chambers answered. "It's a spin used in dancing, assuming you know what dancing is."

"I have a memory of learning how to do that."

"Lori took ballet classes when she was 7," General Katz said. "Does that mean you have her memories from back then?"

"Some of them. They are flowing in slow…"

"Plür? What's wrong?"

"It is you."

"Me? What about me?"

"I feel…She feels so much anger and hatred towards you." Plür walked over to the general. "It is like she wants you… nonexistent."

"Can we not talk about this now!"

"Plür tried to put her hands on his face, but he pushed it away. "Don't."

"I am sorry. This is the bad part of transference. We get the good and bad memories." She walked towards the doctor.

The general went back to watching over Lori. "That's the bad part? I think the bad part is what you've done to my daughter!"

"She will be fine, once we switch back. As long as she stays here and is not exposed to anything too stimulating." Plür felt the texture of the brown hoodie jacket she was wearing. On the pockets where multicolored dancing teddy bears. She ran her hand over the right pocket and felt something crunchy. She put her hand inside and pulled out a piece of paper. She slowly unfolded it and read it. "Casper Cornbread 555-8257." What is this white leaf with numbers on it?

Dr. Chambers took it from her. "It's a phone number of a guy…Casper. I think I know him, Cornbregger, not Cornbread. He was the person that touched you when you first landed."

"Oh yes, the smelly one."

"Smelly, what?"

"And what is this…phone number?"

"It's a way to communicate. Most likely, she made a date with him," the mayor answered.

"Who made a date with my daughter?" The general asked. The doctor handed him the paper.

"Is not a date a measurement on a time keeping device?" Plür asked.

"No." the mayor answered. "By date I mean romantic courtship. She was going to go somewhere with him to find out if they can have a relationship. Does that make sense?"

"Yes. It is part of mating, right?"

"If it's done right."

"Then I would like to go date with Casper 555-8257."

"What!" the general yelled. "Over my flaming, headless dead body!"

"Is there a problem?"

The doctor interrupted. "The general is feeling protective of his daughter…also part of the dating ritual. He perhaps has forgotten that his daughter is the one in ball form and you are not her, correct?"

The general went back to looking at Lori.

"Mating courtships are the easiest and fastest ways for me to analyze a society. This would be a perfect opportunity for our people to bond. Please, help me to find Casper 555-8257."

"And how in the world can we make this happen?" the mayor asked.

"Casper is Ami's roommate," The general said. "I'm sure she knows where to find him. But I'm still not comfortable with this whole date thing. Even if it's not my daughter, this Casper character is a bit of an oddball. We really want to have him as the ambassador of romance?"

"I assume you mean he is not a perfect male specimen." Plür said. "it doesn't matter. All I am interested in is the mating ritual. Unless he tries to cause me physical harm, I have no problems with anything else."

"He tries to get fresh with Lori's body and they'll be physical harm all right!"

"Perhaps one of us can chaperone," the doctor suggested.

"Is chaperone a normal part of your mating ritual?" Plür said.

"It's really not," the mayor said. She got a very nasty look from the general. "I'm sorry, but it's a sign of a lack of trust. I'm very sensitive to society scrutinizing my love life."

The general was about to start arguing, but he was cut off by the doctor "Perhaps we can have a compromise. A long distance chaperone, hiding in the shadows, without interfering?"

"Fine, I'll send a couple of soldiers to…"

"No, thank you," Plür interrupted. "Having humans with weapons nearby means you expect him to harm me or me to harm him. It is not a sign of trust. This is one of the reasons Lori does not like you. I have memories of lots or arguments about it. Finally, she leaves home. There is sadness and…"

"ENOUGH!" the general yelled. There was an awkward silence for a few seconds. "Just go on your date, leave, learn all you want, I don't care…just don't harm her body."

"I'll be the long distance chaperone." the mayor said. "Would that be okay?"

"Yes. As long as you do not interfere,"

The general nodded agreement.

"I'll only be there as an advisor. Other than that, I won't interfere."

"Then let us depart." Plür said.

Aarti was nervous. She was nervous about having snuck Professor Pascal onto the army camp site in the trunk of her car and now she was even more nervous when Professor Pascal walked into the computer lab, tent, wearing a blond wig for a disguise. She quickly got up from her desk and walked over to him. "Lewis!" she whispered loudly. "What in M. Night Shamble-lot are you doing?"

"Don't worry about it."

"Are you insane? One of them are going to turn you in!" She gestured to the three other scientist in the tent, working away on their computers. "That disguise is terrible!"

"I doubt it. The disguise is for the army people outside. Soldiers are trained to look for anything suspicious, in this case Professor Pascal suddenly appearing from the dead, but not a blond-haired, Professor Sven Svengundsun from Sweden. The scientists in here, on the other hand, never looked up from their computers even when I worked here. Unless I'm a walking cup of coffee or a centerfold of a CPU from Wired magazine, I doubt they even know what I look like."

"That's ridiculous!"

"Really? Watch—Hello!" he yelled. "I'm Dr. Sven Svengundson from Sweden. I will be working here from now on!" No one looked up at him. One person did managed to wave hello without looking up. "See."

Aarti sighed and then returned to her desk.

At Don's Café, Darla patiently waited at one of the small outside tables for the very late Casper to show up. When she saw him, it appeared he had not bothered to go home after work to change into nicer clothes and was still wearing his red apron from work. She hated the red aprons from her job and detested seeing them outside of work. Unknown to her, he knew this. He carried a Tupperware™ container full of food. She looked forward to whatever he was carrying and took guesses to what it could be: spaghetti and meatballs? Lasagne? He unceremoniously tossed the container onto the table and sat down with his arms crossed. "Er-Hi? Casper," she said.

"Wut-up?" he said looking away from her.

"You're late."

"Had to work late at the office."

"Ooo-kay." She raised an eyebrow. "So. What's for dinner?" He opened the box. "What is that? She held her nose to protect if from a sulfuric smell.

"Burnt toast and a rotten egg."

"Burn't toast and a rotten egg? Why'd you make that?"

" 'Cause I got a tape worm and that's good enough for 'em!"

Watching the whole scene from across the street were Plür and Mayor Duncan. They had learned from Ami that he was having a date with Darla today at Don's Café.

"Looks like we're too late. Seems he's already on a date." The mayor said.

"This is good also. Perhaps I can observe their actions and learn more about humans."

Darla leaned back in her chair to show more of her outfit with its heaving bodice top. "So…what do you think? How do I look?"

"Casper refused to tell her that she looked hotter than a flaming plastic army man on the sun. "You look 'ight, I guess." He took a bite of burnt toast and then spat it out, nearly hitting a walking passerby in the crotch. "Sorry."

Darla became even more perturbed. "Well. Now that we're alone, with no interruptions…If you know what I mean?"

"Actually I don't." (Truth be known, he really didn't).

"You know…What keeps getting interrupted, between us?… On the bleachers, or near the river?"

"Aliens, Professors, Sue, Newtonian gravitational fields?"

"No! What we were going to do before they interrupted?"

"Oh…Huh?"

"Kissing, you numbskull!"

"Oh, right…huh?"

"You were going to kiss me, you ill-informed ignoramus!"

"She seems to be insulting him," Plür stated.

"Doesn't seem to be going very well for him," the mayor agreed.

"Is this part of the mating ritual?"

"Only in the really kinky relationships."

Darla looked like she was ready to give up on Casper, if not punch him. She leaned back, crossed her arms and thought for a second. She leaned forwards and closed her eyes. "Kiss me!"

"Er-ah."

"Enough with the 'er-ah'. You heard me—Kiss me! If you want a relationship with me, you'll kiss me. Otherwise, I'm tired of your little procrastination games. SO, either you kiss me and be a man or you can make me force feed you your tape-worm sandwich, EXIT first! So what'll it be?"

Casper had to think fast. "Kiss Darla and get thrown into a relationship, or eat a horrible meal—backwards. At least with the meal, the pain would go away faster." He didn't want to deceive her, she was right that he was taking the coward's way out with the attitude and the fake meal but he was never very good at bailing out of a bad relationship. "I guess I can always test it out." he thought looking at her puckering black lips. "She is attractive and fun like a carnival ride…as well as dangerous, barely held together with loose screws and constructed by hillbillies…like a carnival ride. Kiss her, Cornbregger! It doesn't mean you're married. It's just a kiss."

As they watched him agonize on his next move, Plür inquired about what was going on. "She looks like she wants to kiss him, but he doesn't want to." the mayor answered.

"How odd. I've seen some races that kiss. Usually it's a parent regurgitating food into their youths mouth. I want to get a better look." Plür walked across the street, almost getting hit by two army vehicles that came to a screeching halt. The mayor tried to follow but was blocked by a citizen that recognized her and started harassing her about some zoning law and about keeping the dogs out of the park unless they wore pants. After that, a view blocking firetruck and more citizens taking advantage of her availability.

"Are you sure this is wise?" Bosq asked Plür. "You may be interfering too much."

"It will be fine," she said. "All mistakes are teachers." By the time Plür made it to Darla and Casper's table, he was sporting a kissing face with his eyes closed and slowly moving forwards to kiss Darla. He stopped and moved back, his face like someone being tortured with eating a lemon. Plür leaned down and got really close to their faces and studied their expressions.

"I'm keeping my eyes closed until there's a kiss!" Darla said. Casper moved forwards and then stopped. His face was one of anguish and sadness.

'He looks so sad." Plür thought. "Unless there is a kiss, he's going to be in pain. Perhaps I can help him out.'

Casper felt a pair of lips on his. Of course he expected Darla's lips to be soft, but not on the level of a brand new pair off the lips truck. A tingle ran down his spine and the blood left his legs. It was the sensation he got when a contractor's truck cut him off on the freeway and came within two inches of his bumper, but this time it was like he didn't press the brake and he let himself go, crashing. All of his fears about a relationship were gone. He wanted a relationship with someone who could kiss like this. If he had known Darla could do this, he would have kissed her right in front of Sue. He put his hand on her cheek and kissed her deeper. Their heads moved as they kissed passionately. She moaned approval.

"WHAT...THE...HECK?" Darla yelled.

Casper tried to figure out how she had said that while kissing. "What a talented kisser!" he thought. "Wait, a minute—what the heck? What the heck what?" He opened his eyes. He was kissing Plür, who had bent down and intercepted his kiss. He pulled away really fast. She remained in the kissing position." Whoa whoa WHOA!" he yelled. "LORI?"

"O-M-GUACAMOLE!" Darla yelled. I've had guys cheat on me before but never before we even started to date!" Darla stood up. Casper stood up and Plür straighten up.

"Lori!" Casper said. "What the heck?"

"Okay, I get it Cornbregger!" Darla said, raising her hands. "If you don't want to date me, just say so! You didn't have to go through all of this!"

"I didn't plan this—she kissed me!"

"Sure, play the innocent! And I thought you were a decent guy!" Darla turned on her heels and started walking away. "You're nothing but a play-ah!."

"Darla! Wait!"

"She really should hate the game, and not the person playing," Plür said.

Darla raised her hand.

"Is that one digit paw gesture part of the date, too?" Plür asked.

Casper looked at Plür with extreme confusion, as if she were covered in 100 linked sausages. "What-is-with-you?"

"Pardon?"

"First we set a date, then you blow me off, then you throw garbage on me, then you cause a bar fight, then you knock me down, and NOW you kiss me right in front of my date! WHAT'S YOUR MAJOR MALFUNCTION? What have I done to deserve this?"

"I have a memory of the date plan, some kind of fight and knocking you down, but not the garbage story."

"Of course you don't, because you're psychotic! Nice hair, by the way! Is that another wig?"

"It is true, Lori has some problems with an undisciplined mind."

"Speaking in the third person? Oh-yeah, you're sane all right!"

"Plür!" The mayor yelled. "Wait for me!" She was being blocked by another citizen.

"Well, I'm out of here! I guess I should thank you for keeping me from dating Darla, but I'm NOT!" Casper started walking away. A block later, he realized Plür was following him. "HOLY serial killer! Why are you following me?"

"Because I'm supposed to go date with you."

"Wow…Just…Wow. Are you serious?"

"Yes. It is impossible for me to tell lies. It's against my code of morality."

"Morality? YOU? You kneed a bar-load of guys in the crotch. You're like the queen of crotch fu!"

"That was Lori. Not me."

"Oh I get it, you're a changed man."

Plür opened her blouse and looked down at her cleavage. "No. I am still female…Humans can do that?"

"Very funny. But stop following me." Another block and he stopped and looked behind him. She was gone. He breathed a sigh of relief. "What a nut ball…Heck of a kisser though." When he turned around, she was in front of him. He screamed a little "E-ee-agh!' "You're still here?"

"Of course. I'm waiting on the date."

He looked up and was about to scream. He noticed the night sky had some clear views of the stars. He sighed. "What-ever. I'm going home. I'm gonna make some stir fry, then I'm going to go up on the roof and if I don't jump, I'll probably look at the stars. If that's your idea of a date—tag along. Just don't kill me." He started walking towards home. Plür followed close behind.

Meanwhile, blocks away, the mayor frantically looked around while yelling "Plür! Where are you?"

Meanwhile, back at the farm (I've always wanted to start a paragraph with that). Don was watering his coffee bean seeds. He stepped back and breathed in a sense of pride. He felt like a Columbian coffee bean plantation owner. He wondered if he could get ahold of a donkey so he could change his name to Don Valdez. He reached into the bag of seeds Casper had given to him and pulled out a small brown bag of orange seeds. "Okay Mr Cornbregger, where would you want me to plant your orange groove?" He heard a rustling in the bushes. He quickly put the seeds in his back pocket and looked in the direction of the noise. Ami came out of the woods, tripping a little over a stump. "Ami?"

"It's hard to find this place," she complained.

"That's what makes it so great. People won't stumble across it and pick our fruit."

"Wow, look at the—what is that, mint?"

"Some of it. There's also arugula, fennel and..."Don pointed to each crop, "...Illegal drugs."

Ami looked perplexed. "Is that what I think it is?"

"Yep. Believe it or not, it was planted by mistake."

Ami went over and smelled the cannabis. "Mistake, huh," she said skeptically. "You know what we call marijuana in Japanese high schools?"

"No, what"

"Nothing. We don't smoke marijuana. We're too busy getting better grades than drug addict, American teenagers."

"Very funny. You come here to help or to insult the American educational system?"

"Both, I'll help If I can. At least I'll be helpful...somewhere."

"Ami..." Don walked over to her. "I'm sorry for what I said. It was stupid. What you do is really important and like you said, you and the army are gonna be the ones to get us out of here. Not some coffee-slinging barista."

"Don't sell yourself short. Apparently what you do is more important than my job."

"How so?"

"I thought I was part of the team and an equal, but the minute a vey important mission shows up, the first thing they looked at was my race and nationality. I might as well be a Japanese spy in World War Two, as far as they're concerned."

"Ahh, Ami." he put his hand on her shoulder. "Don't you EVER sell yourself short. I grew up with those type of attitudes my whole life, and I was in a liberal city. My people have been here for 400 years and we're still trying to get accepted as equals. You can't let it defeat you. It's not your fault that some people have narrow minds."

"Thanks Don." She patted his hand. They looked at each other for a moment. She cleared her throat. "So, is there anything I can do to help?"

"Help me dig." Ami grabbed a shovel and Don grabbed the hoe. They prepared rows and planted almost all of the seeds

Casper had given them, except the orange seeds. Don secretly glimpsed at Ami working. She looked at him and he quickly looked away. "What is it?" she asked.

"Nothing. You look kinda cute doing garden work."

She turned her head away from him so he wouldn't see her smile. She took a deep breath. "So…Don."

"Yes, Ami–Chan?"

"Hypothetically, have you ever considered dating someone you lived with? I'm asking hypothetically of course!"

"Hypothetically?"

"Hypothetically."

"Well, hypothetically, I like Casper, but I like my men more butch."

"No," she laughed. "I mean if you had a female roommate… NOT ME, just some random girl, hypothetically."

"Hypothetically?

"Hypothetically."

"Well, I think the only way I could date someone I lived with is if I was in love with them."

"And how would you know?"

"I think if it were someone I've known a long time, someone who's been there for me, someone who makes me laugh and I smile whenever I come home because all day I've been thinking about how much I want to see them, someone that likes to put ketchup on her eggs and mayonnaise on her pizza, someone that uses a shampoo that smells like cherry blossoms, brushes her teeth with a Sailor Moon toothbrush, hates it when people eat sushi with chopsticks and especially someone that's my best female friend… Then of course I'd date them…hypothetically of course."

"Of course."

They both went back to tending to the garden.

"Ami."

"Yes?"

"When we were about to die…"

"Which time?"

"Second time, when the comet was coming…Casper's right, it is weird that it's been more than once."

"Yes."

"You said something right when the bright light knocked us out."

"I-I did?"

"Yes. It sounded like I-L-something."

"Really?"

"Yeah. What did you say?"

"Uhh, I don't remember. Maybe it was 'I left the stove on?'" She's unconvincing as a lier.

"Of course…because you don't want the stove on, during an apocalypse." He angrily dug a trench. Ami and Don continued their work. As narrator, I wish I could knock their heads together and just yell "kiss each other you idiots!" but alas, let nature take its course as they say.

Let us go back to the high school gymnasium. The general was resisting the urge to touch the ball which used to be his daughter. She had stopped hovering up and down and now was floating in a circle, five feet off the ground, at a high speed. Sometimes she would describe what was going on inside her head, most of it didn't make sense.

"I see thousands of faces," she said when she made another lap. "A tunnel. There's a tunnel and it goes EVERYWHERE!" The general sadly shook his head.

The sight of Captain Kowalski entering the gym was not too surprising, after all he was a part of the military. What was surprising, he was being escorted by three soldiers, two with machine guns and one with a large duffle bag.

"Kowalski!" the general yelled. "What are you doing here? I didn't call for you."

"So sorry to interrupt, General. I'm afraid the current situation demands immediate action on my part," he said smugly.

"What are you talking about and what are they doing here?" He gestured to the other soldiers. The one with the duffle bag put it down, unzipped it and started building something.

"Don't worry. This will only take but a second. We only want the alien, nothing more. Please offer no resistance and no one will get harmed."

"What?" The general gestured for one of his men to go take Kowalski into custody. Kowalski gestured to one of his men. One fired a quick burst at the general's man. He dropped down dead. The general's other man, in shock, hesitated too long before taking action. He too was shot dead in less than a second. The general almost went into action but Kowalski stopped his man from shooting him and halted the general from any movement by pointing out that his men were aiming at Dr. Chambers.

"Now, now," Kowalski said. "We have no interest in killing anyone else. We only came for the alien."

"Who are you, really?"

"Me? Me, I'm just a loyal soldier carrying out his orders."

"Excuse me," said Dr. Chambers. "But can I tend to those men you shot. They may still be alive!"

"You can check after we leave. Otherwise, you make one move and you'll join them."

"The President told you to do this?" The general questioned.

Kowalski laughed. "That meandering mental midget? No, we did everything we could to make sure he has no hand in anything that goes on in here."

"What are you: CIA, NSA? KGB?"

"I'm not at liberty to say. But I can tell you that we are doing all of this for the common good."

"Common good? Sabotage? Killing my men and trying to harm the first alien visitor to this planet? You don't know what you're doing."

Kowalski laughed again.

"I say something funny? Because I'm not wearing clown makeup."

"Oh, General, do you really think this is the first time this has all happened?"

"What has happened?"

"The ring, alien visitation?"

"I think history would have recorded something as significant as the ring. And don't give me any crap about Area 51, because that was just us trying to invent stealth fighters and iPhones."

"Hhhhhhistory time!" Kowalski said, almost singing. "Siberia, Russia. June 30th, 1908. 7:17 AM. Stony Tunguska River. Large object believed to be a comet, touches town and explodes. Trees and reindeer from miles away are flattened. Case closed."

"So. Doesn't sound the same. This thing exploded but it reconstructed into the ring. Not one object or animal was harmed."

"The first explanation was from the OLD Soviet Union. As time went on, more evidence was uncovered, contrary to their story. Even the original explanation reported that no one ever saw any sign of an impact crater." Kowalski got close to the general's face. "After the fall of the Soviet Union, enter glasnost, a new story emerged. One that said yes, a comet landed and it did explode, but not one thing was harmed."

How would you explain the trees and the lack of ring hovering over Siberia?"

"The old records didn't mention that there was a small town inside the ring, just like Pepper Mill. Occupied by common peasants. All were enclosed in the ring just like us. Things didn't go too well. Old Russia in the 1900s wasn't very good for those cut off from the Tsar's help. They panicked, they ran out of resources; starvation, murder, cannibalism and eventually extinction. The very next second after the last citizen died, apparently by hanging himself, all of the trees inside the ring fell down dead and the ring disintegrated."

"Assuming what you say is true, those people died because there was chaos inside the town. How is what you're doing helping anybody?"

"Those people didn't have an alien to interrogate."

"Plür has nothing to do with the ring! Her people didn't build it; They're trapped just like we are!"

"So she says."

"She's not lying, Kowalski!"

"So she says." Kowalski gestured to the soldier that was assembling something out of his duffle bag. He lifted a large gun and pointed it at Lori.

"Nooo!" the general yelled.

The gun fired. Four black balls came out and spread around Lori. It was a net, attached by cord to the gun. Lori panicked and started moving around.

"Kowalski! That's not Plür!"

"Yes, I know all about the soul transfer. I'm sure whoever is in there will give us far more information than the alien would. If not, we can always blackmail the alien with her body."

"No, it's my daughter!"

Kowalski's face lit up with pleasure. He laughed once again. "Even better!" He pointed a handgun at Lori. "Little Lori? You've gained weight." He looked at the general. "So you won't offer any resistance as we take her away, right?" Two of Kowalski men dragged Lori to the ground and grabbed the net to keep her from floating away. Lori screamed!

"Don't touch her! Plür said not to touch her!" the general yelled.

"That's good to know," Kowalski said. "Take her away. But don't touch her...Unless she doesn't talk." They pulled Lori out the door by the ropes. The general started to make a move but they slammed the door on him and locked it. Dr. Chambers rushed to the fallen soldiers and checked their vital signs. "They're gone," she said sadly.

Casper set a plate of stir-fried ramen noodles on the table in front of Plür. She kept wiggling around in her chair, like an infant trying to figure out the best way to sit. "I know..." Casper said. "Ikea furniture is more form than function."

She found a comfortable position by sitting lotus style. She looked at the food Casper had set down in front of her with great suspicion.

"Sorry about the tofu. Meat is kinda hard to come across these days."

"Oh! This is food!"

"Ha! That's funny," he said sarcastically, "Invite you to my house and you insult my cooking."

"I am sorry. I was not trying to insult you. It has been a long time since I have eaten."

"You poor thing. It must have been tough living on the streets, hiding from the law. You must be starving."

"No. I just don't remember how to eat food."

"Wow, you are starving! Well, eat up." He took a bite. Lori watched him through the whole process and copied what he did, except instead of using a fork, she used her fingers. She put noodles in her mouth and chewed.

"Excuse me, Miss Manners—fork?" He pointed to her fork. She picked it up and ungracefully shoveled more food into her mouth, then put more in and chewed, eventually, there was a mouthful of noodles hanging out of her mouth.

"Uh, you need to swallow there, Tex." Casper pointed at her mouth.

Plür acknowledged his suggestion with a head nod and recalled how to transfer food into the body. Unfortunately, on the last swallow, she started to cough and choke. Casper ran around to her, prepared to do the Heimlich maneuver. It was unnecessary as she spat out the pieces she was choking on.

"You alright?"

"I am not harmed." She reached onto the ground and was about to put the food she had choked on, back into her mouth.

"Eww, Stop! You don't have to eat that!"

"I don't want to insult you by refusing your gift."

"Don't be crazy! Here, let me fix you a new plate." He took away her plate and refreshed it with more noodles. "I can't believe I'm sitting here, eating with you. Darla's right. I am too nice."

"How is that possible?"

"What?"

"Being too nice?"

"Well, you know. Letting people take advantage of me."

"Are we all not here to let others take advantage of us?"

"I guess, to a certain degree, until it get's out of hand."

"Out of a hand?"

"Of course. Like someone steals all your stuff."

"Where I come from, there are no material articles that belong to just the one. We all share, everything."

"Where do you live, at a Burning Man festival?"

"I don't understand."

"That's okay. Nobody gets my jokes."

"Joke. An amusing story? I like those, please tell me one."

"Your sarcasm is on fire tonight, Lori."

"I am not Lori."

"Oh, right, I forgot, you're crazy. I guess being the daughter of a general would make anybody coo-coo. Surprised that he let you roam the streets." Plür was staring at a picture of Casper, Ami and Don on the refrigerator. It was taken on their trip to the Santa Cruz boardwalk. In the picture they are laughing, Don is holding an ice cream cone and Ami has some of it on her nose because at the last minute, before the photo was snapped, Caper and Don had shoved the cone into her face.

"What is that?"

Casper looked at the photo. "Oh that? That's me and my roommates. I think that was last summer."

"I know her."

"Ami? You know Ami? She never mentioned meeting you?"

"Yes. I like Nakajima Ami. She is on a similar path to enlightenment as I am."

"You're a Buddhist? Jeez. Never seen the Dali Lama knee someone in the 'nads…'cept that one guy, but he was being a real jerk." Plür stood up and started exploring the kitchen. Every object was fascinating to her; from the Hello Kitty ™ toaster to the refrigerator magnet from Niagara Falls. "You seem fascinated by our kitchen."

"Yes. I want to learn all about you."

"Is that what you do? Learn about someone, then you chop 'em up and cook them in their own kitchen?"

"Paranoid," Bosq whispered.

"What was that?" Casper asked.

"Ignore that. It will not happen again." Plür furrowed her eye brows in the direction she thought Bosq was and then realized she could move her brows. She reached up and started playing with them.

"Are you off your meds?" Casper asked

"Pardon me?"

"Nothing. So, I'm gonna go get my telescope, The one that cost more than my car…Then again, the gas that went into it was more valuable. You want anything to drink?"

"I remember drinking."

"I bet you do. That would explain your behavior." He went to retrieve his telescope from his room.

In the scientist tent across the bridge, Aarti drew Lewis' attention to her screen. "Look at this…" On it was an overhead map of the local area with red dots in certain areas. Some of the red dots were converging in Pepper Mill."…Apparently there's been lots farm animals escaping from nearby farms and appearing in town."

"Are they crossing the bridge?"

"Some have, but the rest just walked from the West side of town. What do you think the attraction is?"

"Same as us, curiosity?"

"Pigs are some of the smartest animals out there, but none of them have appeared. As well as domesticated animals."

"Cows and chickens?"

"Yes. And a couple of goats."

"Milk and eggs but no bacon."

Aarti thought for a second. "Is it providing?"

"Except for bacon."

"Maybe the ring is Muslim."

"This can also make the case that the ring is not autonomous. Perhaps it's a monitoring device, reporting back to an intelligent life form far away."

"Or, it was just programed to give the inhabitants whatever they need to survive."

"How I wish so much that I was inside with them." he sighed.

"Seriously? You want to be trapped in there?"

"Ground zero, shaking hands with the cosmos? Definitely."

A blond haired gentlemen wearing a white lab coat entered the tent. He was being escorted by an armed soldier. "Excuse me!" the man yelled. "I am looking for Professor Sven Svengundsun!"

Aarti and Lewis looked at each other. He slowly raised his hand. "That's me."

The visitors walked over to them. "Are you Professor Sven Svengundsun?" the guy asked Professor Pascal.

"Y-yes?"

"LIAR!" he yelled.

"Pardon?"

"You are not Sven Svengundsun! Because I-AM Sven Svengundsun!"

Professor Pascal looked at Aarti and then back at the visitors. "Baloney! This man is an impostor!"

"No, YOU are the impostor! Arrest him!" The soldier started to make a move.

"Wait one minute, how do you know he's not the impostor?" Pascal pointed to the blond guy.

"That's true," Aarti agreed.

The Soldier stopped and looked at Sven Svengundsun. "Gotcha there, dude."

"This is preposterous! Look! I have a badge!" He pointed to his picture ID, pinned to his chest.

"And I am so sure of who I am, that I don't even need to carry a badge!" Pascal said.

"Oh snap!" The soldier agreed. "You got burned and served!"

"This is ridiculous! I'm the REAL Sven Svengundsun!"

"No, I'm the real Sven Svengundsun!" Pascal countered.

There was a back and forth arguing until the guard held up his hands. "OKAY, okay, you two, there is only one way to settle this."

"Drivers license?" Sven suggested.

"Naw, too easy. How about a Swed off."

"A what?"

"A Swed-off. Whoever can answer questions about Sweden correctly is the real Sven Svengundsun."

"What-ever. Fire away!"

"Agreed," Pascal said.

"Are you sure?" Aarti asked.

"Of course," Pascal said." Because I'm the real Sven Svengundsun!"

"No, I AM!" Sven yelled.

"Gentlemen!" the soldier interrupted. "Okay, you!" He pointed to Sven. "What's the capital of Sweden?"

"Stockholm."

"Right. He pointed to Pascal. "You, how many days of parental leave do you get in Sweden?"

"480."

"Huh…Right. Okay, other dude. How do you spell Sweden?"

"S-W-E-D-E-N."

"Correct. Now you." He pointed at Pascal again. "How many Kilos of food waste does Sweden gather per year?"

"993,000."

"Right, I guess."

"You guess? Why am I getting the hard ones?"

"This is a waste of time," Sven complained. "Here, look…" He ripped off Pascal's wig. "…He's in disguise!"

"The soldier studied the wig. Okay, I'm gonna have to ask to see your I.D."

"LOOK!" Pascal yelled while pointing. "It's Swedish actor and star of the HBO series *True Blood*, Alexander Skarsgård!"

Everyone, including Aarti looked at where Pascal was pointing. A very fat and confused scientist, eating a pizza with mayonnaise was the victim of the stare. By the time everyone drew their attention back to Pascal, he had managed to duck down and crawl out the side of the tent and escape.

Plür flushed the toilet for the eighth time. Casper took a chance and peeked inside the bathroom. As he had suspected, she was just playing with the toilet. "Uhh, I have a plunger that'll get the big ones down, you know?"

Plür ignored him and moved on to the bathroom mirror. She spent some time looking at her head and checking every part. She was especially interested in the numerous facial expressions she could make, probably the most of any race she has been in so far.

"So anyway, I know I can't compete with whatever you're doing in here, but I thought you'd like to see something on my telescope."

Plür had no idea what a telescope was, so she became very curious and followed him up the stairs to the roof of his building. Seeing the town from this height was exciting enough; all of the lights and sounds below them were very stimulating to someone that came from such a peaceful planet. "It is pretty," she said walking really close to the edge.

Casper grabbed her jacket and pulled her back. "Whoa there, Lucy Lawsuit! Don't get too close to the edge. Fire escape is quite painful to fall onto, learned that fourscore and seven beers ago." He guided her over to his $300 reflector telescope. He checked the eyepiece to see if it was still on target. He guided her shoulders down to it, making sure she didn't jostle it. "Okay, if you look, you can see a really good shot of the planet Jupiter."

Plür took a peek. It was as Casper said. You could see the whole planet, including that ubiquitous red spot. She pulled away for a second and looked up to see if it could be seen with the naked eye. The stars were quite bright and covered the night sky. She looked, through the eyepiece and then looked up again. "I have seen moons in many skies, but never a planet. Where is Jupiter?"

He pointed to an area of the night sky. "It's that bright one, right there. About 365 million miles away."

She stepped away from the telescope and looked up at the Milky Way. "It is beautiful. Is it full of clouds on Jupiter?"

"Very. That red spot is actually a storm that's been raging forever."

"Where I come from, it is full of orange and red clouds like Jupiter, and you can never see the night sky."

"You from Salt Lake City?"

"If I were living on Jupiter, this is what it would be like, seeing my home from far away, correct?"

"If you were from Jupiter, you wouldn't look like you do." He noticed she had a tear running down her cheek. "You okay?"

She wiped her face and looked at the wetness on her hand. "Strange. I am both very sad and very happy at the same time. The universe is very beautiful."

"It is...It really is." He looked at Lori's face. It was so different from the girl he'd had a crush on. So much more soft and gentle. If he didn't know better, he would swear he was out on a date with another person. He wondered if perhaps something traumatic had happened on her homeless adventures while hiding from soldiers. He reached over and felt the back of her head. Bosq started walking towards him, in case he tried to harm her.

"What are you doing?" she asked Casper.

He quickly removed his hand "Sorry, I was checking for bumps, or a sign of a concussion."

"That felt good, when you touched my head."

He did it again. "You mean, this?"

"Yes. I feel a rushing warmth flow into what I think is my stomach when you do that."

"Oh, oh, that must be an acupressure vomit point."

"Please continue doing it."

Casper started massaging her head." Okay, but if you puke, don't blame me." After a moment of giving her a head rub, she closed her eyes and seem to really enjoy it. Casper began giving her a head, neck and shoulder massage. As if her body had become weak, she laid her head back against him with her eyes closed. Her hair was in his face. It was softer than his aunt's mink coat and smelled a heck of a lot better. He knew she was crazy and it was dangerous to do so, but he put his arm around her waist. She lifted her hands and held his hands on her belly. They stayed in this position and enjoyed each other's company.

In the teachers lounge in what used to be the high school, Captain Kowalski and his men were interrogating Lori. The net she was trapped in was now held to the ground by Kowalski's soldiers. The answers she was giving were not the clear and concise ones he wanted. Once again, he asked her if Plür was actually the First Ordinals she talked about.

"I can taste the air, literally!" was her answer before she laughed insanely.

Kowalski growled in anger. "This is getting us nowhere. Her mind must have been like this even before she switched bodies with the alien. It's like talking to that woman from FEMA we got locked up." He got really close to her and examined her surface. "I wonder if she'll respond to some physical persuasion?"

"You mean, torture?" asked one of the soldiers.

"Such an ugly word. Show some respect, soldier. This thing is not some enemy P.O.W." He walked over to Lori. "You see, we won't need any type of torture device to get answers out of

her...."He put his hand next to her. "All we need is the right..."
He touched her and caused her to scream. "...Touch."

"I thought they said, not to touch her?"

"It's probably because it causes her pain." Kowalski put his hand close to Lori again, she tried to move away as much as she could inside the net. "Now then, Lori. Let me ask you this. Is there a way to get out of the forcefield?"

"I've seen twin suns in the sky illuminating a living red ocean," she answered.

"Not what I wanted to hear." He touched her with his full hand. She screamed. "Now again! Tell me something I want to know!"

"All creatures seek secession from suffering."

"Wrong!" Again, a full hand touch and more screams. "Now, the next time I touch you, it won't be for a second, but 10 seconds, after that, 20! How do we get out of the forcefield!"

"You are not the most intelligent, nor the most beautiful!"

Kowalski did as he said he would. At six seconds, he noticed something different. When he tried to pull his hand away, he couldn't do it. He pulled and pulled, but his hand would not come off of the sphere. "What?" He pulled harder and then his hand started to sink into her. The more he pulled the further in his hand sunk into her. "I'm stuck. Get me–Ahh!" he yelled." One of the soldiers let go of the rope that was holding Lori. He grabbed Kowalski"s hand and tried to pull it out of the sphere to no avail. "Agh! It's burning!" Kowalski yelled. The soldier let go of the other rope and tried to aid in removing Kowalski's hand. "Shoot it! Just shoot it!" one of the soldiers took out his pistol and pumped two shots into her. Lori moved, but there was no damage to her. There were two bullet holes on the other side of the room, where the bullets had passed through and hit the wall. Kowalski's hand sunk deeper into her. "Do something!" he yelled. The other soldier took a very large hunting knife and with one quick swoop, cut Kowalski from his own hand at the wrist. He, of course, screamed in agony and fell back against the soldier that was pulling him away from Lori. "MY HAND! MY BEAUTIFUL HAND! WHY DID YOU CUT OFF MY HAND!"

"Sorry...I panicked," was the soldier's excuse.

Lori, now freed of her bindings spat out Kowalski's hand which was burned and she floated up to the ceiling, spouting more thoughts. "I can read your mind! This is like taking acid on a bed made of tongues while God gives me a head rub! More! I want more!"

"Kill that thing, NOW!" Kowalski yelled. The armed soldier pumped at least four shots into her that all passed through to the wall. Lori lunged at him and completely enveloped him. His screams became muffled as he disappeared into her as if he were being eaten by a giant marshmallow.

"YES!" she yelled. "I can see your whole life! Every bit of pleasure, every high, this is so much better than drugs!" Lori lifted up. Standing in the same agonizing position was a completely charred skeleton. Within two seconds, it lost its integrity and fell down into a pile of black dust. Kowalski and the other soldier screamed in terror. "More! I want MORE!" Lori yelled, flying towards Kowalski. He grabbed the other soldier and used him as a human shield. Lori enveloped him while Kowalski used the opportunity to run out of the room to get some help.

Meanwhile in a much more peaceful setting with 99% less burned skeletons (don't ask me about the 1%), Casper and Plür kissed for the third time. Bosq had become bored with their oscular activity and had positioned himself on the other side of the roof, where he observed the comings and goings of the townspeople below.

As good as the kissing felt, Casper's skepticism finally got the best of his hormonal hurt locker and he pulled away from her. His lips felt like they had been massaged by a $500 paintbrush.

"More, please." Plür asked, closing her eyes and puckering up.

"I'm sorry, I'm just a little weirded out right now. It's like you did a full one-eighty on me and now we're making out and stuff. I feel like I may be taking advantage of your mental state or you're just waiting to clobber me when my guard is down…which, right now is the only thing that's down."

"It is difficult for me to understand half of what you have just said, but, if I understand correctly, you are having problems with your trust in me, am I correct?"

"That's exactly what I'm talking about. Also kind of strange the way you don't use contractions."

"It is important to me that I have your trust. Is there anything I can do? Do you wish to mate with me?"

"Whoa-whoa-whooooa! That was both sexy AND awkward! I already feel like a douche for making out with you in your current state. Sex would put me on a bar stool in douce-bag happy hour."

"Again, it is difficult to understand your words. What can I do to gain your trust?"

"I don't know. Not like we can do a trust-fall or anything."

"What is a trust fall?"

"When I went to summer camp, there was an activity where they made one kid turn his back to everyone and fall into the arms of the person behind him. It's a sign of trust that the person behind you would catch you."

"Then we will do that."

"With you? Nooo way! Boy named Rotten Eddie totally ditched me on the ground. Besides, you weigh what, 105-110 pounds? You'll drop me."

"I will not drop you. Let us do a trust fall."

"But...I don't..."

"Trust me, please." The doe-eyed look on her face could have made an invading army surrender and lay down their arms, not their weapons, but actually cut their arms off for her.

"Alright, fine. But don't drop me. Matter of fact, let me get a pillow."

"Is this pillow part of the trust fall?"

"Not really...Fine. Whatever, do it your way," He turned his back to her "Now, you hold out your hands and prepare to catch me. Just tell me when you're ready."

"I am ready."

"So when I fall back you will catch me."

"Yes."

"Are you sure?"

"No, my name is not Sure."

"Funny. Are you ready?"

"Yes."

"Here I go."

"Yes."

"Are you sure."

"Please, I am starting to understand annoyance."

Casper fell back. Now, I'm sure you know exactly what happens here. Casper falls back, Plür either gets distracted by a bird or something or just plain steps away and lets his skull kiss the roof of his building. This is what would be expected in a humorous story such as this one and this is exactly what Casper was thinking when he reached the point where Plür should have touched his back and he kept falling in what felt like slow motion. As his mind said "Oh great, here I go." Something changed. He felt her hands on his back but he kept falling, then he felt his back against her front, a split second later, her arms were around his front and they fell together a short distance and landed on one of the lawn chairs —in essence, she had caught him.

His heart was beating in a panic. "Y-you caught me?"

"Yes. I said I would." She put her hand on his heart. "Your heart is beating strongly. Are you afraid?"

"Not anymore."

In the gymnasium, General Katz tried to kick the front door open with his foot. When he hit it a second time, he knew that he could do it with at least two more kicks. When there was gun fire and two bullet holes appeared in the door, he stopped and stepped back.

"If you come through this door, I'll shoot you on sight!" yelled a voice from the other side.

"Looks like they barricaded the back door and left an armed guard on this one to make sure we don't escape" the general told Dr. Chambers. "We gotta get out of here."

Dr. Chambers looked up at some really high windows at the top of the room. "If we can get up through that window, I think there's an awning below that we can drop down on."

"There's no way we can get up there without a ladder."

"Hmm." Dr. Chambers stepped back and took a look at the window. She took off her lab coat and then her shirt. She now sported a white tank top which revealed the Navy Polar Bears tattoo on her arm. "Cup your hands together and when I step on them, lift as hard as you can."

"Even with a boost, you aren't going to make it up there."

"For someone whose soul-switched daughter was just kidnapped by traitors, you aren't helping by being pessimistic!"

"Sorry, sorry, sure, let's do it."

Dr. Chambers walked all the way across the room, paused, and nodded to the general to say that she was ready. She then ran across the room like a sprinter. Before she reached him, she did a series of somersaults. When she stuck her landing in his hands, he lifted as hard as he could. This sent her into a flip, far into the air. Before she came back down, her arms reached out and grabbed the open windows ledge. Not wasting any time she pulled herself up and crawled out. There was a sound of thumping as the doctor landed on the awning outside. A moment later another thumping sound, the word "hey!" and then silence. A minute later, the doctor opened the front door using a pair of keys. Next to her on the ground lay the sprawled body of one of Kowalski's men.

"I thought you took a hypocrite oath not to kill anybody?" the general asked.

"Hippocratic. He's not dead. I knocked him out by hitting a series of pressure points on his body."

"You learn that in the Navy Polar Bears?"

"No, Xena Princess Warrior. Unfortunately for him, he's going to wake up with a splitting headache and a loss of bowel control."

"Okay, let's go find my daughter...after we put some newspapers under that guy."

In another part of the high school, a medic had finished bandaging Kowalski's stump. He took it upon himself to give his arm a bonus injection of pain killer to numb the pain of his missing appendage. "Dead! I want that thing dead!" he told the medic. Kowalski took out his walkie talkie and made an announcement over the school's PA system: "Attention. All soldiers. The alien ball should be considered armed and dangerous...Well, perhaps not with arms, but it's dangerous and must be eliminated at all cost." At the moment he had said that, Lori had rounded a corner near the science class and came within view of two soldiers. One of them lifted a mop out of a janitor cart and went at her. His yelling "stop where you are!" yielded no results so he started swinging and tried to hit her. The mop hit but caused no more damage than you would give to a soccer ball. The damage she caused him was far more significant as she enveloped him and disengaged, leaving a burnt skeleton behind.

After hearing Kowalski's announcement, General Katz found a telephone on the wall and made his own announcement on the PA system: "Attention all army personnel. Do not, repeat, do NOT engage the alien! Captain Kowalski should be arrested and put in detention immediately! Repeat, Captain Kowalski is to be placed in detention immediately!"

An armed soldier near Kowalski approached him. "Captain. will you come with me, sir?"

Kowalski sighed and then made another announcement. "All soldiers under MY command: Eliminate the alien and anyone else that stands in your way…including General Katz. Operation Red Bandana."

Another armed soldier came up from behind the first and opened fire, freeing Kowalski from custody. He then saluted. All across the base numerous soldiers took red bandannas out of their back pockets and tied them around their necks and left whatever jobs they were doing, much to the shock of the ones that did not do that. In one alarming incident, a red bandana soldier opened up a weapons room and started handing out guns to others like him. The poor soul without the bandana yelled: "Hey! What are you doing?" and was shot dead on the spot. Lori, meanwhile floated around the campus. Those under General Katz command moved away from her as fast as they could. Those under Kowalski's command, opened fire on her. These futile efforts to kill her always ended up with bullets passing through Lori's body and hitting a wall on the other side, if not killing a couple of red bandana-wearing soldiers.

News of his own soldiers killing each other was not making Kowalski happy. "Any soldiers under my command, if you have access to explosive weapons, use them!" he commanded.

Lori was nearing a refueling station. A soldier on Kowalski's team had a grenade launcher in the style of a bazooka used to super-kill your enemies. He aimed it, and in spite of someone yelling "Stop!" fired it. Just like the bullets, it passed through Lori and landed perfectly on the refueling station. A bright flash was followed by a bigger one, followed by a very loud explosion, followed by a fire ball rising in the sky as the army lost its fuel reserves, two humvees and the lives of three soldiers under Kowalski's command.

Before the explosion on the army base, there was another explosion happening with Casper's libido. He and Plür had taken their face-sucking activity inside to the living room couch. Casper was quite forthright about his level of sexual expertise, but while he was kissing Plür, he felt like he was the one who had invented kissing (I think it was a Frenchman named Monsieur Langue). Caper's weak super ego kicked in and told him to apply the brakes to this sex-mobile. When he told it to shut up, it came back with 'Don't you tell me to shut up; if you had listened to me, you wouldn't have ever dated The One Who Shall Remain

Nameless!' "Fine!" he thought, "we'll talk some more, but after that I'm going to Sex Disney Land™ with a three day pass for Magic Mountains!" Casper pulled away from Plür and took a breath. "Okay…sorry, but I think I need to take a breather. We should probably take it a little bit slower. So if you'd excuse me, I have to go stick my pants in the freezer." He stood up and walked to the kitchen. "Do you need anything?"

"I would like more kissing. I like the kissing."

"Later…if not sooner…definitely sooner—excuse me." Casper exited the room.

Even though Plür was not experienced with human relationships, she found it odd for him to leave in their current physical state.

Bosq snuck up to her from the outside and talked quietly: "How is it going in here? Have you completed the mating ritual?"

"I am not sure," she answered. "This body's temperature has risen and I feel uncomfortable."

"Perhaps you should remove some clothing. That's a good way to lower your temperature."

There was far-off sound of an explosion outside.

"What was that?" Casper asked.

"I do not know." Plür answered.

Bosq left to go investigate. Plür stood up and took her shirt off. She was unsure how to take her bra off and ended up pulling it down all the way until she stepped out of it like a pair of panties.

Casper walked into the room holding a glass of ice water. "Hey! You still hungry? I have some leftover chicken—BREAST!" The ice water wasn't in his hand for long after he spotted the topless Plür. "Ooooookay, then. We're doing it your way. I have to get something out of my bedroom. You wait right here. This won't take long…getting the thing, not the thing it's for…I swear I've had lots of practice…sometimes with a partner…excuse me… been a while." Casper left the room again and went into his bedroom.

Again, Bosq snuck up to Plür. "Something bad is going on at the Alpha's complex."

"Is it Lori?"

"I'm not positive. I think we should probably investigate."

"Correct." She grabbed her shirt, opened the door and ran out. Bosq spotted the bra. He had seen human women wearing them and assumed it was important. He grabbed it and ran after her.

Casper came out of the bedroom holding a 100 pack box of Marathon Man contraceptives he had got at a savings club. "Sorry, I wasn't sure how many we'd need so I bought the whole...Lori?" He searched the apartment and ended up outside on the fire escape. He saw a fire happening at the high school, and the mayor wandering the streets yelling: "Plür? Where are you?" There was also a sound of fireworks. He wasn't curious about any of it as he returned to the inside, with his head hanging hug low. "Good job, Cornbregger," he thought. "I guess that's what her plan was all along. Take me to the brink of Funky Town and then run out of here. Women! Sometimes I really wish I were gay. Least then, we could borrow each other's pants.'

Ami and Don passed through the still open front door (It was hard for Bosq to close it while running with a bra).

"Why's the front door open?" Ami asked.

"O-M-G!" Don said. "You won't believe what I saw on the way up here."

"The fire?" Casper asked.

"Not just that, but a white-haired chick running topless down the street being chased by a floating bra!"

"What?" Casper asked.

"He's delusional. I didn't see anything," Ami complained. "Why are you holding that?" She pointed to the box.

Casper threw it on the couch. "That was Lori Katz. We were hanging out in here and when it got hot and heavy, she ran away."

"Lori Katz was HERE?" Don asked.

"Wait," Ami said. "She was here and she ran out—topless?" She walked over, grabbed the box off of the couch and hit Casper on the head.

"Ow! What the cheese, Ami?"

"Did you try to take advantage of her?"

"No! It was consensual...At least it was until I left to go get that box, and she just flaked out on me—again, and ran out! She's unstable!" Ami hit him on the head, again.

"OW! Why god-why?"

"She's mentally unstable! You were taking ADVANTAGE of her! HENTI, baka!"

"No! I swear to the Evangelical god! Things were going great...well, she did interrupt my date with Darla by kissing me... and she didn't know how to use a fork...." Don walked over, took the box from Ami and hit Casper on the head. "OW! ET TU DON!?"

"That's for ignoring my story about a floating bra. Seriously? You and Lori?"

"I know, I know! But now I feel like a dirt-ball. I should't have made out with her." He covered his eyes with his hands. "Probably freaked her out. That's why she ran out of here."

"Well…" Ami said.

"Well what?"

"Her dad is the general, and he does work on the base."

Casper lowered his hands from his face. "That's true! Maybe she was going to make sure that he was okay. I gotta go after her! If anything, I should apologize for being a rake." Don Laughed. "What?"

"YOU? A rake?" Don laughed.

"Hey! I can be a notorious rake!" Casper complained. "Ami thought so too, right Ami?"

"Oh my gosh! I'm so stupid" Ami said.

"You did too think I was a rake!"

"No! I gotta go! If there's a fire, there may be injured people. They're going to need all of the medical personnel there."

"Okay. Let's go!" Casper said.

"Wait, you guys," Don interrupted. "You can't run to that base —that's like a billion blocks away."

"Don't have a choice," Ami said.

"Sure you do…"

Within a few minutes after they left the apartment, they were in Don's Porsche 911 Carrera 4 Cabriolet convertible, zooming down the main road.

"I thought you were supposed to give this back?" Casper complained.

"They can take away my house with a pool, but there's no way they're getting my baby." He pressed the accelerator and made their heads go back.

When General Katz rounded a corner and a man wearing a red bandana aimed a rifle at him, he learned two things: 1) Anyone with a red bandana was now an enemy combatant, and 2) No matter how old he had gotten, he could still disarm a man and kill him in less than two seconds. The doctor also proved to be a formidable ally, even though she preferred to just punch or kick her opponents instead of killing them. As she swiftly applied fist to broken rib of someone she had treated for a groin injury earlier in the week, she thought it would be cruel to inflict him with a new groin injury. So, she applied an elbow to face instead, sending him flying into a brick wall. Unfortunately for him, when he came down, he accidentally unpinned a hand grenade on his belt near his groin which promptly exploded. The doctor scrunched her facial expression. "Sorry," she said.

Wise to the red bandanna soldiers, the regular soldiers had started fighting back and had managed to push the enemy forces to another part of the campus, away from Lori. By this time, Lori had killed at least seven more people and was growing hungrier. The more she consumed the more memories, experiences and knowledge she had absorbed. Lacking someone from the red bandanas to eat, she turned her attention on a female communications officer. Lori slowly approached the woman who had been shot in the leg, and now struggled to get out of the way. When she was almost in killing distance, Plür dropped down from the sky in front of her. Plür hovered in the air for a second and then stepped down. "Thanks for carrying me, Bosq," she said to her friend, who had convinced her it would be much faster if he gave her a ride on his back. Plür slowly approached Lori with her hand up. "It is all right. Everything is peaceful, trust me." Lori stood still. Plür cautiously approached her.

"Be careful, Plür." Bosq said.

"It is impossible for her to harm me." Plür walked over to Lori and put her hand on Lori's surface. "Lori. You must release this body and come back to mine. It is time to rest."

"NO!" Lori yelled. "I feel like a GOD!"

"We are not gods. We are sprits and part of everything. Return to where you belong."

"NEVER! I LKE IT HERE!"

"Release your soul and return to this body."

"You can talk! You've seen so much! We are nothing but bugs compared to you and the Collection of Wanderers. Human life is WORTHLESS!"

"All life is beautiful."

"SHUT UP!"

General Katz and Dr. Chambers rounded the corner and spotted Plür and Lori."

"Lori!" he called out.

"I'm never going back! NEVER!" Lori yelled. She rose up and hurried around the other side of the building.

"Follow her, please!" Plür yelled.

"Yes," Bosq said before giving chase.

The general ran over to Plür. Doctor Chambers helped the female officer with her injury.

"Plür. What happened to her?" The general asked.

"Her soul has become contaminated. I tried to reconnect her with her body but I'm afraid she has absorbed too many lives."

"What do you mean absorbed?"

"She is destroying any life she comes across. She will not stop until even you have been consumed."

"Isn't there anything we can do?"

"There is only one option for someone in her state: Release."

"Isn't that what you were just trying to do?"

"No. This is something that's rarely done with my people. It is only used when one of us becomes contaminated."

"Well, let's do that. What do we need to do?" Just when he said that, a bullet hit the ground near him. Realizing they were being shot at, he started firing back at the enemy who were slowly making their way back to the main building. "Let's go!" The general lead them all around the other side, the doctor helped the officer to walk."What do we need to do for this release thing?"

"I need the white powder."

"The white powder? What white powder? This some kind of magic dust or something?"

"The white powder appears on all planets we have seen with oceans. It is the only substance which can affect my people."

"Salt?" The doctor asked.

"Yes. I have heard it called that. We need...salt. At least this much." Plür held out her hands and cupped them.

"That looks like at least two cups. Where are we gonna get that much salt around here?" The doctor asked.

"Cafeteria?" answered the general.

"I think that was destroyed when the fuel tank exploded."

"Shove a squirrel in me!" he said in anger. "Where else?"

"Do you not have a large food storage building with animal carcasses, nearby?" Plür asked.

"The grocery store?" the doctor answered.

"Right!" the general said. "I'll get a soldier to drive you to the store. When we find Lori, we'll let you know where to find us."

Ami, Don and Casper were almost to the high school. They could see a firetruck operated by FEMA workers spraying foam on the fire and some kind of commotion involving what sounded like fireworks. A soldier stopped their car and told them they couldn't enter the complex because it was too dangerous. "I'm part of the medical team!" Ami yelled.

"Okay, but you have to wait over by the front gate until we get the all clear sign."

Ami stepped out of the car."What exactly is going on in there?"

"I think it's some kind of mutiny."

A humvee drove pass them, headed in the opposite direction. Casper recognized one of the passengers. "Lori! That was Lori in there! Follow her!"

"I'm gonna stay here with Ami," Don said. "Why don't you take the car?" Don slid out of the vehicle.

"You sure? You trust me with your baby?"

"If I'm staying here with my girl, I'm not gonna stop you from going after yours."

"We're both fools in love, aren't we?"

"Yep, the biggest." Don jogged over to where Ami was waiting.

Casper sat in the driver's seat and felt like he had stepped into the cockpit of an X-wing fighter. The only car he had driven for two years was marginally faster than taking a rusty school bus with four flat tires. When he pressed the accelerator too hard, the back tires skidded and smoked. He spun into a U-turn, slammed on the brakes and then took off, once again burning a months worth of rubber off of the back tires. Don, who had watched the whole scene, buried his face into the bottom of his t-shirt and felt like crying. "Now I know how Lando felt when he gave Han Solo the Millennium Falcon."

After a few blocks, Casper was able to compensate for the fact that the pedal actually responded when pressed and was able to drive relatively normal. In no time at all, he caught up with the humvee. "Where are they taking her? You'd think the general would want to see her after all of that time they've been looking for her." He followed them all the way to Big Red Grocery's parking lot. "What the heck are we doing here? Sue's probably already closed up." As it turned out, Sue was actually still inside with the two cashier soldiers (you remember them, right?) What you don't remember is that they now sported red bandanas around their necks. Sue finished closing down the register. One of her soldier cashiers spotted the humvee approaching. He watched eagerly to see if it was one of his or General Katz's men. The humvee pulled up front. The driver got out and started walking to the front entrance. The cashier soldiers opened the sliding doors and fired their hand guns at the driver and the humvee. Casper freaked out. When I say freaked out, I mean imagine you are on a subway watching an old woman across the way picking dead skin off of her feet and eating it. Now, the face you just made; combine that with fear and there you have it. He wasn't sure if he had seen the soldiers kill someone, no more than he was sure he had seen the murderers point their weapons at him, but just to be sure, he ducked down. He overdid the ducking part because his knee hit the accelerator and the car zoomed ahead at double the speed. It jumped the curb and went crashing through the window, right into the two soldiers. Along with lots of glass, metal and a "Pork Sale!" sign, both soldiers went flying in different directions. One ended up in the pharmaceutical aisle (which he's going to need in the following weeks) and the other landed in a shopping cart with his feet bent up to his ears (he should say goodbye to his days of sitting in a normal chair). Casper pushed away the airbag, which had inflated, lifted a bunch of cardboard and pieces of glass off of him and crawled over the trunk of the car. His only thought was to go check on Plür. When he made it to the front window, Sue appeared from behind a register, where she had hidden during the chaos. "You-are-so-FIRED!" she yelled.

Casper reached the humvee and opened the door. Plür was ducked down on the floor. She looked at Casper at first as if he was going to hurt her. She didn't understand what was going on, but she did recognize violence when she saw it.

"Oh, thank God!" he said reaching in and helping her out. "Are you hurt?"

"I am not injured."

"Thank God-thank God-thank God!" He hugged her. His heart was beating fast.

A feeling came over Plür. She was really happy and felt a rush of warmth in her stomach. She hugged him back. It was strange for her to feel this way about a native. She assumed she was just melding more with her host body. "My heart...it is beating fast."

"Because you're afraid?"

"Not anymore."

He kissed her. "I'm sorry. I really shouldn't have done that. I actually came here to tell you I'm sorry for taking advantage of you."

"Do you trust me?"

He nodded yes.

"Then know that everything that I have done on our date and will do for now on are done because I want to do them, understand?

He nodded yes again.

"Now, can you please help me to find salt?"

Dr. Chambers came through the high school's gates. She saw Ami and waved her over. "Ami! We need you in here, we have lots of injured!" Doctor Chambers, Ami and Don started to fast-walk to the gymnasium.

"Is it safe?" Ami asked.

"Yes. The mutineers in here were either killed or captured. A small band are heading into the center of town."

"Can I help?" Don asked.

"Of course...Who are you?"

"Doctor, this is my roommate Don," Ami answered.

"Not THE Don?"

"Uhh, yes? What does she mean by that?" Don asked.

"Nothing. Ignore her!" Ami grabbed Don's hand and dragged him along. As they were walking fast, Don looked down at his hand. He thought about Ami and how reserved she was with her public displays of affection. Holding his hand was actually a big deal for her, if this were anything other than her dragging him along. She moved her fingers from a cupped hand hold position, to an interlocking finger position. In Don's mind, this was like the second base of hand-holding. He felt joy as they walked through a scenery of burning army vehicles, dead bodies and agony.

In the humvee, Casper drove Plür back into town. He was still in shock from watching a guy get shot, getting shot at, and crashing into the store. "I think I'm freaking out. Why did those guys kill your driver and tried to kill you? Is this why you've been running away all of this time, because your life was in danger? I feel like the main character in an action movie—I mean, the army and FEMA have been keeping us away from everything, so you'd think that they were the main characters in the movie, and now, suddenly, I'm making out with cute girls, getting shot at by guys wearing red ascots and wrecking Porsches into store windows—Don is going to super-kill me! And now I'm driving a jeep thingy to god knows where!" Plür was not paying attention. She was examining the box of salt. "You okay?"

She shook out of her deep thought. "Excuse me. I was thinking that this is the most dangerous substance where I come from."

"What? Salt? High blood pressure run rampart in your family?"

A radio announcement came on from General Katz. "Attention all available units. We've found the target..She's being attacked by Kowalski and his men in sector one. Converge at that location, but do not engage the Floater, concentrate fire power on the insurgents."

"I have no idea what he just said," Casper complained.

Plür got a message from Bosq that only she could hear. "Lori is in the center of their town. The Alphas with the red cloth on their necks are trying to kill her. Meet me there."

"Do you know where the middle of town is?" Plür asked Casper.

"I assume in the center of town?... I'm just guessing."

"Please take me to there."

"Sure thing." Casper made a right turn. He overcompensated and ran the humvee up on the curb, almost running over the mayor's foot. "Plür?" the mayor yelled.

"Whoops. This thing must be a pain to parallel park." Casper complained.

"I thank you for taking me to the center of town," Plür said, stroking the box of salt.

"I still think we should have waited around. Not a good idea to leave the scene of a crime—I think Sue is right, double hit-and-run through a store window is a good reason to get me fired." He looked over at her again. "I'm sorry, I'm rambling. I'm nervous. How about you? You all right?"

"I am not sure. I feel nervous about the males with weapons but there is something else...it started when you opened the transport vehicle. When I saw that it was you I got this emotional response..." Plür took his hand and put it on her chest.."...Here."

"Whoa!" Casper said swerving the humvee into the bike lane. He put both hands on the wheel and regained control. "Sexting while driving, not a good idea!"

Lori didn't need the help of any of General Katz's forces. From the guy with the machine gun to the guy with the rocket launcher, their weapons passed through her and they were consumed into an agonizing marshmallow of death (not to be confused with eating Lucky Charms with Jack Daniels instead of milk). The last two standing were Kowalski and his second in command, who tried so hard to stop her that he activated a hand grenade inside of Lori while he was being consumed. She shook but received no damage. Lori noticed Kowalski cowering in the alley near some garbage cans. He was trapped. She slowly hovered towards him and prepared to finish the job of consuming. Bosq was watching the whole scenario. He knew he could quite easily save Kowalski but he also knew that his only job was to protect Plür and Plür alone. Any deviation from his duty would mean expulsion from the Collection as a Soul Guardian. Plür and Casper pulled up and stopped in the middle of the street near a flaming army vehicle.

"Wait, that's the alien," Casper said. "I touched that thing! What's it doing here?"

"She's killing many humans and I'm here to stop her. Can you please open this?" She handed the box of salt to Casper. He opened the pour spout.

"Wait! Her? If that thing is killing people then you can't do anything, unless you're some kind of alien hunter, because that would explain your bizarre behavior and give you like, 500 cool points."

"Can you open it more?" He ripped the top off of the box. Plür got out of the car and carried the box in one hand. Lori came towards her. Casper started to get out of the humvee. "Stay where you are!" Plür yelled at him. He closed the door. She turned her attention back to Lori. "This is salt! Do you know what it's for?"

"You won't do it," Lori said boldly.

"I will do anything to save unenlightened lives."

"You know what will happen to you if you do that."

"Correct."

"Plür?" Bosq asked. "What is she talking about?"

"Hello, Bosq, wherever you are," Lori said with malice and deviancy. "You came to protect Plür? What about him?" Plür and Bosq looked back at Casper. "Bet-cha can't protect him!" Lori navigated around Plür and Bosq and headed towards the humvee at a rapid speed.

"STOP!" Plür yelled.

Lori crashed against the side of the humvee. The force was so much that it turned it onto its side with a loud sound of breaking glass and metal. Casper tumbled around like a tennis shoe inside a Laundromat dryer.

"LORI! Bosq!—Help him!"

"I can't," Bosq said. "It's against my code."

Plür ran over to the wreckage. Lori was crashing into the vehicle over and over, like a wreaking ball. The more she did so, the more the door was breaking. At any moment the vehicle would crack open like a walnut and Casper would join the other collection of burned skeletons. Plür looked at the box of salt and then Lori. She reached in and took about a tablespoon of salt in her hand. "I'm sorry," she said. She tossed it at Lori It dissipated in the air but still managed to hit Lori in a sprinkle. She screamed and immediately backed away from the vehicle and lowered herself to the ground. "I'm sorry." Plür apologized again. "I will not let you cause any more suffering."

HOW CAN YOU SAY THAT!" Lori yelled. You are causing me suffering right now! You know what I've been through!" The spots where the salt hit Lori were sizzling.

"Yes. Your mother died when you were born and your father was always away at war. In your mind, you are alone. But, I have talked to countless others in the Collective whose stories are far more tragic than your own and they thrive. Stop what you are doing, please."

"You don't think I will attack you because if you die, I die? Well guess what, I don't care!" Lori made a fast lunge towards Plür. Plür didn't move. She was not afraid of death. There was a loud humming sound and a wave jellied air struck Lori. She screamed, hit the side of the humvee like a kicked soccer ball, bounced off and flew back into the alley against a brick wall, where she had started.

Bosq walked over to Plür. "Are you alright?"

"Yes. Thank you." While they were talking, Lori took the opportunity to guess where Bosq was and sped towards his location. She guessed correctly and attacked him. For a split second, Plür could see what Bosq looked like. She had guessed correctly. He screamed in pain as Lori tried to consume him. Plür threw a handful of salt at her. Lori quickly withdrew and landed on the ground, in pain.

"BOSQ! Are you injured?" Plür yelled

"I will be fine. I can't say the same for my weapon and my suit. If we don't leave soon. I will be visible to the humans."

"I will finish this and then we will go back to the transport."

Casper crawled trough the humvee's broken back window. "What-a-day!" he yelled.

"You should stay where you are," Plür pleaded.

"I'm sorry, but whenever you say that, that alien comes at me like an old lady at a yard sale. I think I'm safer out here." Plür looked back at him, poured a handful of salt in her hand and started walking towards Lori. Casper followed slowly, unsure what he could do against a rampant alien ball. Within a minute, lots of army vehicles pulled up. Soldiers drew their guns and pointed them at Lori and Plür. General Katz got out of a truck and walked over to her. "What's going on? Did you release her?"

"Not yet. When she comes in contact with this much salt, it will be enough for her soul to be released from the body."

"Wait! Soul release!…" he said angrily. "…You didn't say anything about a soul released from the body."

"Yes, it is a soul release. It is the only way to end her suffering and the suffering of others."

He knocked the salt out of her hand, grabbed the box, and threw it into the alley. "ARE YOU OUT OF YOUR MIND! I'm not going to let you kill her!"

"Death is a rest after hundreds of rotations in a shell."

"I don't give a crap about your view on death! We don't live as long as Aliens!"

"But she is suffering and harming others."

"I'm not going to kill her and that's FINAL!"

Kowalski jumped from between some garbage cans, holding the box of salt with his remaining hand, and ran towards Lori. "Don't mind if I do!" he yelled. He doused Lori with the rest of the box. As if touching dark ink to white paper, where the salt hit, turned black and spread all over Lori's surface. She screamed in agony. Her surface bubbled and she appeared to melt onto the asphalt. Her color returned to white and then silver. Her shape became anamorphic and random. Finally, she settled down into a sizzling puddle of white goo.

The general looked at Kowalski. "What did you do? You-you killed her!"

"You're welcome!"

The general took out his gun and pointed it at Kowalski.

Casper covered his eyes. "Please, no more shooting. My therapy bill is going to be through the roof!"

The general cocked his gun. "YOU SON OF A..."

Before he could finish his insult. The white goo rose up and covered Kowalski like a white blanket of death. He struggled, wiggled and moved around. His muffled scream permeated throughout the alley. Finally, as the goo settled down into a puddle, a burned skeleton of Kowalski stood for a second with his hands to his face like the painting 'The Scream' by Edvard Munch and fell into a pile of black dust. The general fell to his knees and reached for the white goo which had thinned to the consistency of milk and started to flow down the sewer drain. "NO, no, no!" He pleaded as it all began to drain away. He reached for it.

"Don't touch it!" Plür yelled. "It could still be dangerous."

The general choked back some tears and turned his emotions into anger. He looked back at Plür. "You know what's dangerous? YOU ARE!"

"I am sorry. I didn't realize that you had such a connection to this plane of existence."

"SHOVE IT!"

"I do not understand."

"Just go."

"Pardon?"

"GO AWAY! You've caused enough damage! Just-GO!"

"Dude!" Casper said. "Why are you being such a hole to your daughter?"

"She's not my daughter! My daughter is dead! That...THING needs to go back to where it came from!"

"Harsh."

Plür turned around and started walking away. The soldiers tried to stop her.

"Let her go!" The general commanded. They moved out of the way and she continued to leave. Casper gave chase.

"Lori!...Lori!" Casper yelled.

Plür walked down the abandoned street, towards the park. It took her a second to realize that Casper was talking to her. She kept walking and didn't turn around.

"Lori! Where are you going?"

"Home."

"Okay, I'm not sure what park bench you were staying on but, you shouldn't be running away from your problems. Sure, you and your dad have some problems but that's the way families are sometimes. You should see me and my mom when we play pinochle." He continued to follow her from block to block.

"Please, stop following me," she said

"Lori, just stop, so we can talk!"

"MY-NAME-IS-NOT-LORI!" Plür stopped walking.

"Okay, fine—whatever. You're no longer Lori Katz. So what… Just a name, I'll call you Alien Hunter, but you don't have to run away, you can crash at my place."

"I do not understand."

"You know, you can stay at my crib."

"No, I do not understand any of your words: "crash-at-your-place-crib.' I do not understand many words! I am foolish. I was so impatient to impress my elders that I took a risk. As a result, many have perished. I failed my mission." A tear ran down her cheek. She wiped it away and looked at her wet fingers. "The only good part of my time was with you and I almost got you released."

"Right. I totally have no idea what your mission was, and how you knew how to kill the alien—perhaps you can tell me later—but you were right about our time together. So far this year, I've almost got killed by a comet, guns, explosive diarrhea, a rampaging alien ball and collected a handful of skee-ball therapy tickets, but knock on wood…" He tapped his skull with his fist. "…I'm still here and so are you. Come back with me. We can look at the stars, cuddle on the sofa and eat more ramen noodles. I'll even let you eat the noodles with your hands."

She looked up at the sky. "You are a nice human, Casper 555-8257"

"Still not used to the new way you talk. But, we'll work through that."

"Goodbye…Do not follow me." Plür started walking again. Casper started to give chase. "Bosq!" she said. Casper hit something. He looked up to see if the ring's force field was acting up. No matter where he went, the invisible wall was there, as Bosq blocked his path.

"What the? Lori! Lori LOOOOOOOORIIIIIIE!" Casper yelled. She went around the corner and a moment later Bosq let him go. Before Casper could give chase again. Bosq sprayed something in front of his nose and he was rendered unconscious.

"Cap!...Cap!"

Casper heard Don's voice calling him. He opened his eyes and saw Don and Ami's faces. "Lori?" he said. They lifted him off of the sidewalk.

"We've been looking all over for you," Don said. "What happened to you, and where's my car?"

"I'm not—Lori! Where's Lori?"

"We haven't seen her." Ami answered. "We need to get you checked out. Are you hurt?"

"No...I don't think so, we gotta find L..." There was a sound like a high-pitched helicopter engine in reverse. The ring stopped rotating and started doing its light show. Inward ripples of bent light waves flowed into it's center like a drop on a pool of mercury in reverse. Something with glowing orange spinning petals, rose from where the park would be and disappeared through the ring. As soon as it disappeared, there was the quick whale moan sound and then the ring started rotating again.

"Looks like the aliens went home," Don said.

The
End

Wait, hold on, that's not the end! This is only book one! I guess I'm in a bit of a hurry to leave, I have another book to narrate.... fine...here's more...

500 light years later...

Orange and red clouds filled the hot air, the sides and where the ground should be. In the middle of the clouds, a white, circular platform made of what appeared to be white coral contained a nude, humanoid figure, lying down—it was Plür. Suddenly she was illuminated by a spotlight from an unknown source. She stood upright. From up above, a very large white sphere, twice her original body's size, floated downwards towards her. It came within a few feet of her head. Plür reached out her hand and touched its surface.

"I am saddened to see you trapped in that form," the sphere said in a female voice.

Plür looked at her hands. "It is not the most efficient form, but it has a high amount of cognition and stamina."

"From what you have told us, they seemed to be a level three, and yet their behavior was closer to a level five."

"First Mother, you told me not to be judgmental when dealing with those under a level three."

"It was not an insult directed at them, Plür, I am disquieted by the trouble they have caused you."

"I am fully to blame for everything that happened. I insisted on a soul switch, I succumbed to the emotional restraints of the animal called Lorie. I failed to understand their strong connection to a corporeal life."

"We are all students, Plür. Mistakes will be made."

"I would like my mistakes to not cause chaos."

"Than you will not be qualified to be an ambassador for the Collection of Wanderers."

"Perhaps, I should not be an ambassador for the Collection of Wanderers."

"That is for us to decide." Came an simultaneous man and woman's voice from above. Plür and First Mother looked up.

"Have the other's voted?" First mother asked.

"Yes," it answered.

"Is it unnatural death?" Plür asked.

"The vote was close…but no. Plürreannedunadugavas will be allowed a natural death."

Plür sighed. She felt relief but confusion. She touched her chest where she guessed the heart would be. "This body…from what I understand…is very fragile and expires within 100 years. A natural death is going to be faster in this form."

"That is to be part of your punishment for the failure of your purge."

"I understand"

"Plür…I am so sorry." First Mother nuzzled against Plür.

"It is acceptable First Mother. I take responsibility for all damage and disruptions. And what of Bosq? Please do not punish him."

"SG456 Bosq will be reassigned to another ambassador. No other disciplinary action was deemed necessary."

"Thank you."

"Do not thank me, your second punishment has not been communicated."

"Is not a natural death in a primitive shell enough of a punishment?" First Mother asked."

"Negative. Plürreannedunadugavas. As further punishment for the disaster your actions have caused to the class threes on the wanderer known as Dirt, the leaders of the Collection of Wanderers have decided to send you back to the nest of Pepper Mill where you will aid the animals in qualifying to be eligible for membership into the Collection of Wanderers."

"You are sending her back?" First Mother asked.

"Correct."

"After what she did, they will harm her."

"That is a risk she must endure."

"This is the same as an unnatural death."

"It is acceptable, First Mother."Plür interrupted. "I will accept all conditions of my punishment."

"Plür…I may not see you again…" Plür put her head against First Mother's surface.

"I will return to the place called Pepper Mill and help them become enlightened," Plür said. She looked up towards the male-female voice. "I have only one request."

"State your request for consideration."

"Before I return to the nest of Pepper Mill, on the wanderer known as Dirt, I cannot be distracted from my mission and risk endangering the lives of the inhabitants. Therefore I think it is best if you remove all of my memories of the one known as Casper Cornbregger."

To be continued…

NEXT TIME, ON
NIGHT COPTER!

About the Author

Alexander G. J. grew up in Charlotte, North Carolina. He escaped to Atlanta, Georgia to study commercial art, then escaped to San Francisco, California, to bolster his writing and fine arts skills. He currently escapes in Richmond, California.

Novels by Alexander G. J.

Mary & I: The Real Story of Miss Mary Mack
Mary & I: Black Blood
Flaming Jackass: Sex, Drugs, and Pizza
Flaming Jackass: In Love
Flaming Jackass: Returns
Flaming Jackass: Detox
I Hate Art (2023)
A Chicken a Rabbi and an Alien Walk into a Bar (due by ??)

Blog: whydidthechickencrosstheuniverse.blogspot.com
Instagram: rabbookspublishing
Facebook: facebook.com/rabbitstudiosbigpush
Author's page: amazon.com/author/alexanderg.j

www.ingramcontent.com/pod-product-compliance
Lightning Source LLC
Chambersburg PA
CBHW070742120726
47910CB00001B/148